Other books by Ann H. Gabhart

THE BELIEVER

A NOVEL

ANN H. GABHART

Revell
a division of Baker Publishing Group
Grand Rapids, Michigan

© 2009 by Ann H. Gabhart

Published by Revell
a division of Baker Publishing Group
P.O. Box 6287, Grand Rapids, MI 49516-6287
www.revellbooks.com

Printed in the United States of America

Library of Congress Cataloging-in-Publication Data
Gabhart, Ann H., 1947–
    The believer : a novel / Ann H. Gabhart.
      p.   cm.
    ISBN 978-0-8007-3362-9 (pbk.)
    1. Shakers—Fiction. I. Title.
PS3607.A23B45 2009
813'.6—dc22   2009013232

Scripture is taken from the King James Version of the Bible.

Page 296: "Funeral Hymn," George DeWitt hymnal, New Lebanon, 1822.

This book is a work of fiction. Names, characters, places, and incidents are the product of the author's imagination or are used fictitiously. Any resemblance to actual events, locales, or persons, living or dead, is coincidental.

To my sisters both by birth and by marriage—
Jane, Rosalie, Dallas, Patricia, Kathy, and Diane.
Also, in loving memory of Joy, who died much too soon
but whose laugh will never fade from my memory.
Sisters make the very best friends.

A Note about the Shakers

American Shakerism originated in England in the eighteenth century. Their leader, a charismatic woman named Ann Lee, was believed by her followers to be the second coming of Christ in female form. After being persecuted for these beliefs in England, she and a small band of followers came to America in 1774 to settle in Watervliet, New York and there established the first community of the United Society of Believers in Christ's Second Appearing, more commonly known as Shakers.

When religious fervor swept the Western frontier at the turn of the nineteenth century, the Shakers, whose communities in New England were flourishing, found the spiritual atmosphere in Kentucky perfect for expanding their religion to the west. By the 1830s the Shakers had nineteen communities spread throughout the New England states and Kentucky, Ohio, and Indiana.

The Shaker doctrines of celibacy, communal living, and the belief that perfection could be attained in this life were all based on the revelations that Mother Ann claimed to have divinely received. The name *Shakers* came from the way they worshiped. At times when a member received the "spirit," he or she would begin shaking all over. These sorts of "gifts of the spirit," along with other spiritual manifestations such as visions, were considered by the Shakers to be confirmation of the same direct communication with God they believed their Mother Ann had experienced.

Since the Shakers believed work was part of worship and that God dwelt in the details of that work, they devoted themselves to doing everything—whether farming or making furniture and brooms or developing better seeds—to honor the Eternal Father and Mother Ann. Shaker communities thrived until after the Civil War, when few recruits were willing to accept the strict, celibate life of the Shakers, and the sect gradually died out.

In Kentucky, the Shaker villages of Pleasant Hill and South Union have been restored and attract many visitors curious about the Shaker lifestyle. These historical sites provide a unique look at the austere beauty of the Shakers' craftsmanship. The sect's songs and strange worship echo in the impressive architecture of their buildings. Visitors also learn about the Shakers' innovative ideas in agriculture and industry that improved life not only in their own communities but also in the "world" they were so determined to shut away.

1

August 1818

Ethan Boyd didn't like loud voices. Bad things happened when there were loud voices. Now Preacher Joe and the man with whiskers were yelling at one another. Ethan wanted to run outside and crawl up under the porch to hide with one of Preacher Joe's hunting hounds. The one Preacher Joe said was afraid of firearms. The one Preacher Joe said wasn't worth the powder it would take to shoot him. The one that liked to lay his head in Mama Joe's lap when she sat on the porch. She said Birdie was her dog and it didn't matter whether he could hunt or not.

Mama Joe took in strays. That's why Ethan was sleeping on the cornhusk mattress on the little bed in the room off the kitchen. Orphans and strays.

But then this man with his gray-streaked black whiskers was saying Ethan wasn't an orphan or a stray. That he belonged to him. Ethan scrunched as far back in the chair at the table as he could and held so tight to the bottom that the cane cut into his fingers. He darted his eyes to the man and then away to stare down at the table.

The table was made out of two broad planks, worn smooth by years of use and Mama Joe's polishing. Mama Joe liked to polish things. Even Ethan. She was forever rubbing the dirt off his face with the corner of her apron. Ethan's eyes found the circle that was part of what Preacher Joe said was the grain of the wood. It looked like a little head with arms reaching away from it. Mama Joe had let Ethan poke two little holes for eyes in the circle, even though normally she'd wear him out for making holes in any of her furniture.

When Ethan told her the circle was his face, she smiled and ran her hand over it softly the way she sometimes stroked his hair. Then she traced the little bit of lighter wood that surrounded the circle like a halo. "See that," she said. "That's the good Lord's love wrapping around you. Remember that, Ethan, no matter what else might happen, his love is always there. You can count on that."

"But will you always love me too, Mama Joe?" Ethan kept his eyes on her finger tracing the circle in the wood. He was afraid to look in her face. Afraid her answer might not be yes.

She reached over, put her hand under his chin, and raised his face up to look at her. "Yes, my little child." She smiled, and the deep wrinkles around her faded blue eyes softened. She dropped her work-roughened hand down to lay it flat against his chest over his beating heart. "My love will always be right there in your heart." She took his hand with her other hand and placed it over her heart. "And your love will always be right here in my heart. That's the way love is. It stays."

Then she picked up the knife she'd been using to peel

potatoes for their supper and carved a small heart inside a bigger heart right in the middle of her table below the circle. After she dusted away the wood shavings from the hearts, Ethan put his hand over them. He felt warm all over. And safe.

Now as the two men's voices got even louder, Ethan stared at the circle with the two points for eyes and the hearts below it. Mama Joe wasn't there. She'd gone to help one of the church-women who was sick. She did that a lot. Ethan didn't mind. Preacher Joe told him funny bedtime stories, and Mama Joe was most always back in time to cook them breakfast.

All of a sudden the whiskered man slammed his fist down on the table right on top of the hearts. Ethan was sure the wood would splinter and break under the force of his anger, but it stayed strong. Ethan felt his own heart beating in his ears.

Preacher Joe's face was a funny purple color as he pointed toward the door. The other man's eyes narrowed until they weren't much more than two slits in his wind-reddened face. He stared straight at Ethan as he said, "I'll be back."

Preacher Joe stepped between the man and Ethan. Preacher Joe was usually a little stooped over, but now his back was stretched up straight as he faced down the man. "Our door will not be open to you."

"He's my boy."

Ethan gripped the bottom of his chair even tighter as the man's words slid around Preacher Joe to grab at him.

"The Lord says different." Preacher Joe's voice was quiet now. Quiet, but firm and calm and sure.

The man laughed and Ethan was glad Preacher Joe was blocking his eyes from him. "Your God has no say in this."

"The good Lord has say in everything. Your life and mine. And the boy's. He stays with us."

"We'll see about that." The words were more growled than spoken.

The man slammed the door behind him so hard that Mama Joe's Sunday dishes on the shelf over her worktable rattled. Ethan squeezed his eyes tight shut, afraid the plates were going to fall off and shatter all over the floor. She'd brought them all the way from Virginia when she first came to Kentucky. Sometimes she stroked the roses on them the way she'd stroked the hearts on the table. She said they made her think of her dear mother who had moved up to heaven to live with Jesus.

Preacher Joe turned away from the door and lifted Ethan out of the chair and sat down with him on his lap, even though he'd told him many times that a boy of six was way too old to be sitting on anybody's lap. Trembles were shaking through Ethan, and Preacher Joe held him tight against his chest as he stroked his head. "There, there, child," he murmured in his ear. "'The Lord is thy keeper; the Lord is thy shade upon thy right hand. The Lord shall preserve thee from all evil; he shall preserve thy soul.'"

Ethan knew that was from the Bible. Half of what Preacher Joe said was from the Bible. The words were like a soft blanket over Ethan, and the trembles left him. Preacher Joe said he could depend on the Lord's words.

"Will he be back?" Ethan whispered against Preacher Joe's bony chest. He was afraid the trembles would start up again, but he held his breath and they didn't catch hold of him.

"I can't say for sure," Preacher Joe said after a long moment. "But don't you worry your head about it. We'll go see the sheriff in the morning and he'll send the man on his way. You can trust the truth of that. You're our boy now."

Ethan was silent for a moment, not wanting to say the words, but he had to. They were pushing against his mouth so hard they were almost breaking his teeth. "Is he my father? My born father."

"So he says." Preacher Joe's hold on Ethan tightened. "But even if there is truth in his words, he forfeited his right to you when he deserted you and your mother when you were a mere babe in arms."

"I remember my mother." Ethan couldn't really remember exactly how she looked, but he remembered the touch of her hands. Her laugh echoed somewhere in his memory. Sometimes when he smelled blackberry jam he could almost see her face. He had no such memories of a father. "I don't remember him."

"No way you could. You weren't much more than a babe in arms when your mother died. You had no father then and had not for some time."

"Did you know my mother?" Ethan looked up at Preacher Joe. Surely he had asked this before, but if so, he had lost the answer.

Preacher Joe smiled down at him. "No, we had no acquaintance with your mother. It was her sister that brought you to us. She had kept you with her for some months, but then she came up in the family way again, and with the worry of another mouth to feed, her husband began to resent what little you were eating or so she told us. She claimed he was a hard man and she feared he might be unkind to you. She cried when she left you."

He seemed to remember that. Tears. Perhaps it was her

face he saw when he smelled the blackberry jam instead of his own mother's. "I'm glad she brought me here." He lay back against Preacher Joe's chest and felt the man's breath going in and out. Slow and steady. He wished he could stay right there in Preacher Joe's lap all night long.

"So am I. Such a gift you were to us. A wee little blue-eyed lad with a smile brighter than a shiny stone in a creek bed. It's hard to believe that's been nigh on three years ago now." Preacher Joe's arms tightened around Ethan. "The good Lord has a way of blessing us in some surprising ways."

By the time Ethan said his prayers and climbed into bed to let Preacher Joe pull the cover up under his chin, he had almost forgotten the sound of the whiskered man's loud and angry voice. Preacher Joe's voice was calm as he read a few verses out of the Bible by the light of a candle. Mama Joe still wasn't home. Preacher Joe said that the churchwoman was having a baby and that some babies were slow in making their way into the world. That Mama Joe would surely be home by breakfast, but if not, he knew how to fry up some eggs.

He tousled Ethan's dark hair and dropped a kiss on his forehead. "Good night, son. May the good Lord watch over you."

Ethan turned over and went to sleep. He was sure if Preacher Joe asked the Lord for anything, it would be done. After all, Preacher Joe was always saying the good Lord was his best friend.

A rough hand clamped over his mouth jerked Ethan from his sleep. The room was pitch-black, and at first he wasn't sure if he was awake or dreaming. Then the smell of the woods and tobacco smoke and some other odor Ethan didn't know filled the room. The man's whiskers scratched against Ethan's face as he spoke into his right ear. "Not a peep out of you if you don't want your old preacher friend to get hurt. Got it?"

Ethan tried to nod, but he was too petrified to move. The man's hand was mashing into his face until Ethan thought his cheekbones might snap like he'd seen chicken bones do when Mama Joe was cutting up chicken pieces to fry. His wide-open eyes began to adjust to the darkness until he could make out the shape of the man beside him getting ready to swallow him up. Ethan feared he might wet the bed and then what would Mama Joe think when she came home.

"Don't be scared, boy. Your old pa won't hurt you. Not as long as you do as you're told."

Ethan tried to pull away from the man, but his hold was too strong.

"Ain't no use struggling. You're going with me one way or another. Now I'm gonna take my hand away. If you holler, I'll kill the old preacher man." There was the slide of metal on leather and then the man was holding a knife up in front of Ethan's face. He turned the long blade from side to side so that it caught light from somewhere in the darkness and flashed in Ethan's eyes. Ethan lost his breath and his head started spinning.

The man took his hand away from Ethan's mouth and Ethan gasped for air. The ragged sound of his breathing was loud in the silence of the night.

"Put your clothes on." The man wasn't holding on to him anywhere now, but the knife was still shining in the darkness. "If you don't do as I say, you'll be sorry. You and the old man."

Ethan tried not to make a sound as he felt for his clothes on the chair at the end of the bed. Then he searched under the bed for his shoes. He hadn't worn them for days, not since the last Sunday, but he thought he might need them wherever the man was taking him. He didn't aim to knock over the chamber pot that Mama Joe put under the bed for him so he wouldn't have to go to the outhouse in the middle of the night. But he hit it with his foot. He jerked toward it to try to keep it from turning over and banged his head on the bed.

The man jerked him out from under the bed by his ankles. Ethan grabbed his shoes and held them against his chest. The man hissed, "You better hope the old preacher can't hear so good."

But there was nothing wrong with Preacher Joe's hearing. His eyesight was failing, but not his hearing. From the next room they heard his bed creak as he raised up to call, "Are you all right, Ethan?"

The man moved away from Ethan toward Preacher Joe's room. The knife winked in the dark again.

"Run, Preacher Joe, run!" Ethan screamed as loud as he could.

But of course he didn't run. He came straight toward Ethan to save him. The man who said he was Ethan's father clubbed Preacher Joe over the head with the fist that held the knife, but he didn't stab him. Preacher Joe fell to the floor and lay still. Ethan dropped his shoes and ran toward him.

The man grabbed Ethan by the hair before he got there. "He ain't dead, but he will be if you don't come along with me peaceably like."

A sob swelled up in Ethan's throat. He held it back. "I dropped my shoes."

"You won't need them. I've got a horse."

The man yanked him by the hair toward the kitchen door. As Ethan passed by the table, he reached out and touched the hearts. Behind him Preacher Joe groaned, and then the man pulled him out of the kitchen into the dark night and kicked the door shut.

2

The horse moved through the darkness under the trees as if a lantern was showing it the way. The woodsy smell of damp dirt and rotting leaves mixed with the smell of the man tight behind Ethan in the saddle. Ethan jumped when a great horned owl hooted and flew out of a tree before them with a crashing of wings among the branches. He couldn't stop shaking.

Ethan had been in the woods at night. On foot with Preacher Joe and his hunting dogs as they chased after raccoons. He liked the woods, day or night. The good Lord's blessing on them, Preacher Joe said sometimes as he stopped to lay his hand on the bark of a particularly big oak tree. If the hounds hadn't yet found their prey and begun baying to send Preacher Joe and Ethan chasing through the trees after them, Preacher Joe might say a prayer. Something to celebrate the woods and the night and the Lord. Preacher Joe had a lot of celebration prayers. *Praise God from whom all blessings flow.*

Ethan couldn't pray that now. He wasn't being blessed. He was being stolen. Even if the man did say he belonged to him.

Ethan didn't want to belong to him. He wanted Preacher Joe to be his father. He wanted Mama Joe to touch the top of his head while he was eating his breakfast. But instead this man had hold of him, taking him away from them. Ethan squeezed his eyes shut tight and prayed as hard as he could. *Please, I want to go home.*

Remember the way. Preacher Joe had said those words to him plenty of times when they were out in the woods around their house. *Pay attention to where you are so you can find the way home if need be.* They'd even made a game of it at times with Preacher Joe letting Ethan lead the way. He always found home sooner or later.

He would this time too. The man would have to let him down off the horse sometime, and then Ethan could get away. He could walk home. All he had to do was watch for landmarks to guide his trek back to Preacher Joe's. Ethan opened his eyes wide and tried to pick out things to remember about this or that tree they were passing by, but it was different on the horse. The horse's feet—not his feet—were feeling the path. And no moon was shining down through the branches. The woods were always full of moonlit shadows when they went hunting in the night.

That didn't mean he couldn't watch and see. He'd know the way home once he was off the horse and on his own feet. But at daylight, when the man finally stopped beside a creek and let him off the horse, he tied one end of a rope around Ethan's waist and the other end to his belt before he pointed him toward the creek to get a drink.

Ethan scooped up some water in his hands while the man dropped down on his belly and put his face right into the water. The horse was drinking on the other side of them. It was a nice brown color with a white blaze on its face. The horse had made it through the woods in the dark with ease. It could find the way back in the daylight even easier. The horse raised his head and looked toward Ethan as if it knew what he was thinking. Then it shook his head and sprayed water and mouth foam on Ethan.

The man put his head all the way under the water in the creek before he stood up and shook almost the same as the horse.

Ethan looked at him. "You can untie me. I won't run away." It wasn't a complete lie. He aimed to ride away. Not run.

The man snorted and squeezed the water out of his beard. "Didn't that old preacher man teach you it's a sin to lie?"

"I'm not lying." Ethan's voice didn't tremble much.

"And I'm not Hawk Boyd." The man laughed and cuffed Ethan on the side of his head almost playfully. "Go on and re-lieve yourself over there in the bushes. The rope's long enough, but don't be trying to unloose it. I ain't the kind of pa to spare the rod. You best keep that in mind, son."

When Ethan came back from the bushes, the man handed him a piece of dried meat. "This'll have to do till we get to the river. Then the vittles will be better."

"The river?" Ethan had never seen a river. Creeks like the one they were sitting beside, but no rivers. Preacher Joe had seen rivers. Had said he'd even once ridden a boat on a river somewhere in the east. Ethan stored that bit of knowledge. Preacher Joe had taught him his directions and how to look at the shadows of the trees and the sun to figure out which way to go. Except he wasn't sure which way they'd come in the night.

"That's right. Your old pa is a river man. Your ma knew

that when she married me. She knew I couldn't stay on hard ground. Got to feel the water under my feet." He bit off a piece of the dried meat and stared at Ethan as he chewed.

"I don't want to go with you." Ethan spoke the words as firmly as a six-year-old could.

The man's eyebrows scrunched together, making deep lines between his eyes, but he didn't look mad exactly. "I come all this way to get you, to do right by you, and here you are being plain contrary. A boy big as you should want to be with his pa." He stared at Ethan as if he was a puzzle he was trying his best to figure out. Then his frown disappeared as he blew out a breath and said, "And you will. My blood's flowing in your veins. Won't be a week till you'll be thanking me for coming back for you."

"No." Ethan spit at the man. It was the worst thing he could think to do.

The man smacked Ethan on the jaw and knocked him off his feet as easy as he might have swatted down a bothersome horsefly. "First thing, you better learn some respect. Don't be saying no to your pa or the next time I'll use a stick on you." He picked up a fallen branch as big around as Ethan's arm and held it menacingly over Ethan. "Got that, boy?"

Ethan tried to scramble out of the man's reach, but the rope held him.

The man rapped him smartly across the backside with the stick and then laughed again. "Just a taste of what you'll get if you don't jump when your pa says jump. Now get up. We have to reach the river before the sun sets. They won't wait for us longer than that."

A day and a night on a horse. Ethan had no idea how many miles that might be, but he grabbed hold of the information anyway. They rode along the creek until the sun was a couple of hours up in the sky, and then they came out on a road wide enough for wagons. The man kicked the horse into a faster gait. Each time they met somebody on the road he pressed his fingers hard into Ethan's thigh to warn him against making a sound. With the pain still throbbing in his jaw, Ethan kept quiet, but whenever he heard a horse coming up on them from behind, his heart bounded up with hope that it might be the sheriff Preacher Joe had talked about. It never was.

The sun beat down on them until the horse was lathered and the man's shirt behind Ethan's back was soaked with sweat. The man stopped to let the horse drink from a trough in front of a stone house. Then he pushed Ethan in front of him into the building, where he downed a big glass of something that foamed on the top and had that peculiar smell Ethan had noticed the night before when the man stole him out of his bed.

The man bought some apples and cheese for him and Ethan and corn for the horse. Then they were on their way again even though the man at the stone house shook his head and said the man ought to rest his horse through the heat of the day.

"No time for that," the man said as he sat Ethan on the horse and swung up behind him.

Dusk was falling when they left the road and started downhill through another woods. The horse's head had been drooping as they kept to the road, but now he perked up his ears and began to move faster.

"He smells the water," the man said, the first words he'd spoken since they left the stone house. The man pulled in a deep breath. "And it's a mighty fine smell. We're almost there, boy. Can you smell it?"

Ethan raised his head up and took a deep breath in spite of himself. He did smell something different. Dank and fishy and cooler. He couldn't keep from stretching up taller to look for this river the man said was up ahead. When they came out of the trees, the river was bigger than he expected. Four or five times as broad as the biggest creek he'd ever crossed, with brownish green water moving past them. Southwest, according to the shadows made by the setting sun.

"What river is it?" Ethan knew rivers had names.

"The Kentucky," the man said. "It flows into the Ohio. The Ohio flows into the Mississippi and the Mississippi flows into the Gulf of Mexico. That's all the geography any river man needs to know."

A big flat raft with a lean-to shelter in the middle of it was tied up to a tree on the bank. Two men stood on the raft while another was on the bank. At the sound of the horse, they looked up, and the one on the riverbank said, "We was about to shove off without you, Hawk."

"I told you I'd be here before nightfall." The man slid down off the horse and then pulled Ethan down with him. He tied the horse's reins to the saddle horn and pulled the saddle-bags off before he gave the horse a slap on the rump. "Get on home."

The horse went to the river and found a spot to drink before it headed back through the woods.

One of the men on the raft watched the horse go and said, "We coulda maybe tied him to the raft."

"No," the man who had stolen Ethan said. "I told the stable owner I'd send him home."

"When did your word ever matter?" the man on the raft said. "A horse would be more use than that boy there. What you expecting us to do with him, Hawk? We ain't nurse-maids."

"He's my boy and he's going." The man's fingers dug into Ethan's shoulder while his other hand hovered over the knife sheath hanging down from his belt. "Any of you got a problem with that?"

The man on the bank stepped back a couple of steps, held up his hands and answered for all of them. "I reckon a boy should be with his pa. We ain't got no problem with that, do we, fellers?"

The other men stared at Hawk and shook their heads.

"Good to hear." Hawk pushed Ethan forward. "This here's Ethan." Then he pointed toward the men. "That's Bert here on the bank. That one worried you'll be a hindrance is Red, and the other one is Ansel. He can't hear thunder, but he knows every sawyer in the river."

Ethan had no idea what a sawyer was, but he didn't open his mouth to ask. The man kept hold of Ethan's collar as he fished the rope out of his saddlebags and tied it around Ethan's waist again.

The man named Bert frowned. "What's with the rope? I thought you said he was your boy."

"He is, but he's been living with a landlubber." Hawk pulled on the rope to be sure the knot would hold and then hooked it to a post on the raft. "He ain't exactly figured out he wants to be a river man yet, but he will soon enough."

Bert made a sound that might have been a laugh. He waited until Hawk walked away before he eased over beside Ethan. He looked over his shoulder toward Hawk who was digging a bottle out of one of the crates, then got right down in Ethan's face. His teeth were black and his breath smelled worse than Birdie's after the dog had been eating something rotten. He kept his voice low. "I'll tell you two things a river man might need to know straight off. One you probably done know already. That's that your pa is one mean son of a gun. The other is that a *sawyer* is a tree caught in the river that saws back and forth and can catch a raft and dump what's on it into the river. Sometimes everything on it. Sometimes just a thing or two." Bert's eyes narrowed on him. "If you can't swim, boy, you best be thinking on learning."

The frogs and night bugs were in full chorus when they finally pushed off from the bank as night was falling. Mosquitoes buzzed in Ethan's ears, but he didn't pay them much mind as he studied the knot on the rope around his waist. He didn't intend to go down the river. At least not far. Preacher Joe had taught him how to swim in the deep part of the creek out back of their house a long time back. But he had to wait for the time to be right.

All the men except the one named Ansel stretched out on the raft to go to sleep. Hawk checked the knot on the rope around Ethan's waist and took the end off the post and tied it to his arm before he said, "I ain't a heavy sleeper. You try anything, you'll wish you hadn't."

It wasn't long until all three men were snoring. Ethan had to fight to keep his own eyes open. He was so tired. He worked the knot loose enough to slide it down the rope very carefully while keeping one eye on Ansel standing toward the front of the raft watching the river ahead. The man held the long stick he'd used to push them away from the bank.

The sliver of moon sinking in the west reflected a glimmer

of light off the river water. Ethan looked up at the stars that seemed to be right above his head and whispered a prayer in his head. *Don't let Hawk wake up.* He slid the rope down his body and off his feet and then eased it up and around a bundle of furs.

The men kept snoring and Ansel kept staring out at the river ahead of them. Ethan looked toward the bank of the river. It looked a long way and the water was flowing fast. Faster than any creek water he'd ever seen.

He waited until the river carried the raft closer to the left bank, and then with his eye on Ansel, he slipped off the raft into the water. He barely made a ripple in the water. He churned hard with his arms to move toward the bank, but it seemed to get farther away as the river swept him downstream after the raft. His arms turned to rock and his head went under the water.

For a minute he drifted there with the dark silkiness of the river all around him. He couldn't breathe, but it didn't seem to matter. Then a voice told him to kick. He wasn't sure whether the voice was in the water or in his head, but it was a voice he couldn't ignore. He kicked his feet and broke out of the water, gasping for breath. Directly in front of him a tree stuck up out of the water. He wondered if it was one of the sawyers Bert had told him about as he grabbed at the limb and caught it.

Ethan clung to the branch and watched the raft until it was swept around a bend in the river. None of the men on it were yelling. He was safe. And then a lost feeling welled up inside him, and he wondered if he should have stayed on the raft. With the man who claimed to be his born father.

But no, Preacher Joe was the father he wanted.

Ethan began working his way along the tree toward the river's edge by grabbing first one branch, then another, until his feet touched bottom. He climbed up on the rocky bank and collapsed. Morning would be soon enough to worry about how he was going to climb out of the rocky cliffs that rose up from the river.

The next thing he knew, a hand on his shoulder was shaking him awake. Ethan's eyes flew open, but the morning sun was so bright, all he could see was a blurred face and a hat. He scrambled away from the man's hand.

"Easy, little brother," a gentle voice said. "I mean you no harm. How come you to land here on these rocks? Where are your people?"

Ethan pulled in a breath as he squinted his eyes to better see the man. His smile was kind, so Ethan told him the truth. "I don't know. A man stole me from where I live with Preacher Joe and was taking me down the river. I slid off the raft and swam to here."

"And who was the man that stole you?"

Ethan stopped telling the truth. "I don't know," he said.

"So." The man frowned a little as if he knew Ethan lied before he asked his next question. "Do you have a name?"

"Ethan. Ethan Boyd."

"Well, then I'm sure your people will be looking for you, young Ethan." The man's frown disappeared as he reached a hand toward him. "Until then, I daresay you're hungry. How about you come with me to find some breakfast?"

Ethan let the man pull him to his feet and looked up at the rocks rising up from the river. "Is there a way out of here?"

"Yea, for a certainty." The man in the hat laughed. It was a good sound. It reminded Ethan of Preacher Joe. "My name is Issachar Barr. I live in the Shaker village up on top of the hill. You can call me Brother Issachar."

Ethan looked up at the man. Some people called Preacher Joe Brother Joe, and he had the same kindness in his eyes. "What is a Shaker?" Ethan asked.

"Someone who puts his hands to work and gives his heart to God."

"Can I stay with you until Preacher Joe finds me?"

"Yea, that you can. The Shakers never turn away one in need." Brother Issachar knelt in front of him, put his hands on Ethan's shoulder, and looked straight into his eyes. His dark eyebrows were like unkempt bushes over his light blue eyes. "The river has gifted the Shakers with many things in the years since I've been here. But a young believer. You may surely turn out to be the best gift ever." Brother Issachar stood up and took Ethan's hand. "Come, my young brother. A sister will find you some food."

3

October 1833

The day her father died was the worst day of Elizabeth Duncan's life. There'd been other bad days. The day they'd moved from the town to this old cabin in the middle of a wilderness of trees. The day four years past when her mother had died of a lung ailment. The day her brother had come home from a trip to town to relay the message from Ralph Melbourne's father that Ralph had married a girl up in Indiana instead of coming back to Kentucky to keep his promise to Elizabeth. Ralph's father wanted her to know she was free to marry another, Payton said. As if she could just turn to the next man in line.

But watching her father pull in one ragged breath after another and then no more was the worst, when the morning before he'd been laughing and talking with no hint of ill health. Elizabeth lifted the oil lamp to cast more light on the bed where he lay and stared at his chest, willing it to rise again. She was alone with her father in the deepest dark of the night. She'd sent Payton off to bed at midnight with no thought that their father might not make the morning light. A thought she'd been unable to imagine, even though she'd been in sickrooms with her mother and seen death come.

Her mother had learned of herbs and root medicines from her mother back in Virginia, and she'd passed that knowledge down to Elizabeth.

"I don't have the healing gift she had," her mother had told Elizabeth as they walked through the woods in search of the proper roots. "She had an uncanny way of knowing which doses would work best for which symptoms and was much sought in our village back in the old settlement when someone took to their bed with this or that complaint. We had no doctor in the village."

Her mother pointed out a plant of ginseng, and Elizabeth dug its root while her mother leaned against a tree and wheezed as she tried to pull in enough breath to continue on toward their cabin.

Elizabeth put the root in the sack tied to her waist and stood up. "Back in Springfield before we moved here into the woods, people came to you for your potions."

Elizabeth's mother smiled a little sadly. "But now I cannot even heal myself."

"Perhaps the medicine in these roots will be stronger." Elizabeth lifted the sack of roots with dirt still clinging to them.

"Perhaps it will," her mother said as she touched Elizabeth's hair. A deep cough racked her body, and she spit into her handkerchief folding it quickly to hide the tinge of red, but Elizabeth saw it.

The medicine in the roots had not been stronger. Her

mother had died before she saw another spring. And now Elizabeth's father lay on the bed in front of her under the last quilt her mother had pieced, and his chest did not rise.

"Father. Don't leave us, Father." Elizabeth spoke softly. She knew he had already gone beyond the sound of her voice, but she wasn't ready to accept it. She set down the lamp and made herself stand to go to him. She dreaded touching his body and feeling the heat of life leaving him. At the same time she wanted to grab hold of him and push her own body heat into him to keep him there with them.

She turned back the quilt to lay her ear on his chest as she sent up a wordless prayer. The Lord had brought the widow's son back to life and Lazarus after three days. She'd read those truths in the Bible many times. Perhaps he would yet breathe life back into her father. But of course, he did not. Death was not so easily cheated in this day and time.

"Oh my father, what will we do without you?" Tears flooded her eyes and she did not try to stop them. Here in the darkest hour of the night, the darkest moment of her twenty years was the time for tears. Come the sunrise, then she would of necessity push aside the tears.

She thought of waking Payton and Hannah, but what would be the use? Best to let them sleep. Payton would take it hardest. Since he first started toddling across the floor some fifteen years ago, he had followed after their father as oft as he could. As for Hannah, well, who knew what that wild child might do? Probably run off to one of her secret places in the woods.

Since their mother had died when Hannah was four, the woods had been her mother, her friend. Sometimes when Elizabeth went to seek her among the trees, she would find her high in an oak peering down at Elizabeth. Other times she would be dug back into a hole under a rocky ledge.

"You are not a wild animal, Hannah," Elizabeth would admonish her. "You are a girl."

"But can I not be both?" Hannah had asked on one of those occasions. "Are we not animals, and am I not a girl?"

"We are human," Elizabeth said. "Not animals."

"But humans are animals. Father said so. He read to me from one of his books that we are mammals like the horse and the dog or the fox and the squirrel."

Their father told Elizabeth not to worry about Hannah. That she would surely outgrow her wildness. That lacking a mother had opened a window in her mind that not many flew through. He had sounded almost proud. Easy enough for him. He was not the one who had to comb her hair and make her wash her face and teach her to read and do her figures. There was no school anywhere nearby.

Now Elizabeth would have to be mother and father. She would have to see that there was food on the table, wood in the fireplace, fodder for the cow. They did not even own the cabin they slept in. After her mother's death, her father had lost all interest in any kind of commerce. In Springfield, he had hung out a shingle as a lawyer, but no one would walk a half day into the woods to seek legal help. So they had learned to subsist off the land, growing some vegetables and eating the fish her father and Payton pulled out of the Chaplin River that ran past their cabin down the bluff. She traded roots for their few store-bought necessities.

The roof over their head was the charity of Colton Linley who lived in a big house a few miles away. He had delusions that someday Elizabeth would join him in that house. His first wife had died in childbirth, taking the child to heaven with her. His second wife had run back to Virginia after only three months of marriage.

Elizabeth had not known either wife. That had all happened before they moved into his cabin. Colton surely could have married again. He owned land, seemed well-to-do if one could judge by a man's clothes and his horse. Whenever he came to see her father, his brown hair was slicked down with pomade and his shirt pressed. Not exactly a dandy, but a man well aware of his position in life. And if she made herself look at him with an unbiased eye, she had to admit he wasn't really bad looking in spite of a nose that was long and narrow. Or perhaps it wasn't the shape of his nose she found offensive, but the way Colton's flint gray eyes peered down it at others as if the Lord had formed the world for his sole benefit. Even so, he could have captured a third wife with ease.

But if he had courted a woman since his second wife had left him, Elizabeth had no knowledge of it. She wished he had. She wished he had a wife. Instead it chilled her heart whenever she heard him tell her father he was waiting for the right woman—a strong woman in body and spirit who could carry a child without having the vapors. He sometimes added, "A woman like your Elizabeth promises to be."

He was nearly as old as her father, but it wasn't his age that made Elizabeth avoid his very eye on her. It was those eyes and the way they sized her up as nothing more than a piece of property. How strong was her back? How broad her hips to carry his child? He looked at her as if he already owned her and it was only a matter of time before she had to satisfy the payment. She never noted the first hint of tenderness in his eyes.

The year before, after Ralph had gone to Indiana and not returned for her, her father had asked if there could be any chance Elizabeth would ever look upon Colton favorably.

"Colton has land and a fine house," her father had said. "I realize he is old for you, but you would never want for anything."

"Naught but love," Elizabeth answered. She had been building a fire in the cookstove to ready their breakfast, and she dropped the stove lid back in place with a clang before she looked over at her father who was filling the coffeepot. "Colton has no love in his heart for me. He wants to own me. I know not why, but I do know I could not bear his touch on me." She couldn't suppress a shiver at the thought of it.

"Why is he so repulsive to you?" Her father set the coffeepot on the stove before turning to Elizabeth with a slight frown as he tried to understand her aversion to Colton. "He seems decent enough. He lets us stay on here in his cabin without much in return except a few hours' labor now and again. He always says I can pay him later. The man has simply had bad luck with the women in his life."

"Perhaps for a reason." Elizabeth's heart seemed afraid to beat inside her chest as she stared at her father. "Please, I beg of you, don't ask me to encourage his attentions."

"Worry not, my daughter. I would never ask you to marry for any reason other than love." When he reached over to touch her cheek with tenderness, Elizabeth's heart had started beating normally again. "I want you to know love as your mother and I did."

Her father had understood. He had promised to find a way to pay for the cabin, to keep Colton at arm's length. But now her father was gone. Dead in one day. She'd thought to send Payton after the doctor at first light. Even the cholera didn't take its victims so quickly. Two days, three, but not overnight.

Her father feared it was the cholera when he took sick. He'd been to Springfield where in the summer so many had sickened and died from the dreaded illness, but they'd heard of no cholera deaths for weeks. Still, he had vomited until blood mixed with the bile in the basin she held for him.

If it was the cholera, she might not have to worry about what the next weeks would bring. They might all die in the week to come. Cholera oft swept through a family with no pity.

"You're not dead yet," Elizabeth whispered to herself. When she touched her father's cheek, the lifeblood had left it already. She pulled the quilt up over his face and went back to sit in the chair by the bed to wait for the morning light. A person couldn't just sit and wait for the death angel to come for her. She would have to do something. Plan a way to continue to live. She and Payton and Hannah.

"Please, dear God, show me another way besides Colton Linley." She listened intently as if she expected a spoken reply. There was none. Only the dreadful silence of her father's still body under the quilt.

At first light she built up the fire in the woodstove and fetched water from the spring to heat in order to prepare her father's body for burial. She had to wake Payton to help her, because her father was too heavy for her to lift and turn on her own.

Tears streamed down Payton's face as he looked down on their father's body. "Why didn't you wake me so I could tell him goodbye?"

"I'm sorry, but I had no warning. He just stopped breathing."

"Then it was an easy passing."

She saw no purpose in telling Payton about the terrible heaving and ragged breathing. "He did not linger in pain."

"Was it the cholera?" A touch of fear widened the boy's brown eyes that were so like their father's. Their mother used to laugh about how Elizabeth's father and Payton were the pretty ones in the family. They both had long lashes around their deep brown eyes and wavy dark hair falling over their foreheads. Elizabeth looked like her mother, straight brown hair, a no-nonsense square jaw, and green eyes flecked with gold.

Elizabeth met Payton's eyes without wavering and told the truth. "I don't know." Sometimes the truth was all she had.

Hannah came creeping into the room. When she saw their father's body, she shuddered, but she didn't cry. Hannah was not like anyone else in the family. Her almost-white hair sprang out in wild curls around her face, and her eyes were such a light shade of blue that sometimes they looked almost transparent. Elizabeth's mother had called Hannah her fairy child and said that if the midwife hadn't handed her the babe straight from her womb, she wouldn't have believed she was hers. She looked that much different. A throwback to an ancestor no one recalled now.

"He's dead," Hannah said. "Like Mother." Her voice was flat, devoid of feeling. "I don't want him to be dead."

"Nor do I." Elizabeth reached to hug Hannah, but the child backed away.

"You let him die." Hannah's voice was practically a scream now.

"Death needs no permission to enter a house." Elizabeth grabbed Hannah by the shoulders, but the girl jerked loose and ran out the front door.

When Elizabeth started after her, Payton put a hand on her arm to stop her. "Let her go. She'll be sorry for her words and come back to you for comfort later. But it could be that now the only way she can bear it is to run from the truth."

"If only we could." Elizabeth blinked back tears as she turned from the door back to the job at hand.

"Don't we need a box for him?"

"We have no way to buy one."

"Colton might help us."

"No." The word came out harsher than she intended. She pulled in a deep breath and held it a minute before she let it out. "I don't want to be beholden to Colton. Not more than we already are."

"I can make one. I'm good with wood." Payton's eyes went to the wooden dough board he had whittled for her in the summer.

"Where will you get the planks?"

"Off the cowshed out back."

"All right. First help me lay him out proper. Then I'll start digging a grave out by Mama while you build the box."

It wasn't easy digging. The ground was hard and there were plentiful rocks and roots to prise out of the way. Their dog, Aristotle, lay beside the grave with his black head on white paws and watched her with mournful eyes as if he knew why she was digging. Her father had brought the pup in after their mother died. For Hannah, he said, but he had given the dog its name and Elizabeth thought he had loved the animal most of all.

When Elizabeth straightened up to rest her back, she looked at the dog. "I'm sorry, Aristotle. I am so very sorry. For all of us."

Payton finished the box before she got halfway deep enough. She stopped digging and helped Payton lift their father into the box on the porch. Hannah had come back from the woods with her skirt tail caught up full of red and gold leaves and some purple flowers she'd found down by the river. With tears flowing now and dripping off her chin, Hannah laid the leaves in the box on top of their father's body. She gave one of the purple flowers to Elizabeth to place inside the box. Elizabeth kissed the mass of curls on top of the child's head and felt a sorrow for the fatherless child that went far beyond tears.

Payton brought a piece of cedar wood he'd whittled and polished. It had no particular shape, but he treasured it for the red and light tan whorls in the wood. He placed it beside their father's arm and looked up at Elizabeth. "Should we say words now? Out of the Good Book."

"We haven't got the grave ready."

"We need to say the words now so I can nail the top on." Payton looked grim, like someone told he must swim an icy river and so wanting to plunge into the water at once to get the ordeal over and done.

"Very well."

Elizabeth went inside to get the Bible off her father's desk. She found her scissors and some string before she went back out on the porch. With hands she could not keep from trembling, she tied off three locks of her father's hair and cut them from his head. She gave one to Payton and one to Hannah. The last she placed in the Bible beside the lock of her mother's hair she'd put in there four years earlier. She pulled a few strands of her mother's hair loose and laid them over her father's heart. Then she cut a lock of her own hair and Payton's and Hannah's to place on their father's chest alongside her mother's hair.

"Oh, my father, we will miss you so," she whispered.

Payton read 1 Corinthians 13, the same chapter their father had read when they buried their mother. Hannah read Psalm 23, stumbling over a few words that Elizabeth and Payton whispered along with her. Last, Elizabeth took the Bible and found 1 John 2:25. "And this is the promise that he hath promised us, even eternal life."

Aristotle jumped up on the side of the box and howled. The sound was like a knife in Elizabeth's heart. As she let the Bible fall shut to reach for the dog, a piece of paper fluttered out of the pages. After Elizabeth pulled the dog back and Hannah wrapped her arms around him to stop his howls, Elizabeth picked up the paper. It was the envelope for the bean seeds her father had bought from the Shakers last spring. He had stuck the empty packet in the Bible to remember the kind, for they had produced well.

Elizabeth stuffed the paper in her pocket. Springtime seemed forever away.

4

After Payton nailed the top onto the box, they left their father's body on the porch to finish digging the grave. Hannah sat down on the porch steps with Aristotle leaning against her legs and would not budge, even though Elizabeth pleaded with her to come with them and not stay alone with the body.

Hannah crossed her arms tightly over her chest and lifted her chin. "I do not fear my dead father."

So Elizabeth left her there and walked with Payton back to the graves behind the cabin just below their garden plot. They took turns with the shovel, one digging while the other used the grubbing hoe to break loose the roots. The sun climbed high in the sky and reflected off the red and golden trees all around them, but they had no eyes for the beauty of the day. Their eyes were on the dirt as they dreaded the sound of the shovel clanging into a new rock that might prove too big to dig around and heave up out of the grave.

As the shadows started falling toward the east, they had the grave shoulder deep. Payton handed her the shovel and said, "I can't dig more without water. And food."

His face was streaked with sweat and dirt, and Elizabeth knew hers must be as well. She had given no thought to eating, and only after he spoke of it did she realize her thirst. "You're right. I'll keep digging while you go fix something for you and Hannah. There's bread and apple butter in the cupboard. Then you can bring me some water."

Payton looked down at the hard clay dirt under his shoes and back at Elizabeth. "Do you think it might be deep enough already? We could pile these many rocks on top." He waved his hand at the rocks they'd dug out of the grave.

"It would be best to dig another foot." Elizabeth pushed the shovel down into the dirt and shoved it deeper with her foot. She ached all over from the work, and her hands were swollen and red with blisters.

"If it's the cholera, who will dig our graves?"

"It wasn't the cholera. We would have begun to sicken by now if it had been." Elizabeth lifted the shovelful of dirt and threw it up and out onto the pile that loomed larger than the hole.

"Are you sure?"

Elizabeth leaned on the shovel and looked at Payton standing above her. "I am sure. Now go get water."

She was bent over working out yet another rock when she heard footsteps coming back. He had only been gone a few minutes, so she thought he must have decided to bring her the water first. It wasn't until the man jumped into the grave behind her and landed heavily that she realized it wasn't Payton, who was always light as a cat on his feet.

She straightened and whirled around. "Colton. What are you doing here?"

She backed away from him until the cool dirt on the side of

the grave stopped her. Her skin started crawling even before he stepped closer and put his hand on her shoulder. She made herself not shrug it off as she breathed in and out slowly.

"You should have sent Payton to get me. Grave digging is not woman's work."

He sounded cross that she had not asked him for help, but she did not want his help. She wanted nothing from him.

"Payton is helping me," she said briskly. She stared at his face and wondered what about it awoke such dread within her or why his hand on her shoulder was so frightening. Her heart began pounding in her ears. "How did you know of our father?"

"I didn't." He tightened his hand on her shoulder in a gesture of sympathy. "Hannah told me moments ago. I was just coming to talk with him. He stopped by my house yesterday morning about the money he owes me. You did realize he owed me money, didn't you?" He looked pleased by that fact.

"Father rarely discussed his business with me." Elizabeth avoided the answer to his question.

"That's too bad. It might have been something you should know." He moved a step closer to Elizabeth until she could smell the pomade on his hair and feel the heat of his body. "We were working out a way for him to eliminate his debt. And he seemed hale and hearty then. Only yesterday. We shared some fresh cider."

"The sickness came on him suddenly. He died in the night."

"So Hannah told me." He put his other hand on her other shoulder and let his eyes drift from her face down her body.

"It might be the cholera." Elizabeth hoped to scare him back from her. "You best keep your distance."

He actually laughed, the sound as grating as the scrape of the shovel point across rock. "I think not. I think I will never have to keep my distance from you ever again."

She put her hands against his chest and tried to push him back from her, but it was like pushing against a stone wall.

"Get away from me!" She put all the force she could into her voice.

Again he laughed. He lifted one of his hands and rubbed the hard tips of his fingers across her cheek. "You might as well learn to like my touch upon you because you are mine now. You no longer have any other choice. You are the payment of your father's debt."

"He made no such contract with you."

"Oh, but he did. He had no other options. And neither do you. Not if you want a roof over your head and food on the table for your brother and sister." Colton's eyes bore into her.

"We can get by."

"But have you forgotten the debt you owe me? What a shame that the debts of the father can be passed down to the daughter." He pushed his body up against her and shoved her harder against the side of the grave. A root poked into her back. There was no escape.

Elizabeth stayed stiff against him and made her voice icy as she said, "Would you dare violate me in my father's grave? Have you no honor?"

"There is too much weight given to honor in this world," he said, but he stepped back from her. "But perhaps you are right. You need to bury the dead before you can begin your new life with me."

She saw a chance. "Give me a week to grieve my father."

"You don't need a week." His eyes narrowed on her as he considered her words. He might have been making a deal for a horse. "Two days. And when I return you will marry me willingly, without resistance."

She did not nod or say yes, but neither did she say no.

He smiled, taking her silence as consent. "Then it is settled," he said. "Now give me the shovel and I will finish your digging."

It didn't seem right to surrender the job to him, but she could not bear another second so close to him. She handed him the shovel and began to climb out of the grave. He put his hand on her backside and pushed her up, groping her with his fingers as he did. It was all she could do not to kick him in the face.

Payton reached down to help her up. "Are you all right, Elizabeth?"

She had no idea how long he'd been standing there or how much he'd heard, but it would do little good to talk of it with him. He was just a boy yet and no match for a man such as Colton Linley.

"As all right as a person can be with her father dead this day." She looked directly into Payton's pale face. "Colton is going to finish the digging for us, and then I feel sure he will help us carry our father to his final resting place before he leaves to let us grieve in private."

Colton looked up at Payton with a pious look on his face. "Your father was a fine man. So many sorrows in this world, but he's gone on to a better place."

Elizabeth managed not to throw up until she got to the cabin out of sight of the grave. Payton came up beside her.

"So it is the cholera." His voice was flat, resigned.

She wiped her mouth with the cleanest under-edge of her apron she could find. She kept her eyes on the ground away from Payton. "No. It is Colton who makes me ill."

"We don't have to do as he says."

Elizabeth mashed her mouth together. The bad taste of her vomit clung to her tongue, for her mouth was dry as powder. "I need a drink of water." She started on toward the front of the cabin, but then stopped and turned back to touch Payton's arm. "We will talk about this after we bury our father."

"The Lord will help us find a way," Payton said. "Isn't that what Mama always said?"

"All he found for her was a way home to heaven." Elizabeth regretted the bitter sound of her words even before they were all the way out of her mouth. She added quickly, "But I will pray for a way."

"So will I. A way you can bear."

Colton helped them carry their father's body in the box to the grave. In truth, Elizabeth didn't know how they would have managed it without him there. She tried to be grateful as she thanked him for his help after the last prayer was said and the dirt was heaped in on top of her father. Each shovelful had thudded against her heart. But she felt no bit of gratitude until he mounted his horse and rode away, and then she thanked the Lord for the two days she'd been given.

Payton and Hannah looked as wounded and bruised as she felt as they sat around the table eating their meager supper of bread and milk, for Payton had milked the cow. They tried to talk about what they could do, but their grief sat too heavy on them.

Finally she touched Payton's cheek with her blistered hand and brushed aside the curls to kiss Hannah's forehead.

"Perhaps we will see things in a better light come morning."

After Payton climbed up into the loft and Hannah went into the small room off the kitchen where she and Elizabeth had shared a narrow bed since Hannah was three, Elizabeth barred the door and poured water into the basin to wash. The cold water felt good on her hands and face. As she pulled off her dirt-streaked dress, she heard the crinkle of paper in her pocket.

She pulled the paper out and stared at the Shaker seed package that had fallen out of her father's Bible. *One can always find an answer in God's Word.* Her father's voice was so clear in her head that she looked around to be sure he wasn't beside her, but of course, she was alone. *That's where you must look for answers.*

The Shakers. Her father had told her of the Shakers when he brought the seeds in last spring. They lived over in the next county. He had gone there. Said it was a beautiful place with great stone buildings and plentiful crops. A village, he said.

"But what are Shakers?" she had asked.

They were sitting on the porch steps as night fell softly around them. Hannah had fallen asleep in their father's lap and he had carried her to bed before coming back out to the porch. Payton was inside by the lamp, reading the new book their father had brought home with him.

"A religious sect," her father answered as he leaned back against the porch post and stroked Aristotle's head absentmindedly as he talked. In his other hand, he still held the seeds. "They are called Shakers because in their worship they are sometimes so stricken by a feeling of spirit that their bodies shake or they whirl about in a sort of dance."

"That sounds odd." Elizabeth frowned as she tried to imagine it.

"So it is. A bit odd. They claim to be shaking off the sin of worldliness. And they all dress much alike. The women in white aprons over blue dresses with caps to cover their hair, and the men in dark pants and blue shirts. Similar to the Quakers back in the old settlements. Except the Shakers don't believe in matrimony."

"How can they worship the Lord and not believe in matrimony? Doesn't the Bible say to go forth and be fruitful? Surely one should marry to do that."

"As best I could understand, they don't believe in that sort of relationship between a man and a woman. They live as brothers and sisters and claim the Lord revealed this as his will through visions in the last century to someone they call Mother Ann. She set forth their purpose. 'Hands to work, hearts to God.'" He stared down at the seed package as if he saw the words there.

"That doesn't sound so different from what the preacher back in the church in Springfield used to tell us. The part about hearts to God." Elizabeth looked at her father. He seemed very impressed with these people. "Did they convince you of the truth of their ways?"

"No, no," he said quickly. Then he looked away toward the sky. "I did feel a peace there in their village that I have not felt since I lost your dear mother. But no, they didn't convince me of the sin of matrimony. What your mother and I shared was not a sin but a gift of love from God. Nor would I want to give up fatherhood and only be a brother to my children." He reached over and touched her hand with affection.

"But how do they have children in their midst without relationships to produce offspring?"

"They take in all who come to their door. Those they have converted by persuasion and also orphans with the hope that, in time, they will come to trust in the Shaker ways. They don't turn away anyone in need. They have plentiful food and kind hearts. At least so it seemed for the ones I met."

"And must those they feed believe?"

"Not at all. They must work and follow the rules of the Shakers, but they are allowed to leave if they so choose or to sign a Covenant of Belief when they come of age if they decide to join the Shakers as believers."

Elizabeth studied her father's face. She could no longer see his expression for the light had grown dim, but she detected a strange yearning in his voice. "You sound as if you wish you could have believed."

"There was peace there, my Elizabeth. And a school for Hannah. You know yourself she should be in school. There were woodcarvers and architects and many who seemed blessed with great talent and wisdom. I think you are right. I did wish I could believe." He sighed and stuffed the seed packet into his shirt pocket. "But I did not. We will plant their beans tomorrow and see how they grow."

The beans had grown well. Produced more than any beans they had ever planted.

Now Elizabeth smoothed out the packet and laid it on the table. It was her answer. They would go to the Shakers.

5

Ethan Boyd arose from bed at the sound of the rising bell the same as he had every morning since Brother Issachar had found him on the riverbank fifteen years ago. He had picked a good place to be washed ashore. Actually he hadn't picked it. Providence had guided him there. As Brother Martin who had taught him the Shaker way was prone to telling Ethan, he was destined to be a Believer.

Ethan hadn't known that at first. It wasn't that he hadn't liked the village Brother Issachar had led him up the steep road to find. He had. It seemed an almost magical place of light and goodness. The Shaker brothers and sisters were all kind to him as they welcomed him into their midst. They dressed him in new clothes that matched their own and fed him and gave him a bed.

Still, he missed Preacher and Mama Joe, and for months he watched for them to show up in the village to take him home. Brother Issachar did his best to find them as well by going into the towns of the world and asking about a preacher named Joe. But Ethan hadn't known a last name or a place name, and there was no way of determining how far the man who had claimed to be his father might have carried him through the woods and then down the river.

Eventually his memories of the loving Preacher and Mama Joe faded and blended in with his new Shaker brothers and sisters. Brother Issachar was always there with his kind eyes and ready smile. He took Ethan into the forest with him and taught him the different kinds of wood for making the chairs and furniture and tools they needed in the village. Brother Martin filled his mind with knowledge of numbers and letters and the tenets of the Shaker beliefs. Brother Haskell taught him the songs and helped him practice the steps to the worship dances. They all embraced him as the gift Brother Issachar claimed he might be to the Shakers on that first morning so long ago now.

Harmony Hill was just as its name said. Harmony and peace. And work. But Ethan didn't mind the labor. He had grown strong and tall with the Shakers, even taller than Brother Issachar. He enjoyed putting his hands to work, especially working with Brother Issachar, but he gladly did his duty with any work assignment. Sometimes at harvesttimes he imagined every Shaker in the village as the hands and feet on a giant reaping machine going through the field. By himself he could not accomplish so much, but when they joined together for the good of all, much was harvested. They knew no physical wants.

Not only were their biting room tables where they took their meals weighted down with the provisions they grew on their lands, but their industries were booming as well. Every labor of a Believer's hands showed his or her worship of the Eternal Father whether that was weaving a basket, building a drawer, quarrying stone out of the palisades along the river for a new building, or mucking out a barn stall.

While those of the world did not understand or accept the Shaker way, they did seek after the Shakers' seeds and herbs, jams and potions, brooms and baskets. And some of the world came to the village to find the perfect peace and right living of their Society of Believers. The membership at Harmony Hill had climbed since Ethan landed on their riverbank until it numbered over two hundred souls.

Not all were covenant-signed Believers. Some were part of the Gathering Family where they lived as Shakers but had not made a commitment decision. Some only came for the provisions in a time of need and then left the village as their lots improved. Brother Martin spoke angrily of them as "winter Shakers." People committed only to filling their stomachs and running after the lusts of the world, he said. Brother Martin had no use for those of the world.

He had been looking at Ethan in somewhat the same way ever since Ethan turned twenty-one as if he feared Ethan might be lusting after the world. He had expected Ethan to sign the Covenant of Belief and be welcomed into full membership of the Society of Believers at Harmony Hill in October of the year before.

Ethan had brought memory of his birth date to the village. October 15, 1811. He didn't know why he knew that and didn't know so many other things from before Harmony Hill, but he had treasured that one bit of knowledge. Something from the past to remember as his alone.

A birthday had not been an important thing to know as a child among the Shakers. The date of one's birth was not noted in any special fashion among the Believers, but the dates were duly written into the records. Twenty-one was recognized as the age of acceptance when a young person could make a decision about the direction of his life, and Ethan had been ready to make that decision. Had looked forward to making that decision until Brother Issachar had taken him into the woods in the week before Ethan's twenty-first birthday and advised him to wait.

They had sat on a wild cherry log that had fallen in a storm over the summer and that Brother Issachar hoped to use to make cabinets for the Centre Family House.

"You are young, Brother Ethan," Brother Issachar began.

"I will be twenty-one. That is the acceptable age." Ethan took off his broad-brimmed hat and wiped the sweat off his face before he smoothed a few stray black curls back from his face and pushed the hat down on his head again. The October day was warm and they had been hacking the limbs off the cherry log before they had taken a moment to rest.

Brother Issachar took off his hat to cool his head and balanced it on his left knee as he studied Ethan with a steady gaze. Veins traced red lines across his high cheekbones on his long, angular face.

At last he said, "Yea, that it is, but you are still young. You have lived most of your life in our village."

"But is not that good? How better to know the Shaker way?"

"True." Brother Issachar looked around as though concerned someone might be listening from the trees behind them. Age was beginning to droop his shoulders, and his knuckles were knotted with arthritis that made his woodworking difficult.

When he hesitated before continuing, Ethan jumped in front of his words. "Do you not want me to be a brother?"

"You ask the wrong question, my brother. The question is, do you want to be a brother? The Covenant should not be signed lightly."

"I can't imagine any other life," Ethan answered truthfully.

"Have you never looked out toward the world with longing? With curiosity to know how man lives outside the village?" Brother Issachar looked straight at Ethan. "To know how man and woman live as one."

"Nay," Ethan said a bit too quickly. He dropped his eyes to the ground and watched a beetle scramble out of sight under the log. "At least not great curiosity. Brother Martin says all young men feel a stirring in their loins at times. That it is the lust of the world trying to lead us astray, but that such sin and desire can be shaken off us."

"So it can be if that is what a man wants." Brother Issachar looked down at the log and moved his hand up and down its bark. Each fallen tree was a gift to him, a way to make use of every bit of the Lord's providence.

"How old were you when you signed the Covenant?" Ethan had never asked that. It had seemed to Ethan as if Brother Issachar had been born a Shaker.

"I was thirty-two. I joined a community in the state of New York, but I came here when I was thirty-five. That was two years before the river delivered you to us. I had another life before I was a Shaker." Brother Issachar kept his eyes on the pebbled bark of the tree below his hand.

"What sort of life? Did you have a wife?" Ethan asked.

"I did. Her name was Eva."

"So you had the sin of matrimony to rid yourself of before you could be a Shaker. Did she also become a sister?" Ethan had seen many couples come in to the Shakers since he had lived among them. They became brother and sister and no longer had relations one with another once they joined the Shakers.

"Nay. My Eva died trying to bear me a child." Brother Issachar looked up and stared at the trees as if he could see far away back to that other life of which he spoke. "And it was not a sin in that other world."

"But the Believer has taken himself out of that world."

"Yea. That I have done, and with no regrets." Brother Issachar's eyes came back to Ethan. "But I see doubt yet in your eyes. Great or not, it is there. So perhaps it might be better if you wait a year."

Ethan protested. "I see no need in delay. If the doubt you think you see is there, it lies buried so deeply that it will never come forward to cause me problems. I am ready."

"You could be right, my young brother." Brother Issachar pushed up off the log. Then before he began wielding his axe again, he turned to stare intently at Ethan as if searching his soul. "But what is one year in the whole of a man's life? You need to be sure of your decision for a man is honor-bound by the promises he makes."

And so Ethan had waited the year. He had withstood the questions and concerns of the elders and eldresses. He had exercised the dances and sung the songs and read more of Mother Ann's wisdom. He had shaken off the lustful drawing of the world without problem and put his hands to work for the good of the community. He had given himself the time Brother Issachar thought he needed, and the months had passed. He felt no different this October than last. He had been ready to sign his promise to be a Believer then. He was just as ready now.

The elders and eldresses of the Ministry gathered with Ethan after the morning meal for the signing of the Covenant. He read through the document even though he already knew what it said before he signed his name, promising to live a life of purity, to stay celibate, to give his hands to work and his heart to God.

Afterward, Brother Martin clapped him on the shoulder with a big smile spread across his broad face. "You will not regret your decision, Brother Ethan."

Brother Issachar was there as well, and he shook Ethan's hand and spoke no words of concern. But now Ethan thought the doubt was in Brother Issachar's eyes instead of Ethan's. As if Ethan would have to prove his belief. But hadn't it been Brother Issachar's words throughout the years since he had found him on the riverbank that had pushed Ethan along this path? The words that Ethan would be the best gift the river had ever yielded up to the Shakers. He wanted to be that gift. A true Believer.

It was Sunday and the bell rang to signal time for meeting. Out on the paths to the frame meetinghouse, voices began to join together in the Gathering Song. Brother Issachar left the room to join them, but Brother Martin held Ethan back for a moment.

"Don't be concerned with Brother Issachar's reticence. He has a tendency to be too much of an independent thinker for a true Believer. A gift to our Society for sure, with his way with wood and his ability to go out and trade with the world, but sometimes he needs to study the Millennial Laws a bit more devotedly. As you have already, Brother Ethan. You are a gift to us here at Harmony Hill. Of that, there is no doubt."

In meeting, Ethan took part in the back-and-forth steps of

the worship dances passing in lines between his brothers and sisters without having to note once the pegs in the floorboards that helped them to make the right steps. Brother Samuel was gifted with a song and Sister Adele had a whirling gift. Elder Joseph said the spirit was strong in the meeting that day.

Ethan waited for some special manifestation in his own spirit of the step he'd taken, but meeting felt no different this week than it had last week. He told himself that was because he had been a Believer as much the week before as he was this week. He had already made the Covenant promise in his heart. Years ago.

Ethan had never been visited with any special manifestation of the spirit. No whirling. No shaking. No visions or songs. Brother Martin assured him that was not something he should regard with concern. He said each Believer was gifted in different ways, but no gift was more valuable than the next. Mother Ann had treasured the gift to be simple over any other gift, and that was a gift they could all receive as Believers if they humbled themselves and worked for the good of their society.

Ethan was ready to do that. He felt his connection with each brother and sister as they passed one another in the lines of the dance. And best of all, now that he was a full member of the Society, then perhaps the Ministry would allow him to go with Brother Issachar and the other brothers out into the world on the trading trips.

Ever since Ethan was a child, he had enjoyed meeting Brother Issachar when he came back into the village after a trading trip. Sometimes Brother Issachar and the other brothers rode a boat down the river all the way to New Orleans and then walked back after they sold the goods they had. Sometimes they simply took a wagon of goods or seeds into the nearby towns to sell. But whether the trip was long or short, when Brother Issachar came back into the village, he always carried with him some of the air of the world. Air that Ethan breathed in as he wondered about life beyond the village confines. Being curious about that world did not mean that one could not be a true Believer, Ethan told himself, even if part of the Covenant spoke of dividing one's self from the world.

As they stopped their dance to rest a moment, Ethan looked toward where Brother Issachar sat on a bench on the far side of the room. He was not a gifted dancer and sometimes sat out the sets in order not to disturb the order of the dances. Brother Issachar met his eyes. His look on Ethan was kind as always, but his smile seemed tinged with a knowing sadness as if his mind had reached across the room and read the thought in Ethan's head about the trading trips into the world. As if he could see beyond even those thoughts to some deeper fault in Ethan's soul that would cause the Covenant promises he'd made to become a burden.

Ethan shook that thought away. Surely he was reading Brother Issachar's face wrong. It was a time to celebrate when one signed the Covenant of Belief. Not a time to be looking back with doubt. A Believer shook away all doubts. A Believer labored the dances and sang the songs to be simple until his path was clear before him. Ethan had done that. He had no doubts. He was a Believer.

As the meeting broke up, he told himself not to let his mind run after wrong thoughts. *Our thoughts are character molds. They shape language and action.* Brother Martin had taught him that from Mother Ann's teachings years ago. Now he simply had to have right thoughts. A Believer's thoughts.

6

The morning after they buried their father, Elizabeth waited until Payton milked the cow and Hannah fed Aristotle the leftover milk gravy and biscuits from their breakfast. There was no meat and only a crust or two of bread left. She looked at the crock of sourdough starter that her mother had brought with her from Springfield, but Elizabeth had no time to bake more bread. They had some apples left from the tree in back of the cabin, and she had found a few coins in her father's secret hiding places. Perhaps enough to buy food on the way to the Shaker village.

She sent Hannah back out to the woods to gather more flowers for their father's grave before she made Payton sit down and listen to what had to be done.

"I'm not going." Payton stared across the table at her as if she had lost her mind. "We are not going to the Shakers."

Elizabeth smoothed down the seed package she'd left in the middle of the table and leveled her eyes on Payton. "We have no other choice. The Shakers will take us in. They'll give us shelter and food."

"I can catch fish. We won't starve."

"Winter is coming, Payton. The river doesn't yield up its fish all that easily in the cold months. You know that."

"We have the cow."

"The cow also needs food in the winter. Fodder we do not have. Fodder Father would have found for her someway, but now we have to find it and I know not how."

"Colton would help us," Payton said.

"That is my fear," Elizabeth said softly.

Payton's face changed as if he was remembering the scene he'd witnessed the day before. "Is he so bad?" he asked at last with a trace of hope in his voice.

"If he were the only way to keep you and Hannah from starving this winter, I would give myself to him even though his very eyes on me make my skin crawl. I'd rather bed with a snake." Elizabeth couldn't stop the shudder that shook her, but then she sat up straighter in her chair and stared at Payton. "But he is not the only way. The Shakers are our way. It's not so far to their village. Maybe two or three days' walk."

"I won't go." Payton mashed his mouth together in a determined line.

"Please, Payton." Elizabeth reached across the table to touch his arm. "It's our only way of staying together. You and me and Hannah. We don't have to stay with the Shakers forever. Just for a few months until we figure out something better. It is what Father would have wanted."

"How do you know?" Payton asked.

"I prayed for an answer and the Lord gave me this seed packet." Elizabeth held it up. "Father told us about the Shakers. He said theirs is a beautiful village with plentiful food and large houses."

"He said they make everyone work."

"You're not afraid of work. Nor am I."

"What about Hannah?" Payton asked. "Will they understand her spirit?"

Elizabeth sighed deeply. He spoke the worry that had troubled her all the morning. "I don't know, but perhaps it is time she began to rein in her spirit. She needs to go to school. Father said so himself last spring, and he said the Shakers had a school. A good school. And whatever it is will surely be better than her being carried off to an orphanage where we might never see her again. I couldn't bear that. I would go to Colton first."

Payton's face flooded with anger. "Colton is the cause of this. If not for him, we could stay here. We could make our way."

"It is his cabin. His land." Elizabeth pushed the truth at Payton.

His anger settled deeper in his face and changed to lines of sadness as he accepted that truth. "I'll miss the river," he said at last. "When will we leave?"

"As soon as we can be ready. Colton promised me two days, but I don't trust him to stand by his word."

"What can we take?"

"Only what we can carry." Elizabeth had already been grieving over each thing she touched that morning—her mother's rolling pin, the wooden biscuit board carved by Payton, the books on her father's shelves—knowing she would have to leave all of them behind.

"What about the cow?"

"We will loose her in the woods and leave her to pay Colton although I have no idea of the amount he claims is owed him. I searched, but I could find no record of debt in Father's papers." A spark of hope sneaked back onto Payton's face, but Elizabeth blocked it before it could bloom into words. "Even if there is no proof of debt to him, we can't continue to live in his cabin. Not without paying more than I am prepared to pay."

Hannah opened the door and came inside with Aristotle. Her hair was a wild halo of white curls around her dirt-smudged face. The worry grew in Elizabeth that the Shakers would not understand Hannah's spirit. Who could understand the wildness in the child? Not even their father had understood it. He had simply accepted it, as had Elizabeth.

"What of Aristotle?" Payton looked at the dog. "Father said the Shakers didn't have pets. You remember, don't you? How he said it was odd to be in such a large village with no sound of a dog barking."

Aristotle ran over to Elizabeth and pressed his nose against her leg. Why did everything have to be so hard? Why couldn't Colton have been a man she could bear to touch her? She didn't have to love him. Just be able to bear his presence next to her. She stroked the dog's head and blinked back the tears that threatened to spill out and leak her strength with them. She could sacrifice herself to Colton for Payton and Hannah if there was no other way. She could not sacrifice herself for a dog.

"The Lord will help us find him a home on the way."

When Elizabeth told Hannah her plan, Hannah stomped her feet down hard as if attaching them to the floor and crossed her arms over her chest. "I will not leave my mother and father."

Elizabeth stooped down until she was looking Hannah

straight in the eye. "Our mother and father are not here. They are in heaven."

"They are more here than anywhere else we can go."

"No, my Hannah, you have it wrong. They are with us wherever we go. Here in our hearts." She put one hand softly over Hannah's heart and the other hand over her own heart. "We've told their bodies goodbye, but their love is right here inside us forevermore."

Hannah stared at her for a moment while the blue of her eyes seemed to darken with understanding. Then she put her hands over top of Elizabeth's hands. "Your love too?"

"My love too."

"Will I have to comb my hair?"

"Not today, but you must take your comb, for you will have to comb it before we get to the Shaker village. Perhaps we should cut some of it off to make the job easier."

"I care not. It is only hair."

"But what hair!" Elizabeth laughed and hugged her. "Father said the Shakers brought order to all things. We'll see what they can do with your hair."

"Father liked my hair." Hannah pulled back to stare into Elizabeth's face.

"And so did Mother." Elizabeth raked her fingers through Hannah's curls. "She brushed it for you every night before you went to bed and every morning when you got up. She said it was like cotton flax."

"I remember."

"Do you? You were so young."

"I remember," Hannah said again. "Sometimes she comes still to brush my hair in my dreams."

The sun was high in the sky before they had their packs

assembled. The first time they tried to choose what to take with them, they gathered far more than they could carry. In the end Elizabeth left everything behind except her father's Bible and her mother's Sunday handkerchiefs. With her nose buried in the lacy fabric of the handkerchiefs, she imagined she could even yet breathe in a hint of her mother's perfume. The rest of her pack she filled with what food they had, a skillet, her mother's scissors, and the tinderbox.

She told Hannah to choose one stone from her collection from the river and the woods before she helped the child carry the rest to arrange on their parents' graves. She didn't check what else Hannah packed other than to be sure she brought their mother's brush and comb, or what Payton had inside the quilt he'd wrapped around his pack although she could see the edges of books. It didn't matter. If the books got too heavy, he could leave them beside the road.

They hadn't gone more than a mile through the woods when Payton stopped and said he had to go back.

"We can't go back," Elizabeth told him. She had been almost holding her breath fearing Hannah might run off into the trees, but she thought Payton had accepted their new path.

"I forgot something. You and Hannah go ahead and I'll catch up with you. It won't take me long." He would not meet her eyes as they stood on the trace through the trees. He was taller than Elizabeth but so slim that their father used to joke he could tell the direction of the wind by which way Payton was leaning.

Elizabeth gave him a long look. "I don't want to go on without you."

"I promise to come back, Elizabeth, but this is something

I must do." His brown eyes darted up to hers and then away just as quickly.

She didn't like the look on his face. It was furtive somehow, as if he carried a secret he didn't want Elizabeth to guess. But what else could she do but trust him to keep his word? She couldn't hold him on the path beside her.

"Very well," she said. "But make haste. I wish to be far from here before night falls."

"I'll hurry." Payton turned and loped off through the trees with Aristotle on his heels.

Elizabeth watched until he disappeared and then kept staring after him for minutes longer.

Hannah pulled on her hand and asked, "Will we be to the town where the Shakers live by night?"

"No." Elizabeth picked up her pack. "It's a long walk. We'll have to sleep among the trees if we don't find a barn nearby before dark." Elizabeth turned toward the northeast. She needed to keep the directions clear in her head. Once they were farther away from the cabin, she would find a road for them to walk, and then the way would be easier. But now she wanted the trees to hide her from Colton should he come back sooner than he said.

"I hope there is no barn. I want to sleep among the trees," Hannah said, as if Elizabeth had just promised her a special treat.

"That might turn out not to be as much fun as you think. The ground is hard and the air will be chilly once the sun goes down, but at least the sky shows no sign of rain." Elizabeth had prayed about that as she held the seed package in her hand the night before. Rain might be more than they could bear.

The trace of the path they were following got fainter and

fainter until there was no sure sign of the way to continue. Elizabeth stopped.

"We'd better wait here for Payton. He might have a hard time finding us without a path to follow if we venture farther." She looked up through the tree branches to catch a glimpse of where the sun was in the sky. It had surely been more than an hour since Payton had run back toward the cabin. "I thought he would have caught back up with us by now. We've been slow on the path."

"Maybe he isn't coming." Hannah moved closer to Elizabeth as she peered through the trees back the way they'd come.

"He promised." Elizabeth forced confidence in her voice as she added, "He will come. We can rest here and wait for him."

Elizabeth sat down on the ground and leaned back against a maple tree. Hannah dropped down beside her and put her head in Elizabeth's lap. Elizabeth picked out a twig caught in Hannah's curls and smoothed down her hair. The minutes crept by so slowly that Elizabeth counted to sixty five times just so she'd know how much time had actually passed.

"Will the Shakers like me?" Hannah asked without raising her head off Elizabeth's lap.

"They will feed us."

"But will they like us?" Hannah didn't wait for Elizabeth to answer, as if she knew there was no sure answer before she went on with more questions. "Will we have to spin and dance the way Father said they did? Will we have to wear caps on our heads?"

"Perhaps the caps. I know not about the dancing. But Father said there was singing too. You like to sing."

Hannah lifted her head up to look at Elizabeth. "Do you think a cap will stay on my head?"

"Perhaps." Elizabeth smiled and pushed down on Hannah's hair and then let her hand spring away. "Perhaps not."

Hannah laughed and the sound buoyed Elizabeth's spirits. Hannah didn't laugh often. The child's smile lingered as she put her head back in Elizabeth's lap.

Elizabeth was counting to her second set of five sixties when the girl spoke again. "How long has Payton been gone from us?" Every trace of her smile was gone.

"Too long." Elizabeth did not hide her worry from Hannah. The girl would know anyway. She had a way of looking at Elizabeth or Payton and somehow divining their thoughts without them speaking a word.

"Do you think Mr. Linley has caught him?"

Elizabeth took hold of Hannah's shoulders and pulled her up until she was looking into her light blue eyes. "Caught him doing what?"

"I do not know. Whatever he went back to do." When Elizabeth looked at her without saying anything, Hannah went on. "You fear him. Mr. Linley. Is that not why we go to the Shakers? But he only makes Payton angry. You are more like our father."

"What do you mean?"

"Our father feared him too."

"What reason would Father have to fear Mr. Linley?" Elizabeth frowned at Hannah.

"For you, he feared. I know. I saw his face." Her eyes seemed to be looking inward at a memory of their father's face.

Elizabeth pulled in a deep breath and let it out slowly. "Perhaps we should go back to find Payton."

Hannah stood up. "First let me climb a tree to see if I can see him coming. Mr. Linley may not have caught him yet."

Hannah climbed up through the branches of the tallest oak near them. Elizabeth looked up at her far above her head and held her breath as the limbs swayed under Hannah's feet. "Be careful," she whispered under her breath, more a prayer than an admonition.

"I see smoke," Hannah called from her perch high above the ground. "Back to the west."

Back toward the cabin. Elizabeth's heart jumped up in her throat, but she made her voice stay calm as she called to Hannah. "Do you see Payton?"

"Someone comes, but I cannot see who. The leaves hide him." Hannah started down, moving as lightly as a squirrel between the branches.

"Were they on a horse, do you think?"

"No, on foot." Hannah reached the bottom branch and swung out of the tree to let Elizabeth catch her.

Elizabeth set her down on the ground. "Then it has to be Payton. Colton would be on his horse."

No sooner were the words out of her mouth than she heard the crashing through the trees. Payton was running up the path toward them. His eyes were wide open as if he had just witnessed something fearful. His shirt was torn, and he smelled of smoke. He stopped in front of them and leaned against a tree to catch his breath. Aristotle came out of the bushes behind him and ran to Elizabeth. The dog's eyes were glassy with fear the way they were when the sky was heavy with dark clouds and thunder.

"What have you done, Payton?" Elizabeth asked. She dreaded hearing his answer.

Payton stood up straight and looked at her. His gasps for breath were not so desperate now, although his chest still heaved in and out. "Father wouldn't want Colton Linley to have our things."

"But he'll see the smoke, Payton. He will come after us."

Payton stared at her without remorse. "Then we best stop talking and move on toward the Shakers' town."

Elizabeth shut her eyes and tried not to feel panic. She wouldn't allow herself to think of what Colton might do if he knew Payton had set fire to the cabin. Perhaps it would appear to be an accident. A candle they'd forgotten to extinguish in their haste to leave. A spark that had escaped the fireplace and been unnoticed.

She opened her eyes and said, "You must find a creek and wash the smell of smoke off you and your clothes. Then we will find the road and walk into the night. Father said the road went straight through the Shaker village. We can't get lost if we stay on it."

Hours later when even the moon had sunk in the west, leaving only the stars to light the way, and Hannah was leaning against her half asleep, Elizabeth allowed them to stop. They went into the woods beside the road and pushed up a pile of the newly fallen leaves for their bed. And then they slept even as the sky began to lighten in the east.

7

After the morning meal on Monday, Brother Issachar caught
Ethan on the path heading out to the fields to help with the
harvest of the seed corn. "Elder Joseph has given permission
for you to come with me today," Brother Issachar said.

"Do you have a log you wish me to help haul into the village?" Ethan was glad Brother Issachar had sought him out,
glad to feel the same comfort between them as they talked.
He had feared a division between them the day before, even
though Ethan signing the Covenant should surely be reason
for them to draw closer as brothers and not be a reason for
separation.

"Nay. The sisters have a load of spices, potions, and baskets,
and the brethren have brooms ready to be taken to White
Oak Springs. The man who runs the resort there says the
people from the North who come for the healing power of
the springs enjoy carrying back the work of our hands with
them when they leave."

Ethan fell in beside Brother Issachar and tried not to let

his eagerness for this first trading trip show on his face or in his voice. "Do the springs really have healing power?"

"Nay, I think not. While our Eternal Father grants special gifts and powers to those he chooses, I don't believe he has placed such healing power in the springs coming up out of the earth. But some who think the water holds special power are healed by their own thoughts of healing. Or perhaps they weren't so ill as they thought." Brother Issachar smiled and punched Ethan with his elbow. "Better yet, it could be our own Shaker potions that make them well."

Ethan laughed. "That could be. It certainly sounds more reasonable than the water. The potions stand us in good stead here in the village."

"That they do. Along with right living. Look at an old man like me nearly sixty and still able to labor and do my part. With a little help from my younger brothers." Brother Issachar smiled again. He seemed to be in a particularly good mood on this Monday morning.

Ethan had long suspected Brother Issachar enjoyed the trading trips out into the world, although many of the Shaker brethren claimed not to like being away from the fellowship of the Society. But then as Brother Martin said, Brother Issachar was a little different. Even so, he was still a Shaker. So it could be with Ethan. He could take a few peeks at the world without desiring to become part of it.

One of Brother Martin's most oft-repeated warnings was how curiosity could lead a boy into trouble. As it had Ethan many times when he first came to live with the Shakers. He had made his confessions to Brother Martin and paid the price for that trouble. Not with any kind of punishments from Brother Martin, but from the guilt he felt in his own heart for doing wrong. There had even been times when he'd felt so pulled toward anger at one of his brothers, he worried that the seed of the man who claimed to be his father was sprouting meanness in him.

He'd once confessed that worry to Brother Issachar, for Ethan had never told anyone but him about how the man who'd stolen him from Preacher Joe claimed to be his father. He trusted Brother Issachar not to hold that truth as a black mark on Ethan's soul, and he did not. Instead, he assured Ethan that his father's meanness would not sprout inside him.

"A man has many seeds within him. It is the seeds that are watered that grow. We know not what happened to your father that caused the wrong seeds to grow within him. Perhaps it was simply meanness as you say. Perhaps he was treated cruelly himself as a child. Either way, he wasn't in your life long enough to water any of those wrong seeds within you. You were treated with kindness and love by your Preacher Joe and his wife. You have been nurtured in peace here among the Believers. If those cruel seeds were ever within you, they've surely been crowded out by the growth of the good seeds."

It was something Ethan liked to imagine. The good seeds growing in him. The Shakers worked hard to produce good seeds for their crops and their gardens. They cast out the seed from the varieties of plants that didn't thrive in their soil and kept the seed from the plants that produced abundantly. That was what he wanted to do. Cast out the bad seeds within him and cultivate the good seeds so that he could better live the simple life of a Believer. It was a gift to be simple. To take joy in the shaping of a piece of wood into an axe handle or a bowl. To know that the work of one's hands would be used for the good of all the brethren and sisters.

He and Brother Issachar loaded the wagon with the crates of spices and potions. They laid the flat brooms in the wagon bed beside the boxes and filled in the middle with baskets. They covered it all with the heavy cover the sisters had woven especially for the purpose of protecting their baskets from the weather on the way to market.

Ethan looked up from tying down the cover and asked, "Will we also be going into the town?" He'd been in the town a few times. He found it cluttered, without proper planning for the buildings and roads the way Harmony Hill was built. Still, it was interesting to see the people and the different manner of their dress. Some of them carried the same wild look of the men who had carried him down the river.

"Yea, the sisters have need of sugar to finish making their apple butter, and Sister Vera has a list of other necessary supplies since we must go for the sugar." Brother Issachar climbed up on the springboard seat. When Ethan climbed up beside him, he handed Ethan the reins for the team of horses that stood patiently in front of the wagon waiting for the men to be ready. "You drive," he said.

It was a beautiful morning. The air carried that crisp feel of autumn even as the sun warmed their shoulders. Beside the road the maples were yellow and gold with here and there a rose-hued tree that seemed to infuse the morning light with its pink color. The sassafras trees were red as freshly spilled blood while the oaks only showed hints of the dark red that would soon spread through all their leaves. Squirrels chattered at them from the limbs of the oaks where they were gathering their winter provisions.

The few people they met on the road nodded toward them politely with no show of animosity.

"The people are accustomed to us here," Brother Issachar said when Ethan noted the friendliness of a man passing on horseback. "They know our intention is to live in peace."

"But peace is not always in their hearts," Ethan said. At times the Shaker traders were set upon by those who wanted nothing but to cause trouble. Brother Henry had even been robbed of his products on a trip to Louisville the year before.

"We will pray that will not be so on this day. We will pray our trip will be peaceful and profitable."

"Do you always pray such prayers when you go out into the world?"

"Yea. It's only right to do so." Brother Issachar looked over at Ethan. "To pray that the world will do us no harm and that we will likewise do it no harm."

His words surprised Ethan. "How could we do harm to the world?"

"With an unkind word, perhaps. Or an unfair price for our products. Doing anything that might cause strife. By not doing the good that we are able to do."

"But Brother Martin says most in the world don't want the good we can do them. That they reject our ways." Ethan glanced over at Brother Issachar as the horses kept up their steady pace forward. They needed little guidance on the familiar road.

"There are many ways to do good besides converting those of the world to our ways." Brother Issachar reached out and caught a maple leaf off a branch that hung out over the road.

"But is that not what we should do? Encourage those of the world to walk the road of peace with us as Mother Ann teaches." Ethan stared over at Brother Issachar who had placed the leaf on his knee and was tracing the veins running through it. "Brother Martin says the world is a miry pit of sin that swallows up those who don't believe."

"Brother Martin has spent much time studying the Believers' tenets." Brother Issachar kept his eyes on the leaf. "That is as it should be since he has long been a teacher of the young brethren. He suffers greatly each time one of them goes to the world." He suddenly crumpled the leaf in his hand and dropped it on the road.

"Do you not mourn the loss of our brothers to the world?" One of the brothers two years younger than Ethan had left for the world just the month before. He and Ethan had grown up together as brothers. Ethan had done his best to keep William from leaving, but William's head was set. There was no dissuading him from turning and walking away from his life as a Shaker. Ethan missed him.

"Yea, but in a different way." Brother Issachar looked off toward the trees for a moment before he went on. "I have seen much of the world in my time. While Elder Joseph would surely take me to task for saying this, the truth cannot be changed simply because we wish it changed. All cannot be Believers."

"Brother Martin says more could be if they would choose the path of right living."

"So he does," Brother Issachar said mildly. "It could be he is right. It's the path choosing that is difficult for many."

They had delivered their wares to the store at White Oak Springs and were on the way to Harrodsburg before the sun was halfway across the sky. Brother Issachar was telling Ethan of a shady lane not far down the road where they could stop their wagon to eat the midday meal the sisters had packed for their trip when a young woman stepped out of the trees beside the road in front of the horses. She held the end of a rope tied around a black and white dog's neck. The dog barked and jumped forward toward the horses, causing them to shy to the side away from her. She quieted the dog with a word, but didn't move from the road.

Ethan steadied the horses and looked over at Brother Issachar to see what to do next. Ethan had very little occasion to speak with any of his sisters at Harmony Hill. The sexes were kept separate, using separate doors into the buildings and separate staircases to keep even accidental contact at a minimum. He did sing and labor the worship dances at meeting with his sisters along with all the brethren, and at times there was a passing on the walks with polite greetings as they went about their duties. But Brother Martin had advised Ethan to keep such exchanges to the very minimum. A nod was better than a word. So he really didn't know words to say to his own sisters at Harmony Hill. He certainly knew nothing to say to a female from the world.

She didn't have that problem. "Are you Shakers?" she asked, looking first at Ethan and then at Brother Issachar.

"We are," Brother Issachar answered kindly.

Relief flashed across her face, lifting the evident worry for just a moment before it fell back into the lines of her face. She looked behind her toward the trees and then over her shoulder down the road. When she saw the road empty, she turned back to them and pointed the way they'd come. "Is that the way to the Shaker town? To your town?"

"Yea," Brother Issachar said. "Do you seek Harmony Hill?"

"I have heard the Shakers . . ." She hesitated before she went on, changing the words. "I have heard that you will take in orphans. Is that true?"

"We do not turn away those in need," Brother Issachar said.

"You look old to be an orphan," Ethan blurted out. She had to be nearly as old as he. More woman than girl. She certainly little resembled his Harmony Hill sisters with the wisps of her light brown hair blowing across her dirt-smudged face. Her dress was wrinkled and torn in a few places on the sleeves, with a scattering of sticktights on the bottom of her skirt. Her eyes looked tired as she turned to stare straight at him when he spoke. Then he thought "tired" was not the right word. "Desperate" suited better.

"So I am, but I have no home," she said plainly. "And I will be a Shaker if you will take in my brother and sister. I know how to work." She looked toward the woods by the road again and made a motion with her head.

A youth as tall as Ethan and slim as a reed growing in a pond and a small girl with a cloud of white curly hair came out of the trees to step up beside the woman in the road.

She said, "This is Hannah and Payton. My name is Elizabeth. Our father was Marlow Duncan."

The boy stared at them with misgiving. It was easy to see he didn't have the same eagerness as his sister to find the Shaker village. The little girl leaned against Elizabeth, her weariness showing in every line of her body.

"How far is it to your town?" the child asked. "We walked much of the night."

"Will we make it there by dark?" the woman named Elizabeth said. "We are very tired. It's been a hard few days. We buried our father the day before yesterday."

Brother Issachar frowned. "The day before yesterday? And is there reason for your haste to come to our village?"

Again the woman glanced over her shoulder down the road, as though fearing something might be overtaking them. She appeared relieved to see nothing there as she looked back at Brother Issachar and said simply, "We have no food."

"We had apples but we ate them, and Aristotle ate the biscuits," the child with the remarkable hair added. She looked directly at Brother Issachar and then Ethan.

The color of her eyes was the strangest Ethan had ever seen, like the blue of their Shaker cloth faded by the sun until it was more white than blue. Her direct look made him uneasy, and he shifted his eyes to the boy and then the woman. He thought he should drop his gaze down to his hands or off to the trees, but he did not. Something about her attracted his eye, attracted his curiosity. She looked frightened. Lack of food for a few hours would not be reason for fear. And she looked at him boldly as if she not only resented his curiosity but the fact of her fear.

He ordered himself to look away at the trees, but his eyes stayed pinned on her. He was relieved when Brother Issachar spoke to take her attention from him.

"We have food enough to share," Brother Issachar said.

"We don't want to take your midday meal. We aren't that hungry," the woman said. "We only wished to be sure we were heading in the right direction."

"That you are, but it's a good way yet on foot," Brother Issachar said as he climbed down off the wagon. "My name is Issachar and this is Ethan." He picked up his packet of food and handed it toward not the woman but the boy. "Here, take this, my children. I can share with Brother Ethan. The sisters always pack an overabundance for us."

The boy hesitated but only for a bare second before he took the food. "Thank you," he said.

"Yes, thank you," the woman echoed. She looked near tears at Brother Issachar's kindness, but then she mashed her mouth together and blinked them away.

Brother Issachar smiled at them. "Brother Ethan and I must go get supplies in the town, but if you wish to rest here by the road, we will travel back this way in a few hours. You can ride on our wagon into the village with us then."

Ethan spoke up again. "Brother Issachar, you should tell them that we do not have dogs in our village."

Brother Issachar petted the dog's head, setting the dog's tail to wagging so fiercely that his whole body was shaking. "He seems a fine animal. Aristotle, did you say?" Brother Issachar looked at the little girl. "Quite a name for a dog."

"Our father named him such," the woman named Elizabeth said as her own hand fell down to stroke the dog's back affectionately. "And we do know the Shakers have no pets. Our father told us as much after he visited your village last year. We were hoping to find someone in need of a good dog on the way, but we've been staying in the trees and haven't met anyone to inquire about a home for him as yet."

"We have to stay in the trees so Mr. Linley won't find us," the little girl said.

Her sister tightened her hand on the child's shoulder to stop her words.

"Mr. Linley? Is that who you fear might be coming up the road?" Brother Issachar said mildly as he looked at Elizabeth.

She looked reluctant to answer. "I do not wish to see him," she admitted.

"Have you done him some wrong?" Brother Issachar asked.

"He might think so." Elizabeth's voice wasn't much more than a whisper and the boy shifted uneasily on his feet as if he wanted to run away.

The child spoke up, ignoring her sister's tightening grip on her shoulder. "He has thoughts of wedding my sister without caring what she desires. We only fear him for that reason."

"Hannah," the sister said sharply. "These men aren't interested in our troubles."

"But, my sister," Brother Issachar said. "If you become one of us, then your troubles are ours." Suddenly Brother Issachar laughed. "But if it is only matrimony you fear, then the Shaker village is the place for you. There's no problem with matrimony there. Isn't that right, Brother Ethan?"

Ethan nodded his agreement, but at the same time he wished they hadn't come upon these three on the road. The young woman's eyes seemed to reach into him and demand a response that was unsettling. It was just as Brother Martin had warned him often enough. Each time a man stepped closer to the perfect life of a Believer, the devil pushed some worldly temptation in front of him. At next meeting, Ethan would have to labor a special dance to shake this odd feeling off of him.

8

The men took Aristotle with them. The older man, the kind one named Issachar, said he knew a storekeeper who would appreciate a dog with such a fine name. They each told the dog goodbye in their own way. Payton ruffled the dog's ears and scratched his chest before he buried his face in Aristotle's fur to hide the tears in his eyes. Hannah let the dog jump up with his paws on her shoulders and danced a circle with him. Then she gazed deep into his dog eyes without saying a word. It was obvious there was no need of spoken words between the girl and the dog.

Last, Elizabeth knelt in front of Aristotle. She had to remind herself yet again as tears gathered in behind her eyes that she could not sacrifice herself to a man she could not abide in order to keep a dog. "I am sorry to lose you. You have been a faithful friend to our father and to us, Aristotle. You must be a faithful friend to this new man you go to now."

In spite of her best efforts to hold them back, a few tears overflowed from her eyes. Aristotle licked them away and made her laugh as she held out her hand for him to put his paw in it as her father had taught him. Then she stood up quickly and stepped back as Issachar lifted the dog up onto the wagon seat by the younger man and tied his rope to the back of the seat. The younger brother reached out gingerly to touch Aristotle as if perhaps he had never touched a dog's fur before and wasn't sure how it would feel. Aristotle leaned into his touch, begging for more, and the young man's face was a mixture of surprised pleasure and something else. It took Elizabeth a moment to realize his pleasure was mixed with guilt.

"There's a spring-fed creek not far from the road over in that direction." Issachar pointed before he climbed back up on the wagon seat. "You can rest there until we return. It's well off the road."

Elizabeth looked up at him. "You won't speak of seeing us in the town?"

"Nay, I know not why we would have occasion to speak of such," the man said with a smile and a nod toward the young brother beside him to include him in the promise. "The sun will be two hours from setting before we return."

The young Shaker shook the reins to start the horses moving away. Aristotle began whining and scrambling around on the wagon seat to get free, but the older man grabbed the rope around the dog's neck and held him there. Aristotle twisted his head to look back at them beside the road and then he raised his nose to the sky and howled. The sound stabbed Elizabeth's heart and brought forth an answering cry from Hannah that pierced Elizabeth even deeper. Payton put his arms around them both, and they huddled there in abject misery as Aristotle's howls carried back to them long after the wagon disappeared down the road. It was as if they were burying their father all over again.

Then as the dog's howls grew more distant, hoofbeats sounded from the other direction. Elizabeth pulled Hannah and Payton off the road just as a man on horseback came into view. He didn't notice them as they melted back among the trees. Elizabeth's heart pounded until she could see that it wasn't Colton.

She told herself Colton would have no way of knowing which way they had gone. He'd surely think they had gone into Springfield to try to find a place to stay. He'd have no possible way of knowing they were going to the Shakers. And if he did suspect they had set the cabin on fire, he would be going for the sheriff in Springfield, not the one in far-off Mercer County.

Even so, every time she heard a horse her heart jumped up in her throat. She feared Colton's hands on her, his eyes demanding she satisfy the debt they owed him and that had grown larger with the burning of the cabin. He would demand she trade herself for Payton's freedom. She felt safer off the road among the trees.

They found where the spring bubbled up from the rocks into the creek and drank the clear, cool water. Then Elizabeth brushed off the top of a flat rock beside the creek to spread out the food Issachar had given them. A generous portion of ham stacked between thick slices of sourdough bread. Cheese and dried apples. Elizabeth cut the sandwich in half with Payton's pocketknife before cutting one of the halves in half again. She divided the cheese and the apples equally into three piles. As she handed the biggest sandwich to Payton, she said, "We should thank the Lord for his providence before we eat."

Payton had been about to take a bite of the sandwich, but

he pulled it away without taking a taste. "Guess we should. We might as well get into practice. Those Shakers will be a praying bunch or I miss my bet."

"I liked Issachar," Hannah spoke up.

"Yeah, but did you see how that other one looked at us? Like we were worms he wished would crawl back down into the dirt."

"He wasn't that bad." Elizabeth took up for the young Shaker. She didn't know why. "We were just strange to him."

"Strange worms." Payton dropped down to the ground beside the rock. "If we're going to pray, let's get it done. This ham wants to go in my mouth." He raised his hand holding the bread and meat toward his mouth and then pushed it away with his other hand as if his hands were warring.

Hannah giggled and Elizabeth couldn't keep from smiling as she bowed her head. "Dear Lord. Thank you for providing us food. And keeping us safe. Forgive us when we do wrong. Amen."

When she raised her head, Payton was staring at her. "It wasn't wrong, Elizabeth. It was justice."

"So you want to think, but Colton won't think so, and the law will take his side without a doubt."

Payton stared down at the bread and meat in his hand as if he were no longer hungry. "You think I should be sorry for doing it, but I'm not." He looked up at her. "I'm not sorry. I wish I could have stayed and watched the flames climb up the cabin walls."

"And watch our things burn, Payton?" Elizabeth stared at him with concern and confusion. "Is that what you wanted to see?"

"If we couldn't have them, I didn't want Colton Linley

to have them." His eyes were defiant. "And I'm not sorry. I will never be sorry." He took a big bite of his sandwich. He chewed with pleasure before he swallowed and said, "Not about that."

"You must never do such a thing again, Payton. It's wrong to destroy another person's property, no matter what the circumstances." Elizabeth reached across the rock to grab his arm to be sure he knew her words were important. Payton had always been entranced by fire, had once burned away his eyebrows by throwing lamp oil into the fireplace to see what it would do. "You must promise me."

"I know right from wrong, Elizabeth."

"Promise me," she insisted. He tried to pull away from her, but she held tight.

"All right, I promise," he said crossly. "What do you think I am? A firebug?"

She turned him loose and didn't answer as she sat back and began to eat her share of the food. Such a gloomy silence fell over them that Elizabeth could hear Payton and Hannah chewing their food. The hoofbeats of several horses out on the road and then a man's loud laughter carried back through the trees. Elizabeth froze, afraid to even keep chewing for fear the sound would give away their presence there in the trees.

Hannah scooted closer to Elizabeth and said softly, "They cannot see us. The trees protect us."

"But what if they know of the creek? What if they want to water their horses?" She spoke quietly, but even so, her voice sounded too loud to her ears.

"Then there are many places to hide in the woods." Hannah peered up at Elizabeth's face intently. "And Aristotle is no longer here to bark and give us away. He was never good at hiding when we played in the woods. He could seek but not hide."

Elizabeth didn't know which she wanted to do more, smile or cry, as she thought of how she and Hannah used to hide in the woods around their cabin while Payton held Aristotle some distance away. The dog always found them in minutes. The smile won out.

"Besides, it is not Mr. Linley," Hannah said.

"How can you be sure? While I agree the laughter was not Mr. Linley's, he might have gotten help for his search," Elizabeth said.

"It is not the laughter of someone chasing after someone." Hannah spoke with no hint of doubt.

"She's right," Payton said as he cocked his head to better hear the sounds from the road. They were growing fainter as the horsemen passed on by. "I don't know how she knows that, but if you listen, you know she's right."

Relief washed over Elizabeth as she touched Hannah's ears. "Our little sister must have woods ears."

"What are woods ears?" Hannah asked.

"Those that have learned to listen in the woods and know the sounds that mean danger and the ones that are just sounds. Did the squirrels in the trees teach you that?"

The thought seemed to please Hannah. "Maybe they did," she said. "Do you think we can stay in the woods? Not go on to the Shakers' town."

"If the days were all like this, we might." Elizabeth handed one of the dried apples to Hannah. "But winter will come. It always does."

"But a person doesn't have to gather winter to him while the sun is yet warm," Payton said as he stood up. "I'm going down the creek to find a deeper pool." His eyes on Elizabeth dared her to tell him not to go as he put his forearm up to his nose and sniffed. "The smell of smoke lingers."

"Wait." Elizabeth stopped him before he turned away. She dug down into her pack for a piece of lye soap. She smiled as she pitched it to him. "Wash well."

"My sisters," he said with mock irritation. "One with ears like a squirrel's and the other always with a plan like a fox running from dogs." He smiled. "I won't go far."

"Perhaps we should do the same," Elizabeth told Hannah after Payton disappeared down the creek. "I have another bit of soap and it would feel good to wash. Especially my hair." Elizabeth pulled her bun loose at the nape of her neck and shook her head to let her hair fall free down her back.

Hannah combed through it with her fingers. "I wish I had hair like yours."

"I don't know why. My hair is common. Straight and brown like any other girl's. But you have curls of white." Elizabeth tried to smooth back the little girl's curls, but they had a mind of their own. "Perhaps a few too many of them, however. We'll trim some off before we wash them."

She combed and cut, combed and cut until Hannah's hair didn't spring quite so far from her scalp and there was a heap of curls on the ground beside them.

Hannah piled the hair into her skirt tail and scattered it back through the trees. "So the birds can have a soft blanket in the bottom of their nests," she said.

They washed their hair and as much of their bodies as they could without disrobing. Elizabeth didn't feel enough comfort in the woods to take off her dress with the possibility of horses on the road not so far away, but they did take off their shoes and stockings and let the cool water wash over their feet while their hair dried in the sun. Payton came back and sat on the rock they had earlier used for a table and whittled on a piece of wild cherry wood he had found.

Hannah looked at Elizabeth and asked, "Will Aristotle be happy with the man Issachar spoke of?"

"Perhaps not at first. But he will be after a little bit."

"Will he forget us? Forget me?"

"No. He will always remember you just as he remembers Father. But now he'll have a new friend." Elizabeth pulled Hannah's head over to rest on her bosom as she stroked her hair. "Having a new friend doesn't make us forget the old friends. It just adds to the love in our lives."

"I have no friends except for you and Payton," Hannah said. "And the trees back home. They are gone now like Aristotle."

"It's hard to lose so much so quickly." Elizabeth kissed the top of her head. "But there will be more trees and there will be many people at this place we're going. People like the kind brother we met this afternoon. And there will be other children."

"Like me?" Hannah peered up toward Elizabeth with a mixture of hope and concern in her eyes.

"Not exactly like you. There's only one Hannah in this world. But girls your age, no doubt."

"What if they don't like me?"

"How could they not like you?" Elizabeth said. "Now pull your feet out of the water and let your toes air dry while you lay your head in my lap and rest. We should have another hour before the Shaker men return."

Hannah did as she was told and was asleep in two minutes.

The sun was warm on Elizabeth's back and the sound of Payton's knife shaping something out of his stick of wood was somehow comforting. The bright afternoon sunlight sliced down through the trees to glint off the creek water. And that was like a promise from the Lord above that he was watching over them. Weren't things already getting better? Payton no longer smelled even faintly of smoke. He had obviously washed his shirt and pants as well as his body and now wore them while they dried on him. Hannah's hair was a sweeter halo of white around her sleeping face, and they had the promise of a roof over their heads before night fell.

Perhaps her father's visit to the Shakers in the spring had been providential. Perhaps more of the Shakers would be kind like the brother called Issachar and not wary of them like the younger brother. For Payton was right. The younger one had looked at them as if he wished they would disappear. She knew not why, but then she knew so little of the Shakers. Just the bit their father had told them.

What kind of people did not want to have dogs around? That was a worry but one she couldn't allow to sit in her mind. She stared back out at the sunlight on the water and pushed aside the questions about these people that she had no way of answering. At least not yet.

9

They rode into the Shaker village just at sunset. They had been near the road waiting when the two Shaker men came back from the town. The older Shaker brother had pretended not to know them with the dirt washed from their faces as he peered down at them from the wagon seat with a mock frown. "I was looking for three young people, but that can't be you. For the youngest of the three had this great cloud of white hair, and this child only has a bit of a halo of white."

Hannah stepped closer to the wagon and pulled on the ends of her curls to make them spring out from her scalp. "We cut some of it off so the birds could have a soft blanket in their nests for the winter."

"You don't say." Issachar laughed as he took off his hat and ran his hand over the bald top of his head. "So that's what happened to my hair. The birds had need of it."

Elizabeth couldn't help smiling at him, but Hannah looked very solemn as she placed both hands on top of her head to protect her hair. "They can't have any more of mine. I aim to keep the rest."

The younger man laughed so suddenly at Hannah's words that the horses threw up their heads and flared their nostrils in alarm. He calmed the horses with a cooing word, but his smile lingered as he met Elizabeth's eyes. She too was smiling at Hannah's worry, and their smiles met and seemed to make a bridge between their minds. It was as if they already knew one another when there was no way that could be.

His smile faded away, but his intense blue eyes bore into hers as if searching for an answer to a question he had yet to ask. Her heart did a funny skip inside her chest, and she felt suddenly breathless. It was a moment before she realized he had the same look on his face now as when earlier he had reached out to touch Aristotle. As if she were just as much a mystery to him as the dog had been.

Then guilt bloomed on his face and spread color across his cheeks. He jerked his eyes away from hers to peer over at Issachar. He seemed relieved that the older man's attention was still on Hannah. The next time he looked Elizabeth's way, he scooted his eyes quickly past her as though he feared meeting her eyes again.

What did she care, Elizabeth thought as she climbed into the back of the wagon with Payton and Hannah. Her father had said they were a peculiar people. But she didn't have to understand them. She just had to live with their ways until another way opened up. She could do that. They could do that. She looked at Payton and Hannah in the late afternoon light.

Apprehension sat on Payton's face as he kept glancing over his shoulder toward the Shaker men and the horses to see if he could catch a glimpse of their village on down the road. Hannah didn't once look toward where they were going, but instead sadly watched the trees along the road behind them as if she feared she might never again see a tree.

Elizabeth had some of the same feeling. Not for the trees, but that the course of her life was being altered forever. That perhaps she was giving up control of her own destiny and would never now realize her dream of marriage to a man she loved and babies of her own to nurture and love. She was not so young. Already twenty. Her time for finding love might pass her by while she was with the Shakers. She pushed the thought from her mind. It would be better to dwell on the truth that they would have shelter and food—without her having to enter into a loveless union with Colton Linley.

Issachar called back to them when the road began passing through the Shaker lands. Fields of corn stretched as far as the eye could see in one direction, and behind stone fences on the other side of the road were red and white cattle. Then they passed orchards with rows and rows of apple trees and another kind of tree she didn't recognize. When she asked Issachar, he said they were mulberry trees for the silkworms the sisters raised for the making of silk. Elizabeth couldn't even imagine how a person made silk from worms.

"I didn't know people made silk in our country," she said.

"Our sisters do," Issachar said with a laugh. "Very fine silk it is too."

"God is in a Shaker's work," the younger man said.

Payton glanced over at Elizabeth. He looked ready to jump off the end of the wagon and run back down the road the way they had come.

She put her hand lightly on his arm. "We will learn," she whispered. "Perhaps it won't be as odd as it sounds now."

The fields were laid out in perfect angles, and she could

not see even one weed among the rows of corn. Men dressed the same as Issachar and Ethan were spread across the fields cutting the cornstalks and stacking them in shocks for shucking.

"They work as long as they have the sun," Issachar said. "There is much corn to gather before the winter comes. Only a little farther now until you will be able to see the village ahead."

She had a picture in her mind of what the village might look like from what their father had told them after his visit there, but she was still amazed at the impressive three-story brick buildings that came into view as they approached the village. Issachar said they were the families' houses. They rode past one of the houses and toward a large building rising up in the center of the village. Its white stone walls wouldn't have been out of place on a palace, but there were none of the fancy trimmings one might expect on such a structure. There were no fancy trimmings on any of the buildings. Yet in spite of their austere lines, the buildings were pleasing to the eye. Better yet, they looked substantial, strong. The builders of such structures had to be prosperous and industrious.

In fact, the people moving along the walkways between the houses and the smaller buildings scattered in behind them moved with purpose. No one stopped on the pathways to talk with another, as might be expected in a village, and although a few of the people sent curious glances their way, none paused to stare.

The men all were dressed the same as the Shaker men in the wagon, and the women wore blue dresses with large white collars crossed in the front and white aprons over the full skirts. White bonnets covered their heads and shaded their eyes from Elizabeth. The people were different sizes and shapes. Yet there was something so uniform about their look that Elizabeth thought of ants walking a line to their hills.

In the very middle of the village was a white frame building that would have looked large and impressive to Elizabeth except for the great stone building rising so amazingly into the sky opposite it. Both buildings had two front doors, as did nearly all the buildings they passed. The two-story frame building had nothing about it to suggest it was a church, but Issachar said it was their meetinghouse.

"That's where we worship," the young Shaker named Ethan said without looking back at them, as if he wanted to be sure they knew the purpose of the building.

In behind the houses were fields of what looked like strawberry plants, although Elizabeth had never seen such a large patch. In among the buildings were smaller garden patches with herbs that Elizabeth recognized. Some of the same ones that she'd planted with her mother behind the cabin. Others she did not know.

Payton's head twisted back and forth as he tried to see it all. "I know Father told us of this, but did you imagine it so . . ." He hesitated, searching for the right word.

"Big?" Elizabeth offered.

"More even than that," he said with a hint of awe in his voice. "'Grand' might describe it better. What must it take to raise such buildings?"

"Perhaps you will find out. Perhaps you can be a builder." Elizabeth smiled at Payton and then touched Hannah's head. "And one of these buildings is surely a school."

Hannah's eyes were open wide as she took in the Shaker village. Elizabeth sometimes forgot how little of the world

Hannah had ever seen. She hadn't been quite two when they moved to the cabin in the woods and had not gone into the town since their mother died when she was four. All she knew of the outside world was what their father told her and what Elizabeth read to her from books.

"Are we still in Kentucky?" she asked as the young brother guided the horses around behind one of the large brick houses and stopped the wagon in front of a frame outbuilding.

The young Shaker man laughed out again as he had earlier as he looked around at Hannah. "Yea, my little sister. We are yet in Kentucky, but I understand your wonder. I felt the same when I first came into the village as a child. Our land is in the state of Kentucky, but it is not of the world."

"That sounds like a riddle." Hannah kept her eyes on him as he and Issachar climbed down from the wagon and came back to them.

"So it does," Issachar said with a smile.

"A riddle that those of the world cannot solve," Ethan said. He reached up to lift Hannah down from the wagon and then offered his hand to Elizabeth.

She smiled at him as she put her hand in his strong hand that was browned from his work in the sun. "My sister knows little of the world," she said, again meeting his eyes with that strange feeling of a connection that had no way of being. For just a moment as she leaned on him to step down from the wagon, everything around them faded away. There was nothing but her and the young brother speaking without words.

"Brother Ethan," a voice boomed out behind them. Alarm chased across Ethan's face, and he jerked back from her as if fire had shot from her hand to his.

She stumbled and might have fallen if Payton hadn't reached out to steady her.

"Brother Martin," the young brother said. He almost stuttered as he went on. "I did not see you there."

"So it would appear." The man stepped forward. The lines of his broad face were stern and far from welcoming as he swept his eyes over Elizabeth, Payton, and Hannah. None of the sternness left his face as he turned his look back to Ethan. "But you must know that our Eternal Father sees us at all times."

"Yea, Brother Martin, I know it to be true," Ethan answered meekly. "I will strive harder to keep that truth in mind." He stepped away from Elizabeth quickly as if moving away from a steep riverbank about to crumble away under his feet.

"We will speak of it later," the man named Martin said as again his eyes settled on Elizabeth. "What have you and Brother Issachar brought back from the town?"

Not who. What. Elizabeth felt like the worm Payton had spoken of earlier. Perhaps she had gathered winter around her too soon. Perhaps seeking shelter among the Shakers was not the plan the Lord had made for her and Payton and Hannah. Hannah moved over against Elizabeth as if she hoped to hide among the folds of Elizabeth's skirt.

Issachar's voice was as kind as ever as he answered, "These three seek shelter among us. Their father has died and they have no food or place to live." He leveled his eyes on Martin. "It is our duty to be kind to those in need."

"You need not remind me of the duties of a Believer." The Shaker man's eyes narrowed on Issachar.

"Nay, I do not," Issachar said. "We are delivering the sugar we bought for the sisters' apple butter making here at the preserves house. After that, I will find one of the sisters to take charge of the two young sisters. Then I will help the young brother settle among us."

"Yea, it will be your duty. You brought them among us," Martin said.

"Yea, Brother Ethan and I." Issachar didn't look toward the other man as he reached into the wagon bed to pick up a sack of sugar.

Ethan looked as if he were being tugged in two different directions as he stood between the two men. At the same time, Elizabeth felt he was very aware of her standing there by the wagon waiting to be told what to do. Then she realized that the young brother was also waiting to be told what to do.

Issachar must have felt Ethan's discomfort as well, for he looked up at him and said, "I can unload the sugar without your help, Brother Ethan. Go on along with Brother Martin if that is what he desires."

"Yea, it's almost time for the evening meal," the other man said as he stepped between Ethan and Issachar and took Ethan's arm and turned him away from the wagon.

"I will need to wash my hands and face," Ethan said as Martin began hustling him away.

"Pray that is all you need to cleanse yourself of." Martin peered over his shoulder back toward Elizabeth, but Ethan kept his eyes straight ahead.

Issachar turned with the sack of sugar on his shoulder and stood a moment watching the two men walk away with the hint of a frown between his eyes.

Elizabeth spoke up quietly. "I didn't mean to cause your young brother trouble."

"Nay, you did not, my sister." Issachar pulled in a breath and let the frown slip away from his face. "Brother Martin has a fear of any breath of the world touching the young men he teaches. And you are of the world. I think he fears you may be a temptation to Brother Ethan."

"I have no desire to be a problem for him or for any of you."

"Our desires often ask no permission to war within us. Brother Ethan has much yet to learn of such things." Issachar turned to smile at her. "As do you."

"I will try to learn the Shaker way. We all will." Elizabeth put her arm around Hannah to give her courage. "Our father said he felt peace when he visited here last spring. That's all we seek with you. A chance to earn our way and to feel that peace."

"That isn't too much to ask," he said. "Now come, young Brother Payton, and help me unload the sugar. I think the sisters are no longer here at the preserving house. All have gone to the biting rooms for the evening meal. That's dining rooms to you."

"We're not causing you to miss your supper, are we?" Elizabeth asked.

"Worry not, my sister. All will be taken care of in due time." He climbed up the steps and opened the door into the preserving house. "First the sugar must be unloaded, and then we will take you to the Gathering Family house. There you will begin your life among us."

"Can we not just stay with you, Brother Issachar?" Hannah asked.

"Nay, my child. That is not the way of the Shakers."

"I do not know the way of the Shakers," Hannah said. "I only know the way of the woods around our cabin."

Issachar looked at Hannah leaning against Elizabeth and for a moment the shadow of a frown came back between his eyes. But then he smiled. "You will learn, my little sister. I will pray it is not too hard for you."

But it was hard when they got to the Gathering Family house and the two sisters came out to them. One, called Sister Ruth by Issachar, was tall and angular with no smile on her face. Her sharp eyes looked them over as if for signs of the world they had come from yet clinging to them like the sticktights on their clothes. The other sister, Nola, was as short as the first sister was tall and a bit thick around the waist under her apron. She was smiling, welcoming them into the family even before Issachar told her their names. A few locks of gray hair sprang out from under her cap and curled down her neck. Sweat moistened her upper lip and sat in beads on her forehead. She took a plain cotton handkerchief from her pocket and wiped her face dry.

"I spent the day stirring apple butter, and the heat of the stove stays with me," she said almost as an apology. "It is warm for October."

"I left the sugar there for the morrow," Issachar said before he looked at Elizabeth and Hannah. "Have patience, young sisters. And courage."

Everything happened too quickly after that. Payton went with Issachar into the men's side of the house. Payton glanced back at Elizabeth. She saw his worry, but there was nothing she could do. She had chosen this path for them. But it wasn't until Ruth took hold of Hannah to pull her away from Elizabeth's side that she truly questioned the wisdom of her decision. Hannah clung to Elizabeth's hand.

"Can we not stay together this night?" Elizabeth asked.

"Nay," the woman said. "It is better to begin the Believer's way at once. Do not let her hold to you." She yanked Hannah's hand away from Elizabeth.

"Izzy," Hannah screamed. It had been years since she had called Elizabeth that. She jerked loose from Ruth and wrapped her arms around Elizabeth's waist. She held on so tightly that Elizabeth could barely breathe. Sister Ruth put her hands on Hannah's shoulders, and Hannah screamed again. "Izzy, don't let them take me."

"Please, let me talk to her," Elizabeth begged the woman. "Please."

Ruth did not want to give in to Elizabeth's request, but Nola put a hand on Ruth's shoulder. "Give the children a moment."

"She's not a baby," Ruth said. "There's no reason for her screams."

"Just a few minutes," Nola said softly.

"Very well. A moment only." Ruth turned loose of Hannah, but she didn't look pleased.

Elizabeth sat down on the stone steps into the house and pulled Hannah down beside her. Nola took Ruth's arm and moved her a few feet away to give them some privacy.

"I don't want to go with her," Hannah said. "I want to stay with you."

"I want you to stay with me." Elizabeth put her arm around Hannah and pulled her close. "But that must not be the Shaker way."

"Then I don't like the Shaker way."

"It does seem strange to us, but we must try to accept their ways at least for a little while." Elizabeth tipped Hannah's face up until she was looking directly into her eyes. The panic there made her heart hurt. "We can do this, Hannah. We must do this. At least until spring. Can you try to do that? For me?"

"And when spring comes?"

"We'll leave if you remain unhappy with their ways."

"Do you promise?" Hannah dug her fingers into Elizabeth's arm as she waited for her answer.

"Yes, I promise." Elizabeth didn't want to think of what that promise might mean or what she might have to do to keep it, but she made the promise anyway. "Do you promise in return?"

"I will go with the mean one if you say I must." Her shoulders drooped as she let her hand fall off Elizabeth's arm.

Elizabeth glanced over at the sisters, hoping they hadn't overheard Hannah's words. "She is not mean," she said softly. "Only stern. She has rules we must follow."

"I don't like rules." The panic in Hannah's eyes changed to rebellion.

"I know, but you will listen and do as they ask. You promised me." Elizabeth looked at Hannah steadily until the rebellion faded from her eyes and she only looked sad. Very sad and a little frightened. Elizabeth put her hand on Hannah's heart as she had earlier at the cabin. "Remember, my love is always in your heart."

"But my heart hurts, Elizabeth. I'm afraid it will break apart and all the love will spill out."

"That can never happen. Not with my love or our mother's and father's love. It's here." Elizabeth pressed down on Hannah's chest. "Always. Forever."

"I believe you, Elizabeth, but I wish I could run into the woods." Hannah looked past Elizabeth toward the trees that grew in the distance behind the houses.

"That you cannot do," Elizabeth said firmly. "You promised."

Hannah sighed heavily. "I wish I hadn't."

"But you did." Elizabeth didn't look over at the two women waiting for them, but she could feel them watching them. She couldn't put off the parting any longer. "Now it is time to do as they want."

They stood up and Hannah faced the two women as if waiting for some dire punishment as the two sisters moved toward them.

"Worry not," the sister named Nola said to Elizabeth. "Sister Ruth is going to see to your needs, and I'll take care of young sister Hannah. She and I have much in common." Nola jerked off her cap and gray curls sprang out from her head. She touched Hannah's curls and smiled down at her. "See."

Hannah peered at the woman's head and then reached over to softly touch her hair. "They are not as white as mine. Nor as springy."

"Nay, mine are much older. They've lost a good bit of their spring over the years." She smiled as she pushed her cap back down on her head. "Come, we'll find you a clean dress and some supper."

Hannah only looked back once at Elizabeth as she walked down the path away from her. And now it was Elizabeth who had to bite her lip to keep from crying out for her.

10

Ethan confessed to Brother Martin the strange feelings Elizabeth had awakened in him when he and Brother Issachar had picked the young woman and her sister and brother up on the road. He tried not to hold anything back. For true forgiveness, a Believer had need to confess his failings not only to the Eternal Father and Mother Ann but also to his designated confessor. For Ethan, that was Brother Martin, although there had been many times when he wished it could be Brother Issachar instead.

Both men were very dear to Ethan, but they were much different. Brother Martin never stopped teaching, never stopped trying to push the young brothers in his charge closer to the perfect life all Shakers sought. He labored zealously to keep Ethan from straying from the true way of the Believer into ways of the world that would surely land his feet on a slippery slope to destruction.

On the other hand, Brother Issachar had a way of accepting Ethan as he was while trusting he would seek out the right paths to walk on his own. Ethan could never remember

Brother Issachar showing disapproval of any of the brothers or sisters. Not even when the wrong had been so obvious it had resulted in ostracism. That was why, Brother Martin said, that the Ministry did not appoint Brother Issachar as a confessor. A man had to notice fault before he could correct it.

Brother Martin had no problem noticing fault. It was obvious he saw much fault in the feelings the young woman had aroused in Ethan.

"You must not allow yourself to be led astray by a woman who has yet to learn the ways of a Believer such as yourself."

"She did nothing to entice me into wrong." Ethan felt the need to make sure Elizabeth was not blamed for his own failure to control his emotions.

"She reeked of the world." Brother Martin stared at Ethan across the small table in the tiny room he used to work on the lessons for the boys in school. His face showed disappointment in Ethan's lapse of proper thought, but not surprise. A teacher of the young brethren for many years, he claimed there was little that could surprise him.

"She did seem different than the sisters I know here," Ethan admitted. "Weighted down with concern. Brother Issachar noticed as well and asked her about it."

"Did she answer him with truth?" Brother Martin's frown deepened as he waited for Ethan's answer.

"She avoided answering Brother Issachar's question, but I believe the younger sister spoke truth when she said her sister feared a man who wished to marry her." Ethan thought again of the strange eyes of the young child with the white curls. He started to say he didn't think the child could speak anything but truth, but there was no reason to stray from the words of his confession. The little sister had no part in the unsettled way the older girl had made him feel when he looked into her eyes.

"The worldly joining of man and woman in marriage causes much strife. That is why we live a life of purity here at Harmony Hill without the sin of matrimony to cause problems among us. How much better it would be if all could believe! Alas, many of the world are not ready to receive the truth." Brother Martin shook his head in sorrow at the wrongness of the world. "I suppose time will tell if these new novitiates will listen and learn the true way to life, but I would not be at all surprised if they turned out to be merely winter Shakers anxious to leave as soon as the sun warms in the spring."

A protest rose inside Ethan at the thought of the girl leaving the Shakers so soon, but he mashed it down. He surely only felt the same concern he would feel for any among their number who might too readily give up the Shaker way to go back to the world.

Brother Martin was watching him closely as if expecting some response. When Ethan remained silent, he said, "Do you not agree?"

"As you say, only time will tell," Ethan answered carefully. He didn't want to disappoint Brother Martin with a wrong word or thought. "But the girl claimed they had nowhere to go."

"A woman such as her always has an eye out for another way."

"A woman such as her?" Brother Martin's words bothered Ethan. He didn't know why he felt such a compulsion to defend this new sister he barely knew.

"You are young, Brother Ethan. You have only had acquaintance with our gentle sisters here at Harmony Hill, but not all women are such. Some from the world have wrong thoughts and sow strife wherever they go."

Ethan knew he should nod and stay silent, but he couldn't stop his mouth from asking, "How can you tell she has wrong thoughts?"

Irritation flashed across Brother Martin's face. He did not expect Ethan to question him, but simply to listen and accept the truths he taught. He removed his wire spectacles and pinched his broad nose in thought for a moment before answering, "I have helped many learn the Believer's way. My eye is practiced in seeing right motives." Brother Martin tapped the frames of his spectacles on the table as he stared at Ethan. "Just as now I see your curiosity about the world, Brother Ethan, and it worries me. I fear it may draw you away from us."

Ethan was shocked at his words. "Nay, that could not be."

"I have hope it is not and I will pray for you, my brother. But you must fight this seeking after the ways of the world."

Ethan stared down at his hands a moment before answering truthfully. "I do not seek such. I only wonder."

"Perhaps it would be better if you did not go on any more trading trips with Brother Issachar until this confusion in your mind clears up."

Ethan's eyes jerked up to Brother Martin's face. "But I had hoped to go on a winter trading trip down the river."

Brother Martin was silent for a long moment as his eyes probed Ethan's face. "You came to us on the river. We would not wish to lose you in the same way. On the other hand, there might be good in letting you see more of the world to ease your wonderment of it. While we Believers are apart from the world, our village isn't a prison without doors. You have already made your decision to be a Believer. You have signed the Covenant and become a full member of our Society. You are a Believer. A brother in good standing deserves trust."

"Yea, I wish it so, Brother Martin." Ethan looked down at his hands in his lap again. "I will reread the Millennial Laws so that I may keep in mind the proper behavior expected of a true Believer."

"That would serve you well, my brother." Brother Martin put his hands flat on the table and pushed himself up to his feet. "We all should keep in mind Mother Ann's teachings. We must labor with our hands and not allow our minds to be idle, for an idle mind is the devil's workshop."

In the days that followed, Ethan did his best to push away all thought of the young woman he and Brother Issachar had found on the road as he buried himself in the duties assigned to him. He did not see the new sisters and brother again until they were introduced in the meetinghouse the next Sunday. It was obvious they had yet to fit themselves into the Shaker way even though they were dressed in like clothing with all the sisters and brethren. The little girl with her white curls mostly hidden by her Shaker cap looked small and sad while the young brother let no expression sit on his face.

The older girl, Sister Elizabeth, the one whose hand on his had set a fire racing through his soul that continued to smolder somewhere inside him in spite of his every effort to quench it, looked weary and uncertain. She felt his eyes upon her and looked across the room at him. Her lips lifted in a smile of recognition before he hastily turned his eyes from her face. He stared down at the floor for a long moment before he furtively slid his eyes back her way. She looked even more uncertain with some of the same sadness as the younger sister now.

He wished Brother Issachar was there at meeting to gift her with his kind smile, but he had gone to Louisville to get building supplies for a new barn. He had taken another young brother with him after Brother Martin had spoken against Ethan accompanying him.

During the meeting, many sought out the new sisters and brother to welcome them into the village, but Ethan did not. He stayed far from them, for he felt Brother Martin watching him. It was better to not encourage the wrong feelings that were trying to grow inside him. Better for both him and the young sister, for he didn't want to hinder her quest to become a Believer. Even so, he desired to speak with her, to find out how she was adjusting to life in the village. He wanted to move close enough to her to see the flecks of gold in her green eyes. He wanted to say something to her to bring back the smile to her face and chase away her sadness. And he had to admit he was feeling worldly temptations he had never known before.

He missed steps in the dances that he hadn't missed for years. He was glad when the shaking dances began so that he could shake away the feelings. But her face stayed before him even though he didn't look across the meetinghouse floor toward where she sat watching on one of the benches around the wall. She hadn't had time to learn the steps of the dances.

After the meeting was over, Brother Martin found his way to Ethan's side as they went out of the building. "Our new sister is fair of face," he said.

"It is the beauty on the inside that matters to our Eternal

Father," Ethan said the practiced line in rote. He had often been told the same about his own looks. It did not matter if his hair was black and curly and his eyes blue. What mattered was the look of his soul. He couldn't allow anything to soil its purity. That included the memory of the feel of the girl's hand in his, and how it had seemed as natural as breathing to reach up to help her off the wagon. He'd done it without thought, but he should have let her climb down on her own. She had no need of his help. She was not infirm.

"And to our Mother Ann. It is good that you are seeing things with clear eyes again, my brother." Brother Martin smiled. "In time you can become one of our elders. Perhaps even of the Ministry."

Ethan glanced back over his shoulder at the meetinghouse. Those of the Ministry lived a secluded life of prayer and service on the upper floor there as they directed the life of the village. Sometimes during meetings, Ethan caught eyes peering down at him through the peepholes at the top of the stairs put there for those of the Ministry to watch and be sure no one was worshiping improperly. He couldn't imagine being that person, the watcher, but a true Believer served without complaint wherever he was assigned. Those eyes on him had never worried him before. His spirit was simple and pure, but now he feared the probing eyes might see fault.

The next morning, Ethan went out into the fields with his brethren. While Ethan liked best working with Brother Issachar harvesting logs in the woods, the duties were rotated so that no brother had to perform a dreaded chore without promise of relief. But at harvesttime, all the brothers and many of the sisters worked in the fields to get the last cutting of hay up and the broom straw cut before the hard frosts of winter and to gather the seeds to package for sale in the spring. The sale of their seeds, brooms, and other products had enabled them to extend their land until they held title to thousands of acres.

Their very prosperity seemed proof that those in the Society of Believers had chosen a right path. One that most of the world disdained. Mother Ann Lee had been persecuted in England before she came to America in 1774 to find religious freedom, and then again in this country when she began sharing her visions with all who would open their ears to hear. Those visions revealed to her that she was the second coming of the Lord and, as the daughter of God, must establish a new order here on earth. She faced many hardships, but prevailed as she spread the Shaker way to those chosen to become Believers. After her death almost fifty years ago, other Believers carried on her work until now Shaker communities were spread throughout the east and the west with two in Kentucky.

Brother Martin had told Ethan and his fellow students Mother Ann's story many times through the years. Ethan had read about her himself in books written so that all could understand and believe. He read her truths and practiced her teachings, but he'd never felt a visitation from her as some among the Believers did. As Brother Martin had. Once during meeting Brother Martin had grabbed a broom and begun feverously sweeping the meetinghouse floor and benches. He said Mother Ann had ordered him to sweep away every bit of dust or dirt that might have landed in their meetinghouse, for good spirits did not live where there was dirt.

Ethan wavered between wishing for such a visitation and fearing the same. What if he were told to do something he did not want to do? Brother Martin assured him that could not happen. He said if Ethan was gifted with a visitation of the spirit, he would be so filled with joy that he'd gladly do any exercise given him. But Ethan remembered Brother Homer who had once spent the better part of a meeting on all fours braying like a donkey. Ethan could not imagine how that could be an exercise of joy.

If he could be visited with the words to a song or a poem of worship, then that would be one thing. But to be asked to do something that seemed to have no purpose did not seem to be the Shaker way to Ethan. Brother Martin took him to task for closing off the spirit, but Ethan couldn't seem to open the door to let any wayward spirit enter and take over his body.

Yet a wayward spirit did enter into him when he looked upon Elizabeth. And try as he might, he couldn't push it out and shut the door tight against it. Instead he found himself searching through the sisters on the paths between the buildings or working in the fields to see if he might pick out Elizabeth among them. It wasn't that she was more beautiful than the other sisters. She was fair of face, as Brother Martin said, but many of their sisters had unblemished features and clear eyes. None of those faces had ever haunted his dreams.

He didn't even know her, and then he wondered if perhaps it was her strangeness that drew him. She and her little sister with the sun-bleached eyes and her too-slim brother were not the usual orphans to show up at the Shakers' doors. And he had never been the one to actually bring any novitiates into the village before this time. That was why, and only that reason, he kept thinking of her, of them. They were such a mystery. It could be the mystery that attracted him. Or it could be sin. He didn't know which.

So when the elder in the cornfield assigned him to guide Brother Payton in the Shaker way to gather corn, Ethan thought it providential. He would have the opportunity to discover more of their story and perhaps then Elizabeth would only be another sister the same as all the other sisters in the village.

There weren't many opportunities to exchange words with the brothers in the field. The rustle of the dry cornstalks was too loud as they bent to their task of cutting the corn and placing it in shocks. Later they would move the shocks into the barn and have a shucking frolic with teams of brothers going against one another to see who could shuck the most ears free from the stalks. The finest ears would be laid aside for seed.

The young brother bent his back to the task without complaint. When at their first break to get water, Ethan asked him if he was settling in to the Shaker life, the boy looked straight at him and said, "I am not hungry. There is plentiful food as my sister hoped there would be." He dipped a drink out of one of the piggins of water that had been set in spots across the field by the sisters and drank thirstily.

Ethan had never had to worry about enough to eat. Even in his dim memories of the years before Harmony Hill, he had always had food, but he knew that wasn't true for many who came to the Shakers. He smiled at Brother Payton as the boy handed him the dipper. "Then you have no problem Shakering your plate."

When the boy looked puzzled, Ethan went on. "Cleaning your plate. It was one of the first things I was taught when

I came into the village as a young boy. Take all the food I wanted, but eat all I took." Ethan dipped out a drink and then covered the piggin before they turned back to the field of corn.

Payton walked along the rows beside Ethan. Ethan was taller than most of his Shaker brethren, but Payton's head was level with his. "So you were an orphan too?" Payton said before he picked up the corn knife.

"Nay, I had a father, but I fell off a raft and the river washed me up on the Shakers' land."

"Your people didn't look for you?"

"I don't know. Except if they did, they didn't find me. And then these became my people." Ethan looked around at the brothers in the field.

"Sounds something like the story of Moses in his boat of reeds."

Ethan smiled. "I was not so young as Moses. I remember the river."

"So do I." Payton looked wistful as he bent to cut a stalk of corn. When he raised up, he said, "We lived near a river. My father and I fished. Do the Shakers fish?"

"Not often. There's too much work to be done, and the fish don't bite fast enough to feed so many mouths."

Payton looked disappointed. "My father used to say that the good Lord intended for us to fish or why would he have created fishing worms." He pulled the corn stob out of the ground and picked a pink worm out from the dirt to hold up toward Ethan.

Ethan's smile grew wider. "We do not call them such. They are earthworms put into the earth to stir it and keep it rich for growing crops."

"And fishing," Payton insisted as he gently placed the worm back in the dirt.

"Brother Issachar sometimes goes fishing," Ethan said. "Perhaps you can go with him on a day when our duties are not so heavy."

"I hear he also works with wood." Payton dropped his eyes to the ground as he went on in a soft voice. "I like to work with wood. Carve things."

"As do I." Ethan put his hand on the boy's shoulder. "We'll make good brothers."

A smile turned up Payton's lips. It was the first time Ethan had seen the boy smile. "I've never had a brother."

"Well, now you do. A hundred or so of them."

11

Elizabeth wearied of the Shaker rules before many days had passed. There were rules to cover everything, even which foot to step up on a stair first and which knee to bend to the floor for prayer. A Shaker must lead with the right foot or knee. A Shaker sister must not hold a handkerchief in her hand as she knelt to pray. A Shaker must clean her plate. A Shaker couldn't speak while eating. It was the duty of all to put aside personal desires and labor for the good of the community. Relationships from the world were to be cast off with no show of special fondness for any one person among the Society. All were sisters and brothers.

Yet while the Shaker men and women claimed such kinship, they were not sisters and brothers in a way familiar to Elizabeth. No casual interaction was allowed between the sexes. Every building had two doors and twin staircases—one for the sisters and one for the brethren—to negate the chance of those of opposite sex jostling against one another as if even the slightest touch might catapult them into sin. A Shaker woman was not to look upon any man in the community except as a brother.

Elizabeth had a brother. Payton. She had no need of dozens more and an even greater number of sisters. While at times in the past their cabin in the woods had seemed too isolated and a place she might wish to leave behind, now she longed for her quiet home there among the trees. She longed for the loving eyes of her father and for the sound of his voice in her ear assuring her she was right to bring Payton and Hannah to the Shaker village. That it was not a mistake coming to the Shakers.

Every time the bell tolled calling them to a meal, she reminded herself of the plentiful food in what the Shakers called the biting room. Food that would have been hard to come by in their cabin in the woods. They had sturdy clothes to wear, even if there were times when she wanted to throw the irksome bonnet on the floor and stomp on it. She had never liked wearing coverings on her head, but here she had no choice. Wear the Shaker cap she must. There was little choice about anything. Do the chores she was given. Say the required prayers. Learn the Shaker dances even if marching in lines and turning in circles brought no feeling of worship to her. Turn from the world.

Do not let her eyes seek out the young Shaker brother. Elizabeth had no intention of searching through the brethren on the pathways or during the worship meetings for sight of the young Shaker who had found them on the road, but whenever he was near, her eyes seemed drawn to him without any conscious thought on her part. She had never had the mere sight of someone so affect her. Ralph Melbourne, whom she had once thought to marry, had never stirred the feelings within her that one look at Ethan did. Feelings she did not want to feel. Feelings she could not allow herself to feel in this community where such feelings were strictly forbidden.

Feelings Ethan surely did not share even if often as not when her eyes were drawn to him, his face would be turned her way. Still, he never allowed his eyes to linger on hers. Not like he had on their first meeting when it had seemed as if the very sight of her had been of surprising interest to him.

Elizabeth had no desire to be a temptation to Ethan, and truly she didn't see how she could be since they hadn't spoken again since the day she came into the village. And yet the brother with the broad face—the one who had met them at the preserving house and looked through his odd spectacles at her with cold disapproval before he hustled Ethan away—had sent word to Sister Melva to be sure Elizabeth knew not to attempt any sort of contact with the young brother.

Elizabeth was puzzled as she listened to Sister Melva tell her of Brother Martin's directive. She stared at the sister who had been assigned to educate Elizabeth in the Shaker ways and said, "I don't understand. Have I done something wrong?"

"Nay, Sister." Sister Melva touched Elizabeth's hand softly. She was in her middle years and had a kind way, but she was very rigid about the novitiates in her charge abiding by the rules. She'd been a Shaker since childhood and found the Shaker rules natural, not burdensome. She said she felt surrounded by love at Harmony Hill and couldn't imagine living any differently. Now she tried to reassure Elizabeth. "Brother Martin merely wants to be sure no wrongs have a chance of happening. When a young sister like you comes into our community, it is sometimes difficult for her to leave behind her worldly thoughts."

Elizabeth's cheeks warmed in spite of her best effort to hold back the flush by bringing to mind times in winters past when she had to dig wood out of the snow for their fireplace. She stared down at her hands clasped in her lap as she said, "I have only tried to speak to my brother, Payton, since being here."

"All the men and boys are your brothers now." Sister Melva's voice carried a reproving tone. She had already made clear how Elizabeth had erred when she stopped Payton on the walkways to speak with him, but Elizabeth had needed to look into Payton's eyes to be sure he was all right. She'd been surprised by his look of ease in his new clothing.

"Yea, so I am trying to remember." Elizabeth used the Shaker word for yes in hopes it would make Sister Melva think she was turning to the Shaker way. Perhaps even to attempt to convince herself that she might be settling into the peace Sister Melva promised would be hers if she would only accept the Shaker life.

"I find no pleasure in taking you to task, my sister. I see your effort to learn our ways. But both Brother Martin and I have seen many of the young sisters and brothers be tempted by ways of the world. And Brother Ethan is pleasing in appearance." Sister Melva sounded as if that was reason for concern as she sighed before continuing. "While we don't worry with the outward appearance of our bodies except, of course, to stay clean and neat, we aren't blind. We're aware that Brother Ethan's handsome look might be an enticement to one newly from the world who has not yet replaced her more temporal thoughts with proper spiritual ones."

"I will work to have pure thoughts, Sister Melva," Elizabeth answered meekly as she kept her head bowed in seeming submission. That was the surest way to hide the color in her cheeks and the doubt in her eyes that she could ever fully accept the Shaker way or remember the many rules.

But even as Elizabeth chafed under the Shaker rules, she was amazed afresh each day at the village. The house where they had given her a bed was three stories of brick that Sister Melva said was built entirely by the brothers from lumber they harvested from their woods and brick they fired themselves. And the beautiful, almost white stone of the Centre Family House had been quarried out of the palisades that rose up from the river to the east of the village.

Elizabeth hadn't seen the river as yet, but that one time she had talked with Payton, he told her he had. Perhaps that was the reason for his change of attitude. He seemed glad to be at the village instead of resentful as he'd been on the road there. He said the river was wide and Brother Issachar, who had taken him to see it, told him it flowed into the Ohio that flowed into the Mississippi, and that river flowed all the way to the Gulf of Mexico and into the ocean. It was as if Payton could imagine traveling with the water on an endless journey of discovery.

Perhaps that was how she should look on her life with the Shakers. As a journey of discovery for however long she was there. The people were like none she'd ever met. Everyone worked; no one watched. And through their dedicated industry, they seemed to accomplish wonders. They made their own potions and bottled row after row of jars of jams and jellies. They packed thousands of envelopes of seeds. They wove the cloth for their clothes and made silk from the cocoons of worms. They positioned windows in their houses to invite the light of the sun into the darkest corners, even the cupboards. Pipes carried their water to the houses and their laundry house where there were machines to aid in the washing of their clothing.

Each time Elizabeth saw the water flow out of the pipe into the kitchen basin at the Gathering Family house, she felt as if she had entered a different world than the one she'd always known. A world where one didn't have to draw water from a well or fetch it from a spring. A world where dances were holy. A world where everything she'd been taught was natural between a man and a woman was considered sin and denied.

Elizabeth told herself she could accept that. The avoidance of matrimony was one reason she had come to the Shaker village. While she had difficulty accepting that all matrimony was a sin and the bearing of children was not part of God's plan, she didn't have to tell Sister Melva that. Instead she could listen to Sister Melva and pretend to be turning from the world. She could be glad Payton was taking to their new life.

Hannah was a different matter. She was sad through and through, even though Sister Nola was being extra kind to her. Elizabeth could see the child's sorrow in the droop of her shoulders. Hannah hungered after her old ways. She missed her freedom. She missed her trees. She missed Elizabeth as Elizabeth missed her, but it was the decision of Elder Homer and Eldress Rosellen, who were the leaders over the Gathering Family, that Elizabeth and Hannah should not be allowed to be together.

More rules. Rules that Elizabeth wasn't sure Hannah would be able to abide for long, even if she had promised to do so. Sometimes at night when sleep eluded Elizabeth, she would stare into the darkness above her narrow bed in the sleeping room she shared with eleven other women and worry about how she would keep her own promise to Hannah. Elizabeth had no real hope the Shaker rules would be any less odious to Hannah come spring than they were now.

She prayed then. Not to the God of the Shakers, but to the Lord her mother had taught her about as a child. The Lord who knew every fiber of her being and loved her in spite of her failings. A Lord whose love was not dependent on how well she kept a list of rules. And she'd hear an answer out of the night. Not spoken, but in her heart, to take each day as it came and somehow there would be a way. Just as the Shakers' seed package had shown her a way to keep from having to give herself to Colton Linley.

They'd been at the Shaker village three weeks when Hannah ran away. The early days of November had been dreary with a fine mist of rain, but five days into the month, the sun pushed back the clouds and afforded them a gift of Indian summer weather. That morning when the bell tolled for breakfast, Elizabeth and Sister Melva left off their early morning chore of gathering soiled clothing for the laundry to take their morning meal. Sister Nola met them at the bottom of the stairs. Elizabeth knew at once something was wrong.

"Is Hannah all right?" she asked.

"Then you haven't seen her." Sister Nola sighed. "When she wasn't in her bed this morn, I thought that perhaps she had come to you."

Elizabeth's heart felt heavy in her chest. "You don't know where she is?"

"Nay, I fear she may have run away." Sister Nola looked reluctant to say the words.

Elizabeth couldn't imagine what Hannah could be thinking. She had no place to run away to. And while Hannah knew the woods around their cabin like the back of her hand, the forest around the village would be strange with unknown dangers. She could get lost. They might never find her. Elizabeth pulled in a deep breath and closed her eyes a moment to hold away the panic that wanted to grab her.

"Worry not, my sister," Sister Nola said. "After the morning meal, if she hasn't come back, we'll gather some brethren to search for her. She can't have gone far."

Sister Ruth came up to them, her angular face stiff with disapproval. "You know it's not proper to have so much conversation before our morning meal."

"Yea, Sister Ruth, I beg your forgiveness for breaking the silence of the morning, but little Sister Hannah is missing and I thought perhaps she had come to seek Sister Elizabeth," Sister Nola said.

"The child needs more discipline." Sister Ruth's frown deepened. Then she looked at the sisters and Elizabeth. "We could all use more discipline, it appears."

"Yea, it is true. Let us pull silence over us as we go in to our meal," Sister Melva said, looking pointedly at Elizabeth as she moved past her to lead the way to the biting room.

Elizabeth stood rooted to her spot at the bottom of the stairs. She didn't want to stay silent. She wanted to scream at them. Shake them away from the peace they pulled around them like a cloak. How could they expect her to proceed calmly to her morning meal not knowing where Hannah was or if she was safe? Sister Ruth's eyes were burning into

Elizabeth waiting for her to move. To obey. To be a good Shaker worthy of her place at the table.

Sister Nola put her hand under Elizabeth's elbow and, without looking toward Elizabeth, whispered very quietly, "Come, Sister. Give our little sister time to return. She has told me of her love for the woods. She has no doubt run off to the trees. She will be safe with Mother Ann watching over her."

What else could she do but let Sister Nola tow her into the biting room? After they knelt for prayer, Elizabeth put only a small biscuit on her plate, for there was no way she could swallow the fried potatoes and eggs. Sister Melva watched Elizabeth with concern, but she didn't break the silence with speech. Sister Nola had gone to sit in her assigned spot at another table. The only noise was the clatter of the bowls and the scraping of forks against the plates. Now and again one of the benches would creak when a sister moved to get more comfortable. The brothers were on the other side of the room, eating as silently and intently as the sisters. A Shaker must feed his body to better enable him to do his work in a way pleasing to the Lord. A horse needed its feed to pull its load and so did a Shaker.

Elizabeth forced herself to swallow the biscuit, crumb by crumb. At last all were finished eating, and after kneeling once more for prayer, they were allowed to leave the biting room. Sister Nola caught Elizabeth's eye across the room and nodded a bit as if to assure Elizabeth she'd take care of finding Hannah, but Elizabeth wasn't ready to leave that up to her. She made the excuse to Sister Melva that she needed to visit the outhouse.

Sister Melva looked at her with suspicion. "The brethren will search for the child," she said. "She's our little sister now too."

"Yea, I believe it so." Elizabeth used the Shaker talk and looked straight into Sister Melva's eyes as if she didn't have any wrong motives to hide.

She did go to the outhouse and quietly waited her turn among the many sisters making the same visit before they began their morning chores. Sister Melva had told Elizabeth casual talk was not a part of a Believer's day, although the sisters did exchange greetings and news of one of the sisters who was in the infirmary. They paid little notice to Elizabeth and cared not that when she left the outhouse, she moved not back toward the laundry house where she was to work but headed across the field toward the woods in the distance.

12

The woods seemed to welcome Elizabeth as she stepped in under its canopy of branches. In spite of her worry for Hannah, her breath came easier and her spirit calmed. She hadn't realized how much she missed being among the trees. She'd thought she only missed her father and her books, but like Payton, it had been more. Where he had brought the river with him, she had brought the trees. And the freedom to step out among them whenever such thought struck her fancy. Even when she left chores undone at the cabin, she could excuse her time in the woods by gathering herbs.

She'd told Sister Melva of her knowledge of herbs, but Sister Melva said that novitiates could not pick their duty. That simple obedience was the first thing a good Shaker had need to learn. In time she would be allowed to use her talents for the good of the community.

Who knew what they might allow her or not allow her to do now? They would deem it wrong that she left the village to search for Hannah. They would expect her to confess the wrong of it to sour-faced Sister Ruth, her appointed confessor.

Who knew what else they might expect her to do? Some sort of punishment or show of atonement perhaps. They might even ask her to leave the village, and she'd have no choice except to go. Yet at this moment with the trees around her, the crisp smell of the fallen leaves crunching under her feet, the call of a crow in her ears, she could not be sorry she had walked away to find her sister.

Ah, Hannah. How much worse it surely was for her to be confined to the village houses and yards. She had never known confinement. All she knew were the woods and the rules of nature. She knew nothing of the rules people were wont to make when they formed communities.

Before she went too far, Elizabeth stood still among the trees to take stock of where she was. It would do little good for her to wander into the woods without a plan and immediately lose her own way. Then the brethren would be hunting her as well as Hannah. Since many of the trees had dropped their leaves, the sun was shining brightly down through the branches to give her a clear indication of direction. Only the oaks held their dark red leaves in abundance.

Elizabeth pulled her cap off and stuck it into the waistband of her apron. A breeze chased welcome fingers of cool air through her hair. Elizabeth's mother had covered her head and insisted Elizabeth do the same when they attended church before they moved to the woods. She said it was only respectful to do so, and she had often worn a bonnet to keep the sun from her face. But she hadn't always covered her hair or shaded her face. And Elizabeth had done so even less in spite of her mother's warnings that she would end up with freckles across her nose that no amount of cream could fade.

The Shakers weren't worried about freckles or the sun. Just

modesty and self-denial. A woman should cover her head in church and the Shakers were continually worshiping whether they were actually in a worship meeting or worshiping through the work of their hands. Sister Melva had explained it so. She said that, since the word of God dwelt within each Believer, it was only right to stay holy at all times.

Elizabeth shut her eyes and shook her head to rid the echo of Sister Melva's voice from her mind. She cared not what the Shakers believed or didn't believe right now. She only cared about finding Hannah. If she could find her and return to Harmony Hill before the brethren formed a search party that would take them away from their harvest duties, perhaps the Shaker leaders would be more forgiving of their lapse of obedience. For even as good as it felt to be in the freedom of the trees, Elizabeth had no illusions of their ability to find a way to survive outside the village.

She listened intently for some sound that might lead her to Hannah. If only she had Aristotle by her side, but the dog had a new master now. He couldn't help her track Hannah. However, there had been times when Elizabeth thought Hannah somehow read her mind when they were playing their hide-and-seek games in the woods around their cabin. Perhaps if she concentrated enough, she could read Hannah's as well.

"Tell me where you are, little sister," Elizabeth said softly. Then she added a quiet prayer. "Let my feet walk in the right direction, Lord."

A faint path led off through the trees. A deer trace perhaps. She didn't want to think of other animals that might be in the woods. Bears. Rabid skunks or foxes. Coyotes. At least it was surely too cool for snakes. She started deeper into the woods, stopping now and again to call for Hannah. Squirrels chattered at her from the treetops and a blue jay flew ahead to squawk out a warning to his forest friends. While she neither heard nor saw any sign of Hannah, she kept moving deeper into the woods, sure in some unfathomable way that her desire to find Hannah would lead her in the right direction.

The sun was halfway to noon when she spotted a blue raveling on a wild rose bush. Elizabeth picked it up. The thread was not caught on a thorn. It curled like a snake on top of the bush waiting to be found. A few steps farther down the path, a branch, then another, looked freshly broken. She moved slowly now, watching for more trail markers. She stopped at a heap of leaves as high as her knees kicked up in the middle of the faint path. From there the trace wandered off in two directions.

Elizabeth stared first one way through the trees and then the other. Surely after leaving the earlier clues, Hannah had left something to point the way.

"Which way, Hannah?" she whispered. She could almost see the secretive little smile Hannah always had when she waited for Elizabeth to guess a riddle she'd thought up.

Elizabeth searched the paths with her eyes for something out of the ordinary. At last she noted three small rocks laid out in a straight line on the path to the right. Down that path were more rocks scattered a few feet apart like Hansel and Gretel's breadcrumbs. Then there were no more rocks. No trail markers of any kind that she could see. She stopped and stood very still to listen once again. All was silent until a breeze tickled through the oak leaves overhead and some small animal scurried away through the leaves on the ground.

She held her breath and listened deeper. Somewhere in the distance water tumbled over rocks in a creek or river. She heard nothing to make her think Hannah was within sound of her voice, yet she stood and waited. Then something, one acorn perhaps, fell from an oak tree behind her.

"Hannah, are you here?" Elizabeth asked without raising her voice.

Another acorn fell behind her. She turned and looked up at the treetops. Nothing there but a squirrel's nest high in the branches of the towering oak. No white-haired dryad. She was about to decide it was only the squirrel cleaning out his nest when there was a giggle from high above her head to the left. Elizabeth pretended not to hear as she continued to gaze up into the wrong tree. She would play Hannah's game. They had played it often in the woods behind the cabin.

"Oh, squirrel, if you are up there, please tell me if you've seen a child with white curls?"

"The squirrel has no voice to answer you." Hannah's words drifted down to her.

Elizabeth smiled and looked toward the oak to her left. Far above her head she spotted a patch of blue. Her breath caught inside her chest to see Hannah up so high, but Hannah had no fear of heights. She said the trees lifted their branches to her feet and held her up because she was their friend.

Elizabeth supposed she should order Hannah down at once, but whatever harm that might result from her running away had already been done. There was no way to change that with angry words. Better to simply play her game and give her a holiday from rules. A holiday they both needed.

She smiled as she said, "Then it must be the mighty oak who speaks to me with such a fine voice, although not at all the voice one would expect for a tree so tall. One would think a magnificent tree such as this would boom so loudly the thunder in the clouds would be put to shame."

"It is not the tree, but the acorn that speaks. Who is it you seek?"

"I seek Hannah, a girl with squirrel feet and raccoon hands." Elizabeth stepped closer to the tree to peer up through its branches. She could see Hannah's feet but not her face. Her feet were bare and Elizabeth hoped she had not tossed aside her Shaker shoes.

"And who is it that seeks this Hannah?"

"Elizabeth, her sister."

"Her natural sister or one of the Shaker sisters?" Some of the fun went out of Hannah's voice.

"A sister as natural as the sunshine and as true as the rain." Elizabeth waited a moment for an answer, but when there was none, she went on. "Dear little acorn, please tell my Hannah I have spotted her up in the tree and now she must come down to me. That's the way the game is played. Once found, the hider is no longer hidden and the seeker no longer has reason to seek. Those are the rules."

"Rules. I hate rules." Hannah gave up the pretense of being an acorn.

"How about promises? Do you hate promises, and that is why you didn't keep the one you made to me that you would abide by the Shakers' rules until spring?"

Hannah didn't make an answer, but she began to climb down slowly. When she reached the lowest branch, she swung out in front of Elizabeth. Her cap was gone and her hair was in wild disarray around her small face, but her shoes were tied to her waist by their strings. She stared at Elizabeth with a mixture of rebellion and regret in her pale blue eyes. "I did make that promise."

"So you did."

"But I didn't know it would be so hard to keep. You didn't tell me they were going to keep me caged like the canaries our father spoke of that are taken into the dark mines to see if there's air for the miners to breathe." Hannah's lips quivered before she went on. "There was no air to breathe, so the canary pushed open the cage door and flew free."

"There is surely air." Elizabeth worked to keep a stern look on her face.

"Not free air. Only Shaker air."

She yearned to reach out and pull Hannah close. She wanted to say they wouldn't go back, but better to have less free air and more food. "It is air we can breathe for a few months."

"Do we have to?"

"I fear that we do." Elizabeth could not keep the regret out of her voice.

"Can't you find another man besides Mr. Linley to marry?" Hannah looked up at her with hope in her eyes.

"Suitors don't grow on trees like acorns." Elizabeth held out her arms and Hannah walked into her embrace. "If they did, I'd have many to choose from on this day."

Hannah leaned against her. She didn't cry. "Do we have to go back right away?"

"They may be searching for us."

"But there's water to the east. I saw it from my perch high in the oak. Can't we go put our feet in it?" Hannah leaned back and stared up at Elizabeth with pleading eyes. "Please. There could be a spring to get a drink of water. I'm very thirsty."

She shouldn't have given in to her. She knew that, but she felt the same pull to the sound of the water as Hannah. And she'd heard the Shakers speak of a road to the river. If she could find that road, it might be a faster way back to the village. She pushed aside the memory of her father saying a person could rationalize any course of action, right or wrong, if he or she wanted to. Hannah was thirsty. Therefore they should go find water.

"We will go," she said and was rewarded with a squeeze from Hannah's arms around her waist before the child turned loose to spin away from her.

"Look, I'm doing a Shaker dance." She whirled around again.

It was all Elizabeth could do to keep from smiling. She managed to keep her voice stern as she said, "Their dances are holy to them. You mustn't ridicule them."

Hannah stopped and looked surprised at Elizabeth's words. "Sister Nola said I could do it. I like whirling. She says it's how we can let everything but the spirit of love fly off us. Have you tried it?"

"Not yet."

"Then you should." Hannah looked at her seriously for a moment before she whirled around again, then stopped and waited for Elizabeth to join in.

"I'll bump into a tree," Elizabeth said.

"There is room." Hannah grabbed Elizabeth's hand and gave it a quick jerk the way one might pull the string on a top.

Elizabeth gave in and turned in a circle once, twice. The spinning did seem to let a childish joy rise up in her. Perhaps that was what the Shakers were trying to find when they came under operations and were visited with what they called the whirling gift. Spin free from all their worries. But didn't Sister Melva say a true Believer had no worries? True Believers simply trusted Mother Ann to send down balls of love to them from heaven and keep away worldly problems.

Her shoulder brushed against a tree and she put out a hand to steady herself on its trunk. She was far from free of worldly problems and spinning was not likely to make her so for more than the space of time she was too dizzy to think.

She touched Hannah's arm to stop her spinning. "If we want to find the water, we must get started. Once we get a drink we have to go back to Harmony Hill where I will expect you to keep your promise better."

"It will be a promise easier to keep when the sun isn't shining so brightly," Hannah said. "And when Sister Ruth doesn't tell the rules into my ears so loudly the way she did yesterday." Hannah put her hands over her ears.

"School will start after the harvest. That will be good. You have much you can learn."

"So Sister Ruth tells me." Hannah grimaced. "Over and over."

Elizabeth let her smile come out. "She tells me much the same."

Hannah took Elizabeth's hand and held it to her cheek a moment. "I'm glad my true sister found me." Then she turned and started off down the path, tugging Elizabeth after her. "This way."

It wasn't the river they found, but rather a steep cliff with a stream of water flowing out of the rocks and into a pool at the bottom and then into a creek that wound away through the trees. A beautiful place. The kind of place one might imagine God putting in the Garden of Eden for Adam and

Eve, except he would have surely carved steps for them into the stone to make the water easier to reach.

"It's not so steep. We can climb down. There are places we can hold to the rocks." Hannah pointed to the rocky cliff.

"No. We might fall."

"I won't fall." And before Elizabeth could stop her, Hannah stepped from the rock where they were standing to a ledge a few feet lower down and then scrambled down the face of the cliff, loosing dirt and rocks to fall in front of her.

"Hannah, come back."

Hannah stopped and looked up at Elizabeth. "It's easier to go down than up. Once at the bottom we can follow the creek and find a way back." She found a new toehold and dropped down lower. In minutes she was at the bottom lifting water in her hands out of the pool to drink and splash on her face. "Come on, Elizabeth," she called up from the pool. "The water's good."

"I'm not the monkey you are," Elizabeth called back. She stood on the rock and considered her first step. It didn't look like one she wished to take. One slip and she might be delivered from all her earthly worries. She preferred to cling to them a bit longer. She'd have to find another way down to the pool.

13

When Ethan saw the blue of the sister's dress on the cliff, he feared he might be seeing an apparition. He had come with Brother Issachar to the woods after the morning meal to prepare logs from a fallen wild cherry tree. Brother Issachar had run his hands down the rough bark as if feeling the shape of the furniture it would become. He chopped off a limb and breathed in the odor of the fresh cut before he declared the wood worthy of a chest and perhaps a writing desk. Those of the Ministry had declared a need for such, and Brother Issachar was eager to get the log back to the village where the fallen tree could be transformed into useful furniture.

The November day had been unseasonably warm and the work of sawing the log hot. They hadn't conserved their drinking water since they were working so near to the spring pool where they could refill their water bottles. In fact the thought of the cool spring water had pulled at Ethan all morning as he worked. Brother Issachar had first shown him the pool when he was a young boy.

"A man needs to know where to find clear drinking water,"

he told Ethan. But he hadn't seemed to mind when Ethan pretended to stumble along the side of the pool and fell in. Even now Ethan could remember the way the water had come up around him, welcoming him into its cool embrace.

Later when he had to confess to Brother Martin how his shoes came to be so wet, Brother Martin had warned him of the danger of the place. "If one fell from the cliffs there, he would find no pleasure on the rocks below."

And then there had been the sister who had thrown herself off the cliff. Ethan did not remember her name, for he had only been among the Shakers a short time when it happened. Nor did he know the reason why, but he did remember the whispers and the feeling that something so dreadful had occurred that even speaking of it was a sin.

Brother Issachar had been in the group of brethren who went to bury the woman. They didn't bring her body back to the village graveyard, but buried her somewhere in the woods. Brother Issachar looked grim when he came back to the village, and they had not gone to the spring pool for many months. Yet for years after that, Ethan would wonder each time he stood on the cliff above the pool how the poor sister had felt standing there on the edge before she surrendered to the pull of the rocks below.

So when he came out of the trees and saw the sister peering over the precipice, his first thought was of the doomed woman and that his imagination had conjured up her ghost. He stopped and blinked his eyes, but the sister was no apparition. She was really there on the edge of the cliff. She wore no cap, and when the wind ruffled her hair and lifted it away from her neck, he knew her. Elizabeth, the young woman from the road.

For a few dreadful seconds, Ethan hesitated. He didn't want to be near her, for she set off feelings inside him that he struggled to ignore. Just the sight of her made his heart bounce around oddly inside his chest and pushed thoughts into his head only a man of the world would have. Certainly not thoughts a covenanted Believer should entertain in his mind.

During meeting when his eyes caught on her and those unsettling feelings raced through him, he could shake them off by concentrating on the steps of the dances and the words of the songs. But here there were no songs, no other Shaker brethren and sisters to remind him of what was proper and what was not. Here there were only the two of them alone, and that in and of itself was sin. Yet the fear of her falling from the cliff to break her body on the rocks below before he could reach her froze his heart inside him. He couldn't bear that.

She kept her eyes on the pool of water and gave no sign of knowing he was there. The water splashing down over the rocks must have kept her from hearing him run toward her. He couldn't see her face, only the bend of her neck as she kept staring downward toward the rocks just as he had always imagined the long dead sister doing, allowing the wrong spirits to pull her off the cliff.

"Don't jump!" he shouted when he was only a step or two away. She whirled toward him with startled eyes. The sudden movement made her lose her balance, and she teetered on the edge of the cliff with such fear in her eyes that it was plain she'd never had any intention to jump. Her arms flailed the air as she tried to catch herself, but she'd have surely fallen if he hadn't been close enough to grab her and jerk her away from the edge. He fell backward, pulling her down on top of him.

His breath was coming in sharp gasps that had nothing whatever to do with the short sprint across the open space to reach her and everything to do with the feel of her body on top of his. Worldly feelings flooded through him until absolutely nothing else mattered but the sight of her face staring down at him. The panic in her eyes faded away to be replaced by a soft look of wonder.

His hands seemed to move of their own accord. One slid down her back to press into the small curve above her hips and the other reached to touch her hair and then to trace her lips. His fingers trembled as if from the cold, but he had never felt so warm. He slipped his hand to the back of her neck and gently pulled her face toward his. Her breath mingled with his, and his lips parted in anticipation of the touch of her lips.

"Elizabeth! Elizabeth!"

The sound of her name rising up from the pool below broke the spell, and Elizabeth jerked away from Ethan. He scrambled away from her at the same instant as the realization of what he'd been about to do swept through him. How could he have even thought of kissing her? And yet even as he burned with shame, he wished the child, for it was surely the white-haired sister, had waited one more minute to call out.

"You should answer her," he said finally. His voice sounded odd to his own ears.

"Yes," she answered softly, but she didn't move as she stared at him as though his eyes held her captive.

The child called her name again, and at last Elizabeth crawled over toward the edge of the cliff to call down to her. She did not stand up. "It's all right, Hannah. I am here." Her hands clung to the ground as if she still feared falling into the open air.

"I heard you scream," the child said.

"Someone startled me. That is all." Elizabeth's eyes came back to Ethan.

"You are going to come down here with me, aren't you, Elizabeth?" The voice climbing up the cliff sounded small and frightened.

She called an answer down to the child without looking back over the cliff. "Wait there for me. I'll be down as soon as I find a safe way." Her eyes stayed on Ethan. After a minute, she spoke to him. "I wasn't going to jump."

"Yea, I see that now, but when I came out of the trees and saw you standing there, I feared that was your intent." He thought he should stand up, move away from her, but at the same time he owed her an explanation. "I didn't mean to startle you. Are you all right now?"

"Yes, thanks to you. If you hadn't caught me, I would have fallen." She scooted closer to him away from the cliff edge as if she needed more space between her and the air.

"If I hadn't frightened you, you wouldn't have lost your balance and been in danger to begin with." He couldn't pull his eyes away from her face. He could not imagine how he was going to speak of this to Brother Martin when he had to make his confession. He barely knew how to think of it. His eyes went to her lips as he remembered their softness under his fingertips. He forgot about Brother Martin.

"True, but as my father at times said, it is the end result that carries the most weight in our lives. I didn't fall." She pulled her eyes away from him to look around. "Did Sister Nola send you to search for Hannah?"

"Nay. Why would you think so?"

"Because you are here." Her eyes came back to him.

"I came to fill my water bottle. I'm helping Brother Issachar harvest a log from the woods. How come you to be here?" He couldn't remember when he had ever exchanged so many words with anyone except Brother Issachar. The elders frowned on such free communication even between the brethren and certainly not with the opposite sex.

The only free exchange of words allowed between the sisters and brethren were at the Tuesday and Thursday evening union meetings where seven or eight of the sisters would sit in chairs across from a like number of brethren in one of the brethren's rooms to talk of whatever came to mind. Usually the work of the day. Often as not, part of the hour was spent in singing songs, for there never seemed enough talk to fill the whole union hour. Yet here he was talking to this novitiate as if he had forgotten all the proper rules of behavior.

"Hannah ran away, and I hoped to find her and take her back before the brethren had to disrupt their workday to search for her," Elizabeth was saying. "My sister often disappeared into the woods back where we lived, and at times I had to seek her. Of course I had our dog to help me there."

"It appears you found her at any rate."

"She left trail markers," Elizabeth said with a smile. "And then she was thirsty and we heard the water, so we came here. She scrambled down the cliff, but I feared falling if I tried her route."

"I can show you a better way to the pool." Ethan at last made himself stand up. His legs felt shaky as though he might be standing on the precipice now as he looked down at her.

She rose up off the ground a few inches and then sat back

down as if her legs wouldn't lift her. She looked over her shoulder toward the cliff. "I'm not sure I can stand up."

"Are you hurt?" Ethan asked with concern.

"No." She looked a little embarrassed as she dug her hands down into the grass and dirt. "But I feel the air reaching for me. Give me a moment to find my courage." She pulled in a deep breath.

Without thought, he reached down for her hand the same as he had reached to help her out of the wagon when they brought her into the village. He glanced over his shoulder. He wouldn't have been surprised to see Brother Martin stride out of the trees to point out his wrong again, but no one was there. Not even Brother Issachar, who had to be wondering what was keeping him. "Here, let me help you up. I won't let you fall."

She seemed reluctant to put her hand in his, but after a moment she did. The jolt of her touch shook him as he helped her to her feet. It must be Satan who kept throwing her into his path. To challenge his commitment to the Shaker way. He would have pulled away from her then, but she clung to his hand as she stepped away from the edge. "How do we get down?" she asked.

"There is a path around the side. It is steep, but you won't fall," he assured her as he eased his hand free of hers. He couldn't allow her touch to make him forget who he was.

He moved in front of her to lead the way. It was easier to keep the worldly thoughts away from him if he didn't look at her, didn't see her soft lips and sun-flecked eyes. Such would not tempt a true Believer.

As she followed him down to the pool, she said, "I'm causing you trouble."

"Nay, I had need to get water from the pool." He kept

walking without looking back at her. The sooner they got to the bottom and he got his water and she got her little sister, the sooner he could return to Brother Issachar and continue his duties without the temptation of her presence.

"That's not the trouble I'm talking about. I speak of trouble with your other brethren and the elders. I've been told it is wrong for a sister and brother to be alone together, and while I don't feel the wrong in it, I sense that you feel it strongly." Her voice was soft, apologetic. "For that I am sorry. For causing you trouble in your spirit and with your brethren."

"These are not normal circumstances. A Shaker is always expected to help his fellow man in need. One's spirit isn't harmed by that."

"And his fellow woman?"

"Yea. A Believer must do kindness to all. Especially his sisters." In his ears, his voice sounded stilted and cold. He kept his eyes on the path in front of him.

"I thank you for your kindness then, my brother."

Her voice changed, lost its apologetic tone. He knew if he looked behind him, he would see her smiling. He didn't let himself look. At the same time he felt no pleasure in her calling him "brother." He forced out the words. "Give it no thought, Sister Elizabeth. I have done nothing that any of the other brethren wouldn't do."

"I pray your Brother Martin will believe that." And now the smile was evident in her voice. "I won't mention seeing you if you so wish."

More temptations to assault his spirit. It would be good not to have to speak of being alone with her in the woods. To not have to admit to Brother Martin the worldly feelings she made burn in him. Even now he had to fight the desire to turn and look into her eyes again. To see the smile that would be lifting the corners of her mouth. He kept his eyes forward on the path. He could conquer such temptations of the world. He must do so.

"Nay, that is not as it should be," he said. "We must both make confession of our meeting so that it can be seen that no wrong was intended. Or done."

"Yea." She used the Shaker word and all trace of a smile was gone from her voice. "No wrong was done."

The child ran up the path to meet them. She pushed past Ethan to grab Elizabeth around the waist. "Oh, Elizabeth, I was so scared when you screamed."

"It's all right, Hannah." Elizabeth rubbed the child's wet hair that curled as uproariously wet as dry. The little sister must have jumped in the water for she was wet from head to toe. "I lost my balance for a moment, but Brother Ethan caught me."

The little girl glared over her shoulder at Ethan. "I saw him. I thought he was going to push you. He's as bad as Mr. Linley."

"Oh no, dear child. He is nothing like Colton Linley."

"Is Colton Linley the man you ran to our village to be free from?" Ethan asked. He tried not to let the child's words wound him, but they did. He'd never had anyone call him bad before. He was the gift to the Shakers. He was a Believer. He walked the true way. He could not let these two lead him astray.

"He is," Elizabeth said.

"You are safe from him now," Ethan said. "He won't find you here."

"I fear no one will," Elizabeth said as she looked around.

"Is there a way back to the village without climbing that cliff path again? I have heard mention of a road to the river. That is what we hoped to find when we heard the water."

"The river is a ways away. You could follow the creek and reach it, but you can go to the north and find the road not far from this spot. Maybe a mile's walk. I can take you there if you want."

"Brother Issachar will be worried about you. You need to fill your water bottles and go back to where you were working." Elizabeth kept her eyes on the top of the little girl's head and didn't look at Ethan. "I can keep my bearings and find the way. We will be all right at least until we get back to the village, and then we will beg our sisters' and brothers' forgiveness, won't we, Hannah?"

"If we must." The child's shoulders drooped. She peeked up at Ethan. "Will Sister Ruth whip me?"

She looked so worried that Ethan had to smile. "Nay, my little sister, you need have no worry of that. She will merely point out the error of what you did and suggest ways you can correct such faults."

Hannah crossed her arms over her chest and frowned. "I think I'll take the whipping instead."

Ethan couldn't keep from laughing. He knew how the little girl felt. He'd often felt the same as a young boy having to listen to Brother Martin listing his faults. His smile faded. He felt some of the same now.

Elizabeth didn't smile. She gave the child's shoulder a shake. "You will do as you are told, and you will keep your promise to me."

"Yes, Elizabeth." Again the girl's shoulders drooped. "If I must."

"You must," Elizabeth said. "And now we must stop burdening our brother and find our way back to the village. Get one last drink so we can be on our way."

"Can I fall in again?" Hannah asked.

"No." Elizabeth's voice was firm. "It is November. You cannot swim in November."

Suddenly Ethan wanted to throw aside all the rules and not worry about what Brother Martin would say. He wanted to be a boy again running alongside Brother Issachar who did naught but laugh when he fell into the water. He wanted to feel that laughter inside his heart and see it in the eyes of the white-haired child.

"What matters the day on the calendar?" Ethan said as he kicked off his shoes. "It is the warmth of the sun that matters, and today the sun is warm." He gave his hat a sling up on the rocks before jumping into the pool.

The little sister shrieked with joy and fell in after him. Then Elizabeth laughed as she unlaced her shoes, pulled them off, and did the same. For a brief moment in the sun, they floated there, free of all cares and rules. And Ethan knew that of this he could never speak.

14

The week after Hannah made her brief escape from the confines of the village, clouds rolled in to hide the sun and brought a cold rain and piercing winds. Elizabeth spotted snowflakes among the raindrops as they walked back to the Gathering Family house after a day of labor in the laundry, but Sister Melva kept her head tucked down inside the hood of her cloak, claiming she had no desire to see proof of winter so early in the year.

Elizabeth held out her palm to catch one of the snowflakes, but the raindrops overwhelmed it at once, turning it into water to drip off her hand the same as the rain. That's how she felt among the Shakers. Something different. Something apart, but at the same time she was being surrounded and absorbed into the whole. Often at night as she lay in her narrow bed under the same color woven covers as all the other sisters in the sleeping room, wearing an identical nightdress and sleeping cap on her head, having eaten the same food and sung the same songs, she had to fight the feeling that they were breathing in unison and that if she didn't match her breath with theirs, the air in the room, the Shaker air as Hannah had called it, would not fill her lungs. More than once she had awakened gasping for breath after dreaming she was in a grave with the sides falling in on her.

She hadn't seen Hannah except at the Sunday meeting since they had walked back up the river road to the village. Over the course of the week, Elizabeth had found it necessary to bow her head and listen to many words condemning her actions. She confessed her wrong again and again to Sister Ruth, but the sister never heard enough sorrow in Elizabeth's voice and continually warned her of eternal punishment if she did not turn from her worldly ways.

Both Sister Ruth and Sister Melva had shown much concern that Ethan had found them in the woods, as if Elizabeth had set out with such a meeting in mind. As if Elizabeth had been the one to run from the village and not Hannah. When she had quietly reminded them of why she had left the village—to search for Hannah—they let her know that too had been wrong.

The special feeling she carried in her heart for Hannah was not part of the Shaker way. They told her over and over that she must loosen her hold on her little sister of the world. She was sister to all in the village now and not Hannah alone. And as a sister she had the duty to work for the good of all and not think only of her own selfish pleasure or of the relationships she had carried to Harmony Hill from the world.

There was talk of Elizabeth being assigned solely to Sister Ruth to be sure she walked the proper path of an obedient sister. In the end, they had left her in Sister Melva's daily charge, but Sister Ruth's stern eye was never far away. On the Sunday after her lapse of obedience, Elizabeth had to stand before the assembly and admit her wrong. Hannah did not because she was a child and could be more readily forgiven a lapse of judgment. After Elizabeth had said the words Sister Ruth told her she must say, the elders and eldresses chanted a song full of woes as they stomped their feet and circled around her. Then others of the brethren and sisters stood up from the benches to join the elders and eldresses until Elizabeth felt as if she were in the midst of a whirlwind of disapproval.

She kept her eyes to the floor and did her best to appear penitent. She was not. She would leave the village again on the morrow to find Hannah if need be, but these people stomping away evil as they danced around her didn't have to know that. She could only hope Hannah would keep her promise to restrain her spirit at least for a while.

And then as if they had won the battle and pulled her back from the mouth of the evil about to swallow her, they began marching in a more orderly fashion around her. Their faces were transformed now with smiles instead of fury as their feet whispered quietly on the wood floor. They began to sing. "'Tis a gift to be simple. 'Tis a gift to be free. 'Tis a gift to come down where we ought to be."

Sister Melva reached out and took Elizabeth's hand to pull her into the marchers, and Elizabeth knew she had been forgiven. This time.

"Sing with us," Sister Melva whispered in Elizabeth's ear.

So she joined her voice with theirs, and if she didn't feel the spirit they wished her to feel, she did at least feel grateful that they weren't pushing her out of the village.

Ethan's name wasn't mentioned by her or by anyone else in meeting, nor did she see him there. Her eyes had searched

furtively through the brethren as the men entered the meetinghouse through the door assigned to them. She had seen
Payton, but he only allowed his eyes to touch on hers for a
few spare seconds before he turned away. She had continued
to watch him as she wondered at the change in him. Payton
had completely lost the resistance he had carried with him
to the Shaker village. He looked like one of them. He moved
as they did. In unison. In harmony.

She did not wish that different, but she couldn't keep the
surprise of it from rising inside her. And a tinge of sorrow
that he seemed so ready to turn loose of all they'd shared
over the years and become her Shaker brother with no more
attachment to her than the dozens of other sisters in the village. Once more she reminded herself that was good. She had
enough concern with Hannah's unhappiness. And her own.

When she didn't see Ethan among the brethren, Elizabeth
feared he was being ostracized for the confession he had
perhaps made to Brother Martin, for even though they hadn't
allowed their lips to meet, Elizabeth knew he had desired to
do so. Elizabeth had felt no need to speak of such forbidden
desires to Sister Ruth, but Ethan was a true Believer and might
think it wrong to hide even the thought of doing something
considered so sinful by the Shakers. The Bible was plain on
that. A sin in the heart was the same as a sin done. It was the
definition of what was a sin that was different for Elizabeth
and the Shakers marching around her.

Later as Elder Joseph spoke of the activities of the Society,
Elizabeth felt a rush of relief when he stated that Ethan had
gone with Issachar on a trading trip down the river. At least
she hadn't been the cause for him to be punished. And she
did plan to stay away from him as Sister Ruth warned she

must. She was attracted to the young brother, but surely that was all it was. An attraction. Not love. Even though the mere thought of his eyes on her made her legs feel weak.

Her mother had often told the story of how she had known she would marry Elizabeth's father from the first moment she set eyes on him.

"But did you know you loved him right away?" Elizabeth had asked as she tried to understand the great mystery of love she'd read about in books.

Her mother had smiled over at Elizabeth's father as they sat on the porch and watched evening drop its night shadows over the woods around the cabin. It was a secret smile that he met and shared as he reached to hold her hand. "Oh yes, better than that," she said softly, not turning her eyes back to Elizabeth. "I didn't only know I was going to love him from that day forward, but I think I knew I had loved him forever."

"And did you feel the same, Father?" Elizabeth had asked.

"I felt as if the stars had come down and were sparkling in your mother's eyes. I was captivated by her very first smile at me."

Had that been how she felt looking at Ethan that day on the road when he had seemed so reluctant to meet her eyes? Something had flashed between them. But surely that had been nothing more than curiosity of their disparate worlds. He had been from a strange society she wished to join, and she had been coming from that world the Shakers took great pains to shut away from them. The very sight of her represented sin to him. Especially when it appeared all his thoughts weren't brotherly toward her as they were supposed to be.

Elizabeth had no trouble admitting she lacked the proper Shaker feelings toward him. She had wanted Ethan to kiss her. Even now, days later, the thought of his hand caressing her back while his other hand pulled her head down toward his lips made her heart speed up and her breath come faster. She had kissed Ralph Melbourne before he deserted her for life in Indiana. Colton had almost forced a kiss on her. The first she had accepted as part of courtship. The second had been a violation of her person. But with Ethan there had been no thought of yes or no. It had just felt right and natural to feel him next to her, to see his eyes staring into hers, to know he was going to kiss her.

In another world, it might be natural, but not among the Shakers. So even if it was love she felt for Ethan, she couldn't allow it to grow. She didn't want to be a stumbling block in his path of belief. It was good that he was gone from the village for a while. That would give her time to settle in and accept the Shaker rules. For in truth, with winter coming, she had little choice but to embrace the Shaker way and to pray that Hannah could do the same. No choice but Colton Linley.

As they turned up the walkway to the Gathering House, Elizabeth shivered and pulled her cloak closer about her to keep out the cold wind. She told herself she didn't have to worry about Colton anymore. He had no way to find her. She had disappeared from the world as completely as the snowflake had melted on her hand.

Two days later Elizabeth found out how wrong she was. She heard the commotion outside the Gathering Family house, but so much was strange about the village that she found little to be remarkable. Sisters who were sedate all through the week broke out in the strangest of songs and the most feverish of dances at their worship times. Even Sister Ruth was at times gifted with a whirling dance. At those times the older sister was transformed into a different person, but as soon as meeting was over, the stern shield fell back in place over her face. So Elizabeth paid little notice to the noises as she went about gathering the bed linens.

The day was young with the sun not yet breaking through the morning clouds. Elizabeth looked toward the window and hoped it would. She had need of the sunshine. For days the clouds had hidden the sun, and with the clouds, gloom gathered over her and made her hours toiling in the washhouse long and tiresome.

The morning meal had been eaten and the brethren had left for their workshops and some to the fields to finish the gathering of the corn and to sow the last of the fields with a winter crop of wheat. She wished she could be one of the sisters out trimming the dead plants from the gardens to make them tidy for the coming winter months. Order was important in every aspect of a Shaker's life. Perhaps if she were outside, she might feel less out of order. More in tune with those around her. But instead she had another week of service in the laundry, and then Sister Melva said they would be on kitchen duty for a month.

As loud voices rose up from outside the house, Sister Melva, her eyes wide open in alarm, rushed into the room where Elizabeth was gathering the soiled bedclothes.

"You must stay calm," she said in a frightened voice that belied her words. "Men of the world are encircling our house on their horses."

Elizabeth looked up. "Why?"

"Some of the world take pleasure in persecuting us for our beliefs." Sister Melva looked over her shoulder nervously as if fearing one of the men might already be running up the stairs. "Come, we must make a unified front against them and not allow them to desecrate our house."

At the top of the landing, they joined several other sisters standing shoulder to shoulder on the steps, ready to block the upper floor from the intruders. Outside, horses raced around the building and men shouted. Elizabeth couldn't make out any words, only the noise of their voices that was so out of place in this village where peace and quiet was sought at every moment of the day.

Eldress Rosellen turned from the closed door and held her hands out palms down toward the sisters anxiously watching her. "We must remain calm, my sisters." She herself seemed an island of such calm amidst all the worried faces.

Sister Ruth and some of the older sisters stepped up beside her. "What do they want?" Sister Ruth asked.

"What do they always want? To cause us trouble." Eldress Rosellen's face showed a mixture of disgust and dismay. "I went to the door when I first heard them. At his first sight of me, one of the men began shouting all sorts of twaddle about us stealing young sisters from their families and holding them here against their will."

"That is foolishness," Sister Ruth said.

"Yea, but foolishness they cling to instead of accepting the truth."

"What are we going to do?" one of the other sisters asked. Her voice sounded small and timid. "The brethren are in the fields."

Eldress Rosellen squared her shoulders at the sound of banging on the door. "Remember, my sisters, engaged in our duty, we have no reason to fear. Mother Ann will watch over us." She spoke the words quietly but with great assurance as she turned to reach for the doorknob.

Before she could pull it open, a rough-looking man pushed through the door to the sisters' side of the house and came inside, followed by a man in a dark suit and hat. Elizabeth gasped and shrank back at the sight of Colton Linley. She peeked around the sister in front of her, hoping against hope her eyes had deceived her. But no, it was Colton. He swept off his hat and ran a hand over his hair to settle it into place as his eyes searched through the sisters standing in the entry hall. There could be little doubt he was looking for her.

He started toward the stairs, but Eldress Rosellen stepped in front of him to block his way. "You have no proper business here. We must ask you to leave." She pointed toward the door still standing open to the chill air outside.

He stared down at the little woman as if she hadn't spoken. "Where are you hiding them?" he demanded as two more men who looked as rough as the first man came through the door.

"We hide no one." Eldress Rosellen spoke calmly. "All who come to us are free to leave whenever they so wish. We keep no one against her will."

Colton looked twice as big as the eldress and completely out of place in this Shaker house where peace was advanced at all times. The other men were even worse, giving every appearance of being highwaymen with no respect of property or person. They circled around Eldress Rosellen and the other sisters on the bottom floor like wolves around sheep. Elizabeth felt sick. She couldn't let them hurt these women if it was in her power to stop them. She would have to face Colton.

"Don't put on your holy act with me," Colton was saying. "I've been told what you do here. Killing babies and dancing naked and claiming to worship all the time. Stealing girls for your preacher men to do what ought not to be done."

Several of the sisters drew in shocked breath, and the color drained from Eldress Rosellen's face as she stared at Colton. "Nay, there is no truth in any of that. We serve the Lord in peace here."

"Well, you won't be having any peace today." Colton pushed past her and came toward the sisters' stairway with the other men trailing behind him.

The sisters on the stairs moved shoulder to shoulder to block the men. Sister Agnes, who barely stood a head taller than the handrail, stared up at Colton and said, "Get back from me, Satan."

"Satan, eh?" Colton let out a short laugh that did nothing to soften the hard lines on his face. "Well, I'm not the old devil, but I'm more than any of you can handle." He reached out to shove the old sister aside.

Elizabeth pulled in a breath as she summoned up her courage. She forced her feet to move and stepped in front of Sister Melva out where Colton could see her. "Leave her be, Colton."

Colton stared at Elizabeth as if he didn't recognize her. Then he snorted a little as the dark anger on his face changed to condescending amusement. "The cap doesn't become you, Elizabeth." His smile faded as he shook his head. "The man with your dog told me you must be among the Shakers, but I thought he had to be wrong. I couldn't believe you'd join up with these religious fanatics instead of keeping your promise to me. And now here you are in your cap and apron."

"They have taken me into their family." Elizabeth kept her eyes on Colton's face. Around her the sisters were silent and unmoving.

"I'm here to take you away." He made a move to push past the sisters standing between them.

Elizabeth spoke quickly to stop him. "I have no desire to leave with you."

"You owe me a debt." Colton's eyes narrowed on her.

"I have seen no proof of that. I searched through my father's papers and there was nothing indicating he owed you anything. Father was a lawyer. He would have made a contract in regard to any debts."

Elizabeth fought to keep her voice from trembling. But Sister Melva must have heard her fear, for she stepped nearer Elizabeth and brushed against her arm to lend her courage.

Elizabeth pushed out the question she dreaded to hear answered. "Can you show proof?"

"We had an understanding. You were to be payment if he couldn't come up with the money. And now sadly, he has passed on without paying that debt."

Colton's eyes on her made her stomach twist inside her, but she didn't look away from him. "My father wouldn't have made such an arrangement. Not without my permission."

"A desperate man can be forced to do surprising things."

Eldress Rosellen spoke behind him. "A person cannot be given in satisfaction of a debt."

Colton looked at her before his eyes went to Sister Annie's black face as she stood behind the eldress. "What about her? They sell the likes of her as slaves in the town square."

155

"Nay, not here at Harmony Hill. She is as free as the rest of us here. As free as Sister Elizabeth who has joined with us." Eldress Rosellen eyed Colton a moment before going on. "If you have proof of some debt our sister's father owed you in the world before she came to us, bring it and the Ministry will consider payment."

"I said it was an understanding. A deal agreed to with a handshake."

"Then as there is no proof of what you say, I must ask you to leave and not return." Eldress Rosellen stepped over to the door and pulled it open wider.

"I don't think you have it in your power to make me do anything, granny," Colton told the little woman scornfully. "But my grievance is not with you, but with your sweet little Sister Elizabeth as she well knows." He turned back to Elizabeth. He was like a wolf with his paw already on the neck of the choicest lamb, and when his lips turned up in a small self-satisfied smile, it was all Elizabeth could do to stand still and not run from his eyes on her. "Don't you, Sister? There's more than the matter of your father's debt to me, isn't there? There's my cabin burned to the ground."

"Your cabin burned?" Elizabeth tried to sound surprised and then sad. "If that is true, we have lost all we left behind as well."

"Do you expect me to believe you knew nothing of this?"

Colton's eyes bored into her, but she didn't shrink from his look as she answered, "Believe what you like. The cabin was standing when I shut its door behind me."

"Then perhaps I should ask your brother what he knows of it. Perhaps I should have the sheriff come ask the questions."

"Do what you will. We did no harm to your cabin before we left it. And you say it burned? When was that?"

Colton smiled slightly. "As if you don't already know. Our innocent young Payton has always liked fires, but I fear he won't like jail."

"Go away, Colton." She managed to sound sure and determined without letting even a hint of the trembles she felt inside sound in her voice.

His face darkened. "You will come with me, Elizabeth. I've given you much more than the week you asked to mourn your father." He pushed past the first sisters on the stairs as the other men began to throw down the chairs from the pegs.

Suddenly Elder Homer stormed into the house with a pitchfork. He did not hold the pitchfork menacingly, but he did grip it tightly as he said, "What goes on here?" Other brethren filed in behind him to quickly move between the men and the sisters.

The men with Colton looked at the Shaker brethren's somber faces and backed slowly away from them toward the door. Colton stopped on the stairs. Four sisters still stood between him and Elizabeth. He looked down at the brethren, then back at Elizabeth. "I will have you, Elizabeth. One way or another."

"Nay, I will never be yours, Colton. Never."

He made a sound of disgust before he said, "You even try to sound like one of them, but you're not. You're mine. Rest assured of that."

Without waiting for her to reply, he turned and went down the stairs. He looked neither left nor right as he strode out the door.

When Elizabeth heard the horses' hooves carrying the

men out of the village, she looked at Sister Melva. "I didn't mean to bring you trouble," she said. "I didn't think he would find me here."

"Worry not, Sister Elizabeth. We will stomp out the evil brought into our house." And down below the Shakers circled the room in a stomping dance so full of spirit and fury that Elizabeth expected to feel the house shake. But it did not. It was built too solidly.

"Come add your feet to the dance." Sister Melva took Elizabeth's hand and led her down the stairs where she joined the others stomping and pushing with their hands to shove the devil away. If only she could believe it might work.

15

Ethan watched the wheel of the steamship churn the river water, lifting and dropping it over and over. Ever since he'd stepped aboard the riverboat for their trip down the river to New Orleans, he had been aware of the water flowing under his feet. Aware of it taking him away from all he'd known, and yet somewhere within his soul there was a glad yielding to the pull of the water.

It worried him. This feeling of one with the river. This excitement each time they reached a new port. He feared his father's seed had sprouted unbeknownst to him, and now the river was watering it, making it grow. He feared falling from grace.

Brother Martin had seemed to have the same fear for him after Ethan had confessed the struggle he felt whenever he was near Elizabeth. Ethan had told him of his encounter with Elizabeth in the woods. He had to. Unconfessed sin kept one from living the perfect way, the Shaker way. While he hadn't planned to meet Elizabeth in the trees, they had met. Without supervision. Without control.

"You should have gone to get Brother Issachar before you approached her." Brother Martin had taken off his spectacles and rubbed his forehead as if Ethan's confession hurt his head.

"I thought she was going to jump. If I had gone for Brother Issachar, I would have had no chance to save her."

The lines between Brother Martin's eyes deepened. He blew out a puff of air from his nose and sat in thought a moment before he said, "Yet you tell me she was not going to jump at all."

"Yea, but I feared that was what she intended."

"It could be you should have spoken a prayer for guidance to our Eternal Father or Mother Ann. Did you do so?" Brother Martin peered across the table at Ethan.

"Nay, I was only concerned with pulling my sister back from the edge of danger," Ethan admitted.

"I fear you too were on the edge of danger, Brother Ethan. That you teeter there even yet." Brother Martin's eyes bored into Ethan. "This woman has a troubling spirit." He spoke the word "woman" as some might say "harlot."

Ethan felt the color rising in his face, but he dared not look away from Brother Martin's eyes. "Sister Elizabeth didn't go into the woods to seek me nor did I go to seek her. It was merely chance that led me to the spring for water at the same time she was searching for a way down to the pool."

"So you say." Brother Martin tapped his spectacles against the table.

"I have spoken true words." When Brother Martin continued to stare at him without speaking for a long moment, Ethan went on. "Do you not believe me?"

Again Brother Martin tapped his spectacles against the table. In the silent room the tapping seemed loud. At last he said, "It isn't that I think you don't speak the truth. It's more that I sense something hidden, something that's pulling you from the true way."

"I do not want it to be so." Ethan lowered his eyes. He had no answers for the older brother or for himself. He stared down at his hands gripping his thighs. Strong hands. Hands he had always put to work for God and for the good of his brethren and sisters.

Was Brother Martin right? Was the new sister pulling him away from the beliefs he'd promised to be true to? He couldn't deny she disturbed his inner peace. He'd confessed that to Brother Martin, but Ethan hadn't spoken of his desire to touch her lips with his. He hadn't told him of the abandon with which he had jumped into the pool of water with the two sisters. The sound of their reckless laughter echoed in his mind and smote him with guilt. Even so, he didn't seem able to put such sins into words for Brother Martin to hear. Not and risk the loss of his trust. Yet with unconfessed sin in his heart, he surely risked much worse.

After the silence dragged on for what seemed like an hour, Brother Martin sighed. "Wrong thoughts can lead you into sin, Brother Ethan, and sin can bring you low. Nay, not only can. Will. Sin *will* bring you low. Purity in mind and body are required for the salvation of your soul. 'Blessed are the pure in heart for they shall see God.' That's what we want. To live such a life here in our village that we are pure of heart and purpose. That we bring heaven down to us. That is what you want, is it not, my brother?"

"You know it is. I am a Believer," Ethan answered. He had no doubts of that. "I will pray for an increase in the purity of my mind and body."

"Yea, that will be well." Brother Martin pushed out another long breath of air and then propped his spectacles back on his nose. "Brother Issachar has requested you be allowed to accompany him downriver to help with the selling of our products."

Ethan looked up quickly. He had long wanted to go on such a trip, but only days ago Brother Martin had seemed reluctant to give his approval. Other young brothers under Brother Martin's charge had been sent out to the world on trading trips, even to colleges to learn special skills, but for some reason, Brother Martin had always kept Ethan close to the village. Perhaps he sensed hidden seeds of sin inside Ethan. Perhaps Brother Issachar had told him of the father Ethan had never confessed knowing to Brother Martin.

"A trading trip?" Ethan asked.

"Yea, I don't mind telling you that in the past I have had doubts of the wisdom of such a trip for you, but now I am inclined to agree with Brother Issachar that in order to become a stronger, more committed Believer, you must be allowed to experience some troubles of the world. After all, Mother Ann said, 'Souls in order to insure the right temper are heated in the furnace of affliction and plunged in cold waters of tribulation; some come out of the trial pure, elastic, and bright, ready for the highest service. Others come out brittle and ill-tempered, full of flaws and spots of rust.'"

Brother Martin's eyes settled on Ethan with a good measure of kindness now mixed in with the worry. "I will pray for no spots of rust on you, Brother Ethan, when you return from the trip with Brother Issachar and that you will steadily climb the path to that higher service for which you were given to us."

"I will have the same prayer every day when I wake up and before I lay my head down at night while I am away from the village. When will we go?" Ethan tried to keep the eagerness out of his voice, but he feared Brother Martin heard it anyway.

"A steamship should be coming in to our landing any day now. When it does, you must be ready."

The steamship had come that very evening. Ethan had heard the sound of its horn from up in the village, and it had sent a shock through him. He was glad he hadn't had to be in the same room with Elizabeth before he left. He was thankful he hadn't had to stand in front of the assembly and confess his wrong behavior to the whole Society. That would prove how low temptation had sunk him.

The horn had sounded a second time and pushed some of Ethan's worries right out of his head. He could hardly wait to step on the steamship and start down the river. He hoped the water flowing under his feet would make him forget the sight of Elizabeth's eyes looking at him, seeming to understand more about him than he understood himself.

But now as he stood on deck and watched the Mississippi River water sliding past the boat, he realized that he'd brought the thought of Elizabeth's eyes and touch with him. He tried not to think of her, but she kept slipping past his guard. He dreamed of her. How could a man control the images of his dreams? She was in the mist rising off the river when he first woke in the mornings and stumbled out on deck to face the day. She was in the reflection of the setting sun on the water as evening came. He looked at the stars in the dark of the night and saw the sparkle of her eyes. He knew not how or why, but he couldn't deny he carried a part of her with him.

And he wondered about her back at Harmony Hill. He wondered if the elders and eldresses had condemned her for disregarding the rules and causing a disturbance in the village. He wondered what she had confessed to her appointed confessor. He didn't only wonder about that, but at times felt an almost overpowering worry since he hadn't been as truthful in his own confession as he should have been. What if their stories were compared? Would he be asked to depart from his family of Believers if the Ministry learned of those sins he had not confessed to Brother Martin? Was he being tempered in the fire of temptation? Ethan stared down at the muddy river water and felt way too brittle with the corrosion of sin eating at his spirit.

"The river water rolling by can be a balm to a troubled spirit." Brother Issachar joined him at the rail. He didn't look at Ethan, but kept his eyes on the water churning up behind the boat's big wheel.

"Yea," Ethan agreed. He longed to talk to Brother Issachar about his troubled thoughts, but at the same time he was reluctant to speak the words. They had actually done very little talking other than about matters of business. At each landing they carried some of their products off the boats and set them out for sale. Many who came to buy from them called Brother Issachar by name and greeted him with a smile and an eagerness for the Shaker products. Others looked upon them with suspicion, but even they often as not bought something after examining the workmanship of the brooms or hats or reading the labels on the potions. Nearly every buyer asked for seeds and took away a packet of cucumber or bean seed to save for the coming year even though Brother Issachar promised he or another brother would be back in the spring.

Brother Issachar leaned his arms down on the railing. After a long silence, he said, "A man can feel the loss of his roots when he's on the river."

Ethan stared down at the water. "The river pulls at me," he admitted.

"The river pulls at many men when they are within its sight and sound. The water forever rushing on with few restraints."

"The banks hold it in." Ethan looked to the thick growths of trees alongside the river. Here and there the trees gave way to a few houses or shacks.

"But with more water, the banks are forgotten. At times the water does what it wills." Brother Issachar waved away a fly that buzzed his face. "They say the water of the Mississippi flowed backwards during the great earthquake in '12 and that the river heaved up high above the banks taking the boats with it. Those who lived through it couldn't stop talking of the wonder of it."

"You sound as if you might want to see such." Ethan looked at Brother Issachar.

"Yea, I am wont to search after new sights at times," Brother Issachar said. Then he smiled. "But upheavals of the earth might be something I might prefer to witness from a safe perch somewhere."

"It wouldn't be the same watching as experiencing it."

"Nay, nothing is, but oft it is the safer road to travel." Brother Issachar's smile disappeared as he stared down at the water again. "Especially out here among those of the world."

"That's why we shut away the world from our villages, is it not? To keep temptations at bay."

"Yea, temptations are generally easier to avoid than to

conquer once we have invited such into our thoughts. A true Believer aims to live a perfect life of service and worship. To do good to all without falling into sin. To know peace."

"Do you know that peace?" Ethan felt a yearning inside him for the peace of living in harmony with the Lord and his brethren. Peace he'd once thought he had, but he'd surely been wrong. He couldn't have lost it so easily if it had been the true peace of a Believer.

"I do. Such peace is a gift." Brother Issachar turned his eyes to study Ethan's face. "But I see that it's not peace you are feeling at this time. Perhaps that's why the river pulls at you."

"I have many questions," Ethan admitted.

"There's no sin in questions."

"I'm not sure Brother Martin would tell me the same. He says a Believer has the true answers before questions are asked. Answers from the Bible and from the writings of Mother Ann. That a true Believer only has the need to be obedient."

Brother Issachar smiled and shook his head a little before he turned his eyes to the distant shore as if looking for answers there among the trees. "I wouldn't fain to argue spiritual answers with our Brother Martin. He has more of a gift for study of those truths than I. I can only know what I have in my own heart and mind."

"But isn't that the same as what every Believer would have? Don't we all sign the same Covenant of Belief?"

"Yea, so we do. But even as man is the same in many ways, in many other ways he is different. Think of the disparate gifts we are given. Gifts of spirit. Gifts of labor. Gifts of invention and design. Too many types of gifts to name but all can be useful. It brings to my mind the Bible teachings where the apostle Paul says a hand cannot do the job of an eye nor an eye the job of the hand. Each part is necessary for the whole."

"That it is among the Believers," Ethan said. "Each person necessary to work. Each doing his part to make the whole better."

"Yea. It's not a bad way." Brother Issachar put his hand on Ethan's shoulder. "But it's not one the world understands. There will be those who ridicule us and attempt to cause us trouble when we get to New Orleans." He frowned a little. "You'll see things you cannot imagine. Women with no proper modesty calling out to you with wrong motives. Men ready to kill you for the money they think you carry. You must stay alert and cautious."

"My father would be such a man. Do you think he might still be alive?"

"What's it been?" Brother Issachar looked to be figuring a problem in his head. "Fifteen, sixteen years since you came to us? That isn't so long in the lifetime of a man, but a man such as you say he was could have lost his life in any number of ways since then." The lines around Brother Issachar's eyes deepened with concern. "Is he what troubles you?"

"Nay, not so much. I suppose the river brought him to mind. He boasted to the men with him that he would turn me into a river man like him." Ethan hadn't thought much about that night on the raft floating downriver with his father for a long time, but here on the river the memory was as clear as if it had happened yesterday.

"Do you remember how he looked?"

"Yea. I remember." Ethan's hands tightened on the railing at the thought of his father's eyes on him.

Brother Issachar's voice was mild. "Then it could be you

might recognize him in the unlikely event we run into him, but I can almost assure you, he would never recognize you." Brother Issachar stared at Ethan a moment. "Even if there should happen to be some resemblance in your looks. First, he will have thought you dead these many years, swallowed up by the river. Second, even if he imagined you could have made it to shore, he'd never imagine you a Shaker." Brother Issachar squeezed Ethan's shoulder and smiled at him. "I've been with you to see you through the years, and I can barely put the half-drowned, frightened boy I found on the river bank with the strong young man standing before me today. I'm proud of the man you've become."

Brother Issachar held up his hand to stop Ethan's next question before he could put it into words and added, "And it is not being prideful to think such about you. The Eternal Father told Jesus the same after he received John the Baptist's baptism."

"But his peace was never so disturbed by questions," Ethan said.

"There you are surely wrong, my brother. Think of his prayer in the garden."

"Yea, I remember the Scripture. He prayed until his beads of sweat turned to blood. Like our own Mother Ann when she was praying on the ship coming over to America."

"Yea, so it is said."

"And the Eternal Father sent them answers," Ethan said. "I pray but I find no answers and no peace from the questions."

"It will not always be thus. Trust me." Brother Issachar smiled again. "You will find answers. The right answers for you."

"But how will I know if they are true answers?"

"For the kinds of questions you are asking, the true answers are the only ones you can live with." He turned to walk away, but then he turned back to Ethan. "Of one thing you can be sure, I'll always be proud of you no matter what path your feet decide to walk."

After Brother Issachar walked away down the deck, Ethan turned to stare back down at the river. The muddy water continued to roll under the boat carrying them along.

16

The first fire was in the Carpenters' Shop the week after Payton began working there. The brother assigned to help Payton learn the Shaker way was kind of heart like Issachar and had urged the Ministry to let Payton work with wood. Payton told Elizabeth that Brother Micah had such a way of explaining things that it was easy to see the truth in his words.

Elizabeth had happened to meet Payton on the walkway between the buildings when she had been returning from the outhouse before the Shakers' Monday night social time. It was the night Elizabeth most looked forward to, for Elder Joseph read from newspapers of the world as well as the letters reporting the progress of other Shaker societies across the country.

Elizabeth hungered after stories of the world outside the village. News of government issues or the events of cities near and far kept her from feeling so isolated. It was odd how much more cut off from life she felt among the Shakers where she was surrounded by people night and day than she had at the remote cabin in the woods. But here the people around her kept trying to force her mind into a narrow room of approved Shaker thinking with no window out to the world. At the cabin she'd had dozens of windows to the world in the books stacked on every table and shelf. Her father often traded his services for books instead of money. Books of fancy. Books of learning. Books that carried her off to other lands.

Here she was only allowed to read Scripture and Shaker writings. Sister Melva told her that Believers must stay focused on the Shaker way and doing things useful to the growth of the spirit. Made-up stories and even history books had little useful purpose.

Sister Melva had made a sweeping-away motion with her hands as she spoke. "A Shaker sister needs to concentrate on her duties and not worry about past events. We have no need to know what has been in the world. We are not of that world. We only need to know what will be in our Shaker communities, and Mother Ann reveals that to those of the Ministry in her good time."

"But what about the newspapers? Could we not read them ourselves instead of having Elder Joseph read to us from them?" Elizabeth wanted the words in front of her eyes and not just in her ears.

"Nay, we might be bothered by some of the stories from the world. The elders and eldresses judge what we need to know and what we do not," Sister Melva said flatly with a look that plainly said the topic wasn't open for discussion. Little in the Shaker community was. The Ministry made the rules. The Ministry knew what was best for those in the Society.

So the fences closed in around Elizabeth until at times she felt more a captive than a novitiate who'd come willingly, even eagerly, to the village in search of shelter. Each morning when she rose at the sound of the rising bell to go about her duties, she knelt by her narrow bed and said the required morning prayer. At least the prayers were silent so she could pray as she wished.

She prayed for Hannah and Payton. She prayed for the brothers and sisters in the village. Sometimes she even prayed for Aristotle as she longed to feel his cold nose pushing at her hand in search of a kind word and a petting. And she prayed that she would be able to listen with an open mind to the Shaker teachings Sister Melva and Sister Ruth kept pushing at her and put aside her inclination to doubt the truth of much of what they told her she must believe.

Her father had believed in an individual's right to pursue happiness. He had told her many times their country had been established on that foundation. He claimed freedom was the greatest gift any one person could have.

"But what about love?" Elizabeth had asked him. "Is that not the greatest gift?"

"Without doubt, the love of your mother for me was the greatest gift I could ever hope to receive here in this world, and from that love came each of you in turn until I wondered how my heart could hold more love. But it always did." He had smiled at her with the tinge of sadness that was always there when he spoke of her mother. "Ah, but you see, my dear child, if you have freedom, you can seek love where you will and with the Lord's blessings."

The Shakers spoke a great deal about the gift of love. The love for Mother Ann and the Eternal Father. The love for the brethren and sisters that was to be an all-encompassing love with no special attachments allowed between any two individuals. But the love her father had spoken of, the love between a man and a woman, was considered a dreadful sin that took much laboring and prayer to overcome. So the feeling that took Elizabeth's breath when she looked at the young brother was something to be stomped away in special dances that kept such sin from their village.

But it wasn't stomped from Elizabeth's heart even when she went through the motions of the dances Sister Melva was teaching her. Not that she ever spoke to Sister Melva of how her thoughts raced after Ethan. Sister Melva would not forgive such confession nor understand how the simple touch of Ethan's hand had made Elizabeth's head spin. So each time the young man's face sneaked into her mind, she didn't let herself dwell on the blue of his eyes. She didn't let herself imagine how his lips might have felt against hers if Hannah hadn't yelled to pull them both back to their senses that day on the cliff. Instead she concentrated on paring the thinnest peeling off the potatoes for the pot or on kneading the bread into perfect loaves for rising.

Even so, Ethan lingered in the shadows of her mind waiting for an unguarded moment to come back into her thoughts. She simply could not seem to wipe him from her mind any more than she could forget her ties to Hannah and Payton. Not only was she their sister, she had cared for them like a mother for years. Elizabeth could not fathom how the Shakers expected a person to just shrug all that aside and never think of such again, no matter what rules the Ministry came up with.

Sister Melva said the elders and eldresses assigned to the Ministry spent their time continually in prayer and studying Scripture and Mother Ann's precepts so they could better lead the Society. The Shakers considered them only a bit below

Mother Ann herself since they'd been chosen to continue her teachings. Their rules were sacrosanct.

A Shaker had little of the freedom Elizabeth's father had so cherished. One kept a simple mind and did the bidding of the elders and eldresses. Elizabeth told herself she could live the Shaker way day by day without embracing all their beliefs. She could strive to appease Sister Melva and Sister Ruth by owning up to a few small wrongs when they demanded she confess her every sin in order to receive salvation. She could bend her will to the rules of the Society. She could abide the fences by remembering that the fences not only kept her confined with the Shaker brethren and sisters, but they also helped keep the world out. And she did not want to go beyond the safety of the fences. Those very fences were keeping Colton Linley away.

Two of the elders had gone to see the sheriff in the nearby town after the men with Colton had done damage to the Gathering Family house. The sheriff had come to the village and questioned the sisters with members of the Ministry in attendance. Once he was satisfied that no girls were being held against their will, he promised to see that the men gave them no more trouble.

The Shaker leaders didn't hold Elizabeth to blame for Colton's intrusion, although Sister Ruth's hawklike eyes watched her more intently, as if expecting Elizabeth to bring the community of Believers even more trouble. Trouble she was definitely not worth.

Elizabeth had no desire to cause the Shakers trouble. She had good intentions of being humble and obedient, but when Elizabeth saw Payton on the pathway, she gave in to the impulse to put out her hand to stop him. Night had fallen, but the moon gave light to the paths. He seemed reluctant at first to heed her touch as he glanced over his shoulder to see if anyone was watching. Stopping to engage in conversation as one walked toward this or that duty was contrary to the Shaker rules, but then his face changed as he smiled at her. He didn't resist as she pulled him off the path into the shadows next to one of the buildings.

He looked so different in his Shaker hat and clothes as she must as well in her cap and apron, but he sounded like the Payton she knew when he said, "Elizabeth, you were right to insist we come here. I'm sorry for arguing against it." Back at the cabin, he had always been quick to disagree with her, but just as quick to apologize if he was shown to be in the wrong.

"You couldn't know how it would be. You were only worried." She was grateful he didn't call her Sister Elizabeth even though he surely had more reason to address her thus than any of the many others who did so every day. Elizabeth kept her hand on his arm, not to hold him there, but just to have the connection with him. A connection she missed so sorely here among the Shakers.

"Yea, I was being mule-headed. But we couldn't have found a better place. More food than even I can eat, and the houses . . ." His voice took on a sound of wonder. "I know Father told us of them after his visit here last year, but who could have imagined the likes of these? Built solid with nary a crack to let in the winter winds. And the stones for the Centre Family dwelling. I wish I could have been here to see them cut and put in place, but Brother Micah says they'll be building more soon. He says I can learn about raising roofs and laying stone. That I'm a fast learner and that's a gift. A gift that will serve me well here among them."

Elizabeth peered at him. Even in the shadows she could see the excited gleam in his eyes. "So you are satisfied here? Even with their teachings and rules?"

"The rules aren't so bad. They just expect you to work. I don't mind working. And Brother Micah says I can make a chair from start to finish as soon as I learn some more about the tools they use. He has a way of telling me things that's almost like listening to Father. Not that Father knew that much about carving, but he sometimes helped me see things in the wood that I didn't at first see."

"But they won't always let you work with the wood." Elizabeth couldn't keep from trying to temper his enthusiasm. "And you won't be able to carve something just for the beauty of it."

"I know that, but I can see now that the beauty of anything I make is in its usefulness. Brother Micah explained that right away and also how each brother has to do his turn with duties that aren't as pleasant. That's the only fair way, don't you think?"

"I don't know what to think. Perhaps I need Brother Micah to explain things to me." When Elizabeth heard the sour sound of her voice, she felt ashamed. It was wrong of her to spoil the peace Payton was finding here in the village. So she squeezed his arm gently and hurried to add, "But I am glad you're getting along well, Payton."

He was quiet for a moment before he said, "When they give you a work duty with the plants and herbs, you might like it better."

"Don't be concerned about me. I'm willing to work any duty," she said quickly. "In exchange for my keep. As you say, that is only fair."

"It's more than our keep. They wish us to join with them. To follow the Shaker way and receive salvation." He sounded almost as if he were speaking the words in rote.

Her hand tightened on his arm even though he made no move to leave. "So they do, but I've yet to be able to accept their teachings as the only truth as to that."

Payton again glanced over his shoulder as if he feared someone might overhear her words of doubt. "They don't like for you to question their truths," he said in almost a whisper. "But it doesn't seem all that much different from what Father read to us out of the Bible on Sunday mornings at the cabin."

"What of their Mother Ann?" Elizabeth asked with a frown. "They think of her as the second appearing. The daughter of God. Where does it speak of that in the Bible?"

"You can't see everything in the Scripture. Brother Micah says you have to read Mother Ann's writings too. Then you'll understand she was a woman like no other and that the Creator God blessed her with many gifts of the spirit."

"I think your Brother Micah is turning you into a preacher." Elizabeth smiled a little to hide her concern. She had not brought Payton into the Shakers to lose him, only to see that he was fed.

He ducked his head as if she were chastising him before he mumbled, "I'm only trying to understand their ways."

"As we should," she said softly to take the sting out of her earlier words. "But there are many things I have a hard time accepting. They believe so differently from the rest of the world."

He looked back up at her. "Oh, you mean like how they don't believe in marrying. That's different for sure. And the dancing in their meetings seemed pretty odd to me at first, but I'm getting used to it even if I'm not too good at it yet. But I'm learning. At least the regular back and forth steps. Brother Micah says everyone doesn't have to have a whirling gift. That there are many gifts, and I may be gifted by the spirit in some other way that I can't even imagine now."

He stopped as if he sensed Elizabeth's doubting spirit. When she stayed silent, he went on in a faltering tone. "But I mean I don't guess you have to believe it all right away. As long as you stick to the rules and don't cause trouble."

"I suppose I've already caused them some trouble as you know from my confession at meeting. But I had to go after Hannah." Elizabeth didn't know why she was explaining to Payton. He should understand if no one else did that Hannah was not the ordinary child. "Hannah isn't happy."

"I have seen that. She's tried to talk to me at meetings, but the sister in charge of her won't allow it. That's probably for the best. In time she'll settle in and be all right." Again he sounded as if he was repeating words he'd been told.

"We can hope," Elizabeth said, then realized she didn't hope that at all. She didn't want Hannah's spirit to be broken. She didn't want her own spirit to be broken. "I've promised her we will leave in the spring if she continues to be unhappy."

"Then we would be winter Shakers." Payton sounded truly distressed by the thought. "Brother Micah speaks poorly of them."

"If we leave, you would go with us, wouldn't you?"

He hesitated before he answered. "You said yourself we have nowhere to go. Nowhere but Colton Linley."

"He was here. He saw Aristotle with the man in the town and that's how he knew we were with the Shakers."

"So I heard." Payton stared down at the ground a moment

before he looked back at Elizabeth. "Brother Micah says he spoke of our cabin burning."

"He did. What else did your Brother Micah tell you?"

"Nothing. Except that Colton brought some rough characters with him who threatened the sisters and that later the sheriff came to check into the accusations of sisters being held against their will. Brother Micah said that was ridiculous nonsense."

"Yes," Elizabeth said.

Payton let silence fall between them for a moment before he asked, "Did you have to talk to the sheriff?"

"I did."

"Did he speak of the fire with you?" There was the hint of a tremble in his voice.

"He did. I said I knew not how it started." Elizabeth stared at Payton in the near darkness. "And I do not."

"Nay, you do not."

Elizabeth couldn't see in the shadows, but she knew Payton's face would be burning hot with guilt. "It would be best if you say the same if you are asked of it."

"But Brother Micah says I must confess all my sins before I can find salvation."

"That one can wait at least until spring and perhaps forever. That one and this—our talking to each other—they would also call sin, but it's not. You are my brother. It's not wrong for me to speak to you."

"But Brother Micah says—"

Elizabeth interrupted him. "I don't care what Brother Micah says." She stopped at the shrill sound of her voice and took a deep breath before she went on in a quieter tone. "About this you must listen to me and promise. You could go to jail and Brother Micah could do nothing about that."

"Perhaps I should go to jail. I did wrong."

"You didn't think it so wrong at the time."

"That didn't make it not wrong. I let my grief for our father overpower my good sense."

"So you did," Elizabeth agreed. "But perhaps it was no more than Colton deserved after the way he acted. Remember you said so at the time."

"And you said not." He stood up straight and stared down at her. He looked to have grown even taller in the time they'd been with the Shakers. After a moment he sighed a little as he said, "But all right, Elizabeth. If you want me to promise, I will."

"Good." Elizabeth pulled him close in a quick hug that he allowed but didn't return before she turned him loose. He peeked around the edge of the building to be sure no one was in sight before he stepped back up on the path and hurried toward the West Family house. The Shakers had moved him there to separate him from easy contact with Elizabeth or Hannah. Elizabeth watched him from the shadows until she could no longer see his shape in the moonlight. She whispered, "Oh my brother, I do miss you."

The next night during their time of rest after supper before they gathered with their families to practice the dance steps, the bell began tolling. Sister Melva jumped to her feet.

"It must be a fire," she said. "Hurry, we must give aid if we can."

They joined a stream of sisters and brothers rushing out of the house. No flames could be seen, although there was the smell of smoke in the air, but that could have been drifting down from the chimneys.

Word soon flew through the number that the fire was in the Carpenters' Shop. Sister Ruth, who was hurrying along with Elizabeth and Sister Melva, peered over at Elizabeth and said, "Our new Brother Payton is working there now, is he not?"

When Elizabeth made no answer, Sister Ruth went on. "Perhaps he was careless with a lamp. Isn't that what you told the sheriff may have happened at the cabin you left? The one that horrible man of the world said burned."

"I know not how the cabin burned," Elizabeth said quietly. "But we were always careful with our lamps and candles." She spoke the words without letting the worry inside her show. Surely Payton had nothing to do with this. He'd been excited about the chance to work with wood.

Payton was in the center of the men in front of the building when they got there. The smell of smoke was strong now. Different from what would drift down from the chimneys, but the outer building looked undamaged. In the lantern light, Payton's soot-smudged face looked too pale, and his eyes were stretched wide with excitement or maybe fright. Elizabeth breathed easier when she saw the brethren who surrounded him only looked concerned, not angry.

Brother Joseph raised his voice to address those gathering around them. "There is no cause for alarm, my sisters and brethren. There was a fire, but Brother Payton discovered it and put it out before it could burn anything but the floor and one of the tables. Please return to your houses and give thanks in your prayers that we were spared an unfortunate disaster. Surely Mother Ann is watching over us. At our next meeting we will labor a song of thanksgiving."

"But how did the fire start?" one of the brethren asked.

"We'll have to investigate to see if it was due to carelessness on the part of some of our workers or if it was due to those of the world intending to cause us trouble. Now go back to your houses."

Elizabeth tried to catch Payton's eye, but he kept his head down as Brother Micah took hold of his arm to lead him away. The rest of the brothers and sisters began turning away to go back to their houses.

Sister Ruth stayed close by Elizabeth's side. "I see not how one of the world could get into the middle of our village and start a fire without anyone noticing him. A barn on the outer edges perhaps. But not the Carpenters' Shop. I really cannot fathom how that could happen."

"Perhaps it was an accident," Elizabeth said.

"Yea, accidents do happen. Especially when one is careless." Sister Ruth peered over at Elizabeth. "As you said, your cabin may have burned for the same cause. If not with a lamp, some other lapse of caution with fire."

"Nay, that was not what I said. I said I didn't know how the fire in my old cabin started. Any more than I know how this fire started. I see not the connection between the two." Elizabeth met the woman's eyes in the near darkness.

"Nay, no connection." Sister Ruth pulled her cloak closer around her against the chill of the evening. "Nay, none but your brother of the world."

17

The New Orleans dock was such a bustle of activity as Ethan walked down the gangplank, he hardly knew which way to look first. To his right, a bare-chested brown man in pants held up by suspenders strummed a banjo. A passerby pitched a coin at his feet. Another man snaked through the crowd after a rooster that kept one flap of its wings ahead. Laughter followed the man, but nobody made a move to help him capture the bird. A woman with her head uncovered and paint on her face clung to her male companion's arm as if fearing she might fall off the dock.

When a rhythmic beating noise came to his ears, he asked Brother Issachar, "Is that a drum?" While the Shakers often made drumming sounds with their feet to accompany their songs, Ethan had never seen an actual drum.

"Yea, it sounds it. There's always revelry going on in New Orleans. Pay it no mind." Brother Issachar looked over at him and laughed out loud. "Brother Ethan, I fear your eyes may pop clear out of your head."

"Yea." Ethan didn't try to deny his wonder. "I have never seen such."

"It is strange," Brother Issachar said. "And worldly. It has nothing to do with us. We are simply passing through it." He led the way out onto the dock.

Men and women pushed past them to get somewhere urgent or so it seemed by their hurry. They wore every manner of dress, and some looked as strangely out of place as surely he and Brother Issachar did. Ethan peeked over at Brother Issachar, who paid no notice to the crowd teeming around them like ants spilling out of a disturbed anthill as he calmly counted the crates of their products to be sure they had it all.

"Is it always like this?" Ethan asked when Brother Issachar paused in his counting to pull out his recording book to write down the numbers. Even the weather seemed totally wrong for December. It was warm, not at all like it would be back at Harmony Hill where snow would likely be on the ground.

"What?" Brother Issachar looked up from the book. "Oh, you mean the crowd. No, sometimes it's worse." He smiled and looked back at the figures he was writing down. Without looking up again he added, "Have you been listening?"

"Listening?" Ethan was confused by the question.

"Yea, you can't deny there is much to hear." Brother Issachar glanced up at Ethan with raised eyebrows. "Remember how you learned to listen so that you would know the sounds of the woods? You can do the same here, although the songs of man might not put the same peace in your heart as a birdsong can." He laughed as he turned back to his figures. "Now leave me be so I won't lose count again. If I have to keep starting over, we'll be here on the dock all night."

"Sorry," Ethan mumbled as he stepped away to listen as Brother Issachar had taught him to do long ago when each new noise in the woods had made him jump for fear of meeting up with a bear or perhaps his father of the world coming back for him. To hear it all and then slowly pick out the individual sounds.

Among the trees, Ethan could identify most everything he heard. Here the cacophony made him wonder if he should clap his hands over his ears to keep out the noises of the world. He could imagine Brother Martin doing so, but Ethan did not turn from the sounds. He was too amazed by them all, from the blasting of the steamboats' horns to a young boy's shouts as he tried to hawk newspapers. Horses whinnied as they clomped past, pulling wagons with wheels that needed axle grease. The workers on the dock kept up a steady refrain as they hauled crates off the boats. Two hatless men with dark hair and skin browned almost to leather by the sun passed close in animated conversation, not one word of which Ethan could understand.

Ethan looked at Brother Issachar who had finished his counting and was watching Ethan with his mouth twisted to the side as if to keep from laughing.

"We are no longer in Harmony Hill, my brother," Brother Issachar said.

"Don't they speak English here?" Ethan looked after the men who had just passed him.

"Yea, their peculiar brand of English with a smattering of French and Spanish and who knows what else mixed in. In New Orleans you'll find it all." Brother Issachar looked around. "Be thankful it's winter and not just because of the heat that can melt a man. The mosquitoes are big as birds here in the summertime, but in the winter they shrink to more normal size."

"Big as birds?" Brother Issachar must be exaggerating to see just how much Ethan would believe.

"Perhaps not that big, but no matter their size, they are always hungry for a taste of your blood any time of the year. So be wise and rub on the ointment Sister Lettie fixed up for us to keep them away. Best watch for snakes too."

Ethan looked down as if expecting to see snakes at his feet. When Brother Issachar chuckled, Ethan said, "I'm not afraid of snakes." But then he laughed at himself as he added, "Alligators maybe."

"Let your mind rest easy about them. We won't be going out in the bayous. Our customers come to us. Praises be. I'm way too old for alligator wrestling." He looked past Ethan and out at the people. "We'll have need of a wagon."

"Yea, but how do we find one?" There were other men in wagons loading up crates and barrels, but they all seemed occupied with their own business.

"Have no worry, Brother Ethan. I have been to New Orleans many times since we started trading here. I know my way around now, but you can believe I was just as perplexed as you on my first trip. There were times I thought an alligator and a few snakes might be preferable company over some of the people I met here. So remember to mind your own business and step carefully. The two-legged snakes are the most dangerous kind."

As if to confirm his words, a line of five black men and two women came off the gangplank of one of the boats in the harbor. The chains binding them together at the ankle and wrist clattered and dragged on the wooden platform. The

186

Negroes kept their eyes downcast, but their misery was easy to see in the droop of their shoulders and the shuffle of their bare feet. The woman at the end of the line looked aged, and she stumbled and fell to her knees. The white man behind her lifted the whip he carried, but before he could uncoil it, the man chained in front of the woman gently pulled her to her feet and kept his arm around her as they moved on without making a sound.

"Slave traders." Brother Issachar spat out the words.

Ethan knew of the slavery trade. It was spoken of in meetings, and a few of their brothers and sisters back at Harmony Hill were former slaves. Most had been the property of those seeking to become part of the Believers at Harmony Hill. In order to join with the Shakers, the owners had to free their slaves who could then go and do as they wished. Some decided to join with the Shakers where they were given full fellowship among the Believers. Mother Ann's tenets were clear on that. Man or woman, black or white, all were valued and considered equal.

So although Ethan knew of slavery and had seen men riding through their village searching for runaways, he'd never seen men and women in chains. Ethan's hands clenched into fists and the muscles in his legs tightened.

Brother Issachar put his hand on Ethan's shoulder. "Easy, brother. There are many things in the world that we cannot change."

"But it's wrong."

"Yea, that it is, but we are peaceable men. And even if we were not, there'd be little we could do to help those unfortunate souls." Brother Issachar looked sorrowful as he stared straight into Ethan's face. "We're only two. We must leave the righting of many such wrongs to our Eternal Father."

Ethan looked back toward where the crowd had closed in behind the black men and women, blocking them from his sight. "It's different seeing such things with my own eyes than hearing it spoken of."

"Yea, that is so."

"The others, all these of the world, don't seem bothered by it."

"They're more used to the sight. They think it natural."

"Surely they do not." Ethan couldn't believe that seeing men and women in chains could ever be a natural sight. When Brother Issachar only looked at him without answering, he went on. "I don't think I like these people of the world."

"The world's people aren't all slave traders or immune to the cruelty. Many here are much the same as our brethren and sisters back at Harmony Hill. Their outer garments will look different and they'll be of the world, but their hearts will be kind."

The boardinghouse room was small, with dust in the corners and a garish purple and red cover on the bed. The curtains on the small window might have once been white, but it was hard to tell now. Ethan rubbed clean a small circle on one of the windowpanes to look out at the wall of another building so close he could have opened the window and reached out to touch it.

"Mother Ann would tell us no good spirits could live here with all this dirt," he said as he turned back to help Brother Issachar stack their boxes inside the door. There was barely room left to inch between the boxes and the bed.

"Yea, that she would." Brother Issachar pulled one of their

188

brooms out of a bundle and handed it to Ethan. "We can get rid of some of the dirt. And as soon as we sell our goods, we can head home."

"Will it take long?" Ethan looked at the stack of boxes.

"Not so long. Are you homesick already?" Brother Issachar took off his hat and laid it on the boxes.

"Nay, not homesick exactly." It was hard for Ethan to explain as he began sweeping the dust out of the corners. He felt excited and scared and curious all at the same time, and he kept seeing Brother Martin frowning and shaking his head as if Ethan was falling into a pit of sin. "Just sort of out of my skin. I remember little of the world before I came to the Shakers."

"You would have known nothing of this world at any rate." Brother Issachar sat down on the bed. Something neither of them would have ever done at Harmony Hill, but here there were no chairs on the floor or hanging on pegs along the wall waiting to be used as there would have been at the family houses.

"Except the man who claimed to be my father," Ethan said as he bent down to sweep under the bed. The thought that he might run across the man the others at the river had called Hawk was like a splinter of worry embedded deep in his mind that he couldn't seem to pluck out. Worry that was again mixed with something else. Curiosity. The kind of curiosity that could do naught but lead a man astray and bring him trouble.

"Worry not of him," Brother Issachar said. "Even if he still lives, he's not likely to be in the market for a broom or a bottle of our tonics."

The days passed. They kept the dirt swept from their room and folded the garish bed covering and put it out of sight under the bed. Ethan managed to Shaker his plate and eat all he was given at the boardinghouse meals even though the spices in the food sometimes burned his tongue, for he'd been taught not to waste food. He and Brother Issachar were islands of quietude at the table, as the others there hardly stopped their talking long enough to chew.

There was a schoolteacher and a ship's captain—not a steamboat captain, but the captain of a ship that sailed on the seas. A newlywed couple was the object of much bawdy talk until the boardinghouse owner, a large woman with arms as big as the Shaker double rolling pins, put a stop to it by threatening to take away the plates of any who didn't abide by her stated rules of behavior. No guns or hunting knives at the dining table. Eat what she sat on the table without complaint and refrain from saying aught to spoil another boarder's appetite.

Mrs. Davey took a shine to Ethan. Any time he got close to her, she was wont to grab him and enfold him in her beefy arms even after Brother Issachar asked her to refrain from doing so.

"Now, Issachar," she said while Ethan took small breaths to keep from being overpowered by the woman's earthy smell. "The boy needs a hug or two. A body can see that plain as day in his eyes. You shaking Quakers missed the boat on that one. A growing boy needs a daily dose of loving same as food to make him into a real man." She raised her eyebrows and gave Issachar a critical once-over. "You wouldn't want him to turn into a dried-up stick of a man like you, now would you?"

Not a bit bothered by her words, Brother Issachar laughed

as he took hold of Ethan's arm to tug him free. Mrs. Davey patted Ethan's cheek before she let him go and said, "You want a little extra loving, my boy, I can hook you up with some pretty young thing. You're plenty old enough not to need your old Uncle Issachar's permission."

Ethan's face turned red as a tomato ripe for picking. "Nay, I have no such wants."

Mrs. Davey laughed as she pinched his cheek. "So you say, but your eyes say different, dearie. Fact is, those blue eyes of yours put me in mind of a man I once knew. Hawk never got enough of anything." She winked at Ethan. "Leastways nothing wicked."

"Hawk?" The sound of the name sliced through Ethan.

Brother Issachar shook his head the barest bit at Ethan, but it was too late to keep from arousing Mrs. Davey's interest.

She peered at him with narrowed eyes. "So, you know Hawk? Mayhap there's reason for the blue in your eyes?"

"Nay," Ethan said quickly, feeling little guilt at the lie. "Hawk just seems a curious name. I wondered if it was a first or last name."

"Could've been either, I suppose. Back then where we were, a person didn't tell no more than was needed about hisself. Seeing as how we weren't exactly always on the right side of the law." Mrs. Davey seemed suddenly concerned she might have said too much. She smoothed down her apron spotted with grease and sundry other stains. "I've left those days behind, don't you worry. I married Mr. Davey and the two of us lived upright as you shaking Quakers ever thought to."

"And this Hawk? Did he end up paying for his wrongs?" Brother Issachar asked.

"If you mean did the law ever nab him, I'm saying not or

he'd 'ave been swinging from a tree straightaway." Mrs. Davey pulled up her apron tail and fanned her face with it before she spoke again. "I've not seen him these many years, but I hear tell he's still making trouble down on the streets where the likes of you two shouldn't ought to go. They ain't got no use for Shaker brooms down that way, that's for sure."

"Never fear. We'll be sure to keep our feet off those streets," Brother Issachar said. "But perhaps you'd be interested in bartering for some of our room and board. A broom? A jar of tonic? We'll be finishing up our sales and leaving on the morrow. You can plan on letting your room again after that."

Ethan went on out to the front stoop while Brother Issachar and Mrs. Davey made their deal. He stared at the people passing by on the street. Could he be looking straight at his father and not even know him? He didn't want to see him. He feared seeing him, but at the same time his eyes sought out each man who looked to be at least as old as Brother Issachar.

Had he lost all control of his thoughts? First, at Harmony Hill he let his heart chase after the new sister and even desired touching his lips to hers. The very thought of such was sinful. A sin that burned within him yet. And now his mind was entertaining questions about his worldly father. The devil had surely entered into him. Perhaps Brother Martin was right to have never approved him leaving the village. Perhaps he sensed some weakness in Ethan that made him know Ethan wouldn't be strong enough to stand against temptations of the flesh.

Ethan fell in beside Brother Issachar when he came out of the house. They gathered up their goods and headed toward the street without a word. Silence between them was not unusual as they had no need to fill the air between them with senseless chatter, but this silence was not easy and companionable. This silence bore down on Ethan until the weight of it made each breath an effort, as though the pack of herbs and seed envelopes he carried was ten times heavier than it was. Even so, he didn't speak. He had already spoken too readily to Mrs. Davey. He wouldn't compound his sin.

Brother Issachar didn't look to be bothered. He was the same as on any of the other days they'd gone out trading. He spoke kindly to those who stopped them, even the ones who laughed at their clothes, and most carried away some Shaker seeds or herbs. It wasn't much past mid-afternoon when a storekeeper took all their remaining stock.

Back out on the street, Brother Issachar didn't turn toward the boardinghouse. "We can take some time for the sights now that we've done our duty. It's been a good trip. The Ministry will be pleased with the profit."

As they walked, Brother Issachar talked of how fire had burned through the town several times before the turn of the century. "Some claimed it was the Lord's punishment on the city for its wicked ways. They said the same last year when the yellow fever carried off over seven thousand of the citizens here."

"But in that number there had to be good and bad alike, even if they were of the world." Ethan looked over at Brother Issachar. They had stopped at a channel of water, and Brother Issachar was looking out over the water as if he wished there was a boat to take him farther to see more.

"Yea. Fevers take sweet innocent babes as well as their more sinful parents."

"So do you think that was the Eternal Father's punishment

on the parents' wrong living?" He thought Brother Martin would say so, but there were some things Ethan struggled to understand.

Brother Issachar shook his head slowly. "I cannot answer for God. You'd best ask him that question and listen for an answer."

"I can't seem to hear his answers to my questions lately," Ethan said softly as he stared out over the water as well.

"I have sensed your troubled spirit." Brother Issachar put his hand on Ethan's shoulder. "Did hearing the name of your father of the world bring you worry?"

"Nay." Ethan spoke too quickly and then felt shame for his lie. He let out his breath and admitted, "That's not true. I don't know why I'm letting thoughts of him bother me, but I am."

"Sometimes we must find answers before we can find peace. Do you want to go seek your worldly father? I know the streets Mrs. Davey spoke of."

"But it would be dangerous." Ethan met Brother Issachar's eyes directly.

"There are many dangers in the world. All of them can't be avoided." Brother Issachar's hand tightened on Ethan's shoulder. "Remember, engaged in our duty, we need fear no danger."

"Yea, Brother Martin has told me that often enough, but he also always told me to be sure I was engaged in the proper duty. Something I have not been as sure of in the past few months."

"We're all tested at times. Your questions will be answered."

"How will I know I am hearing the right answers?"

Brother Issachar smiled. "You'll know because the answers will feel right in your heart." When Ethan didn't say anything, Brother Issachar went on. "Search your heart now and we will do whatever it says."

Ethan shut his eyes. He didn't pray in words, only in spirit. And then when he opened his eyes and saw Brother Issachar's concerned look as he waited patiently for whatever decision Ethan was going to make, he knew. He didn't need to know anything more about the man whose seed had begun Ethan's life.

"Do we go to seek your father of the world?" Brother Issachar asked.

"Nay, I have no father of the world. I'm looking at my father."

For a moment, Brother Issachar seemed to be at a loss for words as he blinked back tears. At last he said, "It's not the Shaker way to speak of such family relationships, but you've always been a special gift to me." They didn't embrace. It wasn't necessary.

As they turned to go back to their room to pack for their journey home, Ethan felt as if a heavy burden had been lifted from his shoulders. He no longer looked at those they were passing to see if he might recognize a face. That question in his heart had been answered. He would start back to Harmony Hill tomorrow and leave thought of his father behind forever.

Or so he thought until they got back to the boardinghouse and an old man stood up from his perch on the stoop's steps and came to meet them. Even before he spoke his name, Ethan knew him.

18

The man stopped directly in front of them and stared at Ethan with his right eye. The left eye focused on nothing, but wandered where it willed. His eyes were no longer the deep blue of Ethan's, but rather a watered-down blue. The years had not treated him kindly. He was bent in the shoulders and lacking most of his teeth. Matted strands of gray hair hung down below his floppy felt hat. The scar Ethan remembered from years before made a jagged white path through the deep wrinkles on the man's face. When he spoke, his voice was little more than a growl. "I hear you're hunting Hawk Boyd."

"Nay," Ethan answered. "We hunt no one."

"None except those who might want to buy our goods," Brother Issachar added mildly. "Are you in search of some Shaker potions or seeds?"

"Shakers." Hawk Boyd spit out the word. "I've heard of the likes of you back in Kentucky. Never laid eyes on one though till now." He looked Brother Issachar up and down. The two men were probably of about the same age, but Hawk looked to be twenty years older. "I hear you dance in your churches."

"We worship through dance," Brother Issachar said.

Hawk turned his head back toward Ethan. "And the boy here? Does he dance to the gods too like some kind of wild savage?"

"He is a Shaker."

"Does that mean he can't talk for hisself?" The man eyed Ethan before he went on. "Or has the cat got his tongue?"

"A Shaker has no need to talk simply to hear the sound of his voice," Brother Issachar said.

Hawk let out a sound that might have been a laugh. "I think your friend might have just insulted me, boy. And don't many insult old Hawk Boyd and live to tell the tale."

"He meant you no insult," Ethan said quickly. "Brother Issachar is kind to all he meets."

"Even a scoundrel like me?" The man raised his eyebrows and seemed to stare with one eye toward Ethan and one eye toward Brother Issachar.

"We would not know the sort of man you are."

Again the man made a sound that might pass for a laugh. "Oh, wouldn't you? Guess my reputation hasn't carried all the way to your Shaker town up in Kentucky. But take my word for it. Scoundrel is better than most call me."

When Ethan made no answer, Hawk went on. "I was in Kentucky a few times. Went there once to get my boy. He drowned in the river."

"That must have been a sorrow for you," Ethan said. He did not want to think about this man's seed being the reason for his life.

"That it was. I aimed to make something of the boy. Turn him into a man I could be proud to call 'son.' But then the river claimed him, or so I always thought." He slowly licked his lips as he considered Ethan. "But now ol' Velda in there tells me your name is Boyd just like mine. Ethan Boyd. Weird thing is that's the name my crazy wife gave my boy. Ethan. Now that seems to be more than a coincidence to me. How about you, boy?"

"I don't have a father," Ethan said.

"You might wish that was true, but everybody has a father. Everybody. Even Jesus Christ. And I'm thinking you're looking at yours whether you want to be or not." Again the choking cough sound that was Hawk's laugh. He looked to be enjoying Ethan's discomfort at the thought of having him as a father. "That old preacher man you was living with when I came back and stole you away wasn't your papa, and this sorry excuse for a man beside you ain't your papa. That's me and you should be proud of it. Proud that my blood is running through you, giving you some life."

"I have no father," Ethan repeated coldly.

Hawk punched Ethan hard in the chest. "Don't you go being disrespectful of your old pa."

Ethan stumbled backward, but stayed on his feet. Brother Issachar stepped between him and the man. "What do you want from us?"

"My son."

"Even if he is your son as you say, he's a man now. He owes you nothing." Brother Issachar spoke firmly.

"Maybe he doesn't, but maybe you Shakers do. For stealing my son." A crafty look slipped across Hawk's face. "You owe me plenty for the work he did for you all these years when he shoulda been working for me."

"I can check with our elders when we get back to Kentucky to see if some settlement might be made with you for the loss of your son," Brother Issachar said.

"I don't reckon I'm that patient. I think as how you can just pay me now."

"What payment would you deem fair?"

Hawk twisted his mouth to the side as he stared at Ethan, sizing him up the way a man might look at a mule he wanted to buy. "He's grown into a fine, strapping boy from the scrawny pup I thought drowned all them years ago. I doubt you have half enough money on you to make a fair payment to me, but you hand over what you got and we'll consider the debt paid."

Brother Issachar reached into his pocket and pulled out a few loose bills and coins and held them out to Hawk.

Hawk laughed shortly and knocked Brother Issachar's hand aside. "You ain't fooling me, preacher. Velda's done told me you been out trading. You got more money than that or my name's not Hawk Boyd."

"That money is not ours to give," Brother Issachar said. "It belongs to our family of Believers at Harmony Hill."

"I ain't caring who it used to belong to." Hawk fingered the knife hilt sticking up out of his belt. "It's mine now. So hand it over unless you want to fight me for it."

"We are peaceable men. It is not our way to fight." Brother Issachar kept his eyes on Hawk's face.

"No fighting. And no women neither, I've heard." Hawk glanced back over at Ethan. "I must be wrong about you being my son. No Boyd I ever knew could live like that. A man might as well be dead."

"We are dead. Dead to the world," Ethan said.

"Dead to the world, but still walking and breathing, huh? Well, I guess I kin fix that part of it if you don't hand over the money." He pulled his knife out in one swift move and stuck the point of it up under Ethan's chin. "Now, what do you say, preacher man? You either pay for him or he stays here with me. Leastways his body."

Ethan's breath caught and froze in his chest as he stared into Hawk's face. He tried to take a step back, but the tip of the knife pricked his skin.

"Best stand still, son, unless'n you're tired of living," Hawk said.

"You surely wouldn't kill a man you think might be your own son."

Ethan had never heard Brother Issachar sound so frightened. Not the day the tree fell the wrong way in the woods and mashed their water jars. Not the day the rabid skunk charged at them from the bushes. Not the day he found Ethan on the riverbank. He was always in control of whatever befell them, but Hawk Boyd with his knife against Ethan's chin had control now.

"A Shaker son's no good to me. Might mess with my reputation if folks knew my son was the next thing to a preacher. But you give over the money and we'll go back to being family."

Brother Issachar reached into his other pocket and pulled out a pouch of money. He thrust it at Hawk. "Here, man. Take it, but leave the boy be."

"A little zigzag down the boy's face might give him a little character." Hawk moved the knife up to lightly trace a line down Ethan's cheek.

"Take your money and go," Brother Issachar almost shouted as he pushed the money toward Hawk. "The boy has done you no harm."

"He carries my seed."

Ethan stared into the man's face. Anger flashed through

him, burning away the fear, and it kept burning. He had never felt such rage. This man, his father, despising them and playing with him the way a cat might torment a mouse. Ethan threw up his arms and shoved the man back as easily as brushing off an annoying fly. The point of the knife cut into his cheek, but he hardly felt it. "I carry nothing of yours." The words exploded out of him.

Ethan kicked the man in the shin as he fell backward and would have kicked him right in the face if Brother Issachar hadn't grabbed him and jerked him back.

"Brother Ethan!" he said. "Take control of yourself."

Brother Issachar's words came to him as if from far away, but they did penetrate his rage. He pulled in a ragged breath and fought to keep his feet clamped to the ground when all he wanted to do was stomp the old man in front of him into the dirt. And then the man looked up at him and laughed.

"That's more like it, son. I knew there was Boyd blood in there somewhere." He pushed himself slowly up off the ground. "I'm betting you like the ladies too. In spite of what they tell me about them Shaker men."

Ethan just stared at him without saying anything. He wasn't worth words.

Brother Issachar spoke instead. "Take the money and go."

"Don't let him have the money," Ethan said, but it was too late.

Brother Issachar had already pitched the pouch toward Hawk. The man caught it in midair and stuffed it in his pocket in one motion. He still grasped the knife in his other hand.

"Man is more precious than any amount of money," Brother Issachar said. "He can have it. We can make our way home without it. The good Lord will watch over us."

201

"You listen to him, boy. You'll learn a lot today both from your peaceable preacher friend and from me." Hawk slid his knife back in his belt. "You done learned that if you get mad enough, you ain't afraid of dying no more. That's not a bad lesson to know. Can actually stand you in good stead at times, but you've got a lot more to learn."

"I don't want to learn anything from you."

"So you think, but I got three more things you might find useful in the days ahead." Hawk started to move past them out toward the street. Then in one motion he jerked out his knife again and put it against Ethan's ribs. "First, never trust a man with a knife, 'specially an old scalawag like me. And second, always expect the unexpected."

Ethan didn't have time to react before Hawk flashed the knife away from Ethan and stabbed Brother Issachar in the stomach. Hawk yanked the knife out and stepped back from Ethan, who stared at the blood dripping off the knife blade. Even with that proof in front of his eyes, Ethan couldn't believe what the man had done. Color drained from Brother Issachar's face as he staggered to the side. Ethan grabbed him to hold him up as he glared with hatred at the man with the knife. He should have stomped him into the ground when he had the chance.

One corner of Hawk's mouth curled up in something that resembled a smile as he wiped Brother Issachar's blood from the blade onto his pants before shoving it back in his belt. "Last of all," he said. "Never love nobody too much. You can believe your old pa on this one. Won't bring you nothing but grief."

Ethan turned his eyes away from him out to the street as Brother Issachar leaned more heavily against him. "Help. Somebody help us!"

One man turned and looked toward them before ducking his head and hurrying on. Nobody else seemed to even hear him.

Hawk laughed. "Ain't nobody gonna be rushing over here to mess with the likes of me. You'd best quit squawking for help and see to your preacher friend there." Hawk inclined his head a bit toward Brother Issachar. "He looks to be bleeding a mite. Could be he might need a doctor."

Ethan wanted to lunge at him and choke him with his bare hands. But he couldn't turn loose of Brother Issachar.

"Let him go," Brother Issachar whispered.

"He doesn't deserve to live." Ethan spoke the words with force.

"That's not our decision to make." Brother Issachar pulled himself up to stare straight into Ethan's face. "We're men of peace. We must leave matters of revenge in God's hands." In spite of how he had to struggle for breath, his words were strong and sure. "Let him go."

"Best listen to him, son, unless'n you want your blood mixed with his." Hawk's good eye bored into Ethan. "I ain't never been overly sentimental. But it ain't been all bad meetin' up with you." He grinned and patted his pocket where he'd stuffed the money. Then he looked almost sad as he went on. "It's kinda a shame you fell off that raft all them years ago. The two of us coulda made a good team."

"I didn't fall off. I jumped." Ethan stared at him coldly.

"Ungrateful sons. The bane of fathers everywhere." Hawk laughed and ambled away without looking back once. A little way down the street, he tipped his hat at two women who jerked their skirts to the side away from him.

"It will do no good to chase after him with hate. Help me

inside where we can examine the wound and see how bad it is." Brother Issachar took a step toward the boardinghouse door and almost fell. Ethan practically had to carry him inside.

It was bad. Mrs. Davey brought pans of hot water and, amid a flood of tears, professed her sorrow for sending word to Hawk Boyd that his son was at her boardinghouse. "I didn't have no idea he'd do nothing like this. I mean, me and Hawk, we go way back, and I just thought I owed it to him to let him know about a son like the boy here. But I didn't think he'd show up so fast. Maybe not till you were gone. I must have lost my senses."

Brother Issachar forgave her before he sent her to fetch a doctor. Ethan cleaned the wound as best he could, but the knife had gone deep. When the doctor came, he shook his head and spoke of the danger of infection, even gangrene with such a deep knife wound, before he put in stitches. "A bullet wound is oftentimes easier to treat," he said as he closed his bag. "If he gets feverish, send someone for me."

Ethan mixed the powders the doctor left, but Brother Issachar refused them. "The pain is not so bad as long as I'm still," he said. "I'll wait for Sister Lettie's medicine."

"But how are we to get home?" Ethan asked. "We have no money."

"Worry not. He only got today's money. The rest is safe." He groaned as he rose up off the bed far enough to pull up his pants leg. Another pouch was tied to his calf. "We'll start home tomorrow as planned, my brother." He lay back and shut his eyes. He held his side and took shallow breaths.

Ethan wanted to lay his head over on the bed and weep. He had caused this. "I am sorry, Brother Issachar. I am so sorry."

Brother Issachar slowly opened his eyes and settled them on Ethan's face. "You did not put the knife in my side. You have no reason to be so contrite."

"It's my fault. My curiosity about my father led him to us. My anger made him hurt you."

"Yea, there is truth in some of what you say, but there is no profit in dividing out blame once a thing is done. We can only pray some good may come of it."

"How could good come from this?"

Brother Issachar seemed to be searching for an answer. Finally he said, "I know not, but the good Lord knows. Our lives are always in his hands." He reached over to grasp Ethan's hand and shake it a bit. "And I am not dead yet. Don't put me in the grave before it is time to do so."

"But you are hurt."

"Yea, that I am, and I may die from it. But I don't want to die in New Orleans. I want to see Harmony Hill again." He turned loose of Ethan's hand and let his eyes fall shut again. "Now go post a letter to our brethren and sisters so that they can pray and exercise a dance for me."

When Ethan returned from posting the letter, Brother Issachar was asleep. His breath in and out was steady and he only groaned when he moved. Perhaps there was yet hope that he would live. Ethan knelt by the bed and prayed to the Eternal Father, to Mother Ann, to the Christ, and any other spirit that might be listening. Then he took off his shoes and got to his feet. Quietly he marched back and forth as he would have if he'd been in the meetinghouse at Harmony Hill. As he moved his feet in the familiar steps and turns, he closed his mind to the truth that surely he was Hawk Boyd's son.

19

January 1834

The corncrib burned in the wee hours of the morning just after the start of the new year. The crib was out past the West Family's barn on the outskirts of the village, and by the time one of the brethren got up to relieve himself and noticed the flames, the fire had already engulfed the building. Brethren from the West Family went out to make sure the fire stayed contained to the corncrib, but there was no reason to arouse the entire village from their beds to attempt to save what could not be saved. Especially since a light snow was falling that virtually eliminated the chance of sparks igniting any nearby structures.

Elder Joseph reported the loss of the corncrib and its contents at meeting that night. His narrow face was grim as he stood in the middle of the meetinghouse and spoke. "Those of the world continue to persecute us. They don't understand our ways nor do they want to learn the true way to salvation.

They simply seek to cause us harm as they continue blindly on their way to their final destruction. Perhaps they think they are testing our faith and our resolve to stay true to our beliefs, but if so, they are sorrowfully mistaken. We are well familiar with how Mother Ann was persecuted by those of the world, thrown into jail, mocked, and mistreated, but she did not allow it to turn her feet from the true way. Nor will we. With the help of the Lord and Mother Ann, we will overcome each adversity."

When Elder Joseph stomped his foot to emphasize his words, many of the Believers followed his lead as a murmur of agreement rippled through the room. The bench where Elizabeth sat vibrated with the sound, and she couldn't keep from jumping a little, even though it was not unusual for a stomping spirit to take over the Shakers during meeting. They considered it a gift of the spirit to whirl in dance or stomp their feet and shake all over until sometimes they fell prostrate on the floor as if smitten by the Lord. The first time she witnessed a sister shaking violently before she fell to the floor as if dead, Elizabeth was alarmed. With a glowing smile, Sister Melva assured her that Sister Darcie was shaking free from all that was carnal and would rise from the floor a transformed person better equipped to embrace the simple life.

Elizabeth had yet to feel the first tremble of such spirit, which Sister Ruth said showed her lack of belief. At first Elizabeth had argued against that, for she knew the faith in her heart, but she could win no argument with Sister Ruth. She had learned that Sister Ruth's sermon would be shorter if Elizabeth simply nodded and said, "Yea, it must be so. I will seek to open myself more fully to the spirit."

Now she smoothed down the folds in the skirt of her dress

to cover her unease and looked across the room at Payton, who sat beside Brother Micah on one of the benches on the men's side.

His eyes were on Elder Joseph, listening raptly, wanting to believe. He looked like one of them with his hair grown out into the Shaker style, long in the back and in the front cut straight across his forehead. The men on the bench with him were different sizes, different ages, yet they looked as alike as peas in a pod with their identical clothes and hair and attentiveness to the elder's words. Elizabeth wondered if in another month she would even be able to pick Payton out from among the men at meeting. He would be that much like all the others.

She studied his face for even the slightest sign of guilt about the fire and then upbraided herself for her suspicions. Just because the corncrib was close to where Payton was sleeping meant nothing. Her brother had done wrong and set fire to their cabin. She knew that for a truth, but surely he had not done so for the pleasure of seeing the flames. It was his grief for their father and his anger at Colton Linley that had kept him from thinking clearly. He wouldn't set fire to anything else. It was as Elder Joseph said. Someone from outside the village. Someone from the world.

She turned back to Elder Joseph. She hoped no one had noticed her inattention or how her eyes had gone to the brethren's side of the meetinghouse. If so, she would have to confess such a lapse in proper behavior to Sister Ruth. A Shaker believer was expected to confess every sin, from speaking a lie to not hanging up one's apron properly. Novitiates were encouraged to do the same to better prepare their spirits for acceptance of the Shaker way. At times Elizabeth made up this or that minor infraction just to satisfy Sister Ruth's need to hear confession of wrongs she had done.

Elizabeth dared not reveal her actual wayward thinking or resistance to the many Shaker rules that covered even how one climbed the stairs. Often as not, Elizabeth intentionally stepped upon the first tread with her left foot instead of the proper Shaker way of right foot first. Sister Melva had caught her at that more than once, but thus far had believed it was simple forgetfulness rather than willfulness. Sister Ruth was not as forgiving, so Elizabeth was relieved to see out of the corner of her eye that Ruth's attention seemed to be focused completely on Elder Joseph.

The elder was still talking of the Believers' resolve in the face of hardship. "That crib was almost empty and we have others with plenty of corn for our fowl and milk cows. We will have ample time to rebuild the crib before next fall when we have need of it again. With Mother Ann's blessings, we'll continue to give our hearts to God and work with our hands in this place. Now let us go forth in an exercise of peace. Let us labor a dance in hope that those who persecute us will turn from their wicked ways and become repentant."

Elizabeth lined up with the women to dance. The steps had not proved hard to learn, but the first few times Sister Melva had encouraged her to participate in the dancing exercises, she had worried she'd make a wrong step and spoil the unity of the dance by bumping into someone. Perhaps even one of the brethren, for the men and women often marched in parallel lines or adjoining but non-touching circles. But once Sister Melva showed her the pegs and markers in the floor, she had no problem remembering when to turn and change directions in the marches and didn't mind laboring the songs.

She enjoyed the singing. The voices of the chosen singers were clear and lilting. The songs were simple and easy to sing so whenever it was allowed, she readily joined her voice in with the others. But neither the singing nor the dancing made her feel spiritual. Yet she wondered if, like Payton among the brethren, she too looked like any other Shaker sister in her blue dress and white scarf and cap. She was being drawn into the fold, assimilated into the whole. It was not a comfortable thought.

Her eyes caught on dear Hannah on a corner bench, not dancing, not singing, just staring out at the air as if seeing something there no one else could see. A few curls had sprung out from under her cap, and in spite of the child's solemn expression, Elizabeth's spirits lifted. Hannah would never be absorbed into the whole to be just another set of hands and feet on the body of the Shakers. She would always be Hannah.

Elizabeth tried to catch her eye as she marched past her, but Hannah refused to look at her. She knew she was there. Elizabeth could tell by the way Hannah lifted her chin and shifted her eyes purposely the other way. She was angry with Elizabeth. She didn't want to be the good little Shaker sister Elizabeth had made her promise to be. Nor did Elizabeth, who wished she could step out of turn and go pull Hannah up into a whirling exercise that had nothing at all to do with the Shakers or their way of worship. But Sister Ruth was watching, and a bitter wind was whistling outside against the meetinghouse walls. What choice did she have but to continue the dance?

Two weeks later Elizabeth was summoned from her work duty to Sister Rosellen's room at the Gathering Family house. Clouds the night before had dropped several inches of powdery snow on the village, but the morning had brought a brilliant blue sky and crisp, yet bracing air. The brethren had already shoveled clear paths between the buildings, but the fields and garden plots looked pristine as they sparkled in the sunlight, untouched by the feet of man or animal.

Elizabeth wanted to grab up a handful of the snow to feel its coldness in her mouth, but she restrained herself for fear Sister Ruth and Sister Melva who walked on either side of her would think it frolicsome. While they hadn't revealed the reason Elizabeth was being summoned, she doubted it could be good. Even Sister Melva had a deep-seated frown between her eyes. Elizabeth had the unsettling feeling she was being escorted to a prison cell.

Actually, the last two weeks had been the best Elizabeth had spent at the village. She had been assigned to work with Sister Lettie in preparing and labeling the dried roots, barks, and herbs for the sister's medical potions. Sister Melva had been released to other duties since she had no interest in the healing sciences, and even though Melva was kind spirited, it had been a relief to be free of her company and the constant drone of Shaker teachings for a few hours each day. Instead Elizabeth eagerly listened to Sister Lettie explain the curative properties of the different roots and herbs.

Sister Lettie had joined with the Shakers in the state of New York before the turn of the century. Except for the gray hair that peeked out from under her cap and the brown age spots on her hands, Elizabeth might have guessed her much younger than the sixty-five years she proudly claimed. She was small of stature, barely reaching the top of Elizabeth's shoulder, but she seemed to radiate energy and her step was quick. She had little patience with those who came to her with superficial wounds or complaints, but unending patience for those she deemed in real need of her treatment.

The first day they worked together she talked of her path to the Shakers. "My situation was much as yours, Sister Elizabeth. I had no husband nor did I desire one when I sought shelter at Watervliet. My father was a yarb doctor, and after he died, I had no prospects. The Shakers welcomed me and my knowledge of roots and allowed me to continue to learn. That in itself was a gift and one not many young women are given even in this day and age. The Ministry inquired into sending me out to a medical school, but none would allow a woman."

Sister Lettie made a face and threw out her hands as she continued. "Backward. Very backward of those of the world. I offered to masquerade as a man." Sister Lettie laughed a little. "That idea shocked the Ministry a tad, I must say. I had to make confession of my rashness in Meeting the next Sunday. But I could have pulled it off. I've never been very fair of face, and I could have cut my hair in the Shaker style for men and put on Shaker pants. It would have worked."

"But aren't you a little small for anyone to believe you a man?" Elizabeth asked.

"Yea, you have a point." Sister Lettie tilted her head and gave Elizabeth the eye. "You on the other hand are tall as many men, but your face." She clicked her tongue and shook her head with a sigh. "Way too pretty even with your hair all stuffed away under your cap. It appears we'll have to continue on as we've been doing. Never fear. An attentive person can learn much by watching others. My father shared his knowledge freely with me before he died, and there was a sister in Watervliet who knew much about the healing powers of roots and barks."

"But how do you come to be here at Harmony Hill?" Elizabeth asked. Sister Lettie didn't mind questions. Questions were the avenue to learning, she said.

"Some years ago the sister here who had a gift for mixing medicines crossed over the great divide somewhat unexpectedly and without training a new sister to carry on her work, and so they had need of someone. Since I had trained several sisters in the art of physic medicines at Watervliet, I was able to leave them without worry. I had always had a desire to see the west."

"Have you shared your healing gift with sisters here?" Elizabeth looked up from pounding the ginseng root. It was much valued, so she was careful not to let even a speck of the powder escape the bowl.

"I don't think it a healing gift. More a gift of learning. Perhaps a gift of observing to see what works best. Several of our sisters have learned from me, but none have shown the hunger to learn more that I always felt. I have suggested training one of the brethren, but the Ministry say that wouldn't be seemly. Perhaps a doctor will join our Society here and add his knowledge to ours. That would be a true blessing from Mother Ann." Sister Lettie looked heavenward as if entreating Mother Ann to hurry the blessing. She looked back at Elizabeth. "Or perhaps you are the one who has been sent to us with the hunger to learn. I hear it in your questions."

"I doubt that could be," Elizabeth said before she thought. She felt so comfortable with Sister Lettie that she often forgot to speak the proper answers.

"Why is that, Sister?"

Elizabeth hesitated and Sister Lettie went on. "Don't fret. What you say to me stays with me. It is my way. And there are no hidden eyes peering down on us here. I insist it be so in order for those in need of my treatment to feel free to speak of their health complaints."

Elizabeth let out her breath. "I cannot feel the peace here that I see in your face. I don't think I am meant to be a Shaker."

Sister Lettie touched Elizabeth's arm. "Give yourself time, Sister Elizabeth. The Spirit takes longer to grow in some than in others. And while it's growing, we'll keep learning." She turned to look at her jars on the shelf. "Now what root did you say your mother had you dig to treat her lung ailment?"

Elizabeth had almost believed it could be true when Sister Lettie said it. She had almost believed that she could learn to be a Shaker, that she could forget the ties to Hannah and Payton and become a sister to them in the Shaker way. That she could mash down her need to be her own person and conform to the Believer's way. That she might no longer feel the deep regret at facing the prospect of never having a baby grow within her own womb. Instead she would learn to listen to the Shaker teachings without questioning their truth. She would no longer think about how the young brother had looked at her and how the touch of his hand had awakened feelings inside her that went against all the Shaker tenets.

But then she would see Payton or Hannah on the walkways and want to run after them to put her arms around them. Or she would hear Elder Joseph mention Ethan's name at meeting and hardly dare breathe for fear she might miss one word the elder spoke of him.

He and Brother Issachar had been gone for weeks, and instead of forgetting him as she should, she found herself thinking of him more and more. Her spirit was still far from the Shaker way.

So far away that now Elizabeth feared Sister Ruth had called the meeting with the eldress to accuse Elizabeth of having a wrong spirit within her. Sister Melva's worried peeks over at Elizabeth as she did her best to stretch her shorter stride to match Ruth's and Elizabeth's seemed to promise something unpleasant ahead.

But when Elizabeth saw Sister Nola and Sister Josephine sitting with the eldress, she knew it was not her own contrary spirit in question but that of Hannah's. Sister Nola gave Elizabeth a small, worried smile and then went back to studying her clenched hands in her lap. Beside her, Sister Josephine, who had the duty of teaching the young sisters the basic knowledge of reading and writing and proper Shaker behavior, was red of face and very out of sorts as she glared at Elizabeth as though whatever wrong Hannah had done rested squarely on Elizabeth's shoulders.

20

"The child has a demon in her," Sister Josephine said as soon as Eldress Rosellen asked her to state the problem. Sister Josephine prided herself—as much as was proper for a Shaker sister—in always being in control of the young sisters in her care. Until now. Until Hannah. She crossed her arms in front of her ample bosom and stared at the other women gathered in the small room as if daring them to refute her words.

Elizabeth bit the inside of her lip to keep from speaking out against such a ridiculous assertion. Sister Melva had warned Elizabeth not to speak without permission, else she might be ushered out of the meeting. She didn't want that to happen. Especially now that she knew Hannah was the problem.

Sister Nola peeked over at Elizabeth with an apologetic look before she said, "Nay, Sister Josephine. She is but a child."

"Demons are no respecters of age," Sister Josephine said. "Are there not demonized children in the Scripture? One can look at her and see she's not a normal child. With that hair no cap can contain. And the things she says! No child of her age should know such things." Her eyes widened.

Elizabeth could not stop herself from defending Hannah. "She has a free spirit."

Sister Josephine glared at Elizabeth across the room. "A demon spirit."

Eldress Rosellen held up her hand. "Please, my sisters, we are not here to speak rashly at one another. It would be best if we start at the beginning of our problem and wait to speak when asked to do so."

She turned a stern look on Elizabeth, who lowered her eyes to her hands in a show of obedience. In truth she was as tired as Hannah of bending her spirit to conform to the Shaker way. Still, it must be done. Something she would have to convince Hannah of if she were allowed to do so. With snow covering the ground and the possibility of bitter cold, it would not be a good time to be asked to leave the Shaker village.

She thought the Shakers were too kind to send them out of the village in such weather, but she couldn't be sure. She'd heard of others being asked to leave when their spirits seemed to be a disturbance to the family of Believers. Sister Ruth was always more than ready to tell her of such happenings. Elizabeth was fortunate Sister Ruth would not be the one sitting in final judgment on Hannah and her this day or they would surely be pushed out of the community of Believers before the setting of the sun.

Elizabeth peeked up at Sister Ruth, who was giving Sister Josephine a sympathetic look. She didn't let her eyes stay on Ruth but slid them over to Sister Melva, who looked very concerned, and at last to Sister Nola, who reached up with hands that trembled slightly to pull her cap down tighter over her own gray hair that was every bit as springy and uncontrollable as Hannah's. Elizabeth wanted to tell her that wayward hair had nothing to do with wayward spirits, but she kept quiet.

Dear Hannah. She had kept her promise not to run away again. Sadness had set heavy on her face every time Elizabeth had seen her in meeting, but Elizabeth had hardened her heart to it. Hannah had plentiful food to eat. She was warm. She even had shoes. And she was going to school. So what if Sister Josephine had little patience with Hannah's spirit? It was time Hannah learned to discipline that spirit. Even their father had said as much before he died.

Elizabeth had prayed that Hannah might settle into the Shaker life. Perhaps not so completely as Payton, but enough to keep out of trouble. She'd hoped perhaps her prayers were being answered, but the snow had pulled Hannah from her promise. Hannah loved snow. She cared not if her fingers and toes got so cold they were in danger of frostbite. She liked to lie in the snow and wave her arms and legs to make angels. She liked to run through the white fields to leave a trail of footprints behind her.

But most of all she loved to carefully climb up into a tree with snow-laden branches and, when Elizabeth passed underneath, shake down a shower of snow on her head. That is what she had done to Sister Josephine. Just thinking about how Hannah's laugh had echoed in the woods each time she caught her unaware made Elizabeth want to smile, but she mashed her lips tight together and didn't allow it to show.

Sister Nola seemed to agree that the sin was not so bad. "It was a childish prank, Sister Josephine. She meant you no harm."

"No harm?!" Sister Josephine shot an angry look at Sister

Nola. "Let me put a handful of snow down the back of your dress and see if you think it is of no harm."

"Yea, Sister, forgive my thoughtlessness," Sister Nola said quickly. "I meant no lasting harm."

"It isn't this alone." Sister Josephine sniffed loudly as she struggled to regain her composure. She straightened the folds in her apron before she looked back up at Sister Nola. "It's more than this bit of foolishness. You know yourself the child has a delinquent spirit. How many times has she disappeared from your care without permission?"

Sister Nola hesitated before answering, "Twice, maybe thrice."

"Come, Sister Nola." Sister Josephine fixed her eyes sternly on Sister Nola as if she were one of her recalcitrant students. "You do the child no favor covering up her wrongs. Didn't you tell me that on more than one occasion you have found her bed empty in the night?"

"Yea, I may have said so." Sister Nola shifted uneasily in her chair as color rose in her cheeks. "I've not kept count, but only the one time did she go far."

"In the night?" Eldress Rosellen spoke up with a frown. "Where would the child go in the night?"

"I've heard demons are drawn to the full moon," Sister Josephine muttered.

"Sister Josephine, we know you are distressed, but please do not make this more unpleasant than it already is," the eldress said quietly but firmly. "We must call upon the charity of our hearts to help our young sisters." She turned back to Sister Nola. "Did she confess to you where she'd been when she was gone in the night, Sister Nola?"

"Nay, at least not of a truth," Sister Nola admitted with a

small shake of her head. "She spoke of going to the outhouse, but I checked for her there before she returned and didn't find her."

"And did she admit her untruth?" Eldress Rosellen asked.

"Nay, she merely said she felt led by angels to come back to the children's house in a different way."

"She claims to have seen angels?" Eldress Rosellen's eyebrows shot up.

"That's another thing." Sister Josephine spoke before Sister Nola could answer. "She's always jumping up from her chair while we're having lessons and whirling around, saying the spirit has told her to do such, that she has a gift for whirling, but she never has a visitation of the spirit during meetings, I've noticed."

"There are all sorts of spirits. Both good and evil," Sister Ruth put in. "When you think about it, our village has seen many troubles since these sisters came into our family. Men coming into our house with evil purpose in their hearts. Fires. Fleshly temptations."

Elizabeth looked up at Ruth, who met her eyes boldly as if challenging Elizabeth to deny the truth of what she said.

So Elizabeth did not, even as she did dare to speak. "Yea, you are right. We had much trouble before we came here. The sudden death of our father. The burning of our cabin. Perhaps bad fortune did follow us to your village, but we didn't bring it with intent. We were simply looking for the place of peace our father spoke of after his visit here last year." She shifted her eyes past Sister Melva, who was assiduously studying her hands in her lap to Eldress Rosellen. "What would you have me do, Eldress?"

The eldress was silent for a moment before she said, "I

see the sincerity in your eyes, Sister Elizabeth. And Sister Melva has told me how diligently you have attended to the duties assigned to you. Sister Ruth fears you have an unwilling spirit, but perhaps she needs to have more patience with you as a novitiate. Not all can learn the Shaker way without inner struggle."

"Yea, at times I do struggle with emotions I shouldn't entertain," Elizabeth answered honestly.

Eldress Rosellen smiled kindly at Elizabeth as she reached over to touch her hand. "As do we all, my child. That is why we labor our dances and shake away the carnal feelings of the world. The longer you are here, the easier such feelings are to deny and the more peace you will feel in your soul."

"We aren't here to consider the spiritual state of Sister Elizabeth," Sister Josephine interrupted, "but that of Sister Hannah. It is she who refuses to bend her will for the good of all."

The eldress shut her eyes as weariness showed in the lines of her face. After a moment, she pulled in a deep breath and opened her eyes. "Sister Hannah is very young. From what I have been told, before coming among us she always had much freedom in her actions. Nevertheless, willful disobedience cannot be condoned." The eldress looked at Sister Josephine. "But I do not think the child has a demon, and it is very unlike you to say such a thing, Sister Josephine. So I can see the child has been very trying for you."

"Yea, you are right, Eldress. I should have tempered my words." Sister Josephine bent her head with a look of shame.

"Is the child learning her lessons?"

"She already knows more than most of the other little

sisters," Sister Josephine admitted. "That could perhaps be part of her problem. Her mind is too idle and gives her time to think up troublesome things to do."

"The devil can use an idle mind," Eldress Rosellen said.

"I could teach her for a while," Elizabeth volunteered.

Eldress Rosellen gave Elizabeth's words consideration before she said, "Nay, we are all of a family. The stress of individual family ties is the reason for much loss of peace in our minds. You will both learn our ways better apart. But we cannot allow her to torment Sister Josephine, so we will let her skip the lessons for this winter session and assign her to Sister Nola to help with whatever duties she is engaged in."

"I'm working with the silkworms," Sister Nola said.

"Then you can teach her some small chores with the same, but you cannot allow her to disappear in the night even if you have to tie a string to her arm and attach it to yours. You must be more diligent in your duty."

"Yea, Eldress Rosellen. I will watch her more closely." Sister Nola looked as relieved as Elizabeth felt.

"Where is the child now?" Eldress Rosellen peered over at Sister Josephine.

Sister Josephine sniffed again. "Still out in the snow as far as I know. She refused to come down out of the tree when I told her to, so I left her there. A little chill might do her good."

Eldress Rosellen shut her eyes again for a moment as if working to maintain her patience with all of them. "You must show more kindness, my sister. That is the duty of all of us as sisters." She let her eyes fall on each of them in turn. "It is the only way." She settled her eyes on Elizabeth. "Sister Nola is too old to be traipsing about in the snow hunting the child. You go find Sister Hannah and bring her back to Sister Nola's care. And it would be a boon to us all if you could convince her of the wisdom of listening to her elders."

Hannah was not hard to find. Her footprints in the snow were easy to follow from the tree where the original wrong had been committed outside the children's house. Every few feet there was a new snow angel. The footprints stopped at a small stand of trees back behind the Gathering Family house. Elizabeth kept her eyes on the ground as if she couldn't figure what had happened to the trail of prints and waited.

The minutes passed. No shower of snow came down on her head. She began to wonder if the wind had perhaps whipped away the trace of Hannah's footprints in this spot or perhaps she sat up in the tree, too frozen to move. She waited another minute. Then still without looking up into the branches, she said, "Aren't you going to drop snow on my head?"

"No." Hannah spoke from above Elizabeth. She sounded sad. "The good time for snow dropping has passed. The snow has gone."

Elizabeth looked up. She couldn't see Hannah's face as she huddled next to the tree trunk not far above her. "There is much snow still under my feet. Is there not even a smidgen of snow left on the limbs?"

"No. The fun is done." Hannah's teeth chattered as she spoke and she was trembling. "The wind has blown it all away. It would have blown me away as well, but I have turned into a chunk of ice and the wind said I was too heavy. That I had to stay in this fearsome cold place until I died."

"Come down from your branch, little snow bird," Elizabeth said gently. "Let me warm your frozen wings under my cloak."

Hannah sat a long moment without moving before she finally looked down at Elizabeth. "I think I may be frozen to the branch."

"Shall I climb up to break you free?"

"Oh, how I would fain to be free, but Sister Josephine says that such a desire is surely a sin that cannot be allowed. No freedom in this place. Even one's hair cannot be free to grow as it wills."

"Come down, Hannah. Now."

"You're becoming one of them," Hannah said, but she uncurled her body and climbed down to the lowest branch. "Will you catch me?"

"I will catch you. I will hold you." Elizabeth held up her arms and added softly, "I will love you."

When Hannah swung down from the branch, Elizabeth easily caught her slight body and lowered her to the ground. Then she opened her cloak, wrapped it around the child as she pulled her close against her body. It was like embracing an icicle, but she didn't loosen her hold as the child shook against her with chills.

"Will you always love me, Izzy? Always?" Hannah asked through chattering teeth.

"I will always love you, Hannah. Always." Elizabeth kissed the top of Hannah's head. Her cap was gone and there were ice crystals in her curls. She worried about Hannah's cold toes in the snow. She had on shoes, but they were sure to be soaked through. "We need to get you inside by the fire and into dry clothes. You shouldn't have stayed out so long."

"I never want to go back inside. I want to be a real snow bird or a bear in a thick fur coat asleep in a cave. Anything but a Shaker sister."

"Why is it so hard for you? Can't you bend a bit to their will?"

Hannah didn't answer Elizabeth's question. Instead she peered up at Elizabeth. "Our father told me God would always love me. That he would love me even more than Father could or you could. Father said God's love would be like his love and your love and Mother's love from heaven all wrapped up together and then even more than that."

"Many places in the Bible speak of the Lord's great love."

"I know. You have read them to me." Her bottom lip trembled and not only from the cold as she went on. "But Sister Josephine says God doesn't love me. That God couldn't love me because I have the devil in me. So if God can't love me anymore, are you sure you can?"

Tears popped up into Elizabeth's eyes, and she had to swallow hard before she could speak. "Sister Josephine is wrong. I know because nothing can stop me loving you, and as our father told you, God loves you way more than that. Sister Josephine was only angry with you because you've been giving her trouble."

"Sister Josephine says anger is a weakness that cannot be allowed in the garden we are to grow for the Lord and the other one she calls Mother Ann. We must pluck out our feelings of anger and willfulness and envy and plant good seeds."

"Then today she has some plucking to do in her own garden, because when you dropped snow on her head, she got very angry."

A smile sneaked into Hannah's eyes. "I know. I was glad she couldn't climb trees."

"I'd say that was a very fortunate thing for you. And there are more fortunate things to come. Eldress Rosellen has decided you won't need any more schooling this year from Sister Josephine. You will be allowed to stay with Sister Nola and help her with her duties."

"I like Sister Nola," Hannah said.

"As you should. She's been very kind to you." Elizabeth looked sternly down at Hannah. "But you cannot take advantage of her kindness. You must do as she says without argument."

"I will do my best, Elizabeth." Hannah looked up at her solemnly. "At least until spring. How many weeks away is that now?"

"Not so many," Elizabeth said and tried not to worry about how she would keep her promise to Hannah in the spring.

"Do you think Payton will leave with us in the spring? He sometimes looks at me now as if he doesn't remember who I am."

"I know. He feels at home here."

"Do you think he started the fire in the Carpenters' Shop?"

"I do not," Elizabeth answered quickly. "But I don't think we should talk about it."

"Why?" Hannah looked at her curiously. "Do you think the Shaker ears will hear us even here in the snow and blame him for the fires?"

"The Shaker ears hear much," Elizabeth warned.

Hannah pulled away from Elizabeth to peer around. "And the eyes see much, but if they are seeing today, they must be angels. Invisible angels."

"I hear you have been seeing angels." Elizabeth kept her cloak around Hannah but turned her to start back toward the Gathering Family house.

"Only when I get weary of hearing Sister Josephine tell of

the Shaker rules. Then an angel comes to rescue my itchy feet." Hannah looked a little guilty, but then she giggled and spun away from Elizabeth. "But there are really angels all around us here." She flopped down on the snow and waved her arms and legs. "See."

"Your fingers and toes are going to fall off if you don't stay out of the snow."

"Make an angel with me," Hannah begged. "Please. Just one bigger angel to protect my little angel."

She'd have to confess her folly to Sister Ruth later, but Elizabeth turned and flopped back into the snow beside Hannah. The snow was cold as she waved her arms and legs through it, but at the same time she felt a jolt of childish joy. She laughed as she and Hannah got up carefully to keep from spoiling their angels' wings.

As she brushed the snow off her skirt and cloak and pushed a stray hair back up under her cap, she looked back at the snow angels and whispered, "May angels watch over us."

Hannah came over to slip her hand into Elizabeth's and lean against her. "These will melt with the sunshine, but there are other angels. I haven't seen them. Not really the way I told Sister Josephine, but I know they're there."

"Our guardian angels," Elizabeth said softly as she lightly touched Hannah's head. "Every child has one. Yours will surely watch over you." Silently she added, *And please watch over the Shakers who are being so kind to shelter us. Let no more trouble come to them because of us.*

Two weeks later Elder Joseph read the letter from Ethan telling of the man stabbing Issachar in New Orleans. A pall fell over the meeting, for all there had been touched at one time or another by Issachar's kindness. "He was alive when the letter was posted. Hold that in your minds and remember how strong in the faith our brother is. Let us labor for their safe journey back up the river to us and for our brother's healing," Elder Joseph said.

As they stood to form into lines for the exercise, Sister Ruth stared straight at Elizabeth as if this too could somehow be laid to her blame. Elizabeth wanted to shout at her and all the others that there was no way this could have happened because she had come to their village.

She had brought trouble to the village with Colton Linley chasing after her and threatening the other sisters. She could not deny that. But while Ethan's letter didn't say who had stabbed Issachar, she did know it could not be Colton Linley. She'd spotted him just the week before, riding on the road through the village looking right and left, searching for her. Just in time, she'd stepped off the path and behind a building before he could pick her out among the sisters walking on the pathways. For once Elizabeth had been thankful for the sameness of her cloak and dress with all the other sisters.

And now she prayed with every bit as much might as the others in the meetinghouse for the life of Brother Issachar. Not to Mother Ann as they did, but to the Lord she felt in her heart. To the one who had listened to her prayers through all her years.

21

"Eva. Eva!"

The panicked cry yanked Ethan awake. For a brief moment, he wasn't sure where he was, but then Brother Issachar cried out again. The nightmare of the last few days rushed back at Ethan as his eyes focused on Brother Issachar, whose eyelids twitched as if struggling to open while his lips moved in silent conversation with someone in his head.

Ethan wished he had a way to help his brother and friend, but he knew not what to do except keep watch over him through the night in the glow of the candle on the small bedside table. The candle was burning low, and it would be a race between it guttering out and the morning light filtering dimly through the cabin's tiny window up high along the ceiling. The window didn't look as if it had ever been washed, and Ethan thought of the good spirits Mother Ann said would not live where there was dirt.

He wanted to clean away the dirt, invite in hundreds of good spirits to help Brother Issachar get better. He wanted to turn back the clock to that moment on the walkway up to Mrs. Davey's rooming house and step between the knife and Brother Issachar. He wanted the knife to sink into his side instead of Brother Issachar's. It was his fault that his brother lay so gravely wounded on the bed in front of him. His shameful curiosity that had brought them this terrible trouble. His own flesh-and-blood father who had tried to kill the father of his heart.

Ethan had not lain down beside Brother Issachar for fear of shifting in the small bed and causing him pain. Instead he pulled a wooden chair close to the bed to keep watch over him. Ethan hadn't intended to doze off, but the gentle roll of the river water had been too much for him. He hadn't slept in more than fits and snatches since they came aboard the boat.

At first Brother Issachar seemed to endure the steamboat trip back up the river toward Kentucky and Harmony Hill fairly well. He'd walked aboard the boat, leaning heavily on Ethan, but he was on his own feet, pale but determined.

The doctor had come back to the boardinghouse the morning after Hawk Boyd had pushed his knife into Brother Issachar's side and advised against them traveling anywhere. "You should remain here until you're stronger," he told Brother Issachar. "That way if infection sets in we can use leaches to rid the poison from your system."

"Nay," Brother Issachar said in a voice that brooked no argument. "We will begin our journey home on the morrow as planned."

He sent Ethan to book passage on the first steamboat leaving New Orleans for Louisville. It was January yet, so the captain didn't make any promises when Ethan hunted him up to ask how long the trip would take. Instead he said, "Hard to tell. Could be two weeks. Could be two months. Some who've come down the river speak of cold up north. If there's ice, we'll have to put into a port and wait out the winter."

"But we must get back to Kentucky as soon as possible. A man's life might depend on it."

The captain's face was weathered with bone-deep wrinkles. Some of the wrinkles around his lips twitched in what could have been amusement or perhaps irritation. "I'd be glad to accommodate you, sonny. Fact is, I don't turn any coins sitting idle, but I've yet to find any channels to steam around the weather. A river man takes what comes, steers past the sawyers he can see, and prays the engines don't blow." The captain turned to walk away. "We go at eight sharp and wait for no one."

The first days on the river hadn't been bad. The sun was shining and the air was cool but pleasant. Brother Issachar insisted on sitting out on the deck, and Ethan began to think Brother Issachar was right when he'd told Ethan he shouldn't have wasted the Ministry's money booking the cabin. Twice a day he took the bandage off Issachar's wound and washed it out with the Shaker potion for aching muscles Brother Issachar had instructed him to buy back from one of the New Orleans storekeepers before the steamboat left harbor.

The potion bubbled and so burned in the wound that the blood drained from Brother Issachar's face as he gripped the bedding clothes with such force Ethan feared he might rip them. But when Ethan hesitated to do the treatment, Brother Issachar fastened his fingers tightly on Ethan's arm as he said, "You must promise to do this for me. Even should I lose consciousness. If gangrene sets in, I'll have no hope of seeing Harmony Hill again."

The evening before, when Ethan had taken the bandage away, the skin around the wound had looked red and puffy in the light of the candle he held close to it. Brother Issachar tried to raise his head up to look at the wound, but he fell back on the bed. His eyes were glassy and his face hot to the touch.

Ethan wanted to go search among the other passengers to see if there might be a doctor aboard, but Brother Issachar feared the sort of doctor he might find. "Nay, doctors of the world oft as not carry death with them, and we're not long from home now." His voice was so weak that Ethan had to lean close to hear him. "Sister Lettie will know which healing potion to mix for me when we get to Harmony Hill."

"But it will be days before we get there," Ethan protested.

"Worry not, my young brother. I will make it home one way or another."

"Do you speak of heaven?" Ethan felt no joy at the thought of heaven. Not if it took his brother away from him.

Brother Issachar's lips turned up in a little smile. "Do we not claim Harmony Hill as our heaven on earth? Do we not live the same there as we will in heaven?" The smile faded. "Now bandage the wound. My head spins with the need for sleep."

And he had shut his eyes and passed into some sort of slumber. For a while Ethan had bathed Brother Issachar's face with wet rags, but then when his skin seemed cooler to the touch, Ethan sat back to rest a moment and let his eyelids close. Now here in the deepest dark of the night, Brother Issachar's face was burning hot as he raised his head up off the pillow and reached toward the shadows. "Eva! Don't leave me."

Ethan gently pushed him back down on the bed. "Easy, Brother Issachar," he said softly. "I'm here with you." Perhaps he was trying to say Ethan and his fevered tongue couldn't get the sounds out of his mouth in the right way. "I won't leave you."

But Brother Issachar struggled against Ethan's hold as if he didn't recognize his voice. He looked beyond Ethan's face into the darkness of the shadows. "No, you must not keep me from her. Turn me loose. If you have any decency in you, let me go to her. To her and the babe." He sobbed as he uttered the last word.

"Calm yourself, Brother Issachar, before you make your wound worse." Ethan kept his voice firm as he tightened his grip on the man's shoulders, but even in his weakened condition Brother Issachar was strong. He twisted away from Ethan, then gasped in pain and fell back on the pillow.

"My Eva, my Eva." His cheeks were wet with tears. "Oh God, what sin have I done against you to deserve such punishment?"

"Shh, Brother Issachar. You have confessed your sins and been forgiven." Ethan could see the spreading circle of blood on the bandage over the man's side. He prayed for the right thing to say to calm Brother Issachar's spirit. "You are a Believer." He did his best to keep his own voice calm, but he heard the panic edging into it. He cleared his throat and added, "One of the brethren at Harmony Hill."

Brother Issachar seized on the last words. "Harmony," he whispered softly and then coughed. The circle of blood on his bandage grew larger. But he was calmer.

Ethan slid his arm under Brother Issachar's shoulders to raise his head up as he put a glass of water to his lips. The water

233

slid into his mouth and he swallowed. Then Ethan wrung out a rag from the basin of water on the floor to bathe Brother Issachar's face. The rag felt hot in Ethan's hand almost immediately, so he dipped it in the water again. Brother Issachar moved restlessly on the pillow. His eyes flashed open and closed, and his fingers twitched as he fought against the touch of the bedclothes and became more agitated again.

With shaking hands, Ethan poured some of the medicine powders the doctor had given him into the glass of water. He prayed for their healing power as he stirred it and then lifted Brother Issachar's head again to get him to swallow the bitter draught. Some of the medicine dribbled out the corners of his mouth and down on the bedclothes, but Brother Issachar swallowed a portion of it even as he pushed against Ethan's hand holding the glass to his lips.

Ethan began singing softly. "Come down Shaker-like. Come down holy. Come down Shaker-like. Let's all go to glory." Ethan hesitated on the last line of the song he'd surely sung several times every week for the last fifteen years of his life.

When Brother Haskell first taught him the song, he had explained to Ethan that the glory in the song wasn't a hoped-for-someday paradise in the sky, but instead the feeling that came over the Believers as they lived separate from the world in harmony and peace with one another. A Believer didn't have to wait for heaven to have glory. A Believer could sing down glory. A Believer didn't have to stop breathing to get to that glory. He simply had to die to the world.

So singing those words wasn't asking the Eternal Father or Mother Ann to take Brother Issachar on to glory in heaven. Ethan's spirit warred against that thought, but at the same time the sound of the song seemed to spread a peace over

Brother Issachar. His hands were no longer twitching and his breath was coming easier. It could have been the medicine, but Ethan kept singing as he placed the cooling rags on Brother Issachar's forehead. He held the candle closer to the bandage. The bloodstain on it didn't seem to be increasing, so he left it as it was.

If only he could sing Brother Issachar out of this dark cabin and back to the light at Harmony Hill. Back to health. With the thought, new words came to him. "Come down Shaker-like. Come down healing. Come down Shaker-like. Come down healing."

As dawn began to push the first fingers of light through the small window, Brother Issachar's fever cooled and he lapsed into a more restful sleep. Ethan sat back in his chair and let the song die on his lips even as he kept a prayer circling in his head. He prayed for healing and he prayed that when Brother Issachar next opened his eyes he'd know Ethan as his brother instead of being locked in some other time from the past.

The sun was straight up in the sky at midday when Brother Issachar did finally open his eyes and speak. "Brother Ethan."

His voice was shaky, but the voice of the man Ethan knew. Relief swept through Ethan as he turned from the doorway where he'd been standing to get a breath of fresher air to smile at the man on the bed. "Brother Issachar, how are you feeling this day?"

"I have been stronger." He shut his lips and then pulled them open. "And my mouth. It feels as dry as new woven cloth."

"It is good to see you awake." As Ethan helped Brother Issachar lift his head to sip some water, he looked at the bandage. No fresh blood seeped through the cotton. He had thought to change it with the morning light, but he didn't have the heart to wake Brother Issachar for that purpose. Now with Brother Issachar watching, Ethan began to gather the necessary items for dressing the wound.

"The air in this cabin is fetid." Brother Issachar wrinkled his nose and frowned. "I have no memory of the night. How long have we been trapped in here?"

"Only a day," Ethan said. "We need to change your bandage. Your wound bled badly in the night."

"Perhaps that is to the good." Brother Issachar attempted a smile. "A doctor from the world would surely say I needed to be bled." With a groan he raised himself to a sitting position. "Let us go out on the deck away from this bad air."

The wind blowing across the deck was decidedly cooler than it had been the day before, but Ethan welcomed the feel of it against his face as he settled Brother Issachar into one of the chairs on the deck. He'd practically carried the man out of the cabin, but he had made a pretense of believing Brother Issachar could have made it on his own.

The exertion of the night before had pushed some pus and much blood out of the wound, and Ethan wanted to think it looked better as he poured the burning potion on it. His prayer song whispered through his head again as Brother Issachar bore the treatment stoically. *Come down Shaker-like. Come down healing.* After he applied the new bandage, he folded up the old one to discard it. Its odor was foul.

"Have we anything left to eat in our pack?" Brother Issachar asked.

"Yea, Mrs. Davey was generous. We have bread and apples and cheese. And some of our sisters' apple butter."

"Bring us bread spread with the apple butter, and you can

tell me what has put the dark frown in your eyes while we eat."

Brother Issachar broke tiny pieces off the bread to hold in his mouth long moments before he swallowed. He had hardly eaten two decent-size bites when he handed the bread to Ethan. "I will have more appetite when I have the sisters' good cooking. Sister Mable's sweet biscuits could entice anyone to eat."

"Yea," Ethan agreed with a forced smile to hide his worry.

"Tell me what happened in the night." Brother Issachar fastened his eyes on Ethan. "Did I fight against your care?"

"I worried not about that, other than hoping you wouldn't injure yourself more. You were out of your head." Ethan looked down at the remainder of the bread spread with apple butter in his hand. He had little appetite himself, but he made himself take a bite and chew. A Shaker did not waste food.

"Out of my head. I pray I said no hurtful or angry words to you."

"Nay, you knew not that I was there. You called out for Eva." Ethan hesitated before he went on. "That was the name of the wife you had before you became a Believer, wasn't it?"

"So it was. Ah, Eva." Brother Issachar leaned back and rested his head on the pillow Ethan had carried from their cabin. The pillowcase was ripped and stained brown from much use. A Shaker pillow would never be so ill kempt.

Brother Issachar was quiet for a long moment before he went on. He kept his eyes closed. "I wondered why she was walking through my thoughts this day." Again he was silent for a time before he opened his eyes and stared out beyond Ethan at something only he could see. "She was so beautiful.

Even now I can bring her before my eyes just as she looked the day we made a sacred promise to love each other till death parted us. It was an easy promise to make. And to keep. But I never thought death would take her from me so soon. Or that my love would live on for her so long after she was gone."

His eyes came back to Ethan's face. "I suppose that's not a very Shaker-like thing to say. But I have never denied my love for Eva. I told the elders of it when I came into the Society. They said I would come to love Mother Ann more once I gave my spirit over to them, but it's not Mother Ann who walks through my thoughts. It is Eva."

"How did she die?" Ethan asked.

"Trying to birth me a son. The doctor who came said the babe was turned wrong, that there was no way she could have ever birthed him. He tore him from her, but it was too late to save either of them. We buried them together."

"I'm sorry," Ethan said.

"You are the first Believer to ever say that to me." Brother Issachar smiled faintly and looked away from Ethan toward the shoreline. "Others—the elders who knew my past—have always said it was God's way of pointing me toward my true purpose of life as a Believer. That the death of my wife and child was a sign to me, just as the deaths of Mother Ann's four babies were a sign to her of a greater mission for her life. I know not whether it was true for Mother Ann. The number of Believers seems to prove the truth of it for her. But I have never believed it true for me. My God is not such a God."

Brother Issachar's eyes settled on Ethan once more. "He didn't take her from me for any such a purpose. She simply died as many women do in childbirth. But I do believe he led me to the Shakers, for he knew I couldn't bear my life in the world without her. The Believers accepted me even though I never became the sort of brother they hoped I would be. I've had a good life among the Shakers, but if my Eva had lived, I would not be at Harmony Hill."

"Your love for her sounds strong."

"There is no earthly love stronger than that love between a man and a woman."

"I will never know that sort of love." Ethan was surprised to feel a wistful sadness at the words. He was a Believer. He had no need of the kind of sinful love those of the world sought. He only needed his love for his brethren and sisters and the Lord and Mother Ann. He had no reason to think of the one named Elizabeth, but she came to his mind unbidden.

"Such love is forbidden to a Believer." Brother Issachar's look sharpened on Ethan as if he were reading his guilty thoughts. "But sometimes forbidden things seek us out and cause us much anguish."

Ethan pushed aside thoughts of Elizabeth. Didn't he have enough wrongs to worry about without letting his mind run after another? Besides, he knew nothing of how one came to fall into this love for a woman. It surely took more than the sight of a comely face or the touch of a hand. For a moment he considered asking Brother Issachar how such love came to be, but then he clamped down on his wonderings. Thinking on things that had no place in a Believer's life had already caused them much trouble.

He confessed as much now to Brother Issachar. "Yea, just as I let my wrong curiosity about my worldly father lead me into sin. Sin that's causing you much anguish."

"Do not blame yourself, my brother. You weren't the one who thrust the knife into my side. We have a plentitude of sins of our own without shouldering those of others." Brother Issachar shifted in his chair a bit and was unable to bite back a groan.

"Would you like me to mix some of the powders the doctor sent with us? It seemed to ease your pain last night." Ethan half rose out of his chair to go fetch the powders.

"Nay. The pain isn't more than I can bear. We will save the powders for the darker hours." Brother Issachar waved him back down, then pointed toward the riverbank as he said, "I know that barn. We're halfway home. Pray that there will be no ice on the river ahead."

22

Two days after they received word of Brother Issachar's injury in New Orleans, the third fire was discovered during the time for rest and meditation following the evening meal. Again no alarm was sounded. It was a small fire much like a child might set. Or so Sister Ruth told Elizabeth the next morning after the rising bell sounded and Elizabeth was leaving the Gathering Family house to go work with Sister Lettie until the breakfast hour. Each Shaker sister or brother began his or her workday the same time as those sisters who had the duty of preparing the morning meal or the brethren who milked the cows. All worked equal hours.

Elizabeth didn't mind. She'd always liked being up at first light to be witness to the sun's rising and to absorb the special peace of the early morning. It was not much different in the Shaker village. Even though she shared a room with nine other sisters, there was little talk among them as they readied themselves for the day. Needless chatter was discouraged by the Ministry. Conversation for merely social purposes was allowed only during the union meetings or by appointment with permission.

So Elizabeth and the others who had come to live among the Shakers slept and dressed and ate in their own small circles of silence broken only by a nod or word of greeting and perhaps some bit of necessary information about the weather outside their window. They didn't speak of the trials they might be enduring, even though at times Elizabeth heard one or the other of them weeping in the night. Sometimes she thought to leave her bed to console the one who cried, but she knew not what words of comfort to offer or whether such words would be against the Shaker rules. So she stayed in her narrow bed and felt coldhearted as she offered up a silent prayer for a sister in distress.

Elizabeth shed no tears of her own. She had wept for her mother. She had wept for her father. Tears hadn't brought them back to her. It was better to push beyond the tears. To find the best road forward. That was what she'd done. Even though she could not seem to bow her will completely to their way, she felt no regret for being under the Shakers' roof. Three times a day she sat at a table laden with food. She had warm clothes and a bed, albeit narrow and lacking in comfort. Best of all they shielded her from Colton Linley although they couldn't keep him from traveling down the road through their village at least once a week. Even in the snow he had come. Sister Melva said he'd spent the night of the snowstorm locked in the tramp room.

When Elizabeth had asked what the tramp room was, Sister Melva explained. "We turn no one away who asks for a place to sleep and a meal. But we can't have unknown men wandering about our village in the night. We must of necessity take precautions to safeguard ourselves. So we lock any such in after the supper hour and unlock the door when we take them breakfast."

"And Colton Linley allowed that?" Elizabeth was astounded.

"I did not see him, but I heard it was the one who led those men with evil intent into our house some weeks ago. The man who knew you from the world." Sister Melva's eyebrows drew together in a slight frown as she went on. "He did not give the appearance of a ruffian like the men with him, but from the way you trembled at the sight of him, I'm guessing appearances can be deceiving. It was good he was locked in. He has no proper business here."

"I fear he seeks sight of me," Elizabeth said.

"Yea, so it seems. Men of the world are driven by wrong desires." Sister Melva gave her an assessing look. "And you do seem to attract the worldly sort of attention that we are to spurn as Believers. Sister Ruth says that's why Brother Ethan was sent to New Orleans with Brother Issachar. To keep him far from sight of you."

"I have sought no contact with Brother Ethan." Elizabeth wanted to be sure Sister Melva knew that.

"Yea, but sought or not, the two of you seem to have been thrown together in untoward situations that are better avoided. That's why we have separate doors and staircases for the brethren and sisters, you know. To keep away sinful temptations that might awaken within us if we don't stay in our proper places. And while we all have to labor to control our sinful worldly urges, that labor is oft the most difficult for our young brethren."

Elizabeth's cheeks had burned as she lowered her eyes

away from Sister Melva's face. She couldn't deny feeling those worldly urges for the young brother, but she had no desire to be a stumbling block in his path as a Believer. When he returned from New Orleans, she would take pains to avoid him as strenuously as she avoided allowing Colton Linley to catch sight of her in the village.

The weather had broken and the days had an early feel of spring to the air. The snow vanished almost overnight, and so the steamboat carrying Ethan and the wounded Issachar was not expected to be delayed in its river journey to Louisville. Two brethren had been dispatched to Louisville with a wagon to await the men. It was said those of the Ministry who lived above the meeting room were praying without ceasing for Issachar, since prayer and deciding rules were their duties. And watching to be sure those rules were followed.

Their many rules seemed tiresome and often foolish to Elizabeth, but nevertheless sometimes after the rising bell had rung and she was out on the walkways in the crisp air with morning falling gently over the Shaker village, Elizabeth thought it might be possible that she could do as the Shakers wanted. She could forget her worldly urges. She might lose the ache within her to one day hold her own baby in her arms. She could learn to be one with these odd people even if she couldn't quite accept every tenet of their belief.

Sister Lettie had assured her only a few days before that the Shakers didn't require one to believe all spiritual things exactly as they did. While they didn't allow disharmony or words of rebellion, they did exercise much patience in allowing each novitiate plentiful time to make up his or her mind about walking the Shaker way. No one was forced to sign the Shakers' Covenant of Belief, and in truth, even if she did want to, she could not do so until after she turned twenty-one in April. However, their kind patience seemed to evaporate when one of their number did choose to go back to the world, and often they were sent on their way with words of condemnation that made Elizabeth cringe.

She heard no such words from Sister Lettie's mouth. Sister Lettie had a kind heart for all, but she did mourn each time a sister or brother fell from the Shaker way. Sister Ruth was not so silent with her opinions of how the departed sisters or brothers were surely on a slippery slope to eternal punishment where they'd cry for relief from their misery but no help could be had. She almost seemed to gloat as she condemned each one. Elizabeth had no problem imagining her saying the same of her. Gladly, with self-satisfied pleasure.

Elizabeth heard that gladness in Sister Ruth's voice when she called out to stop her on the pathway the morning after the small fire. Elizabeth looked longingly at the door of the medicine shop only a few steps away. Sister Ruth was no doubt chasing after her to berate her for some imagined wrong, but whatever it was could surely wait until after the morning meal. And hadn't Sister Ruth herself often told Elizabeth conversation was not allowed on the pathways? Elizabeth kept walking and pretended not to hear Sister Ruth calling to her.

"Sister Elizabeth!" Sister Ruth's voice demanded an answer as she hastened her steps to catch up with Elizabeth. She grabbed hold of Elizabeth's arm.

Elizabeth stopped and turned with a growing sense of dread. Sister Ruth would not be running after her for any small matter.

Sister Ruth, not accustomed to rushing, had to catch her

breath before she could speak. Her scowl could have bent nails. "You are not to ignore me, Sister. Ever."

"Forgive me. I had my mind on my coming duties and didn't hear you." Elizabeth felt little guilt for her lie. "And you have often warned me it's not proper to talk along the pathways to our daily work, so I didn't expect anyone to call to me."

Sister Ruth's cheeks flushed red as she narrowed her eyes on Elizabeth, who gazed back at her innocently. She poked Elizabeth in the chest with her finger. "You may act humble with the other sisters, but you don't fool me for one little moment. You have no thought of living the Shaker way. You're only here to make trouble."

Elizabeth stepped back away from Ruth's jabbing finger. "Nay, you are wrong. I have no desire to see trouble come to any among you."

"Perhaps you don't, but there is devilment within you that you do not care to weed out of your thoughts. Devilment that grows wicked desires in your heart."

Sister Ruth's words didn't bother Elizabeth. She'd heard them from her many times before and had given up trying to change the woman's opinion that trouble had befallen the Shakers because of her. Perhaps it was true. Elizabeth bowed her head. "I will beg forgiveness of the Lord as I strive to weed out wrong desires from my heart."

"Words are easy for you, are they not, Sister Elizabeth? As easy as striking fire is for your brother of the world."

Elizabeth looked back up at Sister Ruth whose eyes were boring into her. "I know not of what you speak. If you talk of our Brother Payton, he's embracing the Shaker way and would certainly do nothing to harm the village. You have only to look at him during meeting to see that."

"So it would seem. But there was another fire last night. A small one in the West Family men's bathhouse." She paused to give her next words more impact. "Shortly after this brother you speak of had been there."

"I heard no alarm." Elizabeth's heart sank at word of another fire. It couldn't be Payton. It could not. For she had spoken nothing but the truth when she said he was following the Shaker path. "Was the building badly damaged?"

"Nay. The fire was small. Easily extinguished. Almost as if a child had set it. But the brother of whom you speak is not much more than a child."

Elizabeth tried to hide her concern, but the gladness that filtered into Sister Ruth's eyes was proof that she wasn't completely successful. "What do you want of me, Sister Ruth? More words of sorrow? For me to fall prostrate here on the walkway at your feet?" Elizabeth didn't try to hide the anger that pushed up within her as she stared at Sister Ruth.

"Such action might prove you were finally opening yourself to the spirit. Not that any of us expect that to ever happen." Sister Ruth sniffed with disdain as she pulled a handkerchief out of her pocket to touch to her nose. "But it isn't what I want that's important. It's what Mother Ann wants."

"And have you had a vision or message from her that tells you what that is? For I have not." Elizabeth met the other woman's eyes without wavering.

"Nay, and I daresay you will not. A Believer cannot have a strife-filled spirit as you do. Or as the white-haired demon-possessed child you brought with you."

Elizabeth softly blew out her breath and purposely un-curled her fists down at her sides as she stared at Sister Ruth.

The woman was not worth her anger. "You're wrong," she said quietly, but firmly. "Hannah is a child like any other."

"It isn't your place to tell me I err." Now anger flashed in Sister Ruth's eyes. "It's no problem to see the trouble you have brought our village. Trouble that followed poor Brother Issachar to New Orleans. Trouble that won't stop besetting our village until you're gone from us. You with your pretty ways full of vanity and the demon child and the one who has a love for fires. Those of the Ministry will see. They have eyes that watch and they won't be blind to your transgressions forever." Her voice got louder as she spoke, until one of the brethren walking some ways away looked toward them curiously.

The door of the Medicine Shop opened behind Elizabeth. "Sister Elizabeth, I wondered where you were," Sister Lettie said as she stepped out of the doorway. "You do know that such gossiping is not proper, my sisters."

"Yea, you are right, Sister Lettie. Forgive me. Sister Ruth was pointing out the error of some of my ways." Elizabeth turned from Sister Ruth with relief and slid past Sister Lettie into the shop.

"There are better times and places for confession, my sisters," Sister Lettie pointed out.

Elizabeth didn't glance back at Sister Ruth, but she had no problem imagining how the anger must be consuming her. Steam would surely be rising from her head as she said, "Yea, Sister Lettie. I will confess my error to Eldress Rosellen."

"Very well, Sister Ruth," Sister Lettie said. "The morning hour is passing. You do have a duty to attend the same as Sister Elizabeth, do you not?" Sister Lettie stepped back into the Medicine Shop and shut the door firmly behind her, ending any conversation. She looked at Elizabeth. "Are you all right, my sister?"

"Yea, I'm fine." Elizabeth put her hands under her apron to hide their trembling. She didn't know why Sister Ruth's words so upset her unless it was that she heard truth in them. "What work have you for me to do?"

Sister Lettie studied her a moment before she pointed toward two bowls of ground roots. "We have powders to mix, an equal amount of each, and two even spoonfuls of that mixture into each packet. Your measurements need to be exact."

Elizabeth picked up the measuring spoon and dropped it with a clatter. She picked it up again, but then spilled the powder as she tried to put it into the packet.

"That is enough, I think." Sister Lettie put her hands on Elizabeth's shoulders. "Come, child. It's time you shared your troubles." She pushed her down into the chair next to the table where she'd been preparing the medicine packets. "Tell me what has happened to make your hands tremble so?"

Elizabeth didn't know what she should say. She didn't want to burden this kind sister with matters that couldn't be helped.

Sister Lettie was patient. "Take your time. We have a while yet before the bell for the morning meal sounds. There's no hurry, but sometimes it's best to just let the words out instead of searching for the ones you feel are proper. I have a good sifter here." She smiled and pointed at her head. "I'll be able to sort out the words that matter the most."

Elizabeth sighed. "I have no desire to bring you trouble, Sister Lettie. To bring any of you trouble, but that's what Sister Ruth thinks I've done. That a wrong spirit dwells within me that's causing problems in your village."

"A wrong spirit?" Sister Lettie took a chair down from the peg on the wall and sat down directly in front of Elizabeth. "And what problems does she speak of?"

"Brother Issachar being injured. The fires. She says there was another last evening."

"So I've been told, but it was inconsequential. Hardly a concern." Sister Lettie threw out her hand in a gesture of dismissal.

"It's surely a concern that someone is setting fires, intending harm." Elizabeth frowned. "The fires don't seem to be accidental."

"The Ministry thinks it is those of the world." Sister Lettie's light blue eyes probed Elizabeth's face. "Do you have reason to believe differently?"

Again Elizabeth hesitated to speak as she looked down at her hands. Again Sister Lettie waited. Finally Elizabeth said, "Nay."

Sister Lettie laid her hand softly on Elizabeth's arm. "I hear a thousand other words behind that nay. Tell me what worries you, Sister Elizabeth. It will be held in confidence."

"Even from the Ministry?" Elizabeth looked up at Sister Lettie.

"Yea, even from the Ministry. I've told you before there are no eyes watching in this room. A doctor must have the trust of his patients. My father taught me that when I was but a child. He threatened me with his strop if I ever spoke of any of his patients' ills to any other, and he wasn't one to lay his hand on me in punishment."

There was so much kindness in Sister Lettie's face that the words spilled out of Elizabeth. She told it all. How as a child, Payton had had a fascination with fire. How their father had sickened and died in one terrible night. How they had run from Colton Linley, who expected Elizabeth to come to him in payment of a debt he said was owed him, and how Payton had gone back and set the cabin afire.

"I know he set that fire. I saw the smoke and smelled it on his clothes when he came back to where Hannah and I waited for him. He didn't deny it. But he was distraught over our father's death and angry at me for forcing him to leave everything he loved behind. He had witnessed Colton trying to force himself on me on the day we buried our father, and so Payton's anger turned on him. I think he couldn't bear thinking of him touching me with such ownership, and I fear that feeling somehow transferred over to the books and other things he loved so well in the cabin."

When Sister Lettie just looked at her without saying anything, Elizabeth hurried on, appealing to her for understanding. "He is young to have suffered such loss. Our mother and then our father so unexpectedly. But he told me he didn't set the first fire in the Carpenters' Shop, and he would have told me the truth. Besides, he likes it here. He has put his feet on the Shaker path. His spirit doesn't war against it the way Hannah's does." Elizabeth looked back down at her hands and admitted softly. "And as mine does as well. I have promised Hannah we will leave in the spring if she has not accepted life here by then. I know not what we will do, but I will somehow have to keep my promise to her."

"Worry not about the spring. Young Sister Hannah's spirit may soften. I hear she likes working with the silkworms." Sister Lettie laid her hand on Elizabeth's cheek. "The Lord's Word says each day has worries sufficient unto the day. Your first worry is the fires, and I believe you speak truth in that

Brother Payton has no part in those. He did wrong that he will have need to confess before he can sign the Covenant, but he is too young for that by several years. He will grow in the spirit before that time comes and be more ready to admit his wrongs. And you needn't worry he'll be accused falsely. The Ministry will set eyes about to spy out whoever is lighting these fires. Not much stays secret from the Ministry." Sister Lettie patted Elizabeth's cheek one more time and smiled. "Outside of this shop at any rate."

"Thank you, Sister Lettie. I feel easier in my spirit."

"Good." Sister Lettie stood up and hung her chair back up on the peg. "Come, let us get these powders mixed before we are called to the morning meal."

They worked in silence for a few moments before Sister Lettie said, "Tell me what seemed to ail your father that took him from you so swiftly."

"I don't know. He seemed fine when he came in about mid-day. He had been to town the day before. Had stayed with a friend there overnight and then went by to speak to Colton about some business matter on the way home that morning, or so Colton told us later. By nightfall he was deathly ill with terrible heaving and cramps and much pain. Before daylight he passed on. I had no thought he would die so quickly. Not even from the cholera if that was what it was."

Sister Lettie frowned as if considering his symptoms before she shook her head a little. "I doubt the cholera. Wrong time of year in the general way of that horrible disease, and even it rarely takes its victims in a day." Sister Lettie was silent for a moment before she asked, "And he was healthy before this? No other times when he suffered from heaving and such?"

"Nay. He was strong and full of vigor."

"Poison," Sister Lettie said with no doubt. "He must have eaten something that poisoned him. Perhaps the wrong sort of mushroom. Perhaps arsenic, although I know not how he could have gotten enough to make him so ill without it being on purpose. His own or someone else's. He wouldn't have taken his own life, would he?"

"Nay, he loved us. He wouldn't have left us alone. Especially not Payton and Hannah."

Sister Lettie looked up at her. "He surely loved you just as much."

"Yea, but I am older, more able to care for myself than they."

"Then it must have been some sort of accident, but it was surely poison. That is the only thing that could take one in such health so quickly." Sister Lettie carefully stacked her packets of medicine in a wooden tray box. "It was probably a wrong mushroom in something he ate in the town. Some are very deadly, you know, and easily mistaken for those one can safely consume."

The breakfast bell tolled. Sister Lettie stood up and put her hand on Elizabeth's shoulder. "Whatever the cause, I see your sorrow. He must have been a fine man."

"Yea, he was. Brother Issachar reminds me of him." Elizabeth was surprised to feel the prickle of tears in the back of her eyes. "And now he may die as well."

"Death cannot always be cheated. I have seen much of it in my time helping my father and even among the Believers. But at least here, there's little sting to death. It's simply like stepping across a divide. Heaven here. Heaven there." Sister Lettie made a back and forth motion with her hand before she took her cloak off the peg and draped it around her shoulders. "But that doesn't mean we won't try to keep Brother Issachar with us longer. I've been searching my books for the best combination of herbs and roots for the treatment of wounds and the infections they can cause. When he gets here, we will war against such for Brother Issachar. You can be sure of that."

23

Ethan wanted to shout when he caught sight of the first Harmony Hill barn. They were home. For weeks his every thought, his every prayer had been focused on somehow getting Brother Issachar home to Harmony Hill. The afternoon sunlight bouncing off the white stone Centre Family House was like a sign that his prayers had been answered. Surely now things would be better. Surely now the wound in Brother Issachar's side would begin to heal.

Brother Issachar had borne the trip from Louisville over the rough roads with courage, but by the time they entered the village, he was beyond knowing where he was. Often on their long journey home, Brother Issachar had lost consciousness, and each time Ethan wondered if he would ever open his eyes this side of paradise again. But Ethan had refused to give up hope as he spoon-fed him water and broth. Brother Issachar wanted to make it home. Ethan had done everything in his power to make that happen, and now at long last home was within sight.

Ethan leaned over close to Brother Issachar's ear and said,

"We are home, my brother. Home to Harmony Hill. We made it."

Although Brother Issachar showed no sign of rousing, Ethan wanted to believe he heard his words and that the knowledge he was back at Harmony Hill would begin the healing that Sister Lettie would aid with her good medicines. He wanted to believe Brother Issachar would once more need Ethan to go into the woods with him to bring back a tree for a new chest or table. He not only wanted to believe it. He had to believe it. Otherwise, the guilt mashed down on him until he found it hard to breathe.

More than once on the way home when he was not overcome with pain and fever, Brother Issachar had assured Ethan he didn't hold him at fault. But no matter what Brother Issachar in his goodness said, the wound in his side was a wound Ethan had put there as surely as if he had shoved the knife in himself.

He didn't want to think about what Brother Martin would say or do when Ethan confessed his wrongs. Ethan had practiced the telling of them often in the long dark nights as he watched over Brother Issachar and begged the Eternal Father, the Christ, Mother Ann, any merciful being, for Brother Issachar's life and for his own forgiveness. Ethan dreaded the disappointment he was sure to see on Brother Martin's face, but that paled in the face of his fear of losing Brother Issachar. That thought was a thorn in his heart that worked deeper into a more tender area every time he looked at Brother Issachar's pale, pain-ridden face.

The brothers carried Brother Issachar to the sickroom prepared for him in the Centre Family House. Sister Lettie, who must have been told their wagon was coming, was waiting to lend her help along with Elder Joseph. Ethan had expected to see them. He had not expected to see the young sister, Elizabeth, hovering behind Sister Lettie. He was so surprised by her presence there that he stared directly at her. She met his eyes with such caring he could almost feel it wrap around him and offer him rest.

Suddenly as if it had been only yesterday instead of months ago, he remembered the soft whisper of her breath against his cheek and the sweet scent of her hair as they tumbled to the ground together at the cliff on the day he thought he was saving her from the fall. He moistened his lips as a longing rose in him to walk across the room and feel her arms around him, to surrender himself to the caring he saw in her eyes.

The women on the streets in New Orleans had beckoned to him, trying to entice him into sin, and he never felt the first temptation. Not there. But now here back in Harmony Hill where temptations were supposed to be virtually eliminated, he looked at Elizabeth and wanted to loose all the shackles of Shakerism for the imagined comfort of her hand on his cheek. With shame, he realized he had not rid himself of thoughts of her but had only shoved them into a treasure box of sorts in his mind.

He'd seen young brothers come into the Shakers and bring with them some forbidden treasure from the world they didn't want to surrender as they began to walk the Shaker way. A mother's locket. A father's knife. A Bible with family births recorded in it. A shiny stone. An arrowhead turned over by their plows. Such treasures were frowned on by the elders but sometimes allowed for a while as the young brother adjusted to his new life.

Ethan had brought nothing to the Shakers with him. But

now it seemed the treasures he couldn't give up were in his mind. His willfulness. His curiosity. His lack of discipline. His carnal desires. He was a sorry excuse for a Believer. His face hardened in disgust at his weaknesses.

Elizabeth's eyes widened a bit in alarm at the look on his face before she lowered her eyes to the floor. He stared at the top of her white cap and wanted to reach across the divide between them and put his hand under her chin to raise her beautiful eyes back to his. To let her know his anger hadn't been directed at her. To keep the promise of her caring in his heart.

Brother Martin would tell him to shake free of such worldly desires. That is what he should do, but instead he looked at her and remembered the softness of her hand under his. He didn't want to shake free of the feeling that flooded through him.

As they shifted Brother Issachar from the stretcher to the bed, he groaned and the sound pulled Ethan away from his shameful thoughts. He was a Believer. Believers did not look upon their sisters with carnal desires. They did not live un-disciplined lives that brought disaster to their brothers. Not unless they let wrong seeds take root in their souls.

Elder Joseph leaned over and spoke to Brother Issachar. "We're thankful you are home, Brother Issachar. We will labor a song for you this evening in meeting."

Sister Lettie showed no patience for the niceties of his greeting. "I'm sure your words and prayers will be a comfort to him in time, Elder Joseph, but he has no ears for them right now." She moved in front of the elder to put her hand on Brother Issachar's forehead. "He burns with fever." She looked at Ethan. "How long has he been thus?"

"The fever comes and goes. He will be burning with it during the night and then with the morning he'll feel cooler. The wagon ride over the roads was hard," Ethan answered. He hesitated for a second before he added, "The wound festers."

Sister Lettie pulled up Brother Issachar's shirt and peeled the bandage back to study the wound. She didn't flinch from the sight or from the odor the bandage released into the room, but Elder Joseph stepped back with a small gasp of dismay. Ethan looked at Elizabeth, expecting her to be pale, perhaps ready to swoon. There had been a time or two in the cabin of the steamboat when he had to fight to keep the smell from overpowering him, but Elizabeth seemed every bit as calm and collected as Sister Lettie as she moved up beside the older woman to be ready to aid her if needed.

Sister Lettie looked up at Elder Joseph. "We should call in the doctor from town."

"Nay," Ethan said. "Brother Issachar asked me to tell you not to do that if he was unable to speak. He trusts in what you can do for him and fears a doctor from the world will only delay his healing."

"I may not be able to pull him back from death." Sister Lettie stared across Brother Issachar's motionless form on the bed at Ethan. "The wound is very bad."

"Yea, but he made me promise."

She looked at Ethan for a long moment before she let out a sigh and mashed her mouth together in acceptance of Ethan's words. "Very well." She turned to Elder Joseph. "We need hot water and some chicken broth from the kitchen."

"Send Sister Elizabeth for what you need," Elder Joseph said.

"Nay, I need her here. She has a gift for healing and we of a surety need all the gifts Mother Ann will send down to us for Brother Issachar to recover."

Elder Joseph looked a little discomfited, but he turned to do Sister Lettie's bidding with no more argument. And in truth, Elizabeth was already placing cooling cloths on Brother Issachar's forehead and bathing his face and neck with great gentleness while Sister Lettie began to cut away Brother Issachar's shirt. The two seemed to work as one without the need for words to pass between them.

Brother Issachar moaned and then called out. "Eva. Don't leave me. Eva!"

"Eva? For whom does he call?" Sister Lettie glanced up at Ethan.

"The wife he had in the years before he began following the Shaker way. He said she died many years ago in childbirth."

"Ah," Sister Lettie said as she turned her full attention back to pulling the bandage away. She must have heard Ethan pull in his breath, for she spoke without looking up. "Get the young brother a chair, Sister Elizabeth. He is weakened from his long journey home."

Elizabeth quickly lifted a chair down from one of the pegs and pushed it under Ethan. "Have you been eating, Brother Ethan?" Elizabeth asked quietly even as she kept her eyes away from his face. "You look gaunt."

"Worry not about me. I am not the one with the wound." His voice was brusque.

"As you say, Brother." She turned back to tend to Brother Issachar, but her words had brought Sister Lettie's attention to him.

"She's right," she said as she eyed him. "You have spent

much energy in caring for your brother and of necessity have neglected proper care of your own body. Go wash the grime of the journey from you. The dinner bell will soon ring and you need to be ready to eat food that will bring you back to proper strength. Sister Elizabeth and I will care for our brother, and if we have need of help, we'll send for you or one of the other brethren."

Her words brooked no argument, but Ethan didn't want to leave Brother Issachar. He feared leaving him. He had listened to his every breath in the last few weeks until sometimes it seemed as if he had lent his strength to him in order for him to continue breathing. If he deserted him now, would the next he heard be that Brother Issachar had passed over the divide?

"Set down your burden, my brother. We'll care for him." Sister Lettie spoke the first words kindly before she stiffened her voice and ordered him from the room. "Now go. You can come back after the evening meal to check on him before meeting. You will want to go to meeting after so many weeks away."

"Yea, it will be good to shake the sins of the world from me," he said even as he stared at Brother Issachar's still form on the bed and hesitated. He couldn't make his feet turn toward the door.

Without looking up, Elizabeth spoke. "Brother Issachar has much love for you. He would tell you to go eat."

Her words rankled. He didn't need anyone to tell him Brother Issachar cared for him. He already knew that and the knowing made the thorn in his heart stab deeper. He jabbed back at Elizabeth with a hint of scorn in his words. "Do you have a gift for knowing the thoughts of others as well as a gift for healing, Sister Elizabeth?"

Sister Lettie started to speak, but Elizabeth held up her hand to stop her as she lifted her eyes to his face. "Nay, Brother Ethan. I know not another's thoughts, but I did know Brother Issachar's great kindness when he came upon me and my sister and brother on the road and how he looked upon us, three strangers, with compassion and love. He surely has even greater love for you."

"'Greater love hath no man than this, that a man lay down his life for his friends.'" He spoke the Bible verse aloud as it came unbidden to his mind. Preacher Joe had taught him that verse even before he came to the Shakers. And Hawk Boyd had hurt Preacher Joe too.

"And is that what happened?" Sister Lettie asked. "Did he step in front of the knife to save you, young brother?"

"Nay, but I should have done so to save him. It was my sin that brought the man to our door. I am the reason he lies here so gravely wounded."

"Ah, the burden of sin can weigh us down and give us much sorrow if we don't confess our wrongs so that we can be forgiven." The lines of Sister Lettie's face deepened with compassion. "Is Brother Issachar your appointed confessor?"

"Nay, that is Brother Martin."

"Then speak to him at your first opportunity. Unburden yourself, for unconfessed sin can fester in our souls the same as this wound festers in our brother's side." There was a tap on the door. "That will be the hot water," Sister Lettie said as she turned her attention back to Brother Issachar.

Elizabeth turned from the bed to go to the door. As she stepped past Ethan, she said, "All is not yet lost. Sister Lettie will fight to keep him this side of the divide for a little longer." She spoke so softly that Sister Lettie didn't seem to note her words as she tended to Brother Issachar. Elizabeth didn't touch Ethan, but her voice seemed a caress. "As you have been doing." Her eyes touched on his for the barest second before she went on to the door to take the basin of hot water from the sister there.

She understood without him telling her how he had fought to bring Brother Issachar home while he yet took breath. Perhaps she did have the gift of knowing the unspoken thoughts of others, but however she knew his thoughts, her words seemed to finally release Ethan. He was able to turn toward the door and surrender the care of Brother Issachar to her and Sister Lettie.

He went straight to the bathhouse and dropped the water down over him from the barrels above. The water was only heated for the morning baths, but Ethan didn't mind the chill of the water running over his body. He rubbed his arms and chest with the lye soap the sisters made until his skin tingled before he used the last of the water in the barrel to rinse off. The barrel would be filled again from the pipes that ran down from their holding pool. Brother Issachar had shown him how to take his first bath in the bathhouse after the pipes had been run. They had laughed at the novelty of having a waterfall inside of four walls.

"It takes a whole man to be a Shaker," Brother Issachar had instructed him as he dressed after his bath.

"Yea, so Brother Martin has told me. He says that it's wrong to neglect our body or our soul. That Mother Ann has supplied us good food for both and it is a sin not to partake of the blessings she rains down on us from heaven."

"Especially when it's the gift of our sisters' good cooking." Brother Issachar had smiled with a little wink at him.

That was the thing about Brother Issachar. He always had a smile ready. Even if Ethan couldn't see his smile on the outside, he knew he was smiling on the inside. That wasn't something shared in common by most of the Shaker brethren and sisters. Most claimed peace. Most sought spiritual joy during meeting, but frivolity while going about their duties was frowned upon by the Ministry. A Believer gave his hands to work and his heart to God. If one had a gift of laughter, then there were others who might say a gift of silence was better. Brother Martin was one of those. He looked upon any high jinks among the young brethren he taught with great disfavor.

The bell for the evening meal sounded just as Ethan fastened the ends of his suspenders to the waistband of his clean britches. It felt good to be clean again. He looked more the proper Shaker on the outside. But inside he carried guilt and sins he had need to confess. First he would eat.

His brothers nodded to him in silent welcome when he came into the Centre Family House to join them as they filed toward the biting room. They stood at their appointed place at the tables until all were gathered—the brethren on one side of the biting room and the sisters on the other. Then in unison they knelt at their places and offered up silent prayers of thanksgiving for the food they had to eat. Ethan added a prayer for Brother Issachar and then, as he got to his feet, for courage to speak his sins to Brother Martin after the meal.

The sisters who had the duty to serve them sat bowls of beans, meat, and bread out for each group of four. That way all could reach each bowl with no need for words to ask for anything to be passed. The brethren in his group, Will, Henry, and James, let Ethan take his serving out of each bowl first. They didn't speak. Conversation was not allowed in the biting room. There were only the sounds of the spoons on the bowls and the forks on the plates as they ate, but his brothers' eyes showed gladness that he was back among them as well as concern for Brother Issachar.

Yet in spite of the welcome he saw in their eyes, in spite of his relief to be back at Harmony Hill, he didn't feel the peace he had expected to feel back among his brethren. The silence beat against his ears, and he wanted to stand up and have the gift of shouting or speaking in tongues. Perhaps even howling like a dog as he had seen Brother Patrick do once in meeting. Anything but the terrible silence. But he stayed in his place. He continued to spoon food into his mouth.

Such gifts would not be allowed in the biting room. Later at meeting, he could shout. A gift of shouting might be rejoiced in there. But now is when he wanted to break the silence. Now is when he knew that, even though he might look like the proper Shaker on the outside, he was a failure as a Believer on the inside.

He knew he wouldn't be able to empty himself of all his sins when Brother Martin listened to his transgressions. He could confess his sin of curiosity that had ended with Brother Issachar so badly wounded. He could confess his sin of worry and despair as they traveled home. He could confess his sin of gathering worldliness like his britches picked up sticktights and cockleburs in the woods. But he was far from ready to empty everything from the treasure chest in his mind. He carefully put his longing for the young sister, Elizabeth, down into that imaginary chest and shut the lid. He tamped it down tight.

But no matter how much he imagined hammering it closed, he knew he could open it again. He knew he would open it again.

24

Brother Issachar drifted in and out of consciousness over the next several days. Sister Lettie sat with him day and night except a few brief hours when Ethan or one of the other brothers relieved her. She insisted Elizabeth be allowed to stay with her to be her hands and feet. "I'm not so young as I used to be," she told Elder Joseph when he questioned the wisdom of pulling Elizabeth out of the regular rotation of duties. "Our new sister shows a gift for healing. It's wrong to ignore the gifts of our Eternal Father."

"There are many gifts, and the first is our gift to be simple." Elder Joseph frowned across Issachar's bed toward Elizabeth, who bowed her head and did not meet his eyes. "We must not puff ourselves up and celebrate this or that gift as greater than any other. God is a part of all our laboring. He abides in our work whether it's planting potatoes, weaving cloth, or fashioning the inner workings of a drawer for a new chest."

Elizabeth kept her eyes on the floor in a show of diffidence. She wouldn't be allowed to plead her case to stay with Sister Lettie at any rate. Her duty was to be obedient, and since her spirit often chafed at such mindless subservience to whatever the elders and eldresses determined was good and proper, she had found it best to hide her eyes from most everyone in the village except Sister Lettie, who never searched her face for evidence of fault.

Unlike Sister Ruth who tried to glean every wrong thought or deed. Elizabeth had no choice but to endure Sister Ruth's harping on her obvious shortcomings as a Shaker novitiate whenever she had to make confession, but at least Sister Melva was no longer watching her every step. Since Elizabeth was working so closely with Sister Lettie, the Ministry had assigned Sister Melva to a different newcomer to their village.

The village increased in number daily, but Sister Ruth scorned some who joined with them. "Winter Shakers. Mark my words, most of them will be gone as soon as the sun warms and good riddance." Then she stared at Elizabeth as though surprised to find her even yet in front of her eyes continuing to masquerade as a Shaker sister.

Elizabeth wasn't growing in the spirit. At least not in the Shaker spirit. But she was growing in the knowledge of healing, and if she had to dance in a pretense of worship, then what would that hurt? The Bible spoke of King David dancing in the joy of worship. Perhaps such worship was a gift as the Shakers said. And there seemed no real wrong with the idea of shaking off the sins of worldly desires and stomping out boastful pride. Any preacher would expound on the need for a Christian to do that.

As she felt Elder Joseph's eyes boring into her while he considered Sister Lettie's request, Elizabeth said a silent prayer that he'd believe she was shaking off her sinful desires. She wanted to stay with Sister Lettie that much. And with Issachar.

She blocked thoughts of Ethan from her mind. It wasn't the time to be thinking of the young brother. If Elder Joseph guessed at how her eyes feasted on the sight of Ethan's face and how her heart leapt up in her throat each time he came to see Issachar, she'd be sent out to plant the crops or to the washhouse for sure, or perhaps even sent to another Shaker village. She couldn't allow that to happen. She could not leave Hannah behind.

Before Elder Joseph spoke her fate, Issachar cried out and began to struggle with the bedclothes. Without thought, Elizabeth stepped closer to the bed to lay her hand on him. His fever seemed to be rising once more, and whenever that happened, he was tormented with unhappy dreams. Her touch never failed to calm him even as it did now. She dipped a cooling rag into the basin of water and laid it on his forehead as she softly began to sing one of the Shaker songs.

When she heard the door close, she looked up. Elder Joseph was gone, and Sister Lettie was smiling. "You will be allowed to stay. At least until Brother Issachar gets better."

Elizabeth smiled, but then her smile faded when she turned her eyes back to the man on the bed. "Is he getting better?"

Sister Lettie's smile also disappeared. "The wound heals on the outside, but his continuing fever makes me fearful the inner wounds are not healing as they should. Our brother is strong, else the fight would have already been lost, but there are times now I wonder if he wants to come back to us enough to keep on fighting. He seems to be reaching toward a different world than the one he knows here." She stared at Issachar as she spoke directly to him. "Brother Issachar, do you want to come back to us?"

His eyelids flickered, and for a moment it looked as if he were trying to rouse enough to answer her question. But then he threw out his arms and tried to lift himself off the bed as he shouted for Eva. They had heard her name often as they sat with him.

Sister Lettie let out a sigh. "Speak to him, Sister Elizabeth. Hold his hand and calm his spirit before he does damage to himself."

Elizabeth did as Sister Lettie ordered and Issachar grasped her hand with surprising strength. Sister Lettie mixed a draught of medicine.

After she held Issachar's head up to dribble some of it into his mouth, she looked over at Elizabeth. "You do realize he thinks you are his Eva."

Elizabeth looked up at Sister Lettie. "Please don't tell Elder Joseph that."

"Why?"

"He might think I had encouraged some sinful thought."

"It's not your thought. It is Brother Issachar's." Sister Lettie's eyes narrowed on her. "But it is a thought you understand, is it not?"

"Yea," Elizabeth admitted.

"The young brother is very handsome." Sister Lettie's voice carried the same no-nonsense tone it always did. "But he is a Believer, my sister. You must remember that."

"Yea. I have no thought to change that."

"I believe you speak the truth, but it will be better if you aren't alone with him."

"Yea, I wouldn't want to bring him trouble. There are those who think I have brought trouble enough to your village."

"Our village," Sister Lettie corrected gently. "It is your village

269

too. And there has been no more trouble of late. No fires. No disturbances of the spirit that can be laid to your blame unless we speak of the young brother's struggles when he looks at you. And warring against the temptations of the flesh will make him a stronger Believer. If he wins that war." She stared at Elizabeth a moment longer before she sighed. "I suppose that remains to be seen the same as whether Brother Issachar wants to come back to us. Only time will tell."

The dinner bell rang and Sister Lettie stood up and shook her apron as if ridding herself of those worries. "Every dilemma can't be solved before the sun goes down. We move forward one step at a time. And now the bell signals our time to eat. You need to fetch our meals, Sister Elizabeth. And Brother Issachar's broth from the kitchen. But first go to the Medicine Shop and get some slippery elm so I can make a new poultice for the wound."

Elizabeth had the slippery elm and was on the way back to the Centre Family House when a horse suddenly stepped off the roadway into her path. She had been so deep in her own thoughts of what Sister Lettie had said about Ethan and Issachar that she had forgotten to be on the lookout for Colton.

He stared down at her from his horse. "Well, if it isn't a devout little Shaker woman." The flaps of his coat fell down over his saddle, and his boots in the stirrups showed no scuff marks. His broad-brimmed hat shaded his eyes, but she had no trouble imagining the arrogance in them.

Without responding to his words, she turned to walk around him, but he moved his horse to block her way.

"Not yet, Elizabeth," he said as he swept off his hat with a gentlemanly flourish. Now she no longer had to merely imagine his eyes as he peered down his long narrow nose at her, and she had to make herself stand fast and not shrink back from him as he went on. "I've been watching for you for many weeks. I was beginning to think perhaps you'd died. You know, sudden like, the way your father did."

"Nay, I am in health." Elizabeth lifted her chin and stared straight at him. She had no reason to fear him. He could surely do her no harm here in the middle of the village with the Shaker brethren and sisters all around them.

"Nay?" He snorted with derision. "So they've roped you in and got you talking like them now. Do you do their dances and whirls and shake like a leaf in the wind?"

She didn't answer his question. "What do you want, Colton?"

He slid off his horse in front of her. She started to back away from him, but he grabbed her arm and pulled her toward him. "You know what I want." He leaned down so close to her face that she felt the moisture of his words. "I want what is mine."

"We brought nothing of yours with us to this place." She tried to jerk free from him, but he gripped her arm tighter.

"There's you."

She mashed down the urge to fight against him. He was too strong. Instead she made herself stand very still and breathe in and out slowly while she stared at his face. His eyes were cold and hard and showed no concern for her, only anger. "You own no title to me," she said.

"I need no title. You were to come to me when your father died. It was what was supposed to happen. I had a plan for us." His eyes bored into her as he changed his words. "I have a plan for us. You will come with me and marry me as I planned."

"Why would you want to marry me? You know I could never love you."

He laughed loudly and the sound ripped through her as his grip on her arm tightened until she knew the mark of his fingers would be imprinted on her skin long after he turned her loose. If he turned her loose. The smile that lingered around his lips was not pleasant. "You think this is about love?"

"Why else would you want me to marry you?" Elizabeth stared at him with a frown. "There are many women in the world if love is no object."

"I married twice for love or so I thought. The first woman was weak in body and died in childbirth. The second was weak in spirit and ran back to her parents at the first bit of complaint. But you." He stared down at her. "You are strong, with wide hips well suited for child bearing, and you have a strong will. But mine is stronger. I picked you as a girl when your father moved you to the woods. He promised you to me."

"I don't believe that," Elizabeth said.

"Neither did he after you came of an age to marry. He tried to say we'd never had any such understanding, but why else would I have let him live in my cabin, let his cow eat my grass, let him burn my wood in my fireplace to keep his family warm? You were the reason. It wasn't written on a paper, but you are mine."

"I'm not a slave to be bought and sold in payment. My father would have never made such an agreement."

"So he said when last I saw him the day he passed on." His eyes narrowed as he stared down at her. "He thought he could keep me from taking what belonged to me. Nothing can do that. Know that, Elizabeth Duncan. Love may not matter to me, but the desire to have you is strong within me and has been for some years now."

"Let go of me or I'll scream."

Again he laughed, the sound as grating on Elizabeth's ears as before. "What good would that do you? Your Shaker brethren won't help you. Everything's peace with them. Peace. Peace. They won't fight for you."

Elizabeth stared at him with eyes as cold as his and spoke with force. "Let go of me."

Instead he grabbed her with both hands. She pushed against him, but he held her tighter. "I could just throw you over my horse and take you now. Who's to stop me taking what is mine?"

"I'm not yours. I will never be yours." She spat the words at him.

He smiled as he lifted her off her feet. "I won't hold your harsh words about me against you. At least not after I've gentled you down a bit. That might turn out to be as much fun as the other."

She did scream then and fight, twisting and kicking with all her strength to break free of him. She landed a glancing blow to his knee, and when he staggered back, she jerked loose from his hands and fell to the ground. She scrambled to her feet as he came after her with fury on his face.

A strong hand pushed her back gently as the Shaker brother stepped between her and Colton. "Fear not, Sister," Ethan said without looking at her. He stared at Colton. "This man of the world is leaving our village now."

"Who's going to make me?" Colton made a sound of disgust. "You?"

He tried to shove past Ethan, but Ethan stood his ground.

Bigger than Colton and years younger, Ethan looked as immovable as the stone fence along the outer edge of the village as he faced him down. "We do not choose to fight, but we protect our sisters."

He didn't look to the side, but Colton did as five or six Shaker men ran toward them from a barn some ways away. They carried axes and pitchforks.

Colton laughed a little in a show of scorn even as he turned for his horse. Once mounted, he stared down at Elizabeth. "Just as well. It'll be better when you come to me of your own accord." He gathered up the reins of his horse to turn away as he said, "And you will. Perhaps, if I'm feeling forgiving the day that happens, I might take you in."

Elizabeth stared back at him and managed to keep up a pretense of strength until he rode away. Then she shook with such trembles that she could barely stand.

"Are you hurt, Sister Elizabeth?" Ethan asked with concern as he put a hand under her elbow to steady her.

"Nay. Just frightened." She looked up at him shyly. He looked so concerned that a new set of trembles pushed through her that had nothing to do with her fear of Colton. "I thank you for coming to my rescue. He had thought of carrying me away."

"Do you know him?"

"Yea. He was our neighbor before we came here. The one my little sister spoke of on the day you found us on the road."

His eyes changed, hardened a bit as he said, "The one who wished to commit matrimony with you?"

"Yea." She couldn't pull her eyes from his face even though she knew the other men were only a few steps away and would surely note the impropriety of their gaze being locked on one another. "Please don't say who it was. Colton has already caused trouble once in the village because of me, and the Ministry might decide to send me away to be sure such trouble does not happen again."

"Nay, surely not. I . . ." Ethan started and then as a flush rose in his cheeks, changed his word as he dropped his hand away from her elbow and looked at the brethren rushing up beside them. "We won't let him bring harm to you."

As the men gathered around them, Ethan quickly explained what had happened. How before he went to the evening meal, he had carried some broth from the kitchen to Brother Issachar. Sister Lettie sent him after Elizabeth so she would not also fetch broth. That was when he saw the man of the world attacking her and had gone to her aid. It was surely providence that brought the other brothers late from the field so that they saw him standing against the man of the world.

Elizabeth kept her eyes modestly turned down as Ethan spoke. When he fell silent without mentioning that the man of the world was seeking her, she breathed an inward sigh of relief. She let her eyes slide quickly over the men around her as she murmured her thanks. A couple of the older men were frowning as if they thought she'd done some wrong.

She looked back down at the pathway. "I must be about my duty to get Sister Lettie's supper. I am her hands and feet while she cares for Brother Issachar."

"And does our brother's condition improve, Sister?" one of the men asked.

"Sister Lettie says it has not worsened, but he's not showing the improvement she hopes for," Elizabeth answered without looking up. She picked up the packet of slippery elm she had dropped in her struggle with Colton and held it up. "She sent me after medicine for a poultice. I mustn't tarry in my duty." She moved past them without looking back at Ethan even though she wanted to do so. She still felt the warmth of his hand on her elbow and the thought of him standing in front of her, protecting her, made her heart pound in her ears.

She had vowed to stay away from him and not bring him trouble, but it was as Sister Melva said. For whatever reason fate seemed to keep throwing them together.

25

March came in with its usual fickle weather. One day snow would be flying in the air and the next the sunshine would feel warm on Elizabeth's shoulders. She wanted to reach for the warmth of spring, but at the same time she felt the need to cling to the cold gray days of winter. She should have never promised Hannah they would leave the village in the spring. They had no place to go. No relative who might take them in. No money, no possibilities, no luck. Nothing but Colton.

She watched for him more diligently now whenever she had need to walk from building to building, but she hadn't seen him again. He must have meant it when he said she would have to go to him now. He thought she would crawl to him and beg. She'd rather die, she told herself, and then Hannah's forlorn face would be in front of her eyes. She wouldn't rather Hannah died. And she had promised.

Hannah hadn't spoken of the promise again, but then they had little chance to talk except for a brief word now and again at meeting. From all reports, Hannah was beginning to settle into her life among the Shakers. Sister Nola said so. Eldress Rosellen said so. Sister Lettie said so.

But when Elizabeth looked at Hannah, she couldn't keep from remembering the little brown sparrow that had once chased a bug through a small hole in the chinking between the logs of their cabin and found itself trapped. It had flown madly to and fro, banging into the log walls as Elizabeth tried to herd it with her broom toward the door she had thrown wide open for its escape. Finally the bird had landed on the table, sunk its head down into its feathers, and stared at Elizabeth as though accepting its fate. That was the look she saw in Hannah's eyes.

Happiness should not be expected all the time, Sister Lettie told Elizabeth. At least not the giddiness those of the world took for happiness. "True happiness is much deeper," she said. "A gift from our Mother Ann. Her teachings tell us happiness does not depend on our circumstances so much as what lies at the very foundation of our souls."

"Are you happy, Sister Lettie?" They were sitting with Issachar who seemed somewhat improved. He had not burned with fever for two days, but he had no strength. At times he seemed to hover in a sort of wakeful state, but he rarely spoke, as though his voice had retreated somewhere deep within him and could not find its way back to his mouth. And there were moments when Elizabeth saw the hopelessness of the tiny sparrow in his eyes the same as in Hannah's. Now his eyelids flickered open and he stared at Sister Lettie as if awaiting her answer along with Elizabeth.

"Yea," Sister Lettie answered. "At the foundation of my soul. That is not to say I feel that happiness of spirit every moment of every day, but it is there in my center." She put her hand over her heart. "I am content with my place. With my duty. I have peace in my soul. And you, Sister Elizabeth? I sense you don't know this happiness."

"I have known happiness. The kind where the sight of the night sky or the sound of a meadowlark puts joy in your heart, but now I cannot shed the sorrow that settled over me when my father died," Elizabeth answered truthfully. "Or my worry for Hannah and Payton."

Sister Lettie's voice was gentle. "Brother Payton does not need your worry. He is building the Believer's foundation of happiness in his soul."

"Yea, he is changed. He's no longer the brother I knew before we came here."

"But is that not good?" Sister Lettie leaned toward her as if to hear her answer more clearly. "Do you not want him to surrender his will to the true way? Do you not want to attempt to follow his example and do the same?"

"I wish I could say that I do, but in my heart I desire a family of my own."

"We have family here. We are all of one family. So many brothers and sisters with love freely for one another." She stared at Elizabeth intently as if she were trying to force the truth of her words into Elizabeth's unwilling heart, but with kindness.

"But that love seems to turn so quickly to hate when a brother or sister falls from the way and goes back to the world." Elizabeth thought of some of the condemning words she'd heard from Sister Ruth's mouth and from others.

"Nay, not hate. Only sorrow to see our former brothers and sisters falling away to spiritual destruction for a brief flash of pleasure here on this earth," Sister Lettie said. "But never hate. We strive for peace with all and extend love to any who come to us. Mother Ann has instructed us to do good. That's why we never turn any away in hunger no matter what the cost to us."

"Yea, you have shown me much kindness and generosity, but I cannot ignore the sadness of my sister. Or . . ." Elizabeth hesitated, not sure she should go on. She glanced over at Issachar. She didn't wish to remind him of his Eva who haunted his dreams by speaking of marriage, but his eyes were closed now as if he'd wearied of listening to them.

"Or what?" Sister Lettie prodded.

She looked back at Sister Lettie and spoke softly to keep her words just between them. "Or deny my wish for love as the world knows it."

Sister Lettie sighed deeply and looked troubled as she shook her head. "Such love only brings strife. Think of the man who tried to carry you away. He is ruled by that sort of worldly desire. Do you wish to be part of that?"

"Not with him," Elizabeth answered.

"It is wrong to lead another astray." There was an uncommon sound of sternness in her words.

"Yea, I know that is so." Elizabeth looked down at her hands in her lap. "My words were rash. Forgive me, Sister Lettie. I am still learning what is proper and what is not, but I assure you I do not endeavor to tempt any among you to step from your path of belief."

"I know, my child." Sister Lettie's voice was gentle and kind once more. "I see your effort. How you make reasons to go to the Medicine Shop whenever our young brother comes to sit with Brother Issachar. It is only right that you leave the battle up to him. He is the Covenant-signed Believer. Not you. At least not yet. Perhaps someday you'll understand the peace of our love and know the true love of the Lord and Mother Ann. Then you will no longer feel tugged toward the temptations of worldly love."

Elizabeth bowed her head and said no more. She didn't argue that she already felt the love of the Lord in her heart. The Lord had answered her prayer and led her to this Shaker village where she had found shelter. The Lord would be with her if she left this place. Nothing the Shakers had ever said made her doubt that. Mother Ann might condemn her, but the Lord Elizabeth's mother had introduced her to when she was but a child would not. He would keep loving her just as the Bible promised, just as she'd assured Hannah he would the day they made the snow angels.

Even though she didn't look up, Elizabeth could feel Sister Lettie's eyes boring into the top of her cap as she waited for Elizabeth to renounce her worldly thoughts. It was a relief when Issachar moved on the bed and groaned to pull Sister Lettie's attention to him. She stood up to go peer down at him.

"Brother Issachar, are you truly awake?" Sister Lettie said in a voice a bit too loud. "It is good to see your eyes. I daresay you are hungry."

"Nay," he answered weakly.

"Hungry or not, you must eat." Sister Lettie spoke in her no-nonsense voice as, with Elizabeth's help, she lifted him up to a sitting position and propped pillows behind him. "Sister Elizabeth has brought you some soft food from the kitchen. If you're strong enough, you can feed yourself. If not, Sister Elizabeth has had much practice spooning food into your reluctant mouth." She smiled at him.

But he wasn't looking at her. He was staring at Elizabeth as if realizing for the first time who she was. Not his Eva, but the woman he'd found on the road months ago. "Sister Elizabeth," he said, his voice rough from scarce use.

He was as pale as the cases on the pillows behind him. Sister Lettie feared he might be bleeding internally. Elizabeth carried the bowl of food to him, but his hand trembled so much when he tried to hold the spoon that she took it from him. He seemed to have no interest in eating, but he opened his mouth and let her feed him. He shuddered with each swallow.

"Is it so bad tasting?" Elizabeth asked as she offered him another spoonful.

He gave his head a tiny shake and opened his lips to receive the food without fighting against it as he had sometimes when he was more unconscious than conscious. He swallowed four more bites, each seeming to be more of a struggle than the last, before he shut his eyes and pushed her hand away. "Later," he said.

Sister Lettie had left the room to go across the hall to check on Sister Emma, who had twisted her ankle. Through the open doors, Elizabeth could hear Sister Lettie encouraging the injured sister to move her foot. Elizabeth straightened the covers over Brother Issachar's legs and adjusted the pillows behind his head.

When she started to turn away to let him rest, he put his hand on her arm. She looked down at him and asked, "What do you need, Brother Issachar?"

His fingers felt cold even through the fabric of her sleeve, but she didn't pull away from him. Instead she touched his forehead with her other hand to see if the fever was returning to him. He didn't feel hot. "Are you in pain? Sister Lettie can fix a draught to ease you."

"Nay." His eyes fastened on her face and his breath seemed to come harder. "You look like Eva."

"But I am not," Elizabeth said gently.

"I know." His fingers tightened on her arm. "What you said to Sister Lettie. I heard."

A flush of color rose in Elizabeth's cheeks. She shouldn't have spoken so freely in front of him. "I'm sorry to be such a reluctant convert. Perhaps it was wrong for me to come here."

"It's not a bad place." He looked at her a moment before he went on, his voice growing stronger as he talked. "If you are ready to close away the world. I could never think of marrying another after my Eva died, so I was ready. You are not."

"Does that make me evil?" Elizabeth's voice shook a little as she spoke.

Issachar moved his hand from her arm to her cheek as she leaned toward him in her earnest need of an answer. "Nay, you are not evil."

"Then what should I do?"

His hand trembled from weakness and she put her own hand over his to help keep his touch on her cheek. His eyes didn't leave hers as he answered, "Follow your heart."

"But what if my heart leads me wrong?"

"It will not. Not if the love of our Lord dwells there. Trust what he tells you." He smiled slightly as he dropped his hand back down on the covers. "Trust what I tell you. Follow your heart."

"But I see no way," Elizabeth said.

He shut his eyes. Elizabeth watched him a moment in

hopes he would speak more, tell her a way would open, but he did not. He looked even paler than he had a few moments before, as if his words had drained additional lifeblood from him, and she felt guilty that she was thinking of her needs instead of his. She gently stroked his face. "Rest, Brother Issachar."

"Yea," he murmured. "Rest forevermore."

Ethan stood in the doorway and watched Elizabeth smooth down Brother Issachar's bedcovers. Sister Elizabeth, he sternly corrected his thoughts. Not Elizabeth. She was his sister and to be thought of as such. It was a sin to think of her in any other way. A sin he committed daily. Sometimes hourly as thought of her stole into his mind even as he worked to put his full concentration on his duties. Not brotherly thoughts. Nay, far from them.

He had made his confessions to Brother Martin. He'd told him of his sin of worldly curiosity about the man named Hawk Boyd. A man, Brother Martin said, who had nothing to do with Ethan now. Brother Martin had no understanding of why Ethan would have even carried the name in his memory through the years he had spent with the Shakers.

"He should have been long dead to you, Brother Ethan, just as all things of the world are dead to the covenanted Believer." Brother Martin didn't conceal his impatience with Ethan's lack of discipline. "I should have never let you go with Brother Issachar into the world. You seem unready to resist the temptations of the flesh."

Ethan couldn't say he was wrong. Especially not here, standing in the doorway watching Elizabeth tend to Brother

Issachar with such tenderness. He did not think of her as a sister. Instead the desire to feel her hand touching him with that same tenderness swelled up inside him and took away his breath. Brother Martin had cautioned him to stay away from her, but he had to come see Brother Issachar. He had to try to pull him back to life.

And he couldn't simply stand and watch while that man of the world attacked her. No one else had been there to help her. He had pleaded for Brother Martin's understanding. "Surely it was only right for me to protect one of our sisters."

"Yea," Brother Martin had answered, but with a frown. "But why, Brother Ethan, is it always that sister you are called upon to protect? I fear wrong spirits are loose here."

Of course, Brother Martin was right. Ethan had been filled with wrong spirits when that Linley man had grabbed Elizabeth. He had wanted to smash the man in the face and knock him to the ground. Anger had burned through him for hours after the man rode away. At meeting he had tried to shake it off as he went forth to exercise the songs and reclaim the proper peace and love of a Believer, but he couldn't forget how the man had held her so roughly or the man's mocking words and eyes as he stared down on them from his horse. And even as Ethan labored the songs, he feared the seed of Hawk Boyd was sprouting higher within him.

He needed to hear the calming words of Brother Issachar assuring him that was not true, but Brother Issachar had hardly seemed to know Ethan or even where he was in the days since they returned to Harmony Hill. Ethan had been so sure that Brother Issachar would step away from the shadow of death as soon as he got back to his home, but it hadn't happened. So now it was good to see him sitting up, to see him speaking something to Elizabeth, even if the words did seem to bring a look of distress to her face.

He had passed Sister Lettie in the hallway on the way in, and she told him Brother Issachar was sitting up and talking.

"That's improvement," Ethan said as a grateful prayer took wing in his heart.

"Yea, it would seem so." Sister Lettie looked concerned. "Yet he seems weary of the effort."

"To talk, you mean?"

"Yea, that too." She pulled in a deep breath. "Perhaps sight of you will be an encouragement to him. I'm glad the Ministry didn't deny him the comfort of your presence."

"I can only come during the times of rest. All available hands are needed for the planting," Ethan said.

"So you are working in the fields?"

"Yea, planting corn. When I'm not here with Brother Issachar or at meeting. We have many fields this year."

"Mother Ann is blessing us with much prosperity," Sister Lettie said. "There will be plentiful food for our tables." She turned away from him to go on toward the sisters' outside door. "Tell Sister Elizabeth to come help me at the Medicine Shop while you are sitting with Brother Issachar."

It wasn't instructions he would need to speak to Elizabeth. She always rushed out as soon as he came into the sickroom. She seemed anxious to avoid tempting the wrong spirits even if he did not.

"I hear our patient is speaking," he said as he stepped into the room.

Her attention had been so fully on Brother Issachar that his voice startled her. Her eyes flew to Ethan's face and then quickly down to the floor, but not before he saw the same gladness he felt to see her reflected back to him in her eyes.

"Yea," she said softly. "But he's very weak. I'm not sure he knows what he speaks." Red bloomed in her cheeks as if she were worried that he might have overheard their conversation.

"I couldn't hear his words," he assured her.

"Good," she said, then stammered. "I mean, what he said would have been of no interest to you." Those words seemed wrong to her too as she rushed on. "I'm sure he will have much to say to you." She mashed her mouth together as though she feared whatever words might escape her lips next. She tightened the strings of her apron, straightened her cap, and moved purposely toward the door. "I must go help Sister Lettie."

"She told me to so tell you." As she passed by him, Ethan remembered how her brown hair had blown in wisps across her face the day he and Brother Issachar had come across her on the road, and he had the sudden desire to pull off her cap and free her hair to fall down around her shoulders. He shoved his hands deep in his pockets to keep them from the sin of reaching out to stop her. His tongue was not as easily controlled as he tried to delay her leaving by asking, "Did Brother Issachar say something to upset you?"

It worked. She hesitated as she passed him. "Nay, not really. He was sharing advice with me as I struggle to follow the Shaker way."

"And what was that advice?" When she looked reluctant to tell him, he hurried on. "Nay, I shouldn't have asked that. You need not answer."

"I can." She lifted her head and looked straight at him. A

flash like the charge in a lightning bolt shot between them. "He told me to trust the Lord and follow my heart."

"Follow your heart," Ethan echoed. He looked at her a moment before he said, "And do you know where your heart wants to lead you, Elizabeth?"

She slipped her eyes away from his. "Not all pathways are open." She snatched her cloak from the peg by the door and almost ran from the room.

He stared after her until he heard the outer door open and close. He shut his eyes and pulled in a shaky breath. He had to gain control of these worldly urges. He couldn't let his feelings keep catapulting him into sin. He opened his eyes and turned back toward the bed where Brother Issachar sat propped up by several pillows. He was watching Ethan. Not with condemnation, but with his old kindness and something else. Something Ethan didn't quite recognize. A sorrowful longing perhaps for something lost, never to be found again.

Brother Issachar held out a hand toward him. It trembled, but he kept it out, reaching toward Ethan. "Come, sit with me." His voice sounded weak and hoarse as he spoke not much above a whisper. "There are words I need to speak to you while there is yet time."

Ethan took a chair down from the pegs and set it beside the bed. "It's good to see you better," he said as he sat down.

"Nay." Brother Issachar closed his eyes and let his head fall back on the pillows for a moment. "Not better."

Ethan wanted to argue against his words, but the truth was on Brother Issachar's face. His cheekbones practically protruded from his skin as his fight to live had used up every ounce of extra flesh. So Ethan stiffened his spirit and put his hand over Brother Issachar's as he waited silently for him to go on.

"The Eternal Father has given me this gift. Allowed me this moment of clarity to say goodbye. A precious gift." Brother Issachar opened his eyes and looked at Ethan. "Just as you have always been to me. I said when I found you on the riverbank that you would be a gift to the Shakers, but the gift was really to me. You are the son the Lord knew I needed. He supplies our needs. Always."

"And now you're paying for that gift with your life." Ethan couldn't keep the despair from his voice.

"The Lord giveth and the Lord taketh away." Brother Issachar turned his hand over to clutch Ethan's. "I am glad to be the one taken and not you. I've had a good life here at Harmony Hill. I'm ready to step over the divide, but you are not."

"If not for my sin, we would both have many more years here." Sorrow threatened to overwhelm him as he spoke and tears pushed at his eyes.

"Perhaps. Perhaps not. Another misfortune might have overtaken us." Brother Issachar pushed his tongue out in an attempt to moisten his lips. He motioned toward the glass of water on the table. "Let me wet my mouth."

Ethan stood and put the glass to Brother Issachar's lips to help him drink. He held the water in his mouth for a long moment before he swallowed as if he had to force it down his throat. His face grew paler even though Ethan had not thought that possible.

When Ethan stayed standing beside him, Brother Issachar smiled the barest bit and said, "Sit. My spirit lingers yet a little longer, and even if it did not want to do so, you couldn't hold it here by hovering over me."

"I will miss you."

"Yea, that is so." Brother Issachar's voice seemed weaker. He was silent for a moment as if gathering his energy. His next words carried more force. "You must not sorrow over much for me. Nor must you carry guilt. What has happened has happened. Each hardship helps us grow in the spirit."

"Yea, Mother Ann's teachings remind us that is so."

"And we know that all things work together for good to them that love God."

"That's Scripture," Ethan said.

"Yea. Words to remember, and not only for Shakers, but for all men and women."

"But the Shaker way, our way, that is the true way?" Ethan made it a question.

"You want an answer, but some answers we must seek for ourselves." Brother Issachar motioned toward the water again and this time only let it moisten his lips without taking a sip. He closed his eyes and lay back on the pillows.

He was quiet so long Ethan didn't think he was going to say more, but then he began speaking as if he were reading from the Bible. "There is therefore now no condemnation. If our heart does not condemn us, we have confidence toward God." He opened his eyes and looked at Ethan for a long moment before he went on. "Hold that truth."

"But what am I to do with it?"

"I tell you the same as I told the young sister. Follow your heart. It will not lead you wrong."

"Such thoughts as I've been having in my heart have led many to do wrong," Ethan protested.

"The love between a man and woman is not sinful." Brother Issachar's eyes burned into Ethan's. "I know for I have known such love. It too is a gift from the Lord the same as the gifts we know here among the Believers."

"Are you saying I should break the covenant I have made with the Believers?" Ethan could hardly believe his ears.

"Nay, I would not tell you that. I merely tell you to follow your heart. And then whatever you do, there will be no regrets. That is truly the gift to be prized over all others. To look at death and have no regrets."

"And can you do that, Brother Issachar?"

Again the corners of his lips lifted in a smile that this time lingered on his face. "Only because of the little child who washed up on the riverbank that day sixteen years ago. The good Lord's gift to me." He reached for Ethan's hand. His fingers were cold. "Now dwell with me in the richness of silence as I rest, my son. My gift."

26

Brother Issachar passed over the divide into eternity in the wee hours of the morning on the first day of spring. Elizabeth was with him. She and Sister Lettie and Ethan had been taking turns sitting with him day and night, for there had been no doubt his end was near. They felt the need to be there to hold his hand as he crossed over.

Watching his suffering had been a painful repeat of her watch over her father, but her father's death had surprised her. She hadn't thought it possible for a man in such prime of health to depart so quickly. Even if he was poisoned by a mushroom or something else he ate as Sister Lettie said must have happened. In contrast, Issachar lingered so long after they could no longer get him to take any nourishment or even water that the only surprise was in how long he continued to draw breath.

That night as the calendar turned to spring, Elizabeth sang songs and spoke to him of everyday things as though he might yet be able to hear her voice although it had been days since he'd shown any sign of knowing them. He didn't even call out to his Eva anymore. He seemed only a shell of himself lying on the narrow bed as if his spirit had gone on without first convincing his body to surrender to death.

Shortly after midnight when she heard the death rattle in his chest, she hurried to wake Sister Lettie who was sleeping in a room nearby. Sister Lettie woke Elder Joseph who fetched Ethan to stand by Brother Issachar in the final hour.

Elizabeth surrendered her place by the bed with one last squeeze of Issachar's cold fingers. Ethan stepped past her to take her spot with such a look of misery on his face that Elizabeth's heart ached for him. She wanted to lay her hand on him in sympathy, but she felt Elder Joseph's eyes upon her. Still, it seemed to double the pain to have to stand apart in their grief.

Despite how she kept her face downturned, the elder saw the tears on Elizabeth's cheeks. "Weep not for him, Sister. Death has no sting for our brother. His faithful following of the truth will be rewarded in the eternal life even as it was here at Harmony Hill."

Elizabeth swallowed her tears and pulled her handkerchief out of her pocket to wipe her eyes. "Forgive my weakness, Elder Joseph," she murmured softly. "I have grown fond of Brother Issachar."

"As are we all," he went on with gentleness, but she caught a tone of reproof in his voice. "But we must remember that our relationships here, no matter how genial and pleasant, pale next to the greater love we must show our Father and Mother in heaven."

"Yea." She thought it best to say as few words as possible. Plus the tears were balling up behind her eyes. She needed to escape the elder's attention so she could allow a few of them to leak out. Else she feared they might burst through in sobs she would not be able to control.

"Once we know that greater love, then we can love all our brethren and sisters the same with no special feeling for one over another."

Elder Joseph was speaking toward Elizabeth, but she had the feeling his words were no longer for her ears, but for Ethan's. There could be no doubt that Ethan had a stronger attachment to Issachar than he did for others in the village. His grief was almost palpable in the air. His discipline as a Believer was being sorely tested under the stern eye of Elder Joseph.

There was reason for Ethan's great sorrow. It was said the man who stabbed Issachar without provocation on the streets of New Orleans was Ethan's father in the world. There could be no doubt it was without provocation, for Issachar would have never done anything to provoke such a violent act. It was not in his nature. The evil dwelled within the other man. Within Ethan's father. Elizabeth didn't know how this man had found Ethan and Issachar or why, but it was obvious Ethan blamed himself. His guilt crushed down on him like a heavy boulder.

Elizabeth said a silent prayer for him as she moved to stand a bit behind Sister Lettie in case she needed anything. But there was nothing more to do. Nothing to do but wait. When before the break of the day Issachar finally released his last ragged breath and became still, it was almost a relief.

Sister Lettie put her ear to his chest. "He is gone," she said as she straightened up. She mashed her lips together as she stared down at Issachar for a moment before pulling the cover up over his face.

Elder Joseph nodded. "Then it is done. We have seen him over." He looked toward the window. "Morning tarries. Come, Brother Ethan, there is time yet for resting before the rising bell sounds." He moved away from the bed toward the door, but Ethan didn't follow him or even seem to hear his words. He was staring at Issachar's shape under the cover as if he thought he could yet call him back.

"Brother Ethan." Elder Joseph's voice demanded a response and Ethan looked up. The elder's voice softened. "Come, brother. We must let the sisters prepare our brother's body."

The stricken look on Ethan's face pierced Elizabeth's heart and she forgot for a moment to keep her eyes modestly lowered. Sister Lettie nudged her and spoke in a low voice. "We need hot water to prepare our brother's body."

"Yea." Elizabeth tore her eyes from Ethan's face and looked down quickly. It would not do for the elder to see how her heart ran after the young brother. "I will get what is needed," she murmured.

"We leave such preparations in your expert hands, Sister Lettie," Elder Joseph said as Ethan finally stepped away from the bed to follow the elder out of the room. "At first light I will assign brethren to commence digging a grave and building the box to hold our brother's earthly remains. We will commit him to the ground before the evening meal. That way the planting will not be unduly interrupted. Brother Issachar would want us to continue in our duties."

The sun was sinking low in the west when they carried Issachar's body out to the graveyard. It was a peaceful place with a large oak tree lending it shade. A good gathering of Believers had come out to say good-bye to their brother. Sister Adele began singing the funeral hymn. Elizabeth didn't even pretend to sing along as some of the others around the grave joined their voices with Sister Adele's.

> "Our brother's gone. He is no more.
> He's quit our coast, he's left our shore.
> He's burst the bonds of mortal clay.
> The spirit's fled and soars away.
> We now may hear the solemn call:
> 'Be ye prepared both great and small.'
> The call excludes no sex nor age,
> for all must quit this mortal stage.
> Then let the righteous sing,
> when from corruption they get free:
> O death where is thy sting:
> O grave where is thy victory?"

As the last words of the song died away, a few of the brethren and sisters spoke of this or that kindness Brother Issachar had done for them. Elizabeth kept the words she wanted to speak in her heart. She dared not say them aloud. Ethan must have felt the same, for though many eyes went to him as the others spoke of Issachar, he kept his eyes on the box they had lowered into the grave and remained silent.

Elizabeth's eyes came up in surprise when Payton stepped forward to speak. As he told of Issachar finding him on the road and bringing him into the village, he never once mentioned the sisters who had come into the village with him. It was as if he had come alone, as if she had not had to force him along the road to the Shaker village. And she wanted to reach across the grave to where the brethren were assembled and grab him. She wanted to shake him until he looked at her, really looked at her, instead of skimming his eyes across her face as if he did not even recognize her as his sister. She wanted to ask how he could so quickly forget their father, their family.

"My spirit was often troubled in the world. I let anger pull me into sin." He stared down into the grave. His voice cracked and then deepened as he went on. A new Payton. A changed Payton. Not the Payton who liked to stand ankle deep in a creek and catch crawdads. Not the Payton who leaned on her and trusted her to take care of him. "But I have turned from that sin, away from the temptations of the world, and know the peace Brother Issachar had."

At last he lifted his eyes from the grave and looked directly at Elizabeth as she had wished, but now it was she who no longer recognized her brother. She had lost him to the Shakers and who did she have to blame except herself? She had brought him here. She heard the echo of Sister Lettie's words in her head. *Be glad for your brother.* In time perhaps she would be able to find that gladness, but at this moment it seemed to be only a double sadness to know the finality of the loss of Issachar to death and Payton to the Society of Believers on the same day.

Elder Joseph picked up the first handful of dirt to drop into the grave. It scattered on the top of the wooden coffin. On opposite sides of the grave, the brethren and sisters followed after him to do the same. All at once the solemnity of the final goodbye was disturbed by a shout from back toward the West Family House. A shout Elizabeth recognized. She jerked around to see Hannah streaking down the road toward the graveyard with Sister Nola trailing far behind in pursuit. "Elizabeth!"

Without thought of the consequences or even a glance at the others gathered there, Elizabeth went to meet her. Hannah barely slowed as she came through the gateway of the cemetery and slammed against Elizabeth almost bowling her over.

"Elizabeth." Hannah pushed every inch of her body against Elizabeth and looked up at her with a tearstained face. "It can't be true. It's not true. Is it?"

There was such despair in Hannah's face that Elizabeth wanted nothing more than to pull her close and hold her forever. "What can't be true?" she asked with some dread. She wasn't sure she could bear another disaster.

"Brother Issachar. Sister Nola said he died, but he can't have died." Hannah's eyes strayed away from Elizabeth's face toward the open grave. "Not like our father."

Elizabeth let out a sigh. She tucked a stray strand of Hannah's hair back under her cap even as she wanted to yank off the cap and let Hannah's hair spring up under her fingers. "I'm afraid it is true. Brother Issachar died early this morning."

"But why, Elizabeth? He was so nice. He always smiled at me and didn't look at me like he was afraid I was going to sprout horns the way the rest of these people do."

"Now, Hannah, not everybody," Elizabeth said softly as she pulled Hannah off to the side. Even as she tried to deny Hannah's words, she felt the others eyeing them with intense disapproval as they walked past them out of the graveyard. She avoided looking toward them while cringing in expectation of Elder Joseph's voice taking them to task for their uncontrolled behavior. "What about Sister Nola?"

A look of guilt flashed over Hannah's face. "I ran away from her. I shouldn't have done that, I know."

"Sister Nola cannot run after you." Elizabeth looked down the road. Sister Nola had stopped and was leaning against a tree to catch her breath.

"But she wouldn't let me come to the burying. She said I was too young. I told her I had helped bury my own father. That I knew what death looked like." Hannah sniffed and leaned her head against Elizabeth. "But I didn't want Brother Issachar to die."

"I know." Elizabeth stroked Hannah's back. "Nor did I."

"Why does everybody I love have to die?" Hannah's words were muffled as she spoke them against the scarf lapped down over Elizabeth's waist.

Elizabeth searched her mind for some answer that might offer the child comfort, but found no words. All she could do was hold her and hurt along with her as she kept stroking Hannah's back. The silence around them was broken by the sound of the brethren shoveling the dirt back into the grave. The sound echoed in her head as she remembered how she and Payton with Colton Linley's help had piled the dirt in on top of her father. She tightened her arms around Hannah and shut her eyes and wished she were somewhere else. Anywhere but in a graveyard with no way to explain death to a child.

She looked around to see if perhaps Payton had lingered to steal a moment with them, but he was gone. She spotted him walking back toward the West Family buildings. She wondered if Payton had walked by with no concern for his little sister's pain. While she watched, he did not look back.

Nearly everyone had left the graveyard to be ready for the evening meal. The only ones who remained besides the brethren who were filling in the grave were Ethan, Brother Martin,

Elder Joseph, and Sister Lettie. Ethan stared down at the grave so deep in his grief that he had not even noticed Hannah's commotion. The same couldn't be said about the other two men. Brother Martin glowered at Elizabeth and Hannah as if he thought them a blasphemy to the graveyard.

Elder Joseph didn't look much less disapproving as he stepped close enough to speak to Elizabeth. "This is not proper behavior, sisters. I realize you are only learning our way, but we cannot allow such disruptions. I refuse to disturb the sanctity of the resting places of our departed sisters and brothers with harsh words, but you can be sure we will speak of this later."

Elizabeth bowed her head in submission to his words, but she kept her arms around Hannah who had gone stiff against her. As long as he didn't demand she turn loose of Hannah, she didn't care what he said or did. She watched out of the corner of her eye as he turned back to the grave and Ethan. He took one of Ethan's arms and Brother Martin took the other one. Together they ushered Ethan away from the grave.

"There is no reason for such sorrow," Brother Martin was telling Ethan as they hustled him past Elizabeth. His voice was harsh, without sympathy. "You are a Believer, Brother Ethan. To display such grief shows lack of faith."

Ethan let them pull him along without answering him. Before he went out the gate, he looked toward Elizabeth for the barest second. In his eyes, she saw his need to be held as she was holding Hannah, and her arms ached to offer him that comfort. Then they were gone on down the road with the sound of Brother Martin's harping voice trailing back behind them.

Sister Lettie followed them out. "We must clean the sick

room in case there is need of it," she said as she passed Elizabeth.

"I will be there as soon as I take Sister Hannah back," Elizabeth answered. "Please tell Sister Nola I'll bring Hannah to her so she won't have to walk up this rise."

Sister Lettie gave her a long look as if there were more words she thought needed to be spoken, but then she sighed and only said, "Do not tarry, Sister Elizabeth."

"Nay, I will not."

Hannah waited until Sister Lettie turned away, then she jerked away from Elizabeth and tried to pummel her with her fists. "Don't say nay like one of them. You can't be one of them."

"Easy, Hannah." Elizabeth caught Hannah's hands and pulled her tight against her as Sister Lettie looked back with a shake of her head before she walked on down the hill to speak to Sister Nola. When Hannah stopped fighting against her, Elizabeth stroked her back and murmured, "There, there. Calm yourself. I am not one of them. I will always be your sister."

Hannah leaned heavily against her and got very still. "Do you promise, Izzy?"

"I promise." Elizabeth put her hand under Hannah's chin and tipped her face up to look at her. "Always."

"And you won't die?"

"You know I can't promise that. Only the Lord knows the number of our days, but I plan to be here with you for a long, long time."

"They boil the silkworms. Did you know that?" Hannah looked near tears again. "Sister Nola says that I will have to help dump their cocoons in the boiling water."

301

"Why?"

"So they can unwind the silk from the cocoons, but the worms die."

Elizabeth frowned a little as she tried to understand why Hannah was upset. "We used worms for bait to catch the fish at home."

"But we didn't boil them. It's not right to feed them and pet them and love them and then boil them." Hannah peered up at Elizabeth. "I hid some of the cocoons, but they found them. Sister Willena's face got very red and she wanted to hit me."

"She didn't?"

"Sister Nola wouldn't let her. Sister Nola tries to keep me out of trouble." Hannah looked down at her feet. "Maybe I do have a demon the way they say. Even Sister Nola looks at me as if she sometimes wonders."

"I do not wonder. I know." Elizabeth leaned down to put her face directly in front of Hannah's to be sure Hannah listened to her words. "You do not have a demon. I don't want to hear any more such foolish talk from you," she said firmly.

"I know, but I'm not sure that one will not grow within me if we stay in this place." Hannah looked sad. "The sun was warm on my face today, Elizabeth. Is it not spring yet?"

Elizabeth hesitated. How could she answer her? But there was only the truth. "It is spring. Today."

"Then we can leave?" Hope flooded Hannah's face.

Elizabeth did her best to smile. "In a few days. Let me get things thought out."

"It is spring." Hannah's tears turned to laughter as she pulled away from Elizabeth to spin away from her down the hill toward Sister Nola. "I must tell Sister Nola. It is spring."

It was spring. The air was warm. The grass was growing. Soon bees would be flying between the blooms in the herb gardens. But as Elizabeth followed Hannah down the hill, she felt the cold fingers of winter wrapping around her heart. She could not bear to think of what keeping her promise to Hannah might mean.

27

The day after they laid Brother Issachar to rest, Ethan went back out to prepare the fields for planting. Brother Martin said he must. Go clear the new fields of rock and brush so they could work the ground, sow the seeds, and enjoy the fruits of their labor.

That is what a true Believer did. A true Believer continued in his duty to the society as a whole. A true Believer did not dwell in grief. A Believer was already living the heaven life here at Harmony Hill on this side of the divide, so there was no need for great sorrow when one made the crossing over. A Believer did not wallow in self-pity. A Believer put his hands to work and gave his heart to God.

"I told the Ministry some time back that they were allowing you and Brother Issachar to grow too close. He often spoke as if you were a son instead of a brother. Such worldly relationships can only result in a loss of the peace we seek as Believers." Brother Martin's words had pounded into Ethan's head like a woodpecker's beak into a tree trunk. *Wrong, wrong, wrong. Sin, sin, sin. Trespass, trespass, trespass.*

Brother Martin had stayed by his side after the funeral through the hour of rest following the evening meal and during the meeting where they had labored a song for Brother Issachar. It was as if he had a need to encircle Ethan with his reproofs and his instructions. But even as Brother Martin's words pounded into his ears, Ethan heard another voice in his head. *Follow your heart.* He couldn't do that. He couldn't.

He knew so little of the world. Unlike Elizabeth who had come from that world not so many months ago and who, according to Brother Martin, refused to surrender her worldly ways. He had roundly condemned her for what he called the unseemly outburst at the graveyard. Ethan had barely noticed. The little sister's heartbroken cries had merely been an echo of the pain in his own heart, and he had longed to know the same comfort her sister's arms surely gave her. Comfort he could never feel. Not in the only world he had ever really known. His comfort would have to come from the Eternal Father and Mother Ann. Brother Martin assured him Mother Ann's love was all he needed. All any of them needed.

Elizabeth hadn't been allowed to take part in the laboring of the songs at the meeting. Elder Joseph had publicly censored her for not conducting herself with the proper decorum and discipline expected of a Shaker novitiate. He made her stand up in the meeting and ask forgiveness. She seemed to be under an even darker cloud than Ethan as she stood and spoke the required words. Her voice was full of sorrow, but Ethan thought that had little to do with the confession she was making.

The little sister was also made to stand and confess her wrong. She pulled a long face as she spoke the words, but at the same time her eyes held a twinkle as if at any moment she might spin away in a whirling song of joy. After her confession, Sister Nola rushed her out of the meetinghouse. She wasn't required to sit under the eye of censure all through the meeting as Elizabeth was.

Elizabeth had not looked his way all evening even though he often sneaked glances toward her. She sat upright on her assigned bench and watched the dancers with an impassive face. No other sister dared take rest beside her.

Ethan could not stop thinking about how bereft she looked sitting in the midst of the Shakers as they sang the song that begged Mother Ann to drop down balls of her love from heaven into their midst. Many in the assembly trembled and shook with the love they felt falling down on them, while a few of the sisters and brothers shouted as they fell prostrate on the floor with gifts of the spirit. Ethan had felt nothing. His heart had not been touched by Mother Ann's love.

Now as Ethan prodded the rocks up out of the ground to carry to the sled to be hauled off the field, he wondered why he was never visited with those sorts of gifts of the spirit. Was it because his spirit was weak? That is what Brother Martin or Elder Joseph would tell him. He could not deny that was true this morning. He wanted nothing more than to walk away from his duty, to go into the woods where he had spent so many days such as this with the spring sunshine warm on his face helping Brother Issachar find the perfect tree for whatever he planned to build next.

In the woods alone with Brother Issachar he'd never felt any struggling of the spirit. He knew he could ask any question and see no reproof in Brother Issachar's eyes. He had learned about love from him, and now Ethan needed to walk back along the same paths he'd walked with Brother Issachar to seek those answers again. To find the peace he always had there. Brother Issachar told him not to carry guilt for what Hawk Boyd had done, but how could he not? Brother Issachar told him to listen to his heart, but how could he trust what it was telling him?

He was a Believer. He must act like one. He must do his duty in spite of the fatigue and grief that sat heavy upon him.

The sun was past noon and they had eaten the meal the sisters packed for them when Ethan caught the toe of his shoe on a root that was partially pulled from the ground as he got ready to place a heavy rock on the sled. He stumbled forward and the rock fell on his left hand. He couldn't bite back his cry of pain as he jerked his fingers free.

Elder Hanley who had charge of the men in the field frowned at the sight of Ethan's fingers already beginning to swell. "Could be broken," he said.

"Nay, I don't think so." Ethan bent his fingers. It hurt, but he could move them. He held his hand straight up in the air to lessen the throbbing in his fingers. "It's not so bad. I can keep working."

"Nay. Your willingness to continue in your duty is commendable, but a man's hands are vital to his work. For the good of all, we need your fingers to heal properly." The elder looked at Ethan. "There are others to haul the rocks. Go let Sister Lettie put a splint on your hand."

It was a long walk back across the fields to the Medicine Shop. Sister Lettie shook her head when he showed her his hand. His first two fingers were almost double their size. "You appear to have done a fine job on them, Brother Ethan. A rock, you say."

"I don't think they are broken," he said as he let his eyes

slide around the room to see if Elizabeth was there, but Sister Lettie was alone.

"Try making a fist," Sister Lettie instructed. She watched his fingers intently as Ethan curled them in a bit. He could barely move them, but the effort seemed to please Sister Lettie. "The knuckles work. That is good. Give thanks to Mother Ann it wasn't your right hand. There will be some duties you can perform while they heal, although no more rock hauling for a while."

She mixed some powders in a basin of cool water and pushed his hand down into it.

"Soak for a minute while I fashion a splint. That medicinal bath might ease the pain and decrease the swelling."

The throbbing did quit pumping through his fingers quite so strongly. Ethan watched Sister Lettie for a minute before he said, "You have no help today. Is Sister Elizabeth ill?"

He knew it was a question he should not ask even before Sister Lettie turned a considering look on him.

At first she didn't seem inclined to answer, but then she said, "Nay. I have sent her to harvest some roots for our tonics. My knees are getting too old to do the bending and digging. Plus she needed some time alone to think about her behavior among us." Her eyes narrowed on him. "Perhaps you have need to examine your own thoughts, Brother Ethan."

"Yea, Sister Lettie." He stared down at his hand in the water. "I have much need."

The silence that fell over the room thumped against his ears as painfully as the blood thumping through his injured fingers. He could feel her eyes probing him.

At last she sighed deeply and said, "You have been through a great deal, Brother Ethan. Your spirit is vulnerable now with the hurt you feel over the loss of Brother Issachar. It would be wise for you to vow not to do anything rash during this time of weakness. Your spirit will surely heal the same as your fingers, so don't throw away a lifetime of peace for a few moments of worldly temptations."

Ethan looked up at her. "Would you tell me to follow my heart?"

"Your heart?" She smiled the barest bit. "Nay, better to listen to the spirit in you that led you to sign the Covenant."

"Yea, you speak wisdom."

"As would Brother Issachar if he were still here." She pulled Ethan's hand out of the water and gently dried his fingers before she began binding his hand to the splint.

She sent him out to rest until the evening meal. "Tomorrow you will have a new duty that you can accomplish with only one available wing. But today you have need of rest."

He left the Medicine Shop and started down the pathway toward his room in the Centre House to do her bidding, but when he reached the steps of the white stone building, he walked past without hesitation. He needed Brother Issachar's trees around him. He needed to see the river from atop the palisades. He needed time to grieve and to remember. Else he was going to be so soul-sick he would be of no use to anyone.

Elizabeth breathed in the smell of spring among the trees and accepted the warmth of the sun on her shoulders. She had not bothered with a cape even though the morning air had carried a slight chill. The sleeves of her Shaker dress were long and the kerchief across her shoulders was like wearing a wrap. She touched her cap. It would be heaven to strip off the worrisome thing and let her hair hang free, but she had already broken enough Shaker rules for one week.

And soon enough the dress and cap would be gone. She wondered if the Shakers had kept the dress she'd worn into the village. Would they insist she leave as she'd come even though the dress was ragged and torn? She could not imagine them letting her leave with a Shaker dress. All such were owned in common. One's soiled dress went to the laundry. Another dress took its place. One put no mark of ownership on anything.

But then again, the Shakers might be so anxious to be rid of Elizabeth and the trouble she seemed to bring into their midst that they would shove her out of the village with no worry about the loss of one dress.

Sister Lettie said that Elizabeth was forgiven. That once confession had been made in the meeting, she had a fresh start. But that morning as they knelt for their silent prayers in the biting room and sat down to breakfast, Sister Ruth had looked anything but forgiving as she glared across the table at Elizabeth with eyes narrowed to slits and her mouth twisted in a tight circle of disapproval. Sister Melva had kept her eyes on her plate while she dutifully shoveled the food into her mouth to Shaker her plate.

Sister Evelyn, a new novitiate who had just been joined to their group of four, didn't seem to know what to think as a worried frown creased her brow. Elizabeth could sense the questions in the new sister's mind as she looked between them, but no speaking was allowed in the biting room. It didn't matter. Elizabeth had no answers for her. She didn't even have any answers for herself.

Except that she would keep her promise to Hannah. Whatever answer she had to find, they would leave the Shakers before the week was out. She was only delaying their weeping in order to gather the courage for what must be done. She had need of much courage for she saw no choice but Colton Linley.

She hadn't told Sister Lettie she was leaving, but she thought the good sister knew. That was why she had sent her out into the woods to gather roots. She claimed it was because of the spring season when the roots were beginning their growth. Sister Lettie said their healing power was more potent then. But Elizabeth thought it was really because she hoped Elizabeth would find peace for her spirit and choose to stay in the village.

"You have a gift for mixing the potions, Sister Elizabeth, and a comforting healing touch. If you can only settle your troubled spirit, I could apprentice you to take my place here," Sister Lettie had told her that morning as Elizabeth gathered the digging tools and tied the sack for the roots to her apron. "I'm growing old, and it won't be so many years until I follow our Brother Issachar over. It would be good to leave my sisters and brothers in capable hands."

"If only that could be, I would like that, Sister Lettie. You have taught me much."

"It could be if you will let it be, my child." Sister Lettie said the words, but the doubt had been evident in her eyes that it would ever happen. "Young Sister Hannah will learn more control as she ages. She will understand your need to remain here and perhaps, in time, rejoice in that decision."

"Yea, that could be," Elizabeth had said even though she knew it could not. For while she might like to work with

Sister Lettie a little longer, Elizabeth knew that no matter how much she tried, her spirit would never turn completely to the Shaker way. She wanted to marry, to have children, to live the world's way. A way that she didn't feel was contrary to the Lord's will for her life, as the Shakers believed. The only thing contrary that pierced her heart was the thought of living that life with Colton Linley.

She would not think of that yet. Not until her feet were walking up to his door to beg for shelter for her and Hannah. And even then perhaps she could block it away. She could go through the motions, be the wife he wanted, and somehow find a way to get joy out of each day. She would have children. He had picked her for childbearing. She would love her babies in spite of their father.

She spotted a ginger plant just pushing through the rich earth and knelt to dig out its roots. She took one root and left the other for the plant to regenerate. Her mother had taught her that. Never take it all. Leave some for the years to come.

A mushroom was pushing up through the ground beside the ginger plant. Elizabeth touched its sleek top. Could this be what had taken her father from her and landed her in such a spot? She broke off a piece of the creamy top and smelled it. Her mother had tried to teach her the differences in the mushrooms in the woods, but Elizabeth had never been sure she had learned well enough to trust herself to harvest one. Her father didn't like mushrooms at any rate. He would never eat one. Yet Sister Lettie said he had been poisoned with something fiercely deadly.

A mushroom he got in something in the town or something else? She didn't know where he'd gone in the town or his business there. She did know his business with Colton

Linley as he'd returned from town that morning. To deny the man's claim on her.

Elizabeth stood up and stomped the mushroom into the dirt until it was nothing but a smear on the ground. Tears pushed at her eyes as she stared down at it, but she blinked them away. Stomping the mushroom changed nothing, nor would tears.

She moved on through the trees, searching the forest floor for the roots Sister Lettie needed. The nibs of new growth were shooting up everywhere, but not many had leafed out enough to give clue to what they would grow into. Her mother had taught her to only dig roots she was sure of, for there were other poisons in the woods besides mushrooms.

Now and again she looked up to orient herself. She had promised Sister Lettie to return well before the evening meal. She didn't want the Shakers to have to search for her. She purposely walked the same path she'd taken the day she had gone into the woods to find Hannah last fall, since that trail was familiar to her. So she wasn't surprised when she heard the sound of falling water that had drawn Hannah on that day.

She patted her root bag and looked up at the sun. It was several hours past mid-day. She had a good collection of roots. She should head back. She looked over her shoulder at the way she'd come, but then she followed the sound. It drew her as surely as it had drawn Hannah on that day last fall.

With a smile, Elizabeth thought of how Ethan had run out of the woods to pull her back from the cliff edge for fear she planned to jump to her death. That was something she could not imagine doing, however hard life got. The Lord assigned her days. He would help her live them out. And because she felt his presence, she always felt the feather of hope alive within her.

Her smile got wider as she remembered the abandon with which Ethan had jumped into the pool with Hannah. Thinking back on it now, she realized it was at that moment the bud of love for him had flowered in her heart. She had felt giddy as she took off her shoes and laid her Shaker cap and apron on the rocks before she jumped into the cool water of the pool with them. The full skirt of her Shaker dress floated up like a parasol on top of the water and they had laughed like carefree children as she tried to push it down into the water. She almost laughed now thinking about it.

What had Brother Issachar told her? Follow her heart. If only that was possible.

For a minute when she came out of the trees and saw the Shaker brother standing there on the top of the cliff, she thought it possible she might have conjured him up out of thin air. She hesitated, ready to step back in behind the trees, thinking it couldn't be Ethan. But of course it was. That day last fall, Ethan had told Hannah he had been a child even younger than she when he had first jumped into the pool. Someone had to have shown him the pool. Who else but Brother Issachar?

And now his grief had led him back. The fates had once more thrown them together. Or not. She could still turn and walk away. He had not seen her there. She turned back to the trees, but Brother Issachar's words were in her head again. *Follow your heart.*

Perhaps the Lord had given her this moment of grace before she had to step forward toward the rest of her life. What wrong could there be in saying goodbye? No one else was around. There would be no spying eyes this far away from the village. Even if there were, what could they do to her? She was already leaving the village.

She stopped several feet away from the cliff. Ethan showed no sign of hearing her there. His shoulders were slumped and he was deep in his thoughts. When she spotted the bandage on his hand, Elizabeth took a closer look to be sure it was Ethan and not some other brother standing there. But she knew him even with his back to her.

"Ethan." She spoke in a quiet voice. "I trust you have no thoughts of jumping."

He didn't appear startled by her appearance. Instead he turned to her as if he had been expecting her to come.

28

Ethan stared at Elizabeth. It was almost as if she had stepped out of his thoughts to stand in front of him. He started to reach out to touch her to be sure she was actually there, but he stayed his hand. If she was no more than a vision formed by his desires, he didn't want to do anything to make her image disappear. He wanted her there with him. So much that he ached with the longing.

Although he had walked into the woods knowing she was somewhere in the shadow of the trees, he had no thought of finding her. The woods spread out all around their village and there were many paths she might have followed to seek Sister Lettie's roots. Instead he kept his feet on the trails he knew best in search of something he could never find again— Brother Issachar walking beside him once more.

Yet in some ways he had found Brother Issachar there. So many sights brought memory of his words and even better the echo of his gentle laughter. Ethan's spirit was comforted almost as if Brother Issachar was picking him up after a fall. He'd often done that when, as a boy, Ethan had run through the woods with too much eagerness to pay attention to the rocks and snags underfoot. Brother Issachar never berated him for his carelessness.

Instead he simply helped him up, brushed him off, and encouraged him on. "There are many things that can trip us up as we go through life. And while it could be that you should pay somewhat more attention to those you can easily step over, even so you will find no way to avoid every obstacle along your path. The thing is to not let a little stumble stop you. Just run on, Brother Ethan. There is much to discover."

Run on. That was what Ethan heard Brother Issachar telling him as he walked through the woods. He couldn't undo the fall. He couldn't bring Brother Issachar back to him. Not in this world. He could only walk with him now in thought and memory, but the image in his mind was so strong he could almost feel the touch of Brother Issachar's hand on his shoulder and hear the whisper of his voice on the gentle breeze. *Run on.*

Ethan had ended up on the cliff above the clear pool of water where Brother Issachar had let him swim on the hottest days of summer. Another of the many things Brother Martin had frowned upon that Brother Issachar had allowed. A boy did not learn to be a proper Believer by giving in to the reckless impulse for fun, Brother Martin lectured. There were times for pleasure but only after the work was done and as the Ministry directed. Believers were not to be like those of the world with no thought of anything but the moment at hand.

As he stared down at the water, Ethan remembered the last time he was there at the pool and the abandon with which he had shucked his shoes and hat and jumped into the water with the white-haired little sister. And then Elizabeth had jumped in with the same abandon.

He had never confessed that transgression to Brother Martin. He confessed being there with Elizabeth. He confessed being drawn to her in a carnal way. But he hadn't confessed how his heart had pounded with joy as they shared the feel of the cool water in the pool. He had not touched her, but the same water had wrapped around them both and awakened feelings inside him that were both fearful and delightful.

He was thinking on those very feelings when Elizabeth spoke behind him, so it was little wonder he wasn't sure if his desire had merely brought her image to him. But no, she was really there. Her cap was slightly askew and dirt streaked her apron. A few tendrils of rich brown hair hung down on her neck. She was so beautiful standing there in a shaft of sunlight that it took his breath away.

"Are you all right, Brother Ethan?" She stepped closer to him with a look of concern.

He wished the word "brother" from her tongue. He did not want to be her brother. He forced himself to answer. "Yea, you need not worry. I was not thinking of jumping any more than you were when last we were here together."

"That is good to hear." Her eyes caught on his hand. "You have injured yourself."

He held up the splint. His fingers throbbed in a dull, steady way, but he had been almost glad of the pain as he walked through the trees, remembering Brother Issachar. That throb had been something tactile he could focus on instead of the pain in his soul. "I let a rock fall on my fingers," he said. "An inconvenience. Nothing more. Sister Lettie splinted my hand to aid their healing."

"It is good you let Sister Lettie treat you."

"I could do naught else. It takes a whole man to be a good Shaker." He let his hand fall back to his side. The throb beat stronger in his fingertips.

"So Sister Lettie has taught me."

She dropped her eyes to the ground as was only proper for a Shaker sister. Yet he wanted to step closer and reach out to tip her chin up. He desired her eyes on him.

When he remained quiet, she went on. "I should not have interrupted your silence. You were surely thinking of Brother Issachar."

"Yea, that and other things."

Something in his voice brought her eyes back to his. She looked at him for a long moment as if considering what next to say and finding all her words to be lacking. At last she said, "I will leave you to your mourning."

When she started to turn away, Ethan stopped her. "Don't go. Linger here with me a moment, Elizabeth. I have need to talk with someone."

Her eyes widened a bit, but she didn't look away. "Then shouldn't you seek out Brother Martin or one of the elders?"

"Nay, I misspoke. I don't have the need to talk with just anyone. I have the need to talk with you."

Her eyes flashed as if she had trapped sunlight in them, but then the clouds of worry came back. "I have been trouble enough to Harmony Hill. I wouldn't want to be the cause of trouble for you as well."

"I am already troubled. Since my very first sight of you, I have been troubled in my spirit." He stepped toward her then until they were only a pace apart. He wanted to move that last step closer and put his arms around her. He wanted to pull off her cap and let her hair tumble down on her shoulders. He wanted to cover her lips with his. Brother Martin's voice echoed in his head. *Sin, sin, sin.* He closed thought of Brother Martin out of his mind. "Do I trouble your spirit?"

"Not as yours is troubled." She smiled slightly, a thoughtful yet somehow sad smile, and laid her hand softly on his arm as if that was the most natural thing in the world to do. Perhaps in the world she came from it was. "I am troubled by many things. Decisions that must be made. Sorrows that cannot be avoided, but I am not troubled by the feelings I have for you, Ethan. Only by the problems it has brought you."

"What are your feelings for me?" He hesitated for a bare moment before he added, "Is it love for a brother?"

Her smile grew broader. "I have called you brother as the Shakers require, but it has been in name only. You are not my brother." Her smile faded. She shut her eyes a moment, and he feared she wasn't going to say more. Then she opened her eyes and looked at him with boldness. "But I do love you."

Such joy swept through Ethan that he could imagine whirling in celebration of that joy as he had seen many do in meeting. But that was spiritual joy. And this was carnal joy. Strictly forbidden. He should shake off her hand, shake out of him this carnal desire, but instead he reached back for the joy.

She must have seen the storm of his feelings on his face because she said, "I know you Shakers believe such love is wrong. But to me it is as natural as breathing. It's a gift from the Lord more powerful than any gift I have seen at your meetings. I believe the Lord created us with that gift in mind. He gave us these feelings." She paused a moment as if hoping he might speak. When he did not, she went on, her voice sad now. "I know that our love can never be, but knowing that truth doesn't make my love any less."

He gazed into her eyes and felt he might drown in their beauty, but he didn't know what to say. He couldn't love her. He had signed the Covenant. He'd sworn to only know brotherly love. Not this love of passion. The kind of love Brother Issachar had known for his Eva. The love Adam and Eve had shared once they had been thrown out of the Garden of Eden. Had they shared such love while still in the garden? Or was it as Mother Ann taught that before man's original sin, each child was to be a gift to mankind directly from God without the sin of sexual union?

He had no answers. But then he heard Brother Issachar's words whisper through his mind. *Follow your heart.* And without thinking, without considering the rights or wrongs of his actions, he put his arms around Elizabeth and pulled her to him. She didn't resist, but yielded completely to his embrace. He stared down into her face for a long moment as every inch of his body quivered in anticipation. Then as if it were just as she said and as natural as breathing, he bent his head down and covered her lips with his.

A thousand stars exploded in his soul. He didn't want to ever turn her loose. He knew why Brother Issachar had called for his Eva with such feeling so many years after she'd been gone from him. He could imagine why the garden no longer mattered to Adam. But then Brother Martin edged back into his mind. *Will you surrender your eternal salvation for this moment of pleasure? You are a covenanted Believer. Put this sin of the flesh from you.*

He jerked away from Elizabeth and stepped back. "I cannot do this. I am a Believer."

For a moment, Elizabeth stared at him with her arms still outstretched. Then she lowered her arms as sorrowful acceptance came into her eyes. "Yea, so you are."

He wanted to move back into the circle of her arms, to let that joy explode within him again, but instead he took another step away from her.

She reached toward him with alarm on her face. "Careful. Do not back over the brink, my . . ." She hesitated before saying, "My brother."

He looked down at his feet. The rock was solid under him, but the edge was near. He eased away from it even as he felt he had already fallen from the brink and was spinning through the air with nothing to break his fall.

She was speaking again, her words finding the way through the whirlwind around him. "You need not despair, Ethan. I will not lead you into more sin as you see it. On the morrow I will be gone from your village and you can continue on the Shaker path you have chosen."

"I did not choose it. It chose me."

"How so?" Her forehead wrinkled in a frown as she awaited his answer.

He wanted to explain. He wanted her to understand. "When I was six, I jumped from a raft to get away from some bad men and washed ashore here. Brother Issachar found me on the riverbank and took me back to the village. This life is my destiny."

She let her breath out in a little sigh. "And so I must move on to my destiny."

He looked at her a moment before he asked, "But where will you go?"

She mashed her mouth together and straightened her

shoulders to stand taller. The lines of her face grew determined until none of the softness that had been there earlier remained. "There is one who will take us in."

"You will go to the world then." He could hardly bear the thought of her gone forever from his sight. If only there was another way. A way without sin. "I would that you could stay here. Become a Believer."

"Nay, that is not what you want." Her eyes didn't waver on him as she spoke.

He could not deny the truth of her words. She knew his heart. That was not what he wanted. What he wanted could not be.

When he stayed silent, she went on. "You must do what you must do and so must I." She turned away from him then to start across the clearing toward the trees.

"I know nothing of the world," he called after her with despair.

She stopped and looked back to him. She smiled a little as she said, "You have no reason for concern. You will have no need of such knowledge here among the Shakers. May you know a life of peace and goodness."

"Yea, as can you," he said. "If you stay among us."

"No, I have desires in my heart that are unfitting a Shaker. It cannot be."

She shook her head sadly and turned back toward the woods. He watched her all the way across the clearing. She moved with purpose, never once looking back. He stared long at the spot where she disappeared into the trees.

29

The shadows under the trees were deepening as Elizabeth hurried back through the woods to the village. She made her feet keep moving forward as she searched out her trail, even though all she really wanted to do was sit down on a tree stump and just give in to the sadness in her heart.

But no, she had to fulfill her duty to the Shakers and then she would carry out her duty to Hannah. She had always been dutiful. A dutiful daughter. A dutiful sister. With much prayer and forbearance she would force herself to become a dutiful wife to Colton Linley. She shuddered at the thought as the shadows seemed to move from under the trees to enfold and darken her soul. But she could not allow her feet to stray off her path.

At the same time, she didn't try to keep her thoughts from straying back to Ethan. She loved him. She wasn't ashamed of admitting that love to him. Nor was she ashamed of the kiss they shared.

She had followed her heart as Brother Issachar had told her to do, and she had no regrets. She would carry that feeling of complete surrender to the love in her heart to her grave. It was a treasure, a gift that would help her through the days ahead. She might never again be lifted up and swept away by love, but at least she had experienced how love was meant to feel.

The echo of Ethan's words, *I am a Believer*, rang over and over in her head until she had no doubts she was choosing her only possible path in leaving the Shakers. There had been moments since Brother Issachar's funeral when she had wondered if she might continue with the Shakers yet a little longer. With time, Hannah would surely forgive her and understand why going to Colton was a sacrifice too hard for Elizabeth to make. But now the sacrifice was for more than Hannah. It was also for Ethan.

If she truly loved Ethan as she'd told him, then she couldn't remain here and be a stumbling block to his peace. She was a temptation to him. A cause of sin to him as a Believer. Their love was not a sin. The Shakers would never convince her of that, but though that truth was solid in her heart, the opposite feeling was just as solidly in Ethan's mind. In every Believer's mind. If Ethan confessed their meeting in the woods, some kind of chastisement would follow.

She hoped he wouldn't speak of it. Not because she was worried about anything the Shakers might do to her or even of how it might lessen Ethan's standing among them, but because she wanted him to treasure the memory of their kiss and not cheapen it by throwing it out into one of the Shaker meetings for the whole of the body of Believers to stomp out in one of their exercises.

Back at the village, Sister Lettie studied Elizabeth's face with a look of concern as she took the roots Elizabeth held out to her, but she didn't question her. Instead she gently pulled Elizabeth's finds out of the bag and brushed the dirt from them with pleasure. "I knew you would have a gift for finding the healing roots." Her eyes came back to Elizabeth. "You must not allow this gift to die within you."

Elizabeth tried to push a smile out on her face, but how could she smile when she might never again have the chance to be near this woman? She wanted to grab Sister Lettie and hug her. She wanted to lay her head on her shoulder and weep. But she dared not let that first tear slide out of her eyes. Else she might never stop. "I will long remember your teachings and use them any time I can be of help to others."

Sister Lettie mashed her mouth together and closed her eyes for a moment as if willing away her own tears before she reached for Elizabeth's hand and said, "I will miss you, my sister."

Elizabeth caught her hand. "As I will you, Sister Lettie. But I'll carry your loving spirit away within my heart."

Sister Lettie squeezed Elizabeth's hand. "I will pray for you."

Elizabeth looked at her kind face with wrinkles deep around her eyes that spoke more of smiles than frowns. "Please do not condemn me when I'm gone as I know others among you will do."

"Nay, my sister, I would never condemn you. My prayers will lift you up with love."

"That I see the error of my ways?"

"Nay." Sister Lettie shook Elizabeth's hand a bit. "That you will find peace on whatever path you choose. And that you will always know you are loved by the Eternal Father. That knowledge and the gift to be simple, to accept the spirit in a childlike way, will carry you through many troubles."

"May it be true." Elizabeth didn't want to turn loose of Sister Lettie's hand. She wanted to keep her close a little longer. "I do have faith. Just not in the Shaker way as you do."

"Yea, I have seen that. Perhaps someday your feet will turn back to the road to our village. Until then, where will you go?"

"There is a man who will take Hannah and me in."

Sister Lettie's forehead wrinkled in a frown. "Surely you do not speak of that man who tried to carry you away, Sister Elizabeth. Not the one who brings fearful dread to your eyes."

When Elizabeth simply met her eyes without answering, Sister Lettie went on. "You must find another way. You know not what that man might be capable of."

"I see no other way."

Sister Lettie searched her face a moment before she said, "Oh, my sister, the world outside of Harmony Hill can be a fearsome place, but even so, surely there can be another way." She pulled her close in an embrace. She smelled of rose hips and ginger root. "Pray the Lord will lead you to that other way."

Elizabeth did pray as Sister Lettie said while going through the motions of the rest of the Shaker day. In their biting room where the only sounds were the thud of bowls being set down on the wooden tables and the clanking of forks against plates as they ate in the required silence, she avoided Sister Ruth's disapproving stare and kept a prayer circling in her thoughts as she cleaned her plate. She prayed through the time of rest. She prayed as she went through the motions of exercising the dances in the meetinghouse. She did not once allow her eyes to seek out Ethan. That door was closed. It was only a matter of hours before she must walk through the only door open to her in spite of what Sister Lettie said. In spite of her prayers.

Pray believing. Her mother had taught Elizabeth that long before, but then Elizabeth had prayed for her mother. She had believed the Lord would heal her. He had not. Elizabeth hadn't lost her faith after her mother's death, but she had lost her idea of a fairy-tale God who granted her every petition. She had searched the Scriptures and found no passage to say those of faith would not face hardships, but she had seen many promises that the Lord would walk with the faithful through all those troubles. *Yea, though I walk through the valley of the shadow of death, I will fear no evil: for thou art with me.* That is what she had to pray believing.

She did seek out Payton's eyes, but her brother kept his face turned from her. She only wanted to say goodbye. She watched as he did the turns and spins in the dances with purpose and devotion. His face was lit with belief as he listened to Elder Joseph. He had shaken off his ties to the world. His ties to her and Hannah. And even in her sadness, she knew it was better to leave him in peace and not try to tug him away from his new beliefs.

He was young, only sixteen. He wouldn't be allowed to sign the Covenant of Belief until he was twenty-one. Before then, he might question his place here, but she couldn't question it for him. When he did finally meet her eyes as they passed in the lines of one of the dances, she smiled and pushed loving acceptance his way. He looked relieved as he moved past her.

Hannah edged close to her as one of the exercises ended and Elizabeth whispered, "Tomorrow."

Hannah's eyes brightened like a newly lit lamp. Then she looked over at Payton and back at Elizabeth. Elizabeth shook her head a bit, and the light dimmed in Hannah's eyes before she hurried back to Sister Nola's side to be the obedient little sister one more night.

With the decision made, Elizabeth knelt by the narrow Shaker cot in her sleeping room and didn't ask the Lord for any favors other than endurance. As she stretched out on the bed, she refused to let her mind sift through sorrows or vain hopes. There was no turning back. She willed herself to sleep.

At first when she heard Hannah whispering her name, she thought it must be a dream. But no, the hands gripping her arm and shaking her awake were real. Enough moonlight filtered in through the window that Elizabeth could see Hannah's face above her.

"Wake up, Elizabeth. Wake up!" she whispered urgently. Then when she saw Elizabeth's eyes opening. "You have to believe me. I didn't do it."

"You didn't do what?" Elizabeth whispered back as she raised her head up to look around. All the other sisters lay still in slumber.

"The fire. I didn't do it. Not this time. I was thinking about it, but not your house. I would have never done that."

Elizabeth came instantly awake at the word "fire."

"There were men. They had torches." Hannah was almost crying now. "I couldn't see what they were doing, but then the house was on fire and the men got on their horses and rode away."

"What house?"

"This one. We have to get out. We might burn up."

Elizabeth threw back her cover and sat up. She smelled smoke. "Run, Hannah, to the meetinghouse and ring the bell."

"What if I can't reach the rope?"

"Climb on something."

"You have to come with me." Hannah pulled on Elizabeth's nightdress.

"I will come after I wake the others. Now do as I say. Run." She gave Hannah a little push toward the door. Some of the sisters in the beds around them were stirring. Elizabeth pulled her dress on over her nightdress as she spoke to them. "Our house is on fire. We must get everyone out."

Sister Alice, in the bed next to Elizabeth, threw off her covers and jumped to her feet to begin shaking the others awake. Elizabeth snatched up her shoes and ran barefoot out into the hallway. Smoke rising up from the bottom floor stung her eyes as she ran straight across to the brothers' side of the house to the room where Elder Homer slept. She banged on the door and shouted "fire." Other doors were opening now as the house roused. Elder Homer came out of his room, pulling his suspenders up over his shoulders, and sent two of the younger brothers up to the third floor to be sure all were awake there.

At the first clang of the meeting bell, Elizabeth breathed easier. Hannah was safely away from the fire. But what had she meant, she didn't do it this time? Elizabeth shook the question away. There wasn't time to worry about that now. She joined the line of sisters moving down the stairs toward the door. Some like Elizabeth had pulled on their dresses. Others still wore their white nightclothes and caps. Scattered among them were a few carrying candles with flames that flickered high, then low in the drafts and threw elongated shadows on the walls.

Outside the smoke swirled around from the back of the building where a bucket brigade was already forming to fight the flames climbing out of the kitchen up the back wall. Elizabeth slipped on her shoes and joined the line of sisters passing buckets of water from the pipes that carried water to the Gathering Family house. Another line of brothers formed at their side. With their house aflame, they still kept their division of sexes. Even before the men came running from the other houses, they were winning the battle against the fire.

The last of the flames sputtered and died in the onslaught of water from the Shaker buckets. In the light of the moon, a black scar climbed toward the roof on the outside wall of the house, while in one spot near the foundation and the kitchen door, a charred hole gaped. A few of the brethren went inside to be sure no live sparks remained in the kitchen. Others prodded at the exposed timbers to unearth any hidden embers. The thick double walls of the house that kept heat trapped within it in the winter and out in the summer also kept the damaged wall standing.

With smoke hanging heavy in the air, Elizabeth looked around for Hannah. She spotted Ethan, who was scanning the crowd as though looking for one in particular. For a second her eyes stilled on him, but then she moved her eyes on in search of Hannah. What difference would it make if she were the one his eyes sought? That would change nothing.

Payton was also there, staring at the charred wall. Elizabeth couldn't see his face well in the moonlight, but she didn't need to in order to guess the worry that must be building in him. There had been too many fires since they had come to

Harmony Hill. Whispers would start, perhaps blaming him. So many fires could be no mere coincidence. Not with the talk already circling through the village of how their cabin had burned before they came to Harmony Hill.

Payton had nothing to do with the fire. Hannah had seen men on horses. Perhaps the ruffians who had invaded their house in the fall with Colton Linley.

Where was Hannah? Had she slipped back into the Children's House and into her bed beside the sleeping Sister Nola who perhaps would not wonder why she reeked of smoke? But of course, that could not be. The ringing of the meetinghouse bell had emptied out all of the houses. Elizabeth spotted Sister Nola moving in and out of the Shakers looking as intently for Hannah as she was.

Sister Ruth found Hannah first. With her hand twisted in the collar of Hannah's dress, she propelled her toward Elder Joseph.

"Let me go," Hannah yelled as she yanked at her collar and kicked back toward Sister Ruth. "I didn't do it. Let me go!" She had lost her cap and the moonlight bounced off her white curls.

30

"Here is the cause of our trouble." Sister Ruth shoved Hannah so hard toward Elder Joseph that Hannah stumbled and fell on her hands and knees.

Hannah stared up at the elder towering over her and scrambled to her feet. "I didn't do it," she said in a voice not quite so loud now.

Elizabeth pushed through the Shakers toward Hannah, but Elder Joseph held out his hand to stop her. "Wait."

To be sure she obeyed the elder's command, two of the sisters grabbed her arms and held her. Elizabeth might have been able to jerk free of them, but others stood ready to take their place. She couldn't fight them all. "I am here, Hannah," she called softly.

Hannah looked around at her. "Tell them I didn't do it, Elizabeth." There were tears in her voice. "Tell them."

Elder Joseph waved Elizabeth to silence and turned back to Hannah. "You have no need to be frightened, my child," he said in a kind voice. "We won't harm you. What is it that you didn't do?"

"The fire. I didn't start the fire." Hannah's voice sounded very small.

"Why would we think you did?"

"She thinks I did." Hannah glared over at Sister Ruth. "She thinks I have a demon. They all think I have a demon." Hannah swept the Shakers around her with defiant eyes, but then the defiance disappeared when she saw Sister Nola. "All but Sister Nola. She doesn't."

Elder Joseph looked at Sister Ruth. "Speak, Sister Ruth. What is the meaning of all this?"

Sister Ruth pulled back her shoulders and stepped forward. She seemed to relish being the center of attention. "I have been watching. It is part of my duty. To watch to be sure the rules are not broken. The child wanders at night. She knows no discipline. And she carries a lantern."

"Perhaps to see," Elder Joseph suggested.

"Nay, she covers it with a towel. She carries it to set fires. Remember the fire at the West Family bathhouse? That was started with just such a lantern."

Hannah looked down at her feet. Elizabeth's heart sank as she saw the guilt on Hannah's face. "You didn't, Hannah. Surely you didn't," she said.

Hannah looked up at her. "I didn't start the first two fires, but I heard people talking that maybe Payton had. I knew he didn't, but I thought it good for them to think he did. I wanted them to make Payton leave with us. So I set fire to the bathhouse. Everybody was in bed. No one was taking a bath. But my fire didn't burn. It just fizzled out." Big tears rolled down Hannah's cheeks. "I'm sorry, Elizabeth. I know that was a bad thing to do, but I wanted us to be together. I didn't want to lose Payton like we lost our father."

When Elizabeth reached out her arms toward Hannah, the two sisters who had been holding her turned loose. Hannah ran into her embrace. The other Shakers stepped back away from them until they were alone in the middle of a circle with the elder and Sister Ruth.

"See. It is as I said," Sister Ruth declared with satisfaction.

Elizabeth glared over the top of Hannah's head at her. "No, it is not as you say. If not for Hannah seeing the men set the fire and raising the alarm, the house might be burned to the ground and we might not be standing here unharmed. You should be thanking her instead of condemning her." She tightened her arms around Hannah.

Sister Ruth started to speak again, but Elder Joseph stopped her with a look before he turned back to Elizabeth. "There is truth in your words. On the other hand, we cannot condone disobedience, and the child has lacked greatly in obedience since she has come into our midst."

"She has a demon. They both do," Sister Ruth said. Around her several of the Shakers pushed their hands out flat toward Elizabeth and Hannah to ward off their evil.

"Are there any among you to speak for these sisters?" Elder Joseph asked.

There was a moment of silence before Sister Nola stepped forward. "The young one has much love to give."

"Undisciplined love," Sister Josephine spoke up behind her with no charity in her voice.

"But much love," Sister Nola insisted. "She even loved the silkworms. Her heart is pure. There is nothing of the devil in her."

Sister Lettie pushed through to the front of the circle

around them. "Sister Elizabeth shows much healing skill. She has a compassionate heart and is faithful to her duty."

Elizabeth sent Sister Lettie a grateful look. She didn't know why it mattered to her that the Shakers stood ready to condemn her when she had already determined to leave them come morning, but it did.

"Faithful." Sister Ruth spat out the word. "Nay, she is only faithful to her own desires. She has refused to shed the carnal ways of the world. She flaunts the outward beauty of her face and cares not who she might lead astray among us."

"Harsh words, Sister Ruth," the elder said. "Have you proof of this?"

"Nothing I can hold in my hands, but I know it is true." Sister Ruth did not meet the elder's eyes, but instead swept her eyes around those in the circle surrounding them. "You can look at her and see it is true."

Elizabeth shut her eyes as an uneasy murmur rippled through the Shakers. She didn't want to take the chance that she might let her eyes stray toward Ethan and condemn him in front of his brothers and sisters by her look.

She opened her eyes when she heard Payton's voice. "My sisters of the world and I came here seeking food and shelter after the death of our father and in your kindness you took us in. I fought against coming here, but it was surely Mother Ann's guidance that caused Sister Elizabeth to insist our paths led here. While they have not accepted the Shaker way as I have, they mean you no harm. I ask you to forgive them as you have already forgiven me."

Hannah went stiff against Elizabeth as Payton spoke. Then she pulled away from Elizabeth to peer up at her. "He is one of them. No longer our brother," she said sadly.

"No, that isn't true," Elizabeth whispered as she smiled down at her. "He will always be our brother. Just in a different way. So be brave. No more tears." She wiped the tears off Hannah's cheeks with her fingertips.

She kept her arm around Hannah as she turned her to her side so that they were both facing the elder. "Worry not about condemning or forgiving us. We had already planned to leave your village when day dawned on the morrow. Just let us go in peace and with the clothes we wear. That is more than we brought into your village, but we have worked for the good of all in the months since."

The elder looked glad to be relieved of making judgment on them as he said, "We force none to stay with us if the pull of the world is too great, but we sorrow for all who slip back into its carnal pit of sin."

A few woes rose from among the Believers as they began stomping their feet to get rid of any evil that might leak off Elizabeth and infect them.

"We cannot let you return to sleep with those who believe. You will stay the rest of the night in the tramp room. In the morning we will bring your meal and then you can be on your way. May the Eternal Father convict you of the error of your ways before it is too late."

Elizabeth stiffened her back and clutched Hannah's shoulder as one of the brethren came over to lead them to the farm deacon's building where the tramp room was located. Hannah jerked free of Elizabeth's hold and ran to wrap her arms around Payton's waist. He hesitated, but then put his arms around her. Elizabeth thought there were tears in his eyes when Hannah pulled away from him to run back to her.

They walked through a gauntlet of woes and hands pushing

337

against them. The stomping increased in frenzy until the ground shook. Sister Ruth looked at her with triumph as she stomped her feet. Sister Lettie reached to touch her hand. Sister Melva stood quietly with her head bowed, perhaps in prayer. Tears ran unchecked down Sister Nola's cheeks.

And there at the end before they passed from among the Shakers was Ethan. He stood silent and unmoving as he watched them. She let her eyes dwell on his face one last time to set his image in her heart and mind. Then she lifted her chin and turned her eyes forward once more.

❧

Ethan hardly heard the commotion going on around him as Elizabeth and the little white-haired sister followed Brother Millward toward the Farm Deacon's Shop. He had willed her to look at him and she had. One long look of goodbye.

That was as it had to be. He was a Believer. It would be good that she was gone from them. She would find her way in the world and he would continue with the Believers. As it had to be. Perhaps in time he would even forget the way her lips had felt under his.

Brother Martin stepped up beside him. "Are you in pain from your hand, Brother Ethan?"

Ethan lifted up his hand to look at the splint. "Nay, it is not anything I cannot bear."

"Then perhaps the pain on your face is for some other reason." Brother Martin's eyes poked into him. "It might be well if you were stomping down the temptation that threatens to destroy your peace and shaking free of the carnal desires that have no place in a Believer's heart."

"Yea, Brother Martin." Ethan stomped his feet and shook

his arms and hands. The mashed fingers throbbed when he shook them, but instead of surrendering to the pain, he only shook them harder. Brother Martin looked pleased. He saw only the outward display of obedience. He didn't see how inwardly the movements meant nothing to Ethan. Inwardly his heart was chasing after Elizabeth, hoping to slip into the Farm Deacon's Shop and stay with her. Hoping that she would carry memory of his love away with her.

"Do you have the need to make confession of some sin?" Brother Martin asked.

"Yea, I often err and need to clear my soul of sin." Ethan said the words out of habit. He had no intention of confessing anything about Elizabeth. Not yet.

"Unconfessed sin is a burden that will weigh down your heart and keep you from proper worship where you must shake off all pride, lust, self-will. Everything that hinders the free circulation of the pure spirit of Mother Ann. Only then, when you have done thus, will you know true freedom from all worldly things as you put your hands to work here at Harmony Hill."

"Yea, I will do as you say, Brother Martin."

"That is good to hear, my brother." He finally looked as if he believed Ethan. "You must rid your mind of all thoughts of our former sister. She has made her decision for evil and you have made yours for good. That is well."

He wanted to defend her, but instead he said, "Yea, it is as it has to be."

"Good." Brother Martin put his hand on Ethan's shoulder for a moment before he turned back toward the Centre House. "Let us go rest until the morning. I have no doubt there will be no more midnight fires."

"The little sister said men of the world set the fire."

"And you believed her?"

"She seems to be committed to the truth," Ethan said.

"What about the fire she started at the West Family bath-house?"

"She did not lie about it. I think she spoke the truth. That men of the world tried to burn the Gathering Family house." Ethan didn't know why he defended the child when he had not defended Elizabeth, but he didn't back down from his words as he braced himself for Brother Martin's displeasure.

But Brother Martin didn't disagree with him. "You could be right. We will need to keep watch. But even so, those men seem to have followed our former sister into our midst. You know yourself of the man who tried to carry the fallen one away. So Sister Ruth was right about them being the cause of the trouble, even if she did step too far from reason saying they had demons. Of course it is not so far wrong to call unsurrendered worldly desires demons. Such desires can torment a soul and lead only to destruction."

Destruction. Was that where he was headed? If only he could have done as Brother Issachar said. If only he could have found the courage to follow his heart. Then he could be there with Elizabeth waiting for the morning. But what did he know of the world except that every time he ventured into it tragedy awaited?

31

Elizabeth stared out the small window of the tramp room and dreaded the first fingers of dawn lighting up the sky while Hannah slept peacefully against her side on the narrow bed. It had not bothered Hannah to have the Shakers lock them in, but the turning of the key had seemed to echo in Elizabeth's spirit.

She was a prisoner. And while the Shakers were stern but kindly captors, she knew that when the door opened and she was let out to begin her new path, her next captor had no kindness. Colton had slept in this room, had been a prisoner for a night there himself once. Sister Melva had told her so, and it was as if his presence lingered there yet to leer at her from the dark corners of the room. She would never know freedom again.

As the sun began to push light up over the eastern horizon, the rising bell rang. All across the village, the Shaker sisters and brethren were rising for another day of work and worship. Yesterday she had been one of them, hurrying to dress

341

and make her way to Sister Lettie's Medicine Shop. Today she could only sit and wait for the door to be opened.

Sister Melva brought them breakfast shortly after the bell rang for the morning meal. Along with the meal she brought two clean dresses and underclothing for them to wear away for the village. She fussed over the dresses as she laid them out on the bed. "It doesn't have the collar or the cap. Eldress Rosellen said you wouldn't need those in the world, but the material is good. It will last you many months."

"Thank you." Elizabeth touched the skirt of one of the dresses and felt a prickling of tears in her eyes. "That is very generous of you."

"Nay, it's a necessary gift. We couldn't send you away naked." Sister Melva looked down a moment before she went on. "We would that you would stay. Become one of us."

Hannah moved over in front of Elizabeth and gave Sister Melva a hard look as if fearful Elizabeth would be swayed by the sister's talk.

Sister Melva sighed. "But I see that is not to be."

"Nay," Elizabeth said, falling without thinking into the Shaker talk. "But I won't forget your kindness to me. To us."

After they ate the food and donned the clean clothes, Sister Melva escorted them out of the Farm Deacon's Shop. There was only one door instead of the two in most of the buildings. "Normally this building is used solely by the brethren, so there was no need for two doors, but the Ministry made an exception for this day since they could hardly have one of the brethren bringing you underclothing." A flush crept up into Sister Melva's cheeks. "That would have been unseemly."

She didn't walk down the road with them, but stood on the steps to watch them go. They hadn't gone far when Sister Nola came rushing after them. She hugged Hannah and kissed the top of her curls set free now without a cap. "I will miss you, Sister Hannah, and be sure that I have forgiven you for all the times you ran away and didn't do as you were told."

"Thank you, Sister Nola. I wish I could have been a Shaker for you," Hannah said.

"So do I, but perhaps you'll come back someday and see that the Shaker life is the good life. Without the sorrows that may await you in the world."

Hannah looked up at her solemnly. "There are sorrows everywhere. Brother Issachar died."

"Yea, but it was one of the world who attacked him and caused his death."

"I was sorrowful here," Hannah said.

"Yea, so you were. You never bent your spirit to the Shaker way. And perhaps as you say, you could not." Sister Nola sighed and shook her head before she pulled two folded pieces of silk out of her apron pocket. "Here, take these. They are a gift from the silkworms and the sisters here."

Hannah eyed the squares of silk in Sister Nola's hand. "Did you boil the silkworms to get the threads?"

"Nay, not the worms. The cocoons. Their silk threads will exist much longer in these handkerchiefs than they would have without our industry. A sacrifice for something good and useful."

Elizabeth silently willed Hannah to take the proffered gift, but she spoke no word aloud.

"Like the fishing worms and crickets Father used to catch fish for our supper," Hannah said softly as she took the handkerchiefs. "Thank you, Sister Nola. I will think of you and remember the silkworms when I feel these against my skin."

Again they moved on, leaving Sister Nola behind. They had already passed the West Family house when Payton stepped out from behind a tree into their path. Hannah ran to him. "Oh, Payton, you decided to go with us."

"Nay, I must stay here. It is my path," Payton said. "But I wanted to say goodbye and give you this." He pulled a small carved heart out of his pocket and laid it in Hannah's palm. "Smell it."

Hannah put it to her nose. "It smells of the woods."

"It's red cedar. Here, I have one for you too, Elizabeth." He reached into his pocket again.

She took it with a smile. He was more her brother than he'd been since they came into the Shaker village. "But don't the Shakers frown on using time to make something such as this with no useful purpose?"

"Yea, but Brother Micah said I could. That he understood how I still felt pulls toward you both as my sisters of the world and that this might be a way to heal all our hearts. Brother Micah let me work by lamplight before the sun came up so that I could carve them out of a piece of scrap wood for you."

Elizabeth closed her hand around the small heart. It felt warm in her fist. "I have nothing to give you in return." Then she reached out and touched his chest over his heart. "Nothing but my love and my desire for your happiness here."

Hannah sniffled a little and leaned against Elizabeth as she stared up at Payton.

"I'm content here, Elizabeth. The wood comes alive under my carving tools. There is the spirit in the meetings. There is Brother Micah. There's much food and no need for worry about a place to stay warm. I'm sheltered here in body and soul."

"You may make many useful things here, Payton. But you will never make anything more cherished than this." Elizabeth put her hand clasping the heart against her chest. "I'll write to you. The Ministry allows that."

He hesitated as if he didn't want them to walk away. "Where will you go?"

"Colton will take us in. He has told me as much."

"Nay!" A look of alarm spread over Payton's face. "You cannot do that."

"I will do what has to be done." Elizabeth set her mouth in a determined line.

"But are you sure it must be done? I've been praying." He looked a little shy to admit his prayers, but he went on. "I prayed while I did the carvings this dawn. I prayed to the Eternal Father and Mother Ann for you. And for Hannah."

"I've been praying too, but I see no other answer."

"That's because your fear of Colton blinds your eyes."

"Are you saying your eyes are open? That you have answers? A place for Hannah and me."

"Nay, not since you won't stay here," Payton admitted. "Not clear answers, but I kept seeing Aristotle as I prayed. Perhaps he was my answer. The man who took him in surely must have a generous heart."

"Taking in a dog and taking in two females are quite different things," Elizabeth said even as hope wanted to flutter its wings and awaken inside her. Could there be a way besides Colton?

"True enough, but after we came here, I once spoke with Brother Ethan about what became of Aristotle after he and Brother Issachar took him into the town. He said they gave Aristotle to a man who runs a store and also rents a sleeping room to travelers."

"That's all well and good, but we have no money to pay for a sleeping room," Elizabeth said.

Hannah leaned against her, drawing circles in the dirt pathway with the toe of her sturdy Shaker shoe.

"I know that. But he might need a maid or help in his store. You can't just throw yourself away on Colton without at least trying to find another way."

He looked so worried that Elizabeth pushed a smile out on her face and pulled him toward her for one last hug with Hannah in between them. "You are a good brother. I'll miss you." She blinked back tears as she stepped away from him.

He looked near tears himself. "I'm sorry I can't go with you."

"So am I, Payton." She touched his cheek. "But I brought you here. Now it seems I must leave you here."

"You don't have to go. You could stay." His voice was small, his child's voice again.

"No, just as you can't go with us, neither can we stay with you. Goodbye, Payton."

Hannah echoed her goodbye and the two of them started on down the road out of the Shaker village.

"Remember Aristotle," Payton called after them. "Brother Ethan said the man was kind for one of the world. Even to a Believer."

She stopped and looked back at him. "Tell Ethan—Brother Ethan," she corrected and then hesitated as she searched among the words in her head for the proper ones. "Tell him that I hope his pathway here is always free of any stones to trip him up and that I'm sorry if I was such a stumbling block for this brief time."

Payton looked at her a moment before he nodded. "I'll

tell him so when I can." He hesitated. "I won't forget my sisters."

"Nor will we forget our brother. We have your heart." Elizabeth held up her hand with the heart clasped tightly in it. Hannah did the same as tears rolled down her cheeks. Then with nothing more to say, no more reason to delay their leaving, they left Payton behind.

It seemed only right that the last place they passed before leaving the village was the graveyard where Issachar had been laid to rest two days before. *Follow your heart.* She hoped he and his Eva were dancing in heaven.

They were almost past the white plank fences around the graveyard when a Shaker brother moved out from behind a tree in the far corner near Issachar's grave. He stood stock still and watched her. Even before she spotted the splint on his hand, she knew it was Ethan. How could she not know the man she loved?

She didn't let her eyes linger on him. She kept moving down the road, keeping up with Hannah. She would not stop. She could not stop. But she felt his eyes following her, and she knew she was carrying part of him away with her. She wondered how long it would be before he could forget her. Before his dedication to his duty as a Believer pushed her memory from his mind. She wanted to look over her shoulder. She wanted to see him one last time, but she kept her eyes on the road ahead.

When they passed the last Shaker fence post, Hannah jumped up into the air and then almost danced down the road. Elizabeth couldn't keep from smiling at her while in fact she felt some of the same euphoria sweeping through her. She pulled out the pins that had held her hair neatly up off her neck and shook it down around her shoulders. No more would she have to hide her hair. No more would she have to pretend to listen to Sister Ruth. No more would she have to practice the dances that were supposed to bring her closer to the Lord. No more would she have to keep her eyes downcast while she pretended to be obedient to the Shaker will. And her feet wanted to dance like Hannah's.

She ran to catch up with her little sister where they held hands and circled around in the road like two children at play. "It's rather contrary of us," she told Hannah. "We didn't want to dance the Shaker dances, but now we dance."

Hannah laughed out loud. "Those were their dances. These are our dances. Our spring dance." She turned her face up to the sun and spun around in one more circle. Then the smile faded away on Hannah's face as she looked over at Elizabeth. "But I don't wish the sorrow to go from my heart to yours. Do we have to go to Mr. Linley?"

"I don't love Mr. Linley, but perhaps he's not so bad. Our father often went to visit him. Colton said he saw Father on that day he came home from town so sick."

"And then he died," Hannah said.

Sister Lettie's words popped into Elizabeth's head. *It was poison. That is the only thing that would take one in such health so quickly.* "Colton wouldn't have poisoned our father," she said as much to herself as to Hannah.

"He set the fire to burn down the house where you slept."

"What makes you say that?" Elizabeth frowned at Hannah as she waited for her answer.

"I saw him. In the moonlight."

"Why didn't you tell Elder Joseph or one of the sisters?"

"They wouldn't have believed me. They thought I set the

fire. That it was the demon in me. But it wasn't the demon in me. It was the demon in those men. One of them was Mr. Linley." Hannah looked very sure of her words.

"Did he see you?" Elizabeth asked as more of Sister Lettie's words came to mind. *You know not what that man is capable of.* He'd been married twice before. The first wife had died in childbirth and the second wife had run home to her family in Virginia. Or so Colton said.

"I don't think so. I stayed to the shadows until they got on their horses." Hannah came and stood right in front of Elizabeth. "But he will see me if we go to him. He will see both of us."

Icy fingers of fear walked up Elizabeth's spine as she stared down at Hannah. It was one thing to give herself to a man who had little kindness in his heart. It was another to give herself to a man who had such little respect for the life of others that he was ready to snuff it out. Her own life if he had been the one to set fire to the house where she slept, as Hannah said. And perhaps her father's life as well. Had he not told her the day they buried their father that her father had drunk some cider with him?

The sound of horses' hooves came from down the road, and without even thinking about it, Elizabeth grabbed Hannah's arm and pulled her out of sight into the trees. It wasn't Colton, but just the thought that it might be washed fear through her, until now with the horses gone and nothing but silence around them, she had to lean against a tree to gather the strength to keep standing.

Hannah put her arms around Elizabeth's waist. "We can live in the woods. We'll build a shelter out of tree limbs like the settlers did when they first came across the Wilderness

Trail. Soon there will be berries, and you know which roots we can eat." Her face was animated. "We can catch fish and steal turkey eggs from their nests."

Elizabeth managed to smile down at her. "Two wood nymphs."

"That would be better than having to worry about burning up in our beds."

Elizabeth stared off into the trees. Didn't the Bible say the Lord would provide for his children? That he would supply the needs of those who trusted in him. But it didn't always tell how that would happen. One prayed and one got answers. She remembered Payton's prayers for them and felt hope opening up its wings inside her. At least they would have a destination.

Perhaps the man in his kindness would allow them to stay for a few days in exchange for their labor in his store. Or they might find a way to live in the woods through the spring and summer where she could gather roots for sale. Sister Lettie said she had a gift for finding such. It sounded like a desperate plan, but no more desperate than going to Colton with the suspicion awake within her that he could have fed her father poison.

The Lord clothed the world in beauty with flowers and trees and put ample food out for the birds to find each day. Would he not do the same for her and Hannah? Elizabeth ran her hands down the sturdy material of the skirt of her dress. Had he not already begun to supply their needs?

She touched Hannah's springing curls and said, "Let's go see if Aristotle remembers us."

32

They reached Harrodsburg, the settlement closest to the Shaker village, in the middle of the afternoon in spite of stepping away from the road whenever they heard horses. They did not see Colton.

In town, they could no longer avoid people, but at least if Colton saw them, he wouldn't be able to defy the law with so many witnesses on the street. They walked past the courthouse. Somewhere inside would be the sheriff who had come out to Harmony Hill after Colton and his cohorts had threatened the Shaker women last fall. He had seemed a fair-minded man interested in keeping the peace.

Elizabeth hesitated, wondering if she should go in the courthouse and seek the sheriff to tell him about Colton setting fire to the Shakers' house and of her suspicions that her father was poisoned. But she had little besides her suspicions and Hannah's claim to have seen Colton the night before. Would the sheriff trust the eyewitness account of a child of eight? Especially when the only light had been that of the moon. It would be best to find the store first and see if they could obtain shelter there for the night.

The town bustled with activity. People moved along the streets with purpose in their steps, but it was nothing like Harmony Hill. Here people talked and laughed and sometimes shouted at each other across the street. The noise was jarring after the quiet peace at Harmony Hill where the Shaker sisters and brethren went about their work duties with sparse conversation.

Many curious glances came their way. A woman and a girl in homespun Shaker blue dresses without the wide white collars and no caps to cover their hair.

Hannah edged over closer to Elizabeth. "How will we find him? There are so many people."

"Payton said he ran a store."

"But which store?" Hannah looked up and down the street. "We don't know the man's name."

"We do know something." Elizabeth squeezed Hannah's shoulder to give her courage. "Aristotle. Perhaps he will bark a welcome."

"How would he know we are here?"

"Remember how he found us when we hid from him in the woods. His good nose or his ears."

Hannah's face lit up. "I could whistle for him. He always came when I whistled." Hannah pursed her lips, but Elizabeth put her fingers over them before she could blow air out to make a sound.

"It might be better if we don't attract the eyes of everyone in the town just yet. We are already getting more than a few curious stares."

"Maybe Mr. Linley is not here. Maybe he has gone back to his house."

"We can hope," Elizabeth said. "But the town is not so large that we can't find the store without whistling up undue attention."

"How about if I whistle real soft?" Hannah demonstrated. "Aristotle always heard me when I did that in the woods."

So she whistled under her breath so low Elizabeth could barely hear her, but Aristotle's ears were better. They weren't halfway down the street when they heard frantic barks coming from a store two buildings on down the walkway. A man spoke sharply, but then the door was opening and Aristotle bounded toward them. He jumped right at Hannah and knocked her down on the sidewalk. He was trembling all over and his tail whipped back and forth as he licked every inch of Hannah's face before he leaped up on Elizabeth to wrap his front paws around her leg.

A man came out of the store and ran toward them. "Aristotle, what in the world has gotten into you?"

Elizabeth laughed as she scratched the dog's ears while he licked her sleeves. "Do not be concerned. He knows us. He used to be our dog."

"I see." The man gave Elizabeth and Hannah the once-over before he said, "Well, then, any friend of Aristotle is a friend of mine. Come on into the store and we'll sort things out."

Felix Wiley was every bit as kind as Payton had suggested he might be. He looked to be in his sixties, with gray hair lapping his collar and a mustache that didn't hide the deep lines around his mouth. Lines that fell naturally into a smile as he talked about Aristotle. "Your dog has been a godsend to me." He paused while his smile faded and his eyes turned sad. "My wife, she died last summer. Sudden like."

"I'm sorry," Elizabeth said as they followed him into the

store where he sat crackers and cheese in front of them on the counter and waved away Elizabeth's protests that they had no money to pay for the food.

"Well, death comes to us all. And the store keeps me busy, you know," he told Elizabeth as he leaned back against the counter and smoothed down his mustache. "But the people, they all go home at the end of the day, and the night hours stretched out long in front of me before Aristotle came to keep me company. Besides, Aristotle is the best listener I've ever been privileged to know. He's yet to disagree with a single thing I've told him except, of course, about chasing the cat out in back of the store."

"He's always been bad to chase things," Hannah said as she slipped the dog one of the crackers. "Squirrels. Foxes. But we never had cats. I don't know why."

"Perhaps because Aristotle didn't like them," Mr. Wiley said, his smile firmly back on his face again.

A small bell jangled over top of the door as two men came into the store. Elizabeth and Hannah moved to the side out of the way as Mr. Wiley stepped behind the counter to wait on the men. Elizabeth kept her face turned away, but she felt their curious glances. As one of the men picked up his parcels to leave, he asked, "These girls kin to you, Felix?"

"Distant kin," Mr. Wiley told them without a second's hesitation. "Relations of relations of mine."

"They look to be part of those Shakers out at Harmony Hill," the man said.

"You ever see a Shaker woman without a cap and apron? They're peculiar about that sort of thing, you know." Mr. Wiley laughed a little as he walked the men toward the door. He pushed the door firmly shut behind them before he turned to Elizabeth and Hannah and crossed his arms over his chest. "It wasn't a lie. We're both related to Aristotle."

Elizabeth smiled. "We have no problem with that."

"But you do have a problem unless I miss my guess."

Elizabeth's smile faded. "True. It's as your customer said. We were Shakers, but we are no more."

"Did they kick you out?" He eyed Elizabeth. "For an indiscretion?"

Elizabeth looked down at her hands as a blush warmed her cheeks. "Not the sort of which you speak. But there were fires and some thought—"

Hannah interrupted her. "They thought I had a demon because of my hair." Hannah yanked her curls up away from her head. "And because I didn't always want to do what they said. I didn't set the fires. Well, only one little one, but it did no one harm. I saw men setting the other fires."

Mr. Wiley frowned as he tried to sort out Hannah's words. After a moment he asked, "Have you come for Aristotle?" At the sound of his name, the dog wagged his tail and went to the man who reached down and rubbed Aristotle's head.

Elizabeth could tell he cared more about that answer than why they had left the Shakers. "No. We have no way to feed him. We have no money, no place to go. We only hoped that since you were kind enough to take in our dog, you might let us stay in the room we'd heard you rent out to travelers in exchange for us cleaning your house or store." He looked at her without saying anything and she hurried on. "Not forever. Just for a few days until I can find some other way to get by."

Aristotle looked up at him and whined, then went back to nuzzle Elizabeth's hand until she scratched his favorite spot behind his ears. She didn't look at Mr. Wiley. Perhaps she asked too much.

"You're a pretty girl," he said thoughtfully. "You could marry. Best I remember, early on after Issachar brought me the dog, there was a man here looking for you. He saw Aristotle and knew him. He seemed very keen on finding you."

Elizabeth kept her eyes on the dog's head and answered carefully. "That must have been our neighbor from Washington County. He has indicated his wish to marry me, but I do not have the same wish."

Hannah jumped in. "He was the one who started the fire at Harmony Hill last night. We're scared of him."

Elizabeth looked at her and spoke sharply. "Hannah." While there was truth in Hannah's words, some things were best left unspoken.

Tears popped up in Hannah's eyes. She looked very tired. "Well, we are," she said with a little pout. She put her hands over her face to hide her tears. Aristotle tried to climb into her lap as he licked her hands.

Elizabeth reached across the divide between them to touch her shoulder. She too was very tired. If not for the storekeeper watching her, she would have dissolved into tears along with Hannah.

"Is it true? What your little sister says?"

Elizabeth shut her eyes and swallowed hard. Why did she fear admitting the truth? She opened her eyes to look straight at the man. "Yea." She shook her head slightly at her lapse into the Shaker talk. "Yes, I fear him."

"With reason, it seems," Mr. Wiley said. "I knew that man was trouble the first day he stepped through my door. He's done nothing to change my opinion in the weeks since."

"He's still here in town then?"

"I couldn't say for sure. I've seen him out on the streets now and again. He doesn't come in here anymore. Not since he kicked Aristotle and I threatened him with the sheriff. He laughed at me until he found out the sheriff's my cousin. Then he quit laughing. Seems he and John had already had some kind of run-in."

Mr. Wiley went to the door and turned over his closed sign and pulled down the shades. "It is near enough closing time," he said as he went to the counter and began straightening things there without looking back at Elizabeth and Hannah. "Fact is, the room I let out is upstairs here and the whole place could use a good cleaning. Me and the wife lived in the two rooms in back of the store. Of course, it's just me and the dog now, and I never was much for keeping things as clean as I should, and a dog, even a good dog like Aristotle, has a way of tracking in extra dirt. Hilda was always the one who did the cleaning and such. Hilda, that was my wife." He looked up at Elizabeth. "You know how to fry chicken?"

"I can fry chicken."

Her answer seemed to please him. "And pies? How about brown sugar pie? My Hilda could make the best brown sugar pie in the state." Mr. Wiley got a longing look on his face.

"I've baked pies, but mostly apple."

"And blackberry cobbler," Hannah put in. "With whipped cream when the cow was fresh."

"You're making my mouth water." Mr. Wiley rubbed his stomach. "I'd ask you to marry me, but relations can't be marrying relations." He smiled at Elizabeth. "Not to mention I'm old enough to be your granddaddy. But great uncle might be better. You can be the children of my Hilda's long-lost sister's daughter. We haven't heard from that girl since she and her husband moved off some years back. Hilda always figured she died."

"Our mother died," Hannah said. "When I was four."

"Well, see there. The story works."

"The man who was looking for me, our neighbor, he will know who we are," Elizabeth said.

"I never said you'd have to change who you are. Just change who your dear mama was kin to. I'll wager you don't even know who that was anyhow, do you?" He raised his bushy gray eyebrows at them.

"She used to talk about her mother back in Virginia. She was a midwife and herb doctor."

"Not my Hilda's sister for sure then, but we don't have to tell everything, do we? Just until you find that better way. Or the right fellow to marry."

Elizabeth's smile faded as she stared down at her hands. "That might not ever happen."

"Uh-oh," Mr. Wiley said. "Fell for one of them Shaker fellows, did you? Those boys aren't the marrying kind." He put his hand on her shoulder. "But buck up. You've got old Uncle Felix watching out for you now, and in time you'll see there are plenty more fishes in the sea. And a good number of them come right through those doors over there." He pointed toward the front of his store.

"Thank you, Mr. Wiley," Elizabeth said.

He interrupted her. "None of that 'mister' stuff. Uncle Felix, remember."

"Uncle Felix," Elizabeth said with a smile.

Hannah laughed and jumped up to give Mr. Wiley a hug. "I think I like having an uncle." She looked up at him and her laughter died away. "Promise me you won't die like Brother Issachar, Uncle Felix."

Mr. Wiley frowned. "The last Shaker brother who was in here told me Issachar was poorly. I'm sorry to hear he passed on. When did that happen?"

"A few days ago," Elizabeth said.

"A shame. He was a good man. A friend." He patted Hannah's head before she stepped back from him. "I wish my Hilda could have seen your hair, child. You put me in mind of a little lamb."

"Except my wool grows longer," Hannah said. "Did you and your Hilda have a little girl like me?"

"We weren't blessed with children of our own, but my Hilda loved the children who came into the store."

"Do you think she would have liked me?"

"I'm pretty sure she would. She'd have given you a piece of rock candy and maybe a ribbon for your hair."

"I'm sorry she died," Hannah said. "I always wanted a ribbon for my hair."

"What are you talking about, Hannah?" Elizabeth gave her a look. "You know you've always pulled out every ribbon I put in your hair."

Hannah lifted her chin and looked defiantly at Elizabeth. "I wouldn't have pulled them out if our Aunt Hilda had tied them in my hair."

Mr. Wiley laughed. "I think my life just took a turn for the better." He put his hand on Hannah's shoulder. "Come along and Elizabeth can start earning your keep by making us some biscuits."

Elizabeth stood up to follow them back to the kitchen behind the store. She could hardly believe their luck. Not luck, she told herself. She slipped her hand in her pocket and wrapped it around the heart Payton had given her. The providence of the Lord. He had answered their prayers. He had opened up a way for them. A way that had nothing to do with Colton Linley.

33

Ethan watched Elizabeth and the little sister until they disappeared from sight. It was over. She was gone. He could go on about his life as a Believer. He could push away the carnal temptations of the world and concentrate on working for the good of his brothers and sisters. He could listen to Elder Joseph in meeting and not be tempted to let his eyes stray to the benches where the sisters sat. The one who drew his eye would no longer be among the sisters.

He could pray again and have faith the Eternal Father would hear his prayers. Lately his prayers had been running into the stone barrier of sinfulness in his heart and shattering before they reached the Lord's ears. Brother Martin had often reminded Ethan that he who sinned had no reason to expect his prayers to be answered. Not until he made confession of those sins and determined to turn from his wrongs. A man had to make his decision to live the right way, the only way. He had chosen to be a Believer. The one who had enticed his eye off that proper path was gone from their midst.

That was good. His mind knew that. His heart did not. His

heart chased after her, and it was all he could do to stay still and not call out to her. She had seen him, but she had not let her eyes linger on him. She had not lifted her hand in farewell. Her step had not faltered as she walked away from him.

In the woods she had professed her love for him. He hadn't made the same profession back to her, but the kiss had revealed more than his words could have ever said. He did love her. In a worldly way. In a wondrous way. Yet he had not chosen her. He had chosen the Believers and the life he knew. How could he choose other? It was sin to commit matrimony. As amazing as it felt, that fire that raced through him when their lips touched was wrong. A sinful fire that would surely consume him if he kept lusting after worldly ways.

He wanted no part of the world. In the world, men had no peace in their hearts. Men of the world, men like Hawk Boyd, thieved and murdered and lived only for themselves. He could not go into that world. He didn't want to become a man such as his father. He was a Believer. He had told Elizabeth that there on the cliff after they kissed. She hadn't condemned him for lacking the courage to follow his heart. She'd simply opened her hands and set him free, the way a child might release a firefly caught at dusk.

Yet he did not feel free. He felt as if the weight of a whole wagonload of rocks sat upon his heart.

"Our former sister never had intent to walk the Shaker path. That is too bad, for no doubt she will reap sorrow from her worldly choices. Praise Mother Ann that sorrow won't touch us. It is good the fallen one is gone out from us," Brother Martin told him when he found Ethan in the graveyard, staring down at the mound of dirt that covered Brother Issachar.

"Yea," Ethan said. He had no other words.

"You are late to your duty."

"I lost count of the time," Ethan said as he obediently followed Brother Martin away from the graveyard. He would follow the rules. He would put his hands to work and he would strive to be simple in the Shaker way.

"You are to stay with me on this day while your fingers begin to heal. As it is your left hand that is injured, you can help copy some lessons for the young brothers, and then with the morning, you will be assigned to work in the Carpenters' Shop."

"How will I work with this?" Ethan held up his splinted hand.

"Worry not. Until your hand is better, you will only be fetching supplies for the other carvers or sweeping and cleaning. As Mother Ann teaches, good spirits will not stay where we allow dirt to collect. So we must keep our workrooms as clean and neat as we keep our spirits and our hearts." Brother Martin looked at Ethan sharply. "It is good we have meeting this evening, for I sense you have some work to do cleaning out your heart and putting the right feelings back into your spirit."

"Yea," Ethan answered.

But that night at meeting, his spirit was not put right. All he could think of was the darkness falling outside and where Elizabeth might find to lay her head. In spite of the way he stomped and shook as he exercised the dances for Mother Ann and sang the songs begging to be brought low and live the simple life, he longed for only one simple thing. That was to feel Elizabeth's head resting in the hollow of his shoulder and to know she was safe.

He feared such thinking might bring conflict into the

meeting, and so he withdrew from the dances to sit and watch. Some moved with freedom of spirit, but others seemed unsure and unblessed as they went through the motions of the dance. Brother Payton was one of those. He didn't seem able to keep his mind on the proper steps or his eye on the marks in the wooden floor that kept the dances orderly. Once he stumbled and fell, but the brothers around him picked him up and kept him in the flow of the dancers.

They would have done the same for Ethan. They would have carried him forward. Their strengths would suffice for his weaknesses. Yet he had pulled away. A fact noted by Brother Martin if the frown that darkened his face when he looked Ethan's way was any indication. If only Brother Issachar could once more be beside Ethan on the benches. If only he could tell him what to do. Then had he not already told him what to do in his last words before he died? *Follow your heart.* But the stones of sorrow were crushing his heart.

When at last the exercises ended and the brothers and sisters began filing out of their proper doors to retire for the evening, Ethan was relieved. It had been a long day with the fire keeping many of them out of their beds for much of the night. Rest would be a gift. Elder Joseph said as much when he bid them goodnight.

Ethan knelt by his bed to say his nightly prayers, but he found no proper petitions in his head. No "guide these hands to do thy work." No "bless our society." No pleas for love from Mother Ann. No requests for gifts to use for his brethren and sisters. There was only Elizabeth. And so, although Brother Martin would surely say he was compounding his sin, Ethan's silent prayers were for her safety.

But his heart had no confidence in his prayers, and even

after exhausted sleep finally overtook him, he found no rest. In his dreams he was running. At first he seemed to be chasing after someone, but then he was being pursued. He saw the flash of Hawk Boyd's knife in the darkness that pressed in on him. Then there was Brother Martin frowning, shaking his head, turning his back, refusing to help Ethan escape the knife. Ethan stumbled over something. Brother Issachar lay dead at his feet. And far ahead, he heard Elizabeth scream. He could not help her. He could never run so far in time. Not with the way he was having to push his legs forward as if running through a river of molasses. It was pulling him down into it until, like a fly caught in a spider's web, he could no longer move.

He jerked awake and stared at the darkness pushing down on him. Clouds must be over the moon, as scant light came through the windows. That was how it would be for Brother Issachar in his grave, but no. Brother Issachar would have stepped over into heaven. He would be in the glorious light. With his Eva.

At the rising bell, Ethan went to his duty. There had always been a certain comfort in the sameness of his life. He knew what was expected. He knew what was to come. He had not only accepted that, he'd sought that smooth ride through life. Like floating down a serene lake. He had run from the tosses and turns of a stormy river. Then the world had come to him, had found him in spite of his Shaker clothes and promises, had stolen Brother Issachar from him, had pushed Elizabeth into his path. Had dumped him into the river of life where now he must decide which shore to swim toward.

He worked through the day with few spoken words. There was no need for conversation. The carpenters were busy shaping their chairs and chests. He swept up their sawdust and carved leavings awkwardly with his one good hand and helped to sand smooth some of the pieces. Brother Payton was putting together a chair, but though he ran his hands over the spindles lovingly, he looked as if he had slept as poorly as Ethan.

It wasn't until late in the afternoon when it was almost time for the evening meal that Brother Payton came out of the Carpenters' Shop to where Ethan was straightening some lumber that lay ready for the morrow's work. Logs not yet split into planks lay to the side, and Ethan easily picked out the last log he had helped Brother Issachar bring into the village before they left for New Orleans. The brethren had left it through the winter for Brother Issachar, who envisioned a beautiful oaken desk for the Ministry. Now the promise of that log would have to be wrought by another workman.

Payton nodded toward the oak log. "That is Brother Issachar's log. None of the brethren want to cut into it."

"He would want it used," Ethan said.

"Yea, Brother Micah says the same, but he says we can wait until the sorrow is not so sharp." Payton's eyes lifted to Ethan's face. "You could make something from it."

"I'm not a gifted craftsman. I can only do simple pieces. A holding box or a bench. It would be better if the log became the desk Brother Issachar planned it to be."

"I love working with the wood."

"Yea, Brother Issachar told me you have a gift for the wood last fall when he worked with you in the Carpenters' Shop. He said your first chair showed promise."

The young Shaker's cheeks turned red with pleasure. "I would that I could work with the wood all the time, but I know I have to take my turns with the other duties."

"A Believer has many duties," Ethan said.

"I'm learning that is so." Payton looked over his shoulder and around nervously as if he feared they were being watched. He lowered his voice. "I also feel bound by duty to my sisters of the world who left us yesterday."

"They made their choice."

"For evil, many are saying in my ear this day, but Elizabeth and Hannah have no evil in their hearts." Payton stared at Ethan's face a moment before going on. "If they did any wrong, caused any problems, it was not with wrong intent."

"Why do you tell me this?" Ethan asked. "I have said aught against them."

"Because she gave me a message for you before she left. And she was always a faithful sister who loved me without exception. Our mother died when I was twelve."

Ethan shut his eyes. He wanted to walk away from this brother. He didn't want to be opened up to more pain. At the same time he longed to have Elizabeth's words in his ears. He opened his eyes and stared at the brother in front of him. He was so young with the same eagerness for the Shaker way that Ethan had known at his age.

"What is it?" Ethan forced out the question.

Again Payton glanced around. He knew eyes might be watching and ears listening. "She asked me to tell you that she hoped your pathway here was free of stones to cause you to stumble and that she was sorry if she was such a stumbling block in your path."

"She wasn't the stumbling block in my path. My own worldly desires were stones enough to trip me."

Payton looked uncomfortable. "Well, she wanted me to tell you."

"Where did they go? Do you know?"

"I cannot say for a certainty. She spoke of going to Colton Linley." Payton looked stricken at the thought. "Sister Lettie said she spoke the same to her. I begged her not to."

"Colton Linley?" Ethan felt ice cold at the thought of Elizabeth with another man. That had not been in his mind. He had thought to push her aside. He had worried that she might not have shelter. He had not thought of her with another. That changed everything.

"Our neighbor in the world. He has long claimed Elizabeth must be his wife, but she could never bear the thought of it. That's why we came to Harmony Hill. To escape Colton. That is why I burned our cabin with so little guilt to keep our things from his hands." Payton looked down at the ground. "I know that was wrong now."

Ethan didn't care about the burned cabin. He didn't care about anything at that moment except Elizabeth. "You mean that man who tried to carry Elizabeth from here only days ago?"

"Yea, the very one. He's a hard man who thinks only of his own wants and needs. Elizabeth's life will be misery with him." Payton looked up, his eyes awash with tears. "I should have gone with them. Brother Micah said I shouldn't. That I risked eternal damnation if I did, but they are my sisters. So I prayed before they left and I thought I had an answer. Aristotle."

Ethan frowned and shook his head a bit to try to make sense of Payton's words. "Aristotle?"

"Our dog."

"I remember. The one we gave the storekeeper."

"Yea. I told Elizabeth to look for him. That you had once

spoken of the man's kindness in taking the dog when I was worried about Aristotle after we came to the village. I thought perhaps she might even marry him."

"He was old. Older even than Brother Issachar."

"But kind, you said. Anything would be better than her going to Colton. I only had to look into her eyes when she spoke of him to know that. And to remember the way he attacked her in our own father's grave before we came here. I should have gone and gotten my father's gun that day."

"A Shaker does not use such carnal weapons." Ethan thought of Hawk Boyd, who had stabbed Brother Issachar with no compunction. Even if Ethan had been forewarned, he wouldn't have known how to stop it from happening any more than he knew how to stop Colton Linley from hurting Elizabeth. "We are men of peace." His words were a plea to the Eternal Father to show him a way.

"I wasn't a Shaker then. Perhaps I should not be now."

"Nay. You should follow your heart as Elizabeth did."

He heard the echo of Brother Issachar's words in his own heart as the bell began ringing to summon the brethren and sisters from their work duties to their evening meals, each in their own houses. From long habit, Ethan turned at the sound and began walking along the way to the Centre Family House even though his thoughts were in turmoil.

Payton fell in beside him. "She doesn't follow her heart to Colton."

"You are right. It is her love for others that has made her set her feet on that path. For you. For the little sister." Ethan hesitated. "For me."

"The love of a sister," Payton said.

"For you. Not for me."

369

Payton stared over at him. "What are you going to do?"

"What I have to do, the same as Elizabeth." Ethan looked off down the road that led out of the village. He couldn't stay in the middle of the river. He had to swim through the waters, no matter how rough, toward one of the shores.

A man who had been checking his saddle girths beside the road up ahead of them suddenly mounted up and rode straight toward them. Ethan and Payton jumped for the grass beside the pathway, but the man came after them. He reined in his horse with inches to spare. "Payton Duncan," he said. "I have been waiting for you."

It was Colton Linley. The man Payton had feared Elizabeth was going to. Ethan could not bear the thought of this man touching her. Ever.

"Where is she?" the man demanded. "I've been watching all day. Where have these crazy people hidden her?"

Ethan stepped in front of Payton. "You have no business here. Be on your way." His voice shook, not from fear but anger.

"I remember you." Linley leaned down from his horse toward Ethan. "You're the one that kept me from taking her last time I was here, but nobody is going to stop me next time. The woman is mine and I take what is mine. So tell me where she is or I'll burn this whole place down one building at a time."

"You're the one who has been setting the fires?" Payton stared up at the man with big eyes.

"An eye for an eye. You people believe that, don't you? You burned mine. I'll burn theirs." He let his horse prance a couple of steps closer to them. "Now I want to know where she is or some people are going to be very sorry. Starting with you two."

"I don't know where she is," Payton said as he backed up a couple of steps.

Ethan stood his ground. The man's horse was so close that if the horse tossed its head, it would likely hit Ethan and knock him to the side. He looked into the horse's eye and saw the animal's panic. Ethan made a soft sound with his tongue. A horse knew when a man meant to treat it kindly. It wasn't Ethan the horse feared but the man on its back. Ethan looked at the bit pulling back against its mouth and saw flecks of blood. The Shakers would never use such a cruel bit.

"What goes on here?" Brother Micah spoke behind them.

Ethan kept his focus on the horse, but out of the corner of his eyes he saw other brothers coming toward them. The horse skittered to the side away from Ethan.

The man on the horse turned his attention to the new arrivals as he said, "I have come for this boy's sister. She is to be my wife."

"If you speak of our former sister, Elizabeth, we know not where she is. She left our village yesterday," Brother Micah said.

The news seemed to surprise the man and throw him off balance.

Ethan spoke up. "This man admits to setting the fires we've suffered."

Brother Micah glanced at Ethan and then narrowed his eyes on the man on the horse. "Is that true?"

"His word against mine," Linley said even as he gathered his reins to turn his horse away from them.

"And mine," Payton said.

The man stared down at Payton. "Who would believe a boy who has the smell of smoke on him?"

"Our brothers do not lie. If you ever come into our village again, we will have you arrested," Brother Micah said.

A worried look flashed across Linley's face, but then he laughed and pulled his horse sharply back from the men gathered there behind Ethan and Payton. "It's good to know you don't lie. That means the woman I seek will be in the town. No doubt seeking me. I told her she would come to me."

Ethan forgot the brothers around him. "She will never come to you."

The man looked straight at Ethan. "Oh, but she will. One way or another. I've done plenty to make sure of that and no pretty boy like you can stop me. Best stay here and keep dancing." He laughed again as he wheeled his horse around and galloped away.

"We've surely seen the last of him and good riddance," Brother Micah said. "Now our supper awaits. Come, brethren, we must not tarry."

Ethan looked at the men around him. He no longer belonged with them. He was Hawk Boyd's son. He wanted to kill the man on the horse. He was no longer a man of peace. "I must go to her," he said.

"Nay, my brother, your place is with us." Brother Micah looked truly distressed.

"It was, but no more." He stepped away from them.

Brother Micah didn't give up. "Think of what Brother Martin would tell you. You are a Believer. Do not risk eternal damnation for the carnal lust of a woman."

Ethan didn't turn, but kept walking away through the dust the horse's hooves had stirred up on the road. Behind him, he heard them begin stomping and crying, "Woe." He didn't hear Payton's young voice among them.

Even so, the sound mashed down on his heart. He knew not what he would do without his brothers, but he could not turn around. He'd made his decision. He was swimming through the rough waters toward Elizabeth. Pray that he would be in time. Pray that the Eternal Father would still hear his supplications even if the seed of Hawk Boyd was flowering within him.

He had no horse. No weapon. No idea of what he could do to stop the man, but he kept walking toward the town even after darkness fell. He did have one thing the man did not. He knew where Elizabeth was. The storekeeper might help them, and there would be a sheriff in the town.

So he prayed as he walked that he would reach her first. And even though he was walking away from what he had been taught to believe by Brother Martin and the elders, he didn't feel deserted by the Lord. His mind went back to Preacher Joe, who had always walked hand in hand with the Lord. He hadn't been a Shaker, but he had believed. He had taught Ethan Scripture. *And, lo, I am with you alway, even unto the end of the world.*

It was after midnight when he reached the town. He took shelter in a stable to wait for the morning light. The man's horse was there, put into a stall without the proper care. Ethan laid his hand on the horse's nose and spoke into his ear. Then he rubbed him down before he led him to the water trough. The horse had no part of the evil of his owner.

34

Mr. Wiley kept insisting they call him Uncle Felix, and by the end of the first day under his roof, the name rolled off Elizabeth's tongue as if he actually was their uncle. Elizabeth and Hannah cleaned and straightened the back living quarters all through the day. She wasn't exactly hiding from the eyes of Uncle Felix's customers, but at the same time she couldn't keep from worrying what Colton might do when he found out they were there.

Felix assured her she had no reason to fear. That he'd been running the store in the town for many years, and in that time had dealt with more than a few reprobates. His cousin, the sheriff, was right down the street at the courthouse, and he was the kind of sheriff who knew what was going on in his town.

"You're every bit as safe here as you were out at that Shaker village," Felix told Elizabeth. "That scalawag comes around here, we'll send him packing. So don't you be worrying none about that." He smiled at her. "You just think on making some fried pies out of those dried apples over in the cupboard. Then we'll have one fine supper. Could be if we have any leavings, they might even taste good come breakfast. My Hilda did always say I had a terrible sweet tooth. I told her that was why I fell for her."

It was good being with Felix. He laughed as easily as most people smiled. And though Elizabeth would always carry the memory of Ethan in her heart, she had no regrets leaving the Shaker village. She had offered Ethan her love and he had turned from it. Now she had to push thoughts of him aside. She couldn't dwell in sadness. Instead she had to believe the Lord had guided her steps to this place where she and Hannah could begin a new life.

On the second morning, Elizabeth was laying bits of kindling and wood on top of the red coals of the fire in the cookstove to make coffee as daylight began creeping into the kitchen. While no rising bell sounded here as it did at Harmony Hill, the horses in the street had brought her awake. She didn't mind. She was happy to cook for Felix to earn their keep. Besides, it was good to be in a kitchen again where she could cook as she pleased and not just be relegated to stringing up peppers or peeling potatoes all through the day.

Aristotle sat at her feet in hopes she would drop a crumble of bacon or biscuit. It was so much like being in the cabin that for a moment Elizabeth almost thought she might look up and see her father coming in to the table with a book in his hand. With the corner of one of Hilda's aprons she had found neatly folded in a drawer, Elizabeth brushed away the tears that welled up in her eyes. She would talk today with Felix about her suspicions that her father had been poisoned. She had no proof, but perhaps her word of that and Hannah's word that she saw Colton setting fire to the Shaker house would be reason enough for the sheriff to run Colton from the town. Forever.

The bacon was sizzling in the iron skillet and Felix was stirring in his bedroom off the kitchen when Aristotle raised his head off his paws with a low growl as someone began banging on the store's front door.

"What in the world!" Felix came out of his room pulling his suspenders up over his shoulders. "Who the heck could that be?"

Elizabeth grabbed for his arm. "Don't open it."

He paused a minute to pat her hand. "It's nothing, girl. Happens all the time. Somebody gets up and they don't have sugar for their coffee. They think I don't have nothing better to do than wait on them."

But it wasn't that kind of knock. It was a shattering knock. Hannah came running down the steps from the room upstairs and grabbed Elizabeth. "It's him. I looked out the window."

Elizabeth called to Felix, but he was already to the door, turning the knob, letting Colton Linley push into the store. She pulled Hannah back from the kitchen door as she eased it almost shut to keep Colton from seeing them as she said, "Run. Go find the sheriff Uncle Felix talked about."

"It's too early. He won't be at the courthouse." Hannah's eyes were wide and frightened.

"He'll be somewhere." Elizabeth leaned down and spoke directly into Hannah's face as she squeezed her upper arms tightly. "And no matter what, don't come back in here unless he's with you. Don't let Colton see you."

"I don't want to leave you." Hannah looked ready to cry.

Elizabeth shook her a little. "I'll be all right. Colton won't kill me, but I don't trust his intentions with anyone else. He might hurt Uncle Felix." She pushed Hannah toward the back door. "Now go!"

The slight creak of the back door opening and closing was covered by Colton's demanding voice in the front of the store. "Where is she?"

"I don't know who you're talking about. I live here alone." Felix's voice was firm without any sign of fear.

"Then you won't mind if I take a look around."

Elizabeth peeked through the crack into the store. Felix stepped in front of Colton to block his way back to the kitchen. "Indeed I do mind. You've no business here. Now be on your way." He pointed toward the front door.

"She's here. You're hiding her. I see the lie in your eyes." Colton laughed and shoved him roughly to the side. "Did she forget to tell you she belongs to me?"

Aristotle was barking frantically now as he pawed at the kitchen door. In the store, Felix grabbed an axe handle out of one of the barrels. Colton blocked Felix's intended blow with one hand and yanked the wooden handle away from him. He swung it at the old man, who threw up his arm to protect his head. Even in the kitchen over Aristotle's barks, Elizabeth heard the bone crack.

Felix fell backward and hit the floor. He scrambled away from Colton as the man raised the axe handle again. "Run, Elizabeth," Felix yelled.

But she couldn't run. She stepped through the kitchen door and said, "Stop! I'll go with you."

Aristotle ran to stand in front of Felix with his teeth bared at Colton.

"Now is that any way to greet an old friend?" Colton said

to the dog before he turned slowly to Elizabeth. He smiled. "And so you have finally come to me."

"Yes. Just leave Mr. Wiley alone."

"What about the dog? Can I kill him?" Colton slapped the axe handle against the palm of his other hand. "I never did like him much."

"You've killed before." Inside she was quaking, but she refused to let him see her fear as she stared straight at him.

He lifted one side of his mouth in a knowing smile. "You figured that out, did you? About your father?"

"You didn't have to kill him."

"It was self-defense," Colton said.

"You lie."

"Well, near to self-defense. He said he'd see me dead before he let you marry me. So I didn't have much choice, did I? There has never been any doubt that sooner or later you would marry me." Again he hit the axe handle softly in the palm of his hand. "Or perhaps we won't bother with weddings now. I've had much trouble with you. I'm not sure you are deserving of the title Mrs. Linley."

"You don't have to go with him, Elizabeth," Felix said as he pushed himself up off the floor with his good arm and got to his feet.

"Shut up, old man." Colton turned menacingly on the man. "Unless you want another broken bone or two."

Elizabeth kept her voice calm. "Leave him be. I told you I'd go with you." She went over to Colton with sure steps and put her hand on his arm. "We can go right now."

"Eager, are you?" Colton peered down at her with a victorious smirk.

She managed to push a smile across her face. Not a real

smile, but one that was convincing enough. Hannah was not going to get back with the sheriff in time, but at least she would see that no one else got hurt. She let her eyes go to Felix.

"I'll be fine," she said. "Take care of Hannah." And then she couldn't stop the tears as they began to stream down her cheeks.

"Oh yes, little sister Hannah. I forgot about her. Where is the little freak?" Colton looked around. His eyes were cold. "Don't you want her to go with us?"

"She's afraid of you. She doesn't want to go."

"Imagine that." He laughed. The sound stabbed through Elizabeth. "Just as well. I never took to her any better than to your dog over there." He casually threw the axe handle and hit Aristotle in the head. The dog yelped and scooted under a table of bolts of cloth.

Elizabeth didn't look toward the dog. "Just let me get my things." Perhaps she might yet delay long enough. She looked toward the street. The sun was coming up. People would be out and about.

"You're looking for help." Colton sounded surprised as he suddenly grabbed her. "You might as well forget that. It's not coming in time." He pulled her out the door.

Aristotle came out from under the table to grab the back of Colton's leg, but he kicked the dog away. He kept a stranglehold on the collar of her dress as he mounted his horse and then jerked her up in front of him.

"Don't try to get away," he said with his mouth against her ear. "I've got a gun. I'll shoot the old man if you fight me." He pulled her back against him so tightly she could hardly breathe.

It didn't matter. She wanted to be dead.

The sun was pushing its light into the stable when Ethan woke. He hadn't planned to sleep when he'd climbed into the loft and settled down in the hay to wait for the morning, but two nights with little sleep had caught up with him.

Still it was early. The storekeeper might be awake now, but the store wouldn't open for another hour. The man would know where he could find Elizabeth and the little sister. They'd surely gone to him since Linley hadn't known where they were.

Ethan thought he had time until he climbed down out of the loft. He stared at the empty stall where the man's horse had been as his heart began pounding in his ears.

The stable owner came in the door and saw him with hay clinging to his clothes. He pointed the pitchfork he was carrying toward Ethan and studied him with narrowed eyes. "What are you doing in here?"

"I slept in your loft," Ethan answered with the truth.

The man stepped closer to him. "You look like one of them Shaker men."

"I was."

"Well, then I don't reckon you was trying to steal nothing. You fellows got some sorry ways, but pilfering stuff ain't one of 'em." He set the end of the pitchfork's handle down on the dirt floor.

"I needed a place to rest. I'll come back later and clean your stalls to pay you."

"No need in that. Not unless you ate some of the hay up there." The man let out a loud guffaw as if he'd said something particularly funny.

Ethan pushed a smile out on his face as he edged toward the door. He needed to get to the storekeeper before Linley. The stableman stepped in front of him. "You running away from that place out there?"

"I've left them." Ethan pointed toward the empty stall where Linley's horse had been. "When did that horse go out? I didn't hear him."

"I led him out early this morning. Just as it was beginning to get light. The man was all in a stir to get under way. Didn't matter none to me whether he waited till after I fed the horse or not. Same price feed or no."

"What was his hurry?" Ethan asked.

The man shrugged his shoulders. "Men like him are always in a hurry. Never take time to treat their horses right. Act all righteous and uppity but have a mean streak clear through them, if you know what I mean."

Ethan did know what he meant. He ran out the door and down the street as fast as he could. His heart sank when he saw the store at the far end of the street. He was too late. The man was leading Elizabeth out of the store toward his horse. He got on the horse and pulled her up after him to sit sideways in front of him. She wasn't fighting against his hold.

Ethan yelled, but no one heard him. The storekeeper stumbled out of the store behind them, holding the dog by the scruff of its neck but doing nothing to stop Linley. Ethan couldn't let them ride away. He might never find her if they rode away. If only he had grabbed the stableman's pitchfork. But Shakers didn't use weapons.

He pulled in breath and ran faster. A Shaker would not, but the son of Hawk Boyd would. The son of Hawk Boyd could match meanness with the man on the horse and find a way to stop him.

He stepped in front of the horse as the man snapped the reins on its neck. The horse shied to the side. Ethan grabbed the horse's bridle and let his eyes touch on Elizabeth's face for just a second. She looked beaten, without hope, and then when she recognized him, frightened. But not for herself. For him.

He shifted his eyes away from her to stare at Linley. "Let her go."

Looking irritated, the way one might look when bothered by a pesky fly, Linley tightened his arm around Elizabeth and let out a short laugh. "You know how to pick them, my dear Elizabeth. An old man and a peace-loving Shaker boy. Who's next?" He pulled up a pistol with the same hand that held the reins and pointed it at Ethan. "Now tell your little friend to get out of our way. Tell him you want to go with me. You do, don't you?" He moved the gun close to Elizabeth's face to rub the barrel across her cheek in an obscene caress as the reins slid loose in his hand.

Elizabeth looked at Ethan. "It's all right, Ethan. I am going with him." She spoke in a monotone and her eyes looked dull and lifeless. "It is the way things must be."

"Nay, you are wrong, Elizabeth. I won't let you go with him." He held the horse by the bridle while he slipped his other hand over the reins dangling down from the bit in the horse's mouth. He made a soft clucking noise with his tongue to let the animal know he intended it no harm.

Again Linley laughed. "And how are you going to stop me? Are you planning to stomp and shake to try to knock me off my horse?"

The man gathered up the reins, but Ethan's hold on them kept the bit loose in the horse's mouth. The confused horse tried to dance to the side, but Ethan held it steady by its bridle.

"Unhand my horse or I'll shoot you. Simple as that."

"Simple," Ethan muttered. Maybe the answer could be simple. Ethan got a better grip on the reins. He didn't dare look at Elizabeth or at the gun Linley was surely pointing at his head even when he heard the hammer cock. With a sudden jerk, he yanked the reins out of the man's hand and jumped to the side as Elizabeth screamed and banged her head back against Linley's nose.

The gun fired. The shot hit the ground at the horse's feet and it reared in panic, pulling the reins free from Ethan's hands. Linley grabbed for the saddle horn, but Elizabeth knocked his hands away.

Ethan moved in dangerously close to the rearing horse to reach for Elizabeth, who met his eyes and with a sudden twist jerked free of Linley. Ethan caught her in midair and fell backward. They scrambled back from the horse's hooves.

With the dog barking and biting at its tail, the horse did a sidewinder buck to unseat Linley before it raced off up the street. Linley hit the ground hard, jarring the gun out of his hands. It bounced toward Ethan, who let go of Elizabeth to grab it. He cocked it and pointed it at Linley as he lay in the street. This man, if ever a man did, deserved to die.

"You don't have the nerve to shoot." The man laughed scornfully. "But even if you did, it wouldn't matter. That gun's already fired its load." He started to push up off the ground. "You'd know that if you weren't a Shaker."

Ethan was Hawk Boyd's son. His seed had grown and

flowered inside him. He turned the gun in his hand to use as a club. The man had no weapon. Ethan could knock him down with one blow.

Nay, my son. You are the son of my heart. Not his son. Brother Issachar's words whispered through his mind. *My son.*

Then Elizabeth was beside him, her hand soft on his arm. "You are not like him, Ethan. The sheriff is here. Let him do what has to be done."

As if he had just come back from somewhere far away, Ethan looked around. There was a man with a gun pointed at Linley. And there was the little white-haired sister. Hannah, he told himself. Hannah was her name. Behind Elizabeth, the storekeeper watched Ethan while he gingerly held the elbow of his right arm that appeared to be broken. Others were gathering around, staring at Ethan, wondering at him.

He wondered at himself too. He didn't know who he was anymore. He stared at the gun in his hand for a long moment before he let it fall out of his hand back down on the ground. Then he looked at Elizabeth. "I am no longer a Believer."

Elizabeth gently wrapped her arms around him the way one might hold a wounded child. "That's not true, Ethan. I look into your eyes and I see belief. Did you not pray and did the Lord not answer that prayer? Here we stand together. We may not be Shakers. But we are Believers."

35

May 1834

The days passed and became weeks. Ethan cut his hair, put on one of the storekeeper's old shirts, and lost the outer trappings of being a Shaker, but inside it was not as easy. He had washed up on Harmony Hill's riverbank when he was six. He had vague memories of Preacher and Mama Joe from the years before that, but it was the memory of Hawk Boyd stealing him from his bed that was clearest in his mind. Hawk Boyd was the world that the Shakers had shut away from them at Harmony Hill.

And now he was in that world. In the world, no sisters cooked in the kitchens and set bowls of food out on a table for their hungry brothers. In the world, there was no rising bell to tell a man it was time to get up and begin his work. Work that was assigned for the good of all. In the world, a man had to make his own decisions. A man had to make his own way. There was no harmony in the world. Sometimes Ethan worried there was no Lord in the world.

That was what Brother Martin told him when he came after Ethan to lead him back to Harmony Hill. The Shaker brother had found Ethan in the livery stable where the owner had given him a cot in the tack room in exchange for cleaning the stalls in the morning. A rough-talking man, Mel Derbin had little use for Shakers and told Ethan so two or three times a day. His brother had gone to the Shakers years before and turned over his part of the family land to the Society. Mel had never forgiven his brother or the Shakers for that.

Brother Martin didn't seem to have much forgiveness in his heart for Ethan either. He stood in the middle of the small room and visibly shuddered when Ethan offered him a seat on the cot or the upended crate in the corner. He looked about him and said, "You know good spirits won't live in this kind of filth."

"I've been cleaning some on it," Ethan said.

"You can't clean this place, Brother Ethan. You must come back to Harmony Hill. Back to your family of Believers. This way, this place . . ." Brother Martin frowned as he waved his arm around to take in the whole room. "Nothing but destruction awaits you here. The ways of the world will sweep you into rivers of sin that will carry you far from where you need to be. You must not continue on this slippery slope to everlasting condemnation."

Ethan didn't know what to say. There were times when he felt that condemnation in his soul.

Brother Martin must have seen the struggle in his face because his voice softened as he laid a hand on Ethan's shoulder.

"My brother, you don't have to stay here. You can come home to your family. You are a Believer."

"Nay, I am no longer one with the Believers. I have fallen away."

"It is true you have fallen, but you can get back up." Brother Martin leaned toward him and spoke directly into his face. "You don't have to wallow in your sin. With confession, you can be forgiven and brought back into the fellowship of our society."

"I would that I could do as you say, for my spirit is in turmoil. I know not what to believe." But even as he spoke, Ethan saw Elizabeth in his mind. While he knew not how he could live here in the world, he knew he didn't want to live in a world where she was not. Her words whispered through his mind. *We may not be Shakers. But we are Believers.* The man in front of him would tell him that could not be true. And in his heart Ethan wasn't sure it could be true.

As if Brother Martin could see into his mind, he gave a little snort and jerked his hand away from Ethan's shoulder. "It's that woman. She is what has led you astray."

Ethan stared down at the bits of straw and muck that had fallen from his shoes to the floor. He had no Shaker broom to sweep away the dirt. He stared at the straws and said nothing.

"You showed much promise, Brother Ethan, and now you are throwing away your life here and your life everlasting on a few temporal moments of lust."

Ethan looked up and met Brother Martin's eyes. "I have not been with her."

"Perhaps not in your body, but the sin is in your heart."

"Brother Issachar's last words to me were to follow my heart," Ethan said softly.

"Brother Issachar must have been affected by the fever that took him. His words were wrong. If he stood before you this day, he would tell you so. He would tell you that you have planted your feet on the wrong path. He would tell you to confess your sin and turn from this evil world just as he did when he came to Harmony Hill." Brother Martin's voice got louder with each word until he was almost shouting. Out in the stable, a horse whinnied.

"I will not forget your words, Brother Martin," Ethan said. "Or your kindness to me these many years, but now I must find my own way."

The anger on Brother Martin's face drained away. He looked at Ethan for a long moment as if wondering if there were yet words he might say to convince him, but then he only said, "I knew the first time I laid eyes on that woman she was bringing trouble to Harmony Hill. I sorrow that you fell into her trap."

"She laid no trap for me. She set me free to do what I will. Can you not do the same?"

"Nay, my former brother. I cannot sanction sin. The next thing I know, you will be committing matrimony. There can be no peace in such unions. Mother Ann said it herself. Those who marry will know strife. Is that what you want?"

Ethan had no answer for Brother Martin, who left him in his small, unclean room. He had no answer for himself. He only knew that when he got up in the morning and when he went to bed at night, Elizabeth was in his thoughts. He had willingly risked life and soul to free her from Linley.

The judge had sentenced Linley to death by hanging for poisoning Elizabeth's father. The storekeeper had heard him admit to the crime. Linley had denied the truth of it in front of the judge. He claimed to be an upstanding, property-owning citizen of a neighboring county, but the judge was the storekeeper's cousin. Linley hadn't lived long enough to face the gallows. On the way out of the courthouse, he tried to overpower the sheriff, and in the struggle over the sheriff's gun, Linley had been shot. The storekeeper, Felix Wiley, said it was a fitting end for the man.

Felix Wiley was a man of the world. He believed in justice. He believed a man should pay for his crimes. He didn't believe a man could shut away the world to escape evil. He said a man had to look it in the eye and overcome it. He believed in love between a man and a woman and talked about his Hilda a dozen times a day, sometimes wiping away a tear as he did so.

He harbored no ill will toward the Shakers even as he said, "I don't believe a man can dance his way into heaven or shake off his sinful nature. Every man since Adam is prone to sin." He shook his head as he watched Ethan unloading a wagon of new stock for his store. He'd hired Ethan to work for him until his broken arm healed. "Me. You. All of us. It's in our nature, and shutting yourself away out there in that Shaker town and denying all that's natural between a man and a woman isn't going to change that."

"But we have peace there," Ethan said.

"The only ones that have peace are those that don't do no thinking for themselves. That's why Elizabeth and little Hannah couldn't abide the life. Too smart." Felix narrowed his eyes on Ethan. "You're too smart too. You'll see once you shake loose from them."

"I am loose from them already."

"It don't seem that way to me. Looks to me as how you're

like a man in a wagon behind a team of runaway horses. You don't know whether to drop the reins and jump or hang on and try to ride it out. You can't be reaching back and forward at the same time. You need to decide in your heart which way you want to go. Them or Elizabeth."

Felix stood up and came over to make sure Ethan heard his next words clearly. "I'm not really that girl's uncle, but somehow she feels like family. And I don't want to see her hurt. If you love her, tell her. If you don't, be gone with you."

Ethan didn't know what to say as Felix threw out his good hand in a gesture of dismissal and stomped ahead of him into the store. That was the trouble. He didn't know what to say. To Felix. To Elizabeth. How did one go about committing matrimony?

And what if he did find words and then she said no? She had said once she loved him, but that had been weeks ago. Since the wild day when he had kept Linley from carrying her off, she kept her eyes away from his. She spoke to him politely. She put food before him when he was at the store at a mealtime, but she never let her hand touch his. She was more Shaker sister to him now than she had ever been at Harmony Hill.

Ethan put the sack of flour on the shelf next to the counter. When he turned back, there was the Shaker box of seeds Brother Gerard had brought in the week before. He had looked at Ethan as though he didn't know him. And in truth, once Ethan left the Believers, he was the same as dead to them.

Ethan picked up a bean seed packet and stared down at the planting directions written in careful script by one of the sisters. At the village he would not be torn over what to do. He would be told what to do. He would be one of many giving his hands to work for the good of all. Giving his heart to God. Shaking free the sins of the world. Mourning Elizabeth.

From the kitchen in behind the store, he heard her singing. She often sang while she cooked. No Shaker songs, but songs about the Lord that echoed in his mind and made him think of Mama Joe. She sounded happy. She did not need him. He could leave and she would go on singing, go on living. But would he?

Ethan went back out to finish unloading the wagon. When he carried in the last sack of sugar, Felix passed him on his way up the street to the bank. Ethan sat down the sugar and listened for Elizabeth's singing, but it was silent in the kitchen. He walked to the door behind the counter and looked through. She was sitting at the table staring at something in her hand, her cheeks glistening with tears.

His heart constricted inside his chest, and he spoke without thinking whether he should or should not. "Are you all right, Elizabeth?"

She quickly slipped what she had been holding into her pocket and wiped away her tears with an edge of her apron as though the moisture on her face was nothing more than sweat from the heat of the woodstove. "Oh, Ethan, I didn't see you there." She didn't answer his question as she stood up. "Do you want something to eat? I just took an apple pie from the oven."

He hesitated and then went on into the kitchen. He didn't sit down at the table even after she put the plate of pie out for him. "You were crying," he said.

She glanced up at him and quickly away back toward the pie. "My father always said a person couldn't be perfectly happy all the time. Else he wouldn't realize how good happiness felt."

"Have you ever been perfectly happy?"

"I do remember such times when I was younger. Before my father died. And I know there will be such times again." She looked straight at him then without shyness. "How about you? Do you know what perfect happiness feels like?"

"Perfect happiness," he repeated softly as he sat down at the table and ran his hand over the nicks in the wooden boards. He remembered the heart Mama Joe had carved in her table for him. That had been a moment of perfect happiness. He traced a heart on the table with his finger as he told Elizabeth about Mama Joe.

"Is that the last time you felt truly loved?" she asked.

"Nay." He shut his eyes a moment wishing away the Shaker word, but he didn't change it. "Brother Issachar loved me from the first day he found me."

"Like a brother?" she asked.

"No. Like a son." Ethan looked from the table to Elizabeth. "A son of his heart."

She pulled something out of her pocket and laid it on the table for Ethan to see. It was a heart carved out of wood. "You were right. I was crying. I was missing Payton. He gave me this when we left the Shaker village."

He touched the wood warm from her hand. He shut his eyes as feeling flooded through him. It was time to follow his heart.

She spoke first. "I can see you have been troubled, Ethan. I will be forever grateful to you for stopping Colton on that day, but if you want me to stay your sister, that is what I will be. I'll understand if you return to the Shakers."

He squeezed the wooden heart so hard he thought the wood might burst into splinters in his fist. He opened his eyes and stared straight at her. "I don't want you to be my sister."

His voice was so loud she looked startled for a moment. Then she reached over to put her hand over his. "Nor do I want to be your sister."

"I have no money. I have nothing but my hands to work." He opened his hand and laid the heart back in front of her. He felt as if he had pulled his own heart out of his chest to lie beside it. Exposed, beating madly. "It is surely wrong for me to ask you to commit matrimony with me."

She smiled slightly. "You have the most important thing." She reached across the table to put her hand over his heart. "If there is love for me here, then that is all I need. Do you have love for me? Not sisterly love, but the love of a man for a woman?"

He stared into her beautiful green eyes with flecks of golden sunshine. "I love you so much that sometimes I don't think I'll be able to breathe when I look at you." He took her hand in his and pulled it to his mouth to kiss her palm. Her fingers caressed his cheek and sent tingles of joy through him.

"And I love you, Ethan Boyd. Enough to let you go if you think it a sin to marry me. Is that what you think?"

"That is what the elders and eldresses have always told us." Ethan held onto her hand tightly. He couldn't lose her now.

"But what does your heart tell you?"

Ethan took a deep breath. It was time to look inside himself and decide who he was. Not Hawk Boyd's son. There were seeds of Hawk Boyd in him, but he would not let them flourish. Not a Shaker. They had trained him up in the way they thought he should go, but his feet had not stayed on their path.

He was Ethan Boyd. No more. No less. And when he reached upward with prayer, the Lord was still with him. The Lord had led Elizabeth to Harmony Hill. The Lord had put her hand in his. The feeling inside him was not a sin. "My heart wants me to cleave unto you and have you beside me for everlasting. My heart wants to commit matrimony with you." He looked at her. "What does your heart say in return?"

"My heart says yes." Her smile was so bright it was as if the sun had found a new window into the kitchen.

With one accord, they stood and came together. The kiss they had shared on the cliff before Elizabeth left the Shaker village had set his soul on fire, but this kiss was so much better. This kiss was a beginning and not an ending. Together they could face anything. Together they could keep believing.

He raised his head up and looked down into her eyes a moment. "Do you know how a man and woman marry?"

"Usually they stand in front of a preacher and say vows to love and honor one another till death do them part."

"Do you know a preacher?"

She smiled again. "No, but I think Uncle Felix has a cousin who's a preacher."

He laughed as he spun her around, almost knocking over one of the chairs. "I love you, Elizabeth Duncan." He said the words right out loud and somehow, somewhere he knew Brother Issachar was smiling at him.

The End

Ann H. Gabhart and her husband live on a farm just over the hill from where she grew up in central Kentucky. She's active in her country church, and her husband sings bass in a southern gospel quartet. Ann is the author of over a dozen novels for adults and young adults. Her first inspirational novel, *The Scent of Lilacs*, was one of Booklist's top ten inspirational novels of 2006. Her novel, *The Outsider*, was a finalist for the 2009 Christian Book Awards in the fiction category. Visit Ann's website at www.annhgabhart.com.

She lives in a community where
love is forbidden, but will that stop
the passion in her *heart?*

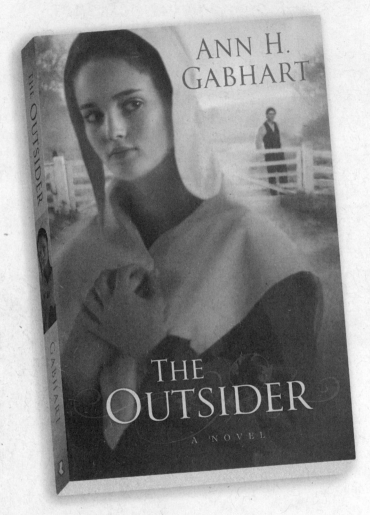

Gabrielle thought she was content—until a love from the
outside world turned her world upside down.

Experience the untamed frontier through the eyes of two spunky and courageous heroines.

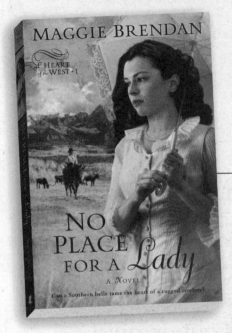

Can a southern belle tame the heart of a rugged cowboy? Fall in love with the Colorado setting and the spunky heroine who wants to claim it as her own in book one of the Heart of the West series.

Her beauty brings admiration and her strong streak stirs up trouble. Caught between the wilderness and civilized society, one young woman must make her way.

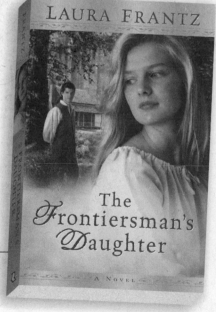